Elephant in the Room

a family saga

JuliAnne Sisung

INFINITY
PUBLISHING

ISBN 978-1-4958-0201-0

Printed in the United States of America

Published August 2014

INFINITY PUBLISHING
1094 New DeHaven Street, Suite 100
West Conshohocken, PA 19428-2713
Toll-free (877) BUY BOOK
Local Phone (610) 941-9999
Fax (610) 941-9959
Info@buybooksontheweb.com
www.buybooksontheweb.com

ACKNOWLEDGEMENTS

T hank you to Larry Hale and Jackie Downey for their excellent editing skills. Your help was amazing. Thanks to Larry for caring so much about my work and making me argue for my words. Thanks also to the characters I've met who have given me creative visions.

Cover by Boris Rasin

FOREWORD

Hersey, a lumber town in northern Michigan, lay in a valley cradled by lush hills large enough to be a challenge to farmers. Milk cows grazed in slanted fashion, two legs always up the hill, and the other two left downside. Farms squatted in between the forests and hills, and small cabins were painted white if the owners were prosperous; left grayish-brown and weathered if nature had not been so kind to the crops.

The Muskegon and Hersey Rivers framed the small town on the east and north sides; one river was large enough to move logs from the hills to the mill, and the other was just right for cooling off in the summer heat. Every Hersey child has escaped chores to grab the end of the knotted rope dangling from a huge oak tree, swing out as far as their weight and agility would allow, and drop into the chilly current. It was a rite of passage to battle the center current and swim back to the rope tree. The young ones floated down to the shallows and walked back on the grassy banks. Only the strong could fight the current.

Going into Hersey from the east, you saw nothing but the forests, but as you approached the top of the last hill, the tip of a white steeple appeared in contrast to the deep green. If you continued on, the steeple grew and then the church appeared, looking whiter than it really was against the green of the hills framing it.

Before the lumber boom, most men farmed to keep their families fed, but the hills and forests battled against easy farming. And winter snows in northern Michigan made for short growing seasons, so the hope was always for next year. Next year would be better, and everyone could have new shoes. Instead, shoes were mostly passed down to the next younger child, and the holes were patched.

All but the most affluent lived in two room homes; one general space for cooking, eating and sitting around the lantern at night, and one for sleeping. As babies were born, rooms were added or the loft was made into bed areas for as many as it would hold.

In the spring of 1890, two men from the east came to Hersey, began buying trees and hiring men to chop them down at unheard of high wages. The giant wheel of the lumber business began to turn. It spun slowly for a brief time and then gained momentum as more and more men left their farms for the more lucrative wage of the lumberjack. The clanging wheel could be heard from dawn until dusk in the ringing of axes and the grinding of the mill.

Hersey was no longer a sleepy town nestled in the arms of green hills and quiet rivers.

CHAPTER ONE

She could hear the trees on their way to earth, limbs crashing through limbs to the forest floor. Rough voices filtered through to where she lay in a bed of trilliums and damp leaves. She was near enough to hear their songs, but hidden from their sight by tall undergrowth. "Sing little lady, sing doo da, doo da," she sang along with the male voices. That wasn't the only song she had learned from the lumberjacks. She knew others, too, ones her mother would have hated. The thought turned up the corners of her mouth a little in some perverse pleasure she didn't totally understand, and at the same time she battled the guilt of knowing she was not behaving in the appropriate young lady manner her mother had tried to instill in her. She tried, but didn't always succeed. Dresses were hard to run in and almost impossible to climb trees in.

But it was spring! Spring was the damp rag wiping the winter slate clean and washed away the winter's dark. Trilliums were scenting the air with sweetness. There were bawdy songs to sing and axes to swing! She crept back a ways to a small rise where she could stand and watch from a distance.

Kate felt the energy of the lumberjacks as they swung their axes and envied them their activity. "I want to take down that tree," she said out loud to the blue jays screaming in the nearby oak tree. "I could be a lumberjack, and I'd be good at it."

For the hundredth time, she wished she had been born a boy. She wanted to feel the axe handle jar in her hand as the blade bit into the tree. She wanted to sing bawdy songs, swear and drink beer.

Kate wasn't supposed to be near the camp. The hills were off limits now. They were crawling with strangers, and her freedom had been sharply curtailed. The town had changed, and she was glad. It's like a giant anthill, she thought. Or a beehive the way it swarms with activity. She pictured her mother's frown.

"It's not an anthill, Kate, and these men aren't ants," she'd say. "They're men and they're lumberjacks, and the ones in town are dandies sporting those silly waxed mustaches and who knows what else."

But Kate liked the way they looked. She didn't think they looked 'rough,' and even if they did, she thought they looked good in their plaid, flannel shirts with their pants tucked into tall, black boots.

"Hey sweet miss," they'd whisper to her if she caught their eye and if her mother wasn't near. Kate never responded, just tilted her head in what she thought was an aristocratic rebuff, but the gleam in her eye did not go unnoticed.

Ignoring her mother's totally unrealistic warning, Kate left her hillside view of the lumber camp and headed for town. She passed shacks hastily erected for the expanding numbers of lumberjacks and cook tents steaming with early morning breakfasts. Smells of maple sausage and biscuits filled the air and had brought late sleepers, men who had spent a late night at the saloon, stumbling from their cots.

"Hey sweet Kate," he called from the front of his tent door. "Your mama's going to rope you to the kitchen if she catches you," he said grinning and running a hand through his long black hair.

His accent pegged him as one of the group who had come from somewhere in the eastern part of the country, one of the 'dandies' her mother disdained.

"She won't know if you don't tell her, Sal," Kate snapped back with a quick grin. Sal was of Italian descent, and his words were a mix of Bronx and old world Italian. He was just one in the strange collection of men lured by the clink of lumber boom coins. There were others. Gamblers in a run of bad luck, lumberjacks from areas already cleared out, city lawyers just wanting a new experience, immigrants working to bring other family members to the land of promise, and just plain drifters. Some worked for a day's wage to spend on the nearest drink or whore, and there were plenty of both in Hersey now, according to Kate's mother.

"It doesn't matter which they get first," Kate's mother would say, her mouth hard and her eyes even harder. "One whets the appetite for the other, Kate. You remember that."

Kate would nod her head in understanding, assuring her mother she also disdained 'that kind of man.' Her eyes spoke agreement, but her head and heart made up her own mind about things of the world, and secretly she didn't think those people were so bad. They were just different. Different was good, wasn't it?

Gathered all together, Kate thought the differences in people weren't so much noticed as expected, like a painting she had seen in school depicting the busy New York Harbor after a ship full of immigrants had disembarked. Already Americanized families in diverse states of change met the newcomers, eyes wide with hope and fear.

Kate liked hearing the Boston accent goading a drawling Tennessee youth boasting his strength in an impromptu arm wrestling contest and losing to Bostonian street smarts. Faces didn't matter so much as the auras surrounding each plaid shirt covering brawny shoulders and reaching down to calloused hands, some accustomed to hard work, some raw from sudden acquaintance with an axe handle. She noted with interest the muscular legs covered in homespun and tucked into muddy boots, and hardened hands holding a variety of saws and axes, all burnished to a shine from use and careful oiling each night.

Mud clung to her shoes, squishing up between boards laid parallel to store fronts, as Kate made her way down Main Street. The spring thaw had brought red mud with the robins and crocuses. The bad with the good, Kate thought. It was all fun. New businesses in various infant states of tar paper and clapboard boasted their wares and services. Baths, haircuts, whiskey and tools headed the list of goods for sale, each demanding prices that should have fed an entire family for a week.

She passed the Tamarack Saloon which was unusually quiet. The men who had work were in the woods; those who didn't have a job couldn't pay for a glass of whiskey either and were gathered elsewhere. She slowed her step, wondering what it would be like to be able to saunter casually in and order a beer, tap her feet to the piano music and smoke cigars.

Kate wandered down the two and a half blocks of Main Street, noting the false fronted buildings, the seven saloons appearing to be held in check by two proud churches standing sentry at either end of town, beacons to all and reminders of the painful fires of hell surrounding whiskey and Sadie's girls.

She peered into the small window of Sadie's Saloon, squinted trying to see past her own tousled blond reflection, past the dust streaks to a world beyond her, one she knew only from her own vivid imagination and her mother's whispered admonitions just the night before to Will, Kate's father.

"That's not a place for a family man, Will," her mother, Ellen, had whispered so the children asleep in the loft would not hear. "Sadie's place is not fit for good folks. I know about those people, and besides, we can't even afford meat for the supper table."

Will had not responded, just nodded and rhythmically tapped his fingers to a song in his head on the scarred, wooden table. Kate had crept closer to the edge of the loft to see her mother look up from her mending to stare in the direction of town. A strange look of concern shadowed her tired eyes as they strayed from the open window to Will, where they momentarily rested.

What was she thinking? Kate mused as she spied from the loft. Then, as if Ellen had shaken herself mentally, she picked up the mending laying abandoned on her apron and angrily stabbed the needle through a torn shirt sleeve.

Still staring into the dusty window of the saloon while she pondered about last night, Kate gave herself a similar mental shake. "Must be a family trait," she whispered out loud, and left the window at Sadie's. "Can't see anything anyway," she mumbled. "They really should wash those windows."

Nestor's General Store was the busiest place in town during the day. Kate strolled down the aisles touching rolls of homespun and brightly colored ginghams. She savored the smell of pickle brine in a keg at the end of the long counter. Kate lingered awhile to hold on to the pungent odor of the brine. She had hidden behind the pickle barrel when she was smaller so she could listen and not be seen. Other kegs held everything from nails to flour. A large potbellied stove in the center of the room drew men from their own home fires to its warmth and the conversation of men.

"Look, Jackson, either you take it at that price, or you don't," Nestor, the owner of the store, said. "There's men waitin' in line, so make up your mind."

He looked anxious to finish his deal with the farmer and kept glancing to the waiting lumbermen. They had money in their pockets.

"John, can't you put it on my bill?" Mr. Jackson pleaded quietly. "I'll get it paid in the fall like I always do."

John Nestor looked at him impatiently at first and then with annoyance. He shook his head noting the desperation in Jackson's stance, the wide spread feet. The fists clenched and unclenched showing red knuckles fading to white then back again. He knew the plight of the area farmers, the costs skyrocketing in sync with the lumber boom, the failed crops from three years of drought. But there was money to be made, and only a fool would let the moment slip by. And Nestor was no fool. This opportunity would not last forever; trees don't grow back overnight. Before you knew it, as quickly as it had started, the boom would be over. As badly as he felt for men like Jackson, he intended to be one of the winners, one of the prosperous.

Kate watched Jackson turn and leave, a glint of fury in eyes set in a face lined by years of sun, wind and worry. The heavy slap of his boots on the wooden floor matched, but no one else noticed his departure. Conversation around the stove was not interrupted. Trees, money and women were more important than the problems of one farmer.

Farmer Jackson and his family were well known to Kate. Jackson had eight kids to feed on his small holding. In the two years they had been in the area, he had worked like a man demented, from sun up to sundown in the fields, and after dark by the light of a lantern, making repairs to the barn and what little equipment he owned. He, like Kate's own pa, was feeling the strain of trying to meet the new high prices on short crop yields.

Kate felt a small sense of betrayal just by being in Nestor's. She loved eavesdropping on exciting conversations, hearing the barter between buyers and sellers, but knowing good, hard working farmers were taking the beating, her father included, dampened the thrill.

She slipped from the store unnoticed, her eyes glued to her brown oxfords showing the strain of two year's wear in gaping places between sole and top, and the muddied socks poking through at the toes gave attention to feet grown too large for the shoes and had defied restraint.

Later, Kate's penchant for having to know everything going on in the world once again moved her to the edge of the loft to eavesdrop on conversation. "I'm not either nosy," she whispered quietly in rebuttal to an imagined scolding from her mother. "I just want to know what's going on." What she heard made her question her need to know. It didn't feel good.

"Ellen," Will said, "this man is offering awful good dollars for each acre of our wooded land. He's done this before and knows what he's talking about."

Ellen just sat. No movement. She just sat staring with her hands on the table in front of her. Her fingers were clasped lightly together in an attitude which might be seen as prayerful or supplicating except for the tenseness evident in their very stillness. The knuckles were deeply lined, reddened from coarse soaps, and enlarged from early hereditary arthritis, much too large for the slender fingers which should have done nothing more strenuous than play the piano she so loved.

No wonder Mama looked worried and sad, Kate thought, and she understood the shadow of fear she had seen on her mother's face. Sounds like Papa wants to move on again, she thought. He's had a bounce in his step lately. That's most likely why. Moving on made him happy, energized by thoughts of the unknown.

Will got up from his chair and moved around the table to place a gentle hand on Ellen's shoulder, willing her to hear him and bend to his excitement. She had once shared his dreams, but time and failure had dampened her enthusiasm, and Will knew he was asking the impossible; once again, for his sake, she should put their future, their family, at risk.

"Ellen," he pleaded boyishly, his blue eyes begging a return to their youthful flight of dreams. "I know I promised this move to Hersey would be our last, but I'm not asking you to move again. I wouldn't do that," he crooned.

Ellen felt his charm, recognized the man she had fallen in love with, and steeled herself against it.

"There's money to be made here," he continued. "Let me try to give you all the things I promised I would when you agreed to be Mrs. Will Hughes."

He perched lightly on the table in front of her, gingerly took her hands in his, and a boyish smile lit his features, a look so charming, she marveled her mother could resist him anything – and she couldn't. Ellen's face warmed and flushed a red-gold hue which startled Kate, and she knew then her seemingly staunch mother could not say no to her husband.

Kate recalled past moves they had made and watched them parade through her mother's eyes, vying for dominance over her love for Will. She had listened to frequent schemes from other lofts in other towns and other states; mining towns from Maine to Montana where her father was to make his fortune in ore booms; prairie lands where irrigation was to build his fame; from tents and tar paper shacks where children were born and wind and snow fought for entry through the cracks between the boards.

Kate, the oldest of three children, had watched her mother make the moves in unspoken fear, but each time she grew more quiet, more tired, less inclined to laugh and sing. Her mother laughed, but some quiet demon waited for the laughter as a cue to move on to another dream, another failure. She was afraid to laugh.

The gleam in her father's eyes made even Kate wary, knowing with each new venture, her mother grew a little less youthful, a little more stooped at the shoulders.

Kate wrapped her quilt tighter, more from the chill of the unknown, or possibly what was known about the past, than from the chill of the night. She watched her mother silently finish putting the supper dishes away, trying to put away her husband's words, pretend they had not been spoken, wishing with her very soul the logging business had never come to Hersey to disrupt her much longed for peace. Ellen finally turned to Will.

"Kate will be a young woman soon," she said. "She's finally getting the proper schooling so when she's done she can teach. Willie and Ruth are doing so well now we've finally settled. Don't spoil it for them, Will."

"I can make it this time, Ellen. I know it. I can feel it." He reached a tentative hand to her shoulder, willing her to hear him, to understand. The intensity of his plea almost shook the room. Kate felt it reverberating up through the chilly air to her loft, and she sensed the power of his blue eyes upon her, as they were upon her mother.

"Tom Reeves is selling his farm land," he said quietly, "and he wants me to go in as a full partner. This town needs its own saw mill. They're floating logs a twenty mile trip right now, all the way to Big Rapids. That little snip of a town has a mill, and we don't. It's not right."

"You don't know anything about saw milling, Will," she pleaded half-heartedly.

"I know I don't, but Tom's got the know-how. He worked in a mill over in Chippewa Township three years ago. He was head man under the owner." He shrugged his shoulders playfully. "Besides," he said, "when did not knowing ever stop me?"

Will took the dish towel from her and placed it carefully, deliberately on the table. He moved his calloused hands down her arms to her hips and then further around to pull her against him.

He nuzzled her face and whispered, "I'll leave this to you, Ellen. I won't push it as I have in the past, but this time it's different. It truly is." Then he nudged her chin with one finger and forced her to look up at him. He towered almost a foot above her, and her stubbornness showed in the tenseness of her neck muscles as she strained to look in his face. Her jaw clenched and tightened as she fought for her place, her family's place in their small world – her opponent was her husband's dreams.

"We don't have to move," he repeated in a whisper. "The kids will still go to school. I'm just changing the way I earn our living."

Ellen's feelings were sensed in her posture. She had not succumbed to Will's body against hers, but the rigid stiffness was easing. Her body said what she couldn't voice. She resented but couldn't resist Will's desires.

"What if this new dream fails, Will? What if it doesn't work?" she spoke in a voice almost devoid of hope, a voice battling love and desire for the man pressed against her and sure knowledge born of experience with his dreams.

"It won't, honey," he crooned into her hair. He sensed acquiescence in her body and spoke more rapidly now. "The time is right," he said, and in the loft, Kate scooted back to where she did not have to watch and listen anymore.

She knew the story, and on one hand, like her father, she was enamored by a new adventure. On the other, she was conflicted by her mother's feelings. Why could she not just say no if she wanted to? Why did she always do what he wanted? She did not understand the play of feeling she had just seen. It was a puzzle, and she went to sleep trying to make the pieces fit.

Below the loft, Ellen was engulfed in a bear hug by the tall man she called husband. The strands of gray in his hair did nothing to dispel his youthfulness. Graying at the temples, but exuding childlike faith in the impossible and trust in everyone, Will's face exploded with excitement in the new adventure.

In August, Will and his partner, Tom Reeves, hauled saws and coal, oiled belts and gear shafts, checked and rechecked the engines and machinery for slicing logs into boards and then into railways and buildings and money for the Hughes and Reeves families.

Tom Reeves was a large man with a slow, hulking walk. He wasn't much of a talker, more of a doer kind of man. He and Will were as different as a butterfly and an ox. Tom's deep brown eyes were watchful, cautious. The bluntness of his chin and square jaw gave the impression of sturdiness, like a brick building made to withstand violent storms and stay put.

While Will was whizzing around town, charming the lumber camp owners and taking care of business in Sadie's Saloon where many business deals were signed and sealed, Tom was steadily installing saws, planes and wheels. They were a good team, cut from different cloth and complimented each other. It began to appear as if one of Will's dreams might finally work.

On August 19, 1890, Kate's birthday, the new mill was ready to run its first paying log. Logs had been floated down the Muskegon River right up to Hersey's first mill. Men with long handled hooks snagged the logs and guided them to a staging area where sure footed horses dragged them up the ramp. Will, the sleeves of his usual white shirt rolled up past his elbows and Tom in brown homespun, guided the first log together and looked typically dichotomous, but happy. Saw dust flew, covering machinery, floor, walls and men. A cheer rose around them, backs were slapped and hands were shaken again and again. Then the work of the day began in earnest. Log after log was guided into the holding area, hooked, and run through the blades. It was a good day and ended with a celebration at the Hughes' house. The mill was up and running! And it was Kate's sixteenth birthday . . .

Mark Ramey, from the Landmark Timber Company, was with them when they went home to celebrate.

"Ah, so this is Kate, our lovely birthday girl," Mark said, bowing playfully in the gallant manner which was an innate part of his nature. He kissed the back of her hand, and Kate's face flushed with the first stirrings of womanhood.

"Good evening," she responded with what she thought was equally elegant repartee.

"It's kind of you to come to our small celebration."

Her mother, startled by Kate's strange manner, stared at her wide eyed and wondering. She would never understand this daughter. One moment she was wishing to be a boy and the next she was a princess.

"Not at all," Mark said, glancing up from her hand. "It is my great pleasure to be in your company."

Kate could not keep up the act and somewhat ungracefully yanked her hand from his, her face a rosy hue from neck to hairline.

At dinner, Mark was seated by Ruthie who chattered on in her magpie manner and kept Mark amused and occupied. "Have you ever killed anybody?" she asked in unbridled awe.

"Well that depends," he teased. "Do you mean with a gun or an axe or a joke?"

"With anything," she said seriously.

"Well, once I saw a man rolling on the floor like he was about to die after hearing one of my jokes. I'm pretty funny, you know." He looked conspiratorially at Ruthie and leaned closer to half whisper in her ear. "I'm pretty sure he died laughing, so I guess I killed him."

Ruthie looked thoughtful and then agreed. He had killed a man. A joke wasn't as good as a gun or knife, but a killing was a killing.

Will and Tom filled in the conversation in the brief moments when Ruthie had food in her mouth until Ellen made it clear there was to be no mill talk at the table.

Kate glanced his way when she couldn't help it and wondered why she had ever wanted to be male. At the moment she only wanted to be beautiful, and a woman. She saw her dusty blonde hair in the sideboard mirror and compared it unfavorably to her sister's golden brown. She wanted to hide her small pointed nose and chin, wishing she had the rounder features, the womanly softness of her mother.

Kate was used to the company of men because unlike most Hersey men, her father did not believe women's place was the home and most especially, the kitchen. Will had led her to believe she was any man's equal. But she didn't feel confident at the moment. Every move she made, every attempt to say something sensible was somehow off kilter.

'What's wrong with me,' she asked herself. And then she wondered if she had said it out loud and glanced around the table to see if they were all staring at her. 'Am I slouching?' She felt her mother's imaginary knuckle pressed against her backbone and heard her voice saying 'Stand up straight. There's a string hanging from the sky, and it's attached to your head, pulling you up.'

'Am I sitting too straight and looking like Miss Prim?' She'd been teased by some of the other girls in school about her erect posture, but she didn't know how she should stand to blend in with the others. Straight? Slack? Life had just become too confusing, and trying to figure it out was simply making it worse.

'How the hell am I supposed to use this fork correctly? Oh, my gosh, did I just say hell? Did I say it out loud?' Kate rolled her eyes and silently whispered a prayer to slide off her chair unnoticed, slither through the cracks in the floor and disappear – live with the raccoons who had made their home under the house.

She watched his hand curl around a glass of amber colored port he had brought as a thank you gift, long slender fingers ending in manicured, clear nails. His brown hair was curling just slightly over the edge of a snow white collar.

'He's not so remarkable,' Kate told herself. 'Average hair color, not like it was jet black or anything really fine.'

Mark tilted his head to respond to some new inane remark from Ruthie, and Kate saw the sparkle in his eyes as they paused to catch her watching him. She quickly looked away, not happy she had been caught, and thought she understood what might be going on in her crazy mind. Mark reminded her of her father, and she was Ellen. The treacherous gleam . . .the spark of fire causing her mother to concede all to her husband . . . it was there now as he looked at her intently across the table and spoke.

"Kate," he teased. "I'll bet all the young men in town will be begging for your hand now you're sixteen. Have you set your heart on one?"

Kate knew he was teasing, but suddenly she was serious. "No," she said resolutely. "I'm not interested in marriage."

Ellen's head jerked up to look sharply at her daughter.

"Come now," Mark continued. "You can't disappoint us all. One man has to be the lucky winner." He leaned back in his chair, crossed his long legs, and watched her face once again flush rose-colored.

"There's a fine young man nearby who's made it clear he has intentions for our Kate," Ellen interjected quickly, trying to plant a seed of knowledge. In Ellen's heart, Kate was spoken for.

"I knew it," Mark said grinning. "Who is the lucky man?"

"Mel Bronson," Ellen answered, "a young farmer nearby. He's a good man and a good provider for his family. He's worked night and day taking care of the farm since his father was killed in a hunting accident. Five brothers and sisters, plus his mother, are a lot of responsibility, but he's no dreamer. He does what needs to be done."

Ellen suddenly stopped for breath, realizing she had gone on a bit in extolling Mel's virtues. He truly was the total opposite of her own husband; no rambling for him; no dreaming about something better over the next hill. There would be no need to search empty pockets for money to buy shoes or seed for the spring planting. Everyone knew Ellen was pinning her hopes on Kate's marriage to Mel. The whole town knew it, and now Mark did, too.

Will watched as she abruptly began clearing the table and knew she had been comparing him to the steady young Mel. Well . . . he wasn't Mel. Never would or could be. As hard as he tried, it just wasn't in him, and it made him a bit sad to know just how much he was a disappointment to her.

"How about a cigar on the front porch," he said to Tom and Mark, "and a bit of lumber discussion? Hate to put a damper on the party, but we've got some business to take care of."

Mark worked for Landmark Lumber, and the Landmark contract meant the difference between struggling with the new mill venture and starting out on firm ground. The nearest logging camps were owned by Landmark, and Mark was acting agent for all of Michigan and the surrounding Great Lakes states. He was also trouble shooter for camps making labor union threats, lease agent for land holders who wanted to clear their forests for farming, con man to those who were reluctant to have their prime forests felled, and payroll agent for all the Landmark camps. He could make or break a mill with a pen and a contract.

"Big Rapids has done a good job for us," he said to Will and Tom. "I'll need a good reason to contract here."

"It's closer, that's why," Tom replied in his terse manner. "Manpower will be cheaper for you."

"True, but how do I know you can handle the production quantity?"

"What I say we'll do, we'll do," Tom reassured, not so confident on the inside, but disinclined to give evidence to his fears.

Will stepped in to help persuade, eager to be part of cementing the negotiations.

"We have new equipment and men eager for work," he said. "We can run all day and night if needed. What can go wrong? It's a beauty of a set up, and we're your mill. We'll beat your Big Rapids price by two percent," Will said, and slapped Mark's shoulder as if the deal was done. He didn't see the frown on Tom's face when he cut the price without consulting his partner. He was wrapped in the moment and the heady flush of making the deal.

"Done," Mark said. "I'll have your contract at the mill first thing in the morning before I take off for the Wisconsin Thatcher Company."

He reached out a hand to Tom first, seeing the agitation in his eyes. 'Some you win; some you lose,' he thought, and he wanted no hard feelings in this man. Mark had long understood the win-lose endings. In his twenty-five years, he had done many things, always striving for the most, perhaps the impossible, wanting what was not always in his power to get or already belonged to someone else. But he was usually not irritated when the impossibility failed to yield. There was always another time, another place, other people.

Kate was eavesdropping on the conversation, loving the give and take of bargaining and wishing she could be a part of it instead of doing dishes. It's not fair, she thought once again. Then she heard Mark would be leaving for Wisconsin in the morning and thoughts of gender inequity fled.

"Fool," she mumbled loud enough for Ruthie to hear.

"What?"

"I said food. I ate too much."

"No you didn't. You were too busy trying to sneak a look at Mark," Ruthie shot back.

"That is not true. I wouldn't look at him because he is a dandy. Probably has all the women in town after him because he's such a flirt."

"He was looking at you, Kate. I saw him."

Kate pulled her shoulders back and squared her jaw. "I wouldn't even consider him as a beau. Besides, I am not his type. What would he want with a sixteen year old girl whose most exciting moment has been playing piano at church? And I don't care," she spouted at her sister, irked Ruthie had seen something she had hoped was hidden.

She thrust her shoulders back again trying to defy the night and stepped out to the porch, determined to join the men whether she was wanted or not.

Mark, ever the gentleman, stood when she joined them and waited until she sat before resuming his seat. In the moonlight Kate noticed the fine lines of his face, the gentle sloping cheek bones and deep set blue eyes which were alive with the fire of life.

"Kate," he said, "your father tells me you play piano and sing. Would you honor us poor, hard working men with a song?"

Not wanting to play badly in front of him, and knowing she'd be too nervous to play well because of him, she tried to side step.

"I just play hymns, Mark. I can't do any of the new tunes." She grasped her fingers in her lap to still their movement. You're being an idiot, Kate, she berated herself. You can play for anyone, anytime, and you know you're pretty good.

"That's great. I really like church music," he said, and without consent, firmly slipped his arm under hers and propelled her inside and over to the piano. Tom and Will stayed on the porch, and the rest of the family joined them to listen to the music under the stars. The night was unusually warm, and stars were blinking on and off like candles in the window as they flicker back and forth in a gentle breeze.

Kate settled at the piano and tried frantically to think of some song he might like. From the corner of her eye, she saw him watching with an unsettling look, and not a single song came to mind. Noticing her discomfort, he grinned and turned to look at a picture perched on the piano, giving her a moment to gain composure.

She finally chose a hymn she frequently played in church and began to sing. Soon her fingers relaxed on the keyboard and she gave herself to the music, almost forgetting he was near.

Through *Precious Lord, How Great Thou Art,* and *In the Garden,* she was alone with her music until somewhere in the middle of *In the Garden,* she heard Mark's soft baritone faintly in the background. He was harmonizing to her melody in a true, deep voice which made up in mellowness what it lacked in knowledge of the words. Kate moved without pause into another hymn, trying not to break the magic of the moment. She listened intently as he warmed to the song and lost himself in the music as she had.

When Kate finally stopped playing and looked up at Mark, he was not yet aware the music had finished. One arm was braced on the piano, and he was staring into space, not really seeing anything. His naked face revealed more than Kate would know about him in years to come. She saw eyes not lit by fire, but soft, gentle, even confused. They were strangely childlike, innocent and yet too sad.

Kate wanted to cradle his head to her breast, protect his innocence from the realities of a world that turns the child into a cynic. Instead, she sat quietly, fingering the keys softly, watching and feeling a little like she was prying into his intimate life, a place she innately knew he would not eagerly share.

He finally turned to her, and the mask slid back in place. "That was beautiful, Kate." His voice had only the slightest trace of huskiness, and in an instant he was back to teasing. "Almost pretty enough to send me off to church on Sunday just to hear you play and sing."

"Thanks," she responded abruptly. She went back to being the flustered young girl and quickly stood to join the rest of the family on the porch.

The night was soon over, too soon for Kate, yet somehow much too long. She longed to be in her loft thinking, carefully sifting through the evening's events, savoring the touch of his presence. And then she knew the thoughts must go.

She listened with half an ear to the conversation on the porch, knew Mark would be at the mill in the morning with the contract, and knew, too, he would be leaving soon after. She watched as he shook hands with Will in the gentlemen's seal of a closed bargain, made the rounds with Tom and little Willie, bowed slightly to Ellen and complimented her on the superb fried chicken. He brought a flush to Ruthie's golden skin by telling her he would be back on a white stallion to sweep her away to his castle in the forest, probably even have to kill someone to rescue her and then turned to Kate. Once again, he claimed the night by kissing the back of her hand.

"Kate, you are a lovely young lady," he whispered. "Happy sweet sixteen."

He promised to see them in the spring, but he didn't.

CHAPTER TWO

1892

An elderly man with a ramrod straight back and bushy grey hair stood at the platform, banging a wooden gavel and trying to bring order to the brawl called a town meeting. The men were all on one side of the room and the women, of course, on the other.

"Order, order!" Gordon Tilmann's raspy voice shouted. "Please! Let's settle down!"

Tilmann, largest land owner and the power behind events in Hersey, was ineffectually trying to maintain some semblance of protocol. Tilmann had taken over the work of leading town meetings since Bob Mann, the mayor, was frequently slurring his words with too much celebration, although what he was celebrating was unknown. However, he loudly proclaimed to anyone who had the misfortune to mention the smell of whiskey on his breath, "I'm just celebratin' a little today. It's a good day to celebrate."

Only the month before, he had tried to cut the ribbon at the opening of the new town hall and had accidentally jabbed the sharp point of the scissors into Agatha Pennington's skinny thigh. She was not a lady to anger, no matter if you were the mayor. In her imperious way, shoulders back, head held at an angle which allowed her to peer down her sharp nose at the offender, she boxed Mann's ears as if he had been a child and demanded Gordon take over the mayoring responsibilities. Since then, those duties have been assumed by the most sober, available and willing man.

Hersey had developed into a real town, and meetings had become necessary but difficult given the variety of personal stakes and interests. Shacks had sprung up when the lumbermen first came, and some had changed into substantial buildings, mostly made of wood freshly cut at Will's mill. The churches finally received their stained glass windows, and a deep toned bell now rang every Sunday morning from the Congregational Church steeple.

Kate, Ruthie and Ellen had worked bazaars and socials for the last two years, raising money for the windows and bell. It seemed to Kate her mother was almost demonic in her intent to elevate evidence of the churches. She had giggled privately at the thought of demonic in connection with Ellen and her churches, but she did seem crazily possessed at times.

Most fund raising projects were held in the park by the Hersey River where Mel Bronson always found the time to help with the heavy work. How he found time, no one knew, but everyone took advantage of his willingness to supply muscle and common sense. Since his father's death in the hunting accident a few years back, Mel had taken on the responsibility for his family's farm. Five younger siblings made the duty a heavy one, but Mel, in his typical manner, shrugged his wide shoulders, hitched up the team, and moved forward. Work was work, according to Mel. Something you just needed to do.

"We need a volunteer committee," shouted Tilmann. "You all want a fire department, and we can't just keep letting the town burn. It might be your house next!" he wailed. He pointed to Ed Miller, owner of the bank next to the new town hall.

"Ed," he yelled, "As of right now, you're the new fire department chairman. And," he grinned, "since I see you and George Simms together at the card table in Sadie's all the time, he's your assistant. You can talk about how we're going to get this fire department in between deals." There was a great deal of hearty laughter at this and as many grateful, heartfelt sighs in knowing they had been bypassed for the job.

Typically, many complained about circumstances but did little to rectify them if it did not seem to directly impact them at the moment. The men did a lot of knee slapping and hawing at George. His wife, June, was sitting on the other side of the room, an embarrassed frown spreading over her face. It was well known she was continually trying to keep George behind the counter of their hardware store instead of behind a glass of beer and waiting for the impossible inside straight. For most, this made Tilmann's choice all the more appealing.

"Oh, come on now Tilmann," George whined, growing red in the neck and ears, a trait he had abhorred in his youth and could never outgrow. It was one of the reasons his card cronies loved to have him at the table. They could read his cards better than he could. George plucked at the sides of his pants like an overgrown schoolboy preparing for a church recital he had, once again, forgotten to memorize. "I ain't got time for that right now. I got all I can handle in the store."

Tilmann knew it wasn't true, but also knew they needed someone who would get the job done. They really needed protection from the growing number of fires since the town had sprouted so haphazardly with the lumber boom. He nodded his bushy head and groaned out a plea.

"Okay, okay. Who will help Ed?" He stood looking intently as the hall grew silent with waiting. Many heads were bowed, eyes studying the toes of their boots. You didn't see such prayerful supplication in church, even on Easter Sunday. It seemed every breath was held in anticipation of their names being called, like the devil calling his children home.

Finally, a voice in the back was heard. "Alright. I'll help if Ed can meet after supper. I've got too much going on during daylight." Of course, it was Mel.

Kate heard the voice and a kind of disgust came over her, even though it was mixed with a strange pride. She knew the kind of man Mel had become and knew, also, with him in charge, they would finally get their fire department and be safe. With Mel on the committee, things would happen. If anyone could keep the mixed mess of men on track, Mel was the one.

Tilmann touched his gavel to the table and said, "Meeting's over. Goodnight." A sudden rush of relieved voices filled the room, along with fresh night air as the door swung open and neighbors flooded out.

Outside, Mel found Kate in the crowd and asked if he could give her a ride home. Kate nodded agreement.

"Just let me find Pa and tell him to go on without me," she said.

Mel silently held the reins in his large calloused hands, letting the two old work horses take their time. It was a restful trip along a road lined with trees just beginning to show their fall colors. Branches touched in the middle of the road, making a canopy enfolding travelers, a tunnel, a lover's lane designed by nature for impulsive caresses or a trap for the wayward to ambush the unsuspecting. Kate's imagination saw both, and she wasn't sure which was the more appealing.

"Kate," Mel said quietly, "When do you start teaching?"

"September fifth. I'm looking forward to it, but I'm still a little nervous," she responded.

"You'll do just fine," Mel said and covered her hand with his. They rode in silence. Kate was comfortable with Mel. She knew he cared for her much more than she could find it in herself to return, and it sometimes made her uneasy and, for some unfathomable reason, a bit angry with him. But not this night.

"Mel, you shouldn't have volunteered to head the committee tonight. Why not let someone else take over for once?" she said.

Mel sighed in his quiet way, "Oh, I can help out. I like it. We're going to be a big town some day, and I should be part of it."

He pulled on the reins and drew the wagon to the side of the road.

"But I don't want to talk about that, Kate," he said, and putting his arm around her shoulders, he gently drew her toward him, lifted her chin, and touched his lips to hers, kissing her softly at first. Then suddenly he pulled her tightly to his chest. She could feel the pulsing of his heart against her own. A strange mixture of emotions coursed through her body, and she kissed him back with more feeling than she knew was in her.

With a start, Mel pulled away and turned his face into the darkness. Kate could see he was trying to say something and knew she did not want to hear his words. She just wanted to feel the intensity of the shivers streaming through her. She wanted the feelings to be free, disconnected to words and the attachments they would bring. She knew she shouldn't, but she did. And it felt good . . . and bad, exhilarating and irritating. And she wanted Mel not to speak, just to make her feel shivery again. She waited for the moment to pass.

"Kate, you know how I feel about you?"

"I think so," she whispered without looking at him, silently praying he wouldn't go further, wouldn't ask anything of her she could not freely give, wouldn't offer something she couldn't return. Still, she didn't want to release Mel, give him up to someone else. It was selfish, she knew, but she had a need of him. Losing him was too dear a price to pay for total honesty. And she would have to be honest with him if he spoke the words.

With a deep breath, Mel turned to face her. "I can't make any commitments right now, Kate. My family's needs are great, and it wouldn't be fair to you, but I want you to know . . ."

Kate put her fingers over his lips, silencing him, stopping the question and the declaration.

"I know," she said. "Don't talk, Mel, please. The night is too beautiful." And she turned to rest her head on his shoulder, gazing past the leaves to the bright stars peeking through.

They sat in silence, his arm around her shoulder and his free hand softly stroking her fingers. Kate breathed a sigh, contented and relieved. After a time, Mel spoke in a voice too husky for the words.

"Your folks will be wondering what happened to us if we don't get moving." He slowly pulled away from her, hesitating for just a moment to brush her hair with his lips.

When they were on their way again and his voice was in control, he said, "Did you hear about the trouble in one of the lumber camps?"

Kate hadn't and wasn't really paying close attention to Mel's words until he casually said, "I think it was the Landmark camp."

Her ears perked up. "What happened?" she asked with sudden interest.

"Well, they're not too sure yet. I hear the men have been waiting, sometimes a week or more after payday, for their wages. That's been going on for quite a time now."

"Why?" she asked, real concern behind her question. "Is Landmark in financial trouble?"

"Some think so. And it's the only reason I can come up with," he responded, "unless it's just poor management. Today a rumor went around camp that the timber agent was bringing a special payroll on today's train, specifically to make sure the men got paid. He didn't show up, and the men are fired up mad."

Kate unconsciously grabbed Mel's arm. "Who was bringing it? Do you know? What happened to him?" she demanded, not aware alarm was obvious in the sound of her voice.

Mel turned and looked at her, questioning her sudden near panic. He couldn't know she was thinking about Mark, didn't even know she knew him.

"No one knows," he said. "There's talk he skipped with the payroll. It's a lot of money, you know."

Trying hard to control her fears, Kate whispered forcefully, to herself as much as to Mel, "No! He wouldn't do that."

"He? Who do you mean, he?"

"Oh, I just mean . . . whoever they think it was, something must have happened to just delay him. No one would just take off like that with all those poor men's wages, especially when everyone knows how much their families need it. Besides they'd have to know their name would be connected with the money. They would have to be afraid . . . well . . . " Kate was babbling, not really conscious of what she was saying until Mel stopped her mid-sentence, patting her hand and smiling like an adult placating a child.

"You're sweet and innocent, Kate. Stay that way, okay?"

Normally, his words would have made her angry, but her mind was too filled with the horror of what she'd heard, so she ignored it. When they pulled into the yard and the horses stopped, lowering their heads to nibble at the grass, Kate questioned him again. She just couldn't leave it alone, had to know more. She tried to be nonchalant in her questioning, but felt Mel could see through her false composure to the real turmoil boiling inside.

"What are they doing to find this man," she asked cautiously. "Maybe he's sick or hurt. Maybe someone robbed him?"

"Well, I'm sure they have checked to see if he got on the train at all. I don't know what they found, but the answer to that will determine their next moves." Kate was staring at him intently, so he continued. "Something has to be done because the men have put down their saws and are waiting for their wages before they will pick them up again."

"No," Kate burst out, angry at herself for not thinking of her father before. "Without Landmark trees, the mill will practically stop."

"Don't worry," Mel comforted. "Landmark has too much to lose to let the men stay idle for long."

He jumped down and moved around to help Kate. Mel was so strong, so solid, she thought. She could feel the muscles of his shoulders tighten under her hands as he easily lifted her from the wagon. With his flannel shirt open at the neck and drawn tight across as it was now, she thought he looked very appealing. Still, while her stomach sent warmth coursing through her body, tinting the skin of her neck pink, some demon in her couldn't resist comparing Mel's roughhewn, if sensual, appearance to Mark's casual elegance. She battled the thought, but it won, and she briefly hated herself for it.

"Will you come in for awhile?" Kate asked. "I'm sure Pa will want to know all you have heard."

Will had already heard the camp had stopped work, but he didn't know all the details. He had planned on going to the camp early in the morning to see what he could do to get the men back to work. It was obvious he was worried. Landmark meant a lot to his mill.

While the men talked, Ellen listened without speaking. Her face was a blank, saying more than words could. She just sat there, her back so straight had she been touched, she would crack; snap like a dried twig under some careless foot, with bark shattered leaving the tender tissue inside exposed and injured. Will and Mel both felt her silence and the unspoken judgment, whether fair or not. It crowded the room, strained the conversation, and they were all grateful when Ruthie broke the silence by bouncing into the room.

Kate's sister Ruthie had turned fifteen her last birthday and had changed with the coming of new womanhood. She sashayed across the room, planted herself on Mel's lap, and all conversation stopped as they waited for what she would do next. Ruthie had the undeniable ability to take over a room. When she entered, she knew all eyes would be on her, validating what she knew. She was queen of the moment. And it was true. She dazzled them with her impish charms, tossed her brown curls, and flashed her wide, toothy smile until they were captured – willing victims or not. She was not predatory or evil. She was Ruthie, with eyes that spoke whatever the victim wanted to hear or see. At the moment, those shining eyes were staring into Mel's.

"Come on," she teased. "Say you'll jilt Kate and marry me." She had the most seemingly unconscious ability to tease, without a hint of embarrassment. Nothing out of Ruthie's mouth seemed inappropriate, or if it did, it was 'just Ruthie.' It was a part of her charm.

Mel smiled and responded in his unaffected way, "The only thing I'll give you, young lady, is the same I'd give any one of my sisters – a licking for being impertinent and not knowing her place."

Ruthie gave her best impression of a pout, knowing she had the room captivated.

"You're getting too pretty for your own good," he said as crossly as he could muster while hiding a grin.

Ellen interrupted from across the room where she was fixing coffee. "Don't flatter her, Mel. She already knows it too well."

With a twinkle belying his frown, Will added, "Pretty? That skinny face? How could she be pretty? She looks just like her pa."

Ruthie saved the evening because news of the Landmark events were never far from the surface for Kate and Will, and most of the time was spent in casual conversation, avoiding more serious thought. Kate only heard half. She responded when addressed, wondering if the missing man was Mark and, if so, where he was. Somewhere deep inside, she was certain Mark would not steal. She didn't know why she knew. She just did.

The next morning, Will went to the Landmark camp and talked with the foreman. All the men were at the camp, but their saws were silent, and their axes were wedged in tree stumps with the handles sticking into the air like monuments at a grave site. They appeared to proclaim absence of faith. To some, the death of a dream.

Matt Keller, the foreman, told Will he'd heard the sheriff had checked the station where the Landmark agent was to board and found he had. They were following the rail route to try to determine when the man had gotten off.

"Who was the agent," he asked. "Any of the men who were here before?"

Matt thought for a moment, scratching his red beard. "I think so. Yea, he was here a couple of years ago, I believe. If I got his name straight, it's Ranny or Ramey, Mark Ramey, something like that."

Matt stooped to pick up a blade of grass, stuck it between his teeth and slowly ran it back and forth between the wide spaces separating his front teeth.

"They ain't sure that's what happened yet," he mumbled. "They think maybe he was robbed and shoved off the train. Nobody knows."

"Well," Will said. "I guess we'll just have to bide our time. It'll come out. Meantime, how soon can you get the men back to work?"

Matt stammered a bit and shuffled his feet, looking at them as if they were new to the ends of his legs.

"I don't know, Will. They're pretty fed up with waitin' for their pay. Right now they say they're not movin' til they see money in their hands."

Will placed a gentle hand on Matt's shoulder, trying to portray friendliness he did not feel, understanding instead of frustration and anger. He thought of Ellen and her sure knowledge his venture would fail, or more, he would not succeed. This was more than the success of a mill. It was a promise he had made to Ellen twenty years ago and had yet to fulfill.

"Matt," he said more calmly than he felt. "You know I'm on your side about the wages. Those men have earned every dollar. They have families to feed, too. But man, without Landmark logs, I might as well shut down. Puts my men out of work too."

Matt flushed knowing he would be betraying good men no matter what stand he took in the argument. He'd had a long friendship with Will, but his loyalty had to be to his men at the camp. He was responsible for them and their work.

"I'll see what I can do, Will. I just can't promise anything."

At home later, Will gave Ellen some of the details concerning the Landmark camp and the missing payroll. He didn't want to. He had really wanted to go to Sadie's, drink a glass of whiskey with other men who shouldn't be there, get a cheerful greeting from Sadie herself. It tore at him to see Ellen's sad, knowing eyes. It was a physical pain to confirm her lack of faith in him. But she was right. He would fail, just as he had always failed.

Kate was quietly listening and couldn't keep still when she heard Mark's name. "No! Pa, Matt's wrong. It couldn't be Mark. He wouldn't!"

"Hold on, hold on," he soothed. "That's what I told him, but he was pretty sure Ramey was the name he heard. They know Mark and a lady got on the train in Wisconsin. What they don't know is where they got off or where the payroll is now."

Will went on to explain it might not mean Mark had stolen the money. He could have been robbed or any number of things could have happened.

Kate hardly heard the rest of the explanation – after hearing the words 'Mark and a lady.' Stupid girl, she chided. Of course he had women. Why wouldn't any woman be enamored by his attention? And then she chided herself again for feeling jealousy instead of concern for their safety. As soon as she could, she went to her loft and slid beneath her quilts. She needed to be alone, to think, to chide herself for her foolishness, and to . . . something. She just didn't know what.

Kate's dreams were a kaleidoscope of bad pictures; Mark clubbed over the head and thrown from the train; Mark skulking away from a train station with a huge bag of gold coins; Mark and an unknown, and of course, beautiful woman. The vision woke her; perhaps the idea of him and the beautiful woman was more disturbing than the one with him as a crook or wounded. Once again, in the wee hours of the morning, Kate did not like herself very much and vowed to try to be less imaginative and intense about everything, more stoic . . . more Christian, more Ellen-like.

She had tried many times before, but it was hard, she thought. How do you just squash feelings? And did you really want to go through life without those glorious senses turning the world red and gold and all the brilliant colors?

"Ah," she whispered to herself, too honest to blame someone or something else. "There's the rub. I don't really want to be less Kate and more Ma. I like to feel like dancing with the first sound of spring song birds. Their joy infects my feet, and my heart sings with them. I like – well most of the time I like to feel like crying when songs break my heart." After a time, Kate was able to smile at her silliness and drift back into a light sleep just before dawn broke into the darkness of her loft.

CHAPTER THREE

He was good looking, a slender man, mid-twenties, confident. A dark brown coat hung from wide shoulders down to sharply creased trousers, all casually elegant. He walked with light, swinging steps, head held high and tilted at what could be described as an arrogant angle. Passing through the throng of people, he listened to the squall of babble accompanying the depot and surrounding the travelers. People amused him; there was something interesting about each of them. He threaded his way through the crowd; his left hand cleared a path for the woman with him, and his right held a satchel carefully by his side.

The train depot in Madison, Wisconsin, was crowded with passengers waiting to board or be picked up by families, friends or cart drivers making a dollar. Scattered stacks of luggage spoke various states of economy, from the healthy glow of oiled leather to cardboard boxes tied carefully with dingy grey string.

Mark noted the variety and the smells emanating from hampers full of home cooked food. Pipe tobacco and coal assaulted his senses. He loved the vitality which entered him through the people coming and going. Looking around, he pretended, as he always did, he could guess where these people were going and why. The why mostly, as the whims of the world intrigued him and the motives urging men to do the things they did. He gave the men imaginary wives and children, jobs and homes, angers and joys. He heard their conversations at dinner tables and in the bedrooms. He loved to walk depot platforms and peer at the emotions tucked inside people and spilling out of their eyes and lips. He created whole worlds for them.

At the steps of the train, after it had whistled and puffed into the station and finally spewed the last of its incoming travelers onto the platform, Mark watched a young woman try to hoist a crying child and two battered suitcases up the steps. Her worn brown, cotton dress showed signs of long ago ironing, the creases still evident in the sleeves, but the hem had been muddied, and stains spotted the front. The face of the girl-woman showed similar signs of wear as she struggled with the child and her load.

Mark maneuvered his way to her, and smiled. With his free hand, he picked up the child who stopped crying at the shock of being lifted high into the air by the strange, smiling man. She patted his face and squirmed with delight. Mark giggled with her and grabbed up one of the suitcases to carry along with his satchel. He followed behind the young woman and stowed both child and suitcase in the rapidly filling day car.

In his private compartment, he carefully stowed his own satchel and sat opposite Lorraine who silently stared out the dusty, coal streaked window. She was beautiful, with raven black hair and matching eyes. The expensive traveling dress she wore molded to a perfect body. Lorraine knew all eyes had admired her as she walked through the cars to their compartment. Adulation was expected.

Mark watched her as she patted already perfect hair and smoothed the already perfect lines of her dress. His brow wrinkled in a frown, and he absently picked at a loose thread on his glove. In fact, a closer inspection would reveal many loose threads and worn spots, not only in his gloves, but in the jacket and trousers, as well.

Silence crowded the compartment during the two hours the train had been traveling, a silence more palpable than a dense and enveloping fog.

"I'm going to the dining car for a few minutes. Can I get something for you?" he asked as he prepared to leave. Lorraine requested a glass of sherry and turned back to the window. "I'll just be a few minutes," he said. "I need to leave a telegraph with the porter to send at the next station."

Mark found the porter, gave his telegraph request, got Lorraine's sherry, and headed back to the compartment. It had taken longer than the expected few minutes, but he was not worried. Lorraine was not the type to wander through crowded cars filled with humanity's masses. She was more the kind who would demand one of the masses fetch for her while she waited for her needs to be fulfilled.

But the compartment was empty when he got there. Mark wasn't immediately concerned, thinking she had probably needed the powder room, and for that she couldn't get a lackey to do it for her. A grim sort of smile crossed his lips at the idea.

"You can't use someone else for all your needs, Lorraine," he murmured to himself a bit wickedly.

Mark nestled her sherry into the specifically designed notch in the table bolted to the floor and settled in. A short while later, he began checking his pocket watch. Looking alternately at his watch then out the window, he wavered between irritation and pleasure in her absence. A sense of freedom followed in the wake of Lorraine's leaving. He'd known loneliness in her company since shortly after they were married, and it had become more intense with the passing of time.

When an hour had passed, Mark began to stew, perhaps even worry a bit some harm had come to her. As much as he wanted to be free of her, as much as her self-centered nature disgusted him, he would not have wanted her harmed.

One last glance at his watch convinced him to look for her. Perhaps she had just gotten confused about the location of their compartment and was wandering about, lost. Perhaps she had gotten tired of waiting for her sherry and decided to get one herself, perhaps more than one. He pictured her sipping several, all gifts from traveling gentlemen who were instantly charmed by her beauty. He started down the aisle to the door connecting their compartment to other cars, and then abruptly re-traced his steps, thinking about the satchel. No matter their space was private, he thought, it could not be left unguarded, just in case. One never knew.

He opened the luggage compartment door, searched for the satchel amid their other baggage, and couldn't find it. Fear gripped him. He searched again, knowing it was not there, but hoping he had somehow missed it. It was gone. He just stood there, thinking, sweat beading his grim face. Refusing to believe things had gone so awry, Mark rationalized.

"Lorraine took it with her," he said out loud. "That must be it." For once, he thought, she was trying to be responsible and protect an important piece of luggage. It was stupid, though, to take it to the liquor bar – or the powder room, but so like her. She couldn't or wouldn't wait for anything she wanted.

Mark started down the hallway again, angry and re-sentful. Her needs always came first, no matter the con-sequences to anyone else. He thought of the payroll, the men waiting for their well-earned dollars, and Land-mark's reputation as he threaded his way through ham-pers and strewn baggage. Every few feet he stopped to describe Lorraine and ask if anyone had seen her go by.

Finally, a portly, red-faced man grinned indicating he had definitely noticed Lorraine, pointed and said, "I saw her alright. She was heading toward the dining car. Have a little spat did ya? She decide to dine by herself?"

"You're sure she was going to the dining car, sure it was the woman I described?" Mark questioned, and a sigh of relief mixed with aversion escaped him. She was getting her damned drink.

"She's a looker, that one," the man drooled, ignoring Mark's questions. "Bet she gives you a real chase, huh?"

Mark quickly pivoted to leave the repulsive man while he was still talking.

"Walking right smartly, too. Pretty little . . ." he heard as he left.

He was still searching for her along the length of the train when he heard the whistle blow for the next short stop. Almost immediately, the train began rolling again, and Mark found a porter to aid in the search. Fear had begun to grip him in earnest.

Their collective search proved futile. Lorraine was not on the train. Neither was the satchel.

"Maybe she got off at the last stop," the porter offered. Mark's head jerked up, and he stared at the man, light dawning in his eyes. "But," he stammered, "That wasn't even a real stop. That was just a mail exchange, wasn't it?" he asked hopefully.

"Yeah, but people can get on or off. There just usually isn't anyone that wants to. It's a podunk town."

"How far is it to the next one?" Mark asked.

"Thirty miles. Want me to report her missing?" the porter asked, trying to be helpful, concern showing in his half smile.

"No!" Mark swung around abruptly. "Don't do that. Uh, I'll take care of it. She probably didn't like the train fare and just got off to get food more to her liking," he said, trying to smooth over the problem. "She most likely just didn't get back in time." He saw the porter eye him, not believing any of it, but Mark couldn't explain his wife had just run off with the company payroll. He'd have to find her on his own if he was to keep the mother of his children out of jail. And he might be implicated as well. What a mess, he thought, rubbing his hands over his face and through his hair. "Damn her," he spat, but the tone was almost sad, "damn her selfish, no good hide. Damn my stupidity for leaving the satchel anywhere near her greedy hands."

At the next stop, Mark left the train and found a broken down rig he could afford to buy. Whatever money left in his pocket had to last. For thirty miles, he bumped and jostled toward where he hoped to get his hands on Lorraine and the satchel. His fear and anger kept him moving, and the long distance gave him plenty of time to dwell on the travesty of a marriage he and Lorraine had endured. Stopping for neither food nor rest, he fed on his hurt and stupidity. How could he have been such a fool as to trust her near the payroll? He should have known better.

They had married when he was only seventeen and thought he could fix the world; nothing was beyond his capabilities. Lorraine had beauty, great beauty, and knew how to use it to her advantage. She had manipulated him, played the fragile, injured innocent. When her black snapping eyes had flooded with unshed tears and she flung her arms around his neck, pressing her fragile body to his, he had jumped at the chance to play knight to her needs. She was beautiful and convincing.

Her influence over him ended ten years and two children ago. Since then, she had spent every cent he could earn on whatever whim happened to catch her at the moment, from clothes to jewelry – to trips to God only knows where and doing God only knows what. In the beginning, she turned sad eyes on him, and he forgave her. Later, she didn't even bother to pretend. She merely tossed her long, black hair, ignored his words of caution and restraint, and laughed at him.

For a long while, Mark made excuses for her behavior. She had always been so poor, and now she was caught up in having nice things. She was social. She needed friends. He used all of the blinders infatuation creates to not see who Lorraine really was, down deep.

But over the years, he had come to know the truth. Lorraine's only interests were herself and what she wanted: money and adulation – male adulation. Mark could not recall a single woman friend, not one. There might be early interest from a new female acquaintance, but they quickly grew wary when they saw her flirtatious behavior with any male in attendance, even their husbands. The head tilted just so, peering up at him through thick, fluttering black lashes in false innocence and feigned adoration. Her face had fooled many a man into believing every word she spoke. Mark didn't blame them. Her veneer was too fine, too cultivated; her lies too cleverly close to the truth. Her smile was too diabolically angelic.

Anyone who happened to hear the lonely, grim chuckle emanating from Mark's rig would have hastened quickly away and pondered the sanity of the inhabitant. It was a harsh half-laugh torn from his guts, a mixture of raw emotions he had never allowed to surface: pain at his own failure to make a good home for his children, sorrow at Lorraine's final duplicity, and anger at himself for being a fool so many times over. The laugh was at himself.

As Mark rode, he chided his weakness for Lorraine's beauty. When she had wanted to turn on the charm, she was sweet and beguiling, and at those times, he had not been able to deny her anything. It had only been in the later years, after he had learned not to trust what he saw, he had learned to turn away. In a small way, he was sorry for her. She was never happy with what she had, and when she learned – very early in life –men could be moved to provide for her every wish, it was an easy task to become adept at tactics to move them.

What she had not yet learned was the impermanence of her talents. Payment would come due. It has a way of happening without notice. Mark knew Lorraine was running from time and the mirror. She hadn't lost her beauty or her ability to set men's blood churning.

But she saw the sand running quickly through the hour-glass and more and more felt the need to grasp it. What he saw now when he looked at her perfectly carved face and deep black eyes was a sad, spoiled, greedy woman who would too soon be old. The injured innocent had long since gone.

Mark's features lightened in the dim light of night as his thoughts took the natural course through his marriage and centered on his children; Jamie, his two year old son; and Flossie, his three year old golden girl. They had been staying for a good part of the summer at their grandparent's home near Marne, Michigan. It was good for them, he thought, to be in the country for awhile; the fresh air, the comfortable solidity his parents provided. He and Lorraine were to pick them up after dropping the payroll in Hersey at the Landmark camp. He made a mental note to wire them if he could not find Lorraine quickly.

After thirty miles of worrying and talking to himself, and five hours of bumping over dusty roads, he at last drove into the small town where he believed Lorraine had left the train. Mark found the depot and began asking questions. He gave a description of what she had been wearing and the satchel she would have carried.

"Everyone who gets off this train is wearing brown or grey and is carrying something, Mister. Is that all you can tell me about this person?"

"Well, she has jet black hair and dark eyes," he continued. "You really can't miss her; she's quite beautiful."

"Yep," drawled a man in a filthy overcoat, two sizes too big. "I saw her. Believe she hired old Mosey and his rig. Musta been in a hurry. Had a pretty sharp tongue on her. Was givin Mosey one sure hell of a time."

Mark interrupted him. He feared the old fellow was settling in for a long chat. "Did you hear where he was taking her?"

"Nope, I didn't hear that, but I did hear a long list of how shiftless old Mosey was, not helping her with her bag and stuff." The man kicked at the dirt, sending clouds of dust in the air to settle on Mark's trousers. Mark turned to leave, heading to where someone might know her whereabouts.

"You might check the hotels," said the man to Mark's retreating back. "Ain't but two of 'em in town."

"Is this Mosey in town now?" Mark asked, turning briefly back to the old geezer. "Maybe I could talk with him?"

"Nope, well, I ain't seen him anyways. But that don't mean nothin'. Sometimes he don't come in to town for days at a time, maybe even a week if he's got a full snoot goin," he continued in his irritatingly slow drawl. "Say," he stopped, looked suspiciously at Mark, squinting his ferret eyes. "You ain't a lawman or something?"

"No, she is my wife," Mark answered quickly. "We were accidentally separated at the last stop. Just a mix up," he said, trying to voice a surety he did not feel. He turned, once again, to leave.

Mark asked for Lorraine at the two hotels, or at least what they were calling hotels. From the looks of them, Mark could not imagine anything would induce her to stay in either of them. He described Lorraine to every person he passed, getting more and more weary of saying the same things over and over, and of getting the same response. The long day was beginning to tell in his sluggish walk and red rimmed eyes. By now, he was growing doubtful about his ability to find her on his own and fearful of her future – and his own.

He finally checked into one of the hotels, cleaned off some of the accumulation of travel dust, ate a meager dinner and lay down to rest for a couple of hours. He awoke groggy and stiff a few hours later and resumed the search. It was a frustrating experience. How could she just disappear? Except for the old man at the station, there was no recollection of her anywhere. It was as if she had never been there, and he knew better. Mark finally accepted the duplicity. Lorraine had talked old Mosey into driving her much farther than town right after leaving the train. But where? He had no idea, and his frustration, along with his fear, mounted.

At the town's small telegraph office, Mark wired his parents. "Trouble with Lorraine. Stop. Keep Jamie and Flossie with you please. Stop."

He felt there was no need for further explanation. His parents were well aware of Lorraine's indiscretions, and while they kept their thoughts pretty much to themselves, Mark knew they had not long been fooled by her.

He was momentarily buoyed by accomplishing something, even something as small as the wire. The search had been defeating. He hated this filthy town. He hated Lorraine. And he hated his failure. But, at least his kids were safe from her.

He went back to the hotel, had a drink which immediately made him a bit woozy, went to his room and collapsed on the bed. He slept restlessly and woke to a grey drizzling day – and the realization there was most likely a warrant out for him.

The possibility of arrest had always been in the back of his mind, but he had thought Lorraine would be more easily found, and the payroll back in his hands where it should have been. He should have notified the authorities. But he just couldn't– even now. For the present, he had to locate Mosey, find out where he had taken Lorraine, and stay out of sight. He had to become invisible.

Mosey finally turned up. He had left his rig tied to the back of a rundown shack inhabited by old men with nothing to do but talk the day away and sip at the jugs on the floor near them. Mosey was bleary eyed and sipping on bottled whiskey when Mark found him, just as the old man at the depot had said he would be.

"Yep," he said, grinning. "I took a lady – well, not that she was one, you know. She looked it, but damn that woman could spit nails."

Mark prodded. "Where did you take her?" he asked again, trying for patience he did not feel.

"She didn't talk all that much, after the lashing she first gave me," he drawled. "She just sat there ignoring the bumps and the dust like she was sittin' in a fancy parlor."

"I'm sure that's the lady," Mark said encouragingly. "We were separated by mistake," he lied. "I am sure she is worried, and I need to find her. Did she have all her luggage with her?"

"Yup, she had a bag with her. Wouldn't even let me put it away for her." He turned to the other old men near him, looking for some understanding and empathy. "Yelled all the while I wasn't doin' things right and weren't fast enough. I tried to tell her if she didn't slow down some she was gonna drop dead from hurry."

Frustrated, Mark again asked where he had taken Lorraine.

"Nope, she didn't listen, just kept on blabberin for me to get movin." He turned back to Mark. "She's your wife and all, but, well, I'm telling you what I'd do . . ."

"Where?" Mark shouted, fists clenching and looking around him, trying to remain invisible.

"Oh, yeah," Mosey said, scratching his greasy grey hair, hurt Mark didn't seem to want his advice. He had seen women like her before and knew the trouble they caused. The young fellow at his side seemed a decent sort. He could have saved him some sorrows if he'd just listen.

"Berville," he said sullenly. "I took her to Berville."

"Thanks, Mosey," Mark said with a sigh of relief, and slipped a dollar piece in the old man's pocket. "Can you tell me how to get there?"

Mosey told him, again taking many side trips in his explanation. Mark wanted to run off and collect his broken down horse, leave the rig so he could ride faster, and head for Berville. But he walked casually away. Mosey talked to his back for as long as he could see Mark, and perhaps even after.

"What I'd do is let her go. You don't need her voice naggin' hurry, hurry all your days . . . It'll tie your innards in knots and kill ya . . . I know, young fella . . . I been there. Only reason I ain't dead is cause . . ."

Behind him, Mark heard the old man's voice trail off and had to grin. The old man was right, he thought. A woman surely will tie your innards in knots and could even get you killed. Look where he was right now because of Lorraine.

Mark tied what bags he could to the horse. He'd prefer taking the rig, but thought he might be more able to avoid notice on the way to Berville with the horse. He'd ride off into a woods, if he had to – if he saw a badge following. He arrived late at night after a grueling ride. He was tired and edgy from straining to see other riders in the darkness. He figured they were most likely looking for him and the satchel by now. They had to be.

Berville could hardly be called a town, it was so small. Why on earth, he wondered, would she stop here? Perhaps old Mosey wouldn't take her any further. Maybe he'd had enough.

He backtracked to the edge of town till he found the stream he had spotted earlier almost hidden between the tall white pine and tamarack trees. They would provide some shelter from the eyes of any passing strangers, as well as from the night's dew. It was cool under the canopy of tangy smelling pines, and his footsteps made soft rustling sounds as needles were brushed from beds long settled. He made his way to the creek and washed the dust from his face and hands, then lay down on his jacket and slept.

When dawn was just beginning to turn the dark silhouettes of tamarack leaves to green, he rose, went to rinse in the stream again, and rode into town. Berville didn't have a train depot, so he stopped at the only hotel in town, a broken building which boasted shutters hanging at odd angles, windows with cracked and missing panes, and a mud walkway to an unpainted door.

"She wouldn't stay here," Mark murmured to himself in despair. "Not even for a night."

He checked, anyway, and was wrong. He'd been wrong a lot lately, he mused. Lorraine had stayed and had gone at first light the next morning. She must have kept a low profile, because anyone who had seen her just walking through this broken town would have remembered, but Mark's questions went unanswered until he went to the stable. There, Mark finally found someone who at least knew her direction.

"Do you know where she was going," Mark asked, "and who she went with?"

A grey bearded man with what was surely last week's catsup covering his shirt stared belligerently at him.

"Why do you want to know?" he growled, then turned his back to Mark and continued scraping a horse's hoof, precisely and almost lovingly trimming the edges of the hoof as if it belonged to his child. He ignored Mark and spoke in soothing tones to the leg he was holding propped on his knees. The angle of the leg looked awkward, but the sleek brown mare merely glanced back at the man, nickered and blinked her huge brown eyes. If it had been a cat, Mark thought, it would have been purring.

As anxious as he was, Mark had to silently watch for a few moments, bemused by the man's obvious dislike of people and love for the muscled creature he was caring for so tenderly.

"Look," he said more gently. "The woman I asked about is my wife. We . . . uh, had a little spat. That's all. You know how it is."

The man looked up from the hoof, took aim and spit a solid stream of tobacco juice at a fly resting on a near stall rail. The fly dropped to the straw, thrashed in circles, and then it flew off in an unsteady exit toward the open door.

"Well," the old man finally dragged out. He turned and stared at Mark as if to draw information from his eyes. After interminable moments, he seemed satisfied and returned to the hoof still resting on his knee. Mark began to wonder if the man had forgotten the question, or if he even remembered Mark was there.

Finally, "Sure, I saw her."

Again, Mark waited, thinking he couldn't push this man, but no more information was forthcoming. He wanted to put his strong hands around the old coot's neck and squeeze, yet, at the same time, he found the man intriguing. His obvious love of the animal, his distrust – dislike of fellow humans, his reluctance to speak to a stranger about another. But he was pressed for time.

"Look," he said. "I'd like to buy the grey in the next stall. Is she for sale? I have an old nag. She won't go much further, and she's yours for pennies on the dollar."

When the man nodded yes, Mark again tried to question him. She was heading south the old man said, and his words came out slowly as he gently stroked Mark's old horse, soothing her into the stall. Mark smiled, thinking the old horse didn't realize how good she was going to have it in the hands of this man. His bet was the rest of her days would be golden. He should have it so good.

Without a certain destination, Mark was lost. He just headed south on the horse he had purchased from the man. At least the new horse didn't look like she was about to fall over. He didn't know what else to do. Three weeks of dodging strangers to stay clear of lawmen, of staying in towns just long enough to catch wind of her possible direction, had worn him out. It seemed she was moving just to keep out of his way, which was probably smart because he wanted to strangle her – badly. What money he'd had in his pocket when he left the train was almost gone, and his hope of a quick resolution was wearing thin.

He lay under the stars at night, far from the noise of town and stared at the sky. He would turn her in, he determined, get help in tracking her and the payroll. Clear his name of the crime. She wasn't worth the effort, and who would believe he hadn't taken the money? Who would believe Lorraine was the thief, and he was merely trying to find her and bring the payroll back to Landmark? But with each star, he changed his mind. To the north, where the brightest one blinked in the indigo sky, he saw innocence, Jamie and Flossie. And in the next moment, he saw their need of a mother and knew he couldn't turn her in. Not for her, for them. The desire to see her pay was strong, but it couldn't outweigh his desire to protect his kids – unless it meant prison for himself, leaving them alone with her. He would not entrust them to her. If it came down to it, he would not hesitate to incriminate her. He just hoped it wouldn't.

It was near the end of the fourth month of searching. He had made the usual rounds of train depot, hotel and dining room. He was tired and sick of asking the same questions, describing the same woman. It was all becoming a blur. By this time, all depots looked alike; the attendants all carried the same knowing smirk; the answers all added up to the same thing. Between hems and haws, shuffled feet and suspicious leers, there was no Lorraine. She was always one step ahead.

Mark's despair showed in his growing lack of caution. The air was brisk, but the sun warmed his back, streaming over his shoulder and taking over his tired senses. He idly watched a slender woman cross the road, noted her sturdy good looks, and his eyes softened in appreciation. His mare slowed to a stop near her, and the woman turned, sensing his eyes upon her.

She looked at Mark with pleasure on her open face, an honest statement. She also liked what she saw. Wordlessly, Mark swung his leg gracefully over the saddle and landed lightly in front of her. Then he reached for the packages she carried and asked if he could help.

It had been a long time since he had enjoyed the pleasure of a lady's company, and this one was worth it. Her bright green eyes slanted in the sun, looking feline, but friendly.

"I am able to carry my own packages, Sir," she said, her voice a husky whisper. But her grin belied her words as she released them to Mark. She started walking, and Mark followed, carrying her wrapped goods.

"I smell fresh bread," he remarked lightly.

"I don't bake," she answered.

"What do you do?"

Without missing a step and looking straight ahead, she responded, "Anything I really want to."

She held the white gate open for him and led the way up a flower edged path. The house was small, but neat. Chintz curtains showed through sparkling windows and lent an air of cozy primness. She led Mark inside, took the packages, and began putting them away in sparsely filled cupboards. Finished, she turned to him, looked him squarely in the eyes, and waited silently.

Never had Mark met such a firm, unclouded gaze. She seemed so self-assured, so unselfconscious. No coyness here. He was unused to being in the position of having to think of something to say, and for a moment he couldn't. He was a bit uncomfortable and faltered.

Then he grinned at his foolishness and extended his hand to her. "I'm Mark Ramey. New in town." He waited and watched a slow smile spread over her face.

"Ginny," she said and shook his hand in a slow, vigorous grasp. "Hungry?"

"Starved," he answered.

She laid the table with cheese, fresh bread, canned pears, and topped the meal off with an apricot cognac. The drink she had made.

"It's good," Mark said, sipping from the small glass of golden liquid. "And potent." He could feel himself beginning to mellow. A light fuzziness enveloped him. He was surprised, but pleased with the feeling. Most likely it wasn't as much the potency of cognac as the long days of riding and even longer nights of sleeping on damp leaves.

"It's the only thing I make, my cognac. I don't cook." She shrugged her shoulders slightly when he asked how she lived – ate.

Sunlight streamed through the porch windows, warming the room. Conversation was brief; not stilted, but comfortable. Nothing needed to be said and so it wasn't. Questions went unasked for lack of need for answers. Mark felt warmed – by the sun – by Ginny's placid acceptance. She led him to the living area, and waving an arm at the overstuffed couch, left him to rest while she picked up the lunch things. Hours later, when dusk was beginning to settle over the room, he awoke.

They sat on the screened porch, talking in broken sentences, taking in the lonely night and the momentarily filled emptiness. His hand brushed her neck, lifted the wisps of soft, gold hair which had fallen from the tie at the back of her head, and she nodded.

The next morning, Mark rode lazily through town, enjoying the early morning breeze and the sun which was making an infantile show of its real power.

A man waved at him from the doorway of the train station as he passed, calling him over. Mark slowed his mare and rode in his direction.

"Mister," he called. "You the one who was lookin' for the woman? I remembered something last night you might want to know." Then he turned and went back into the station.

Suddenly alert, Mark rolled off the saddle, looped the reins around the rail and practically ran to the man who had spoken.

"What?" he eagerly shouted at the man's retreating back, his face lit with new hope. "What did you remember?"

In a flash, Mark's mind played with visions of a time when this nightmare would be over, when he could sleep in clean sheets every night, hold his children, sit with them at breakfast every morning, wake and not have to saddle a horse to ride to strange places and question strange people. In a split second, he knew he would leave Lorraine no matter what and make a real home for his kids, a place free of her influence.

Mark ran into the depot after the man and found him, peering from behind the broad back of a man with a shiny star on his chest.

CHAPTER FOUR

K ate saw the sun's first rays from the window of her loft. It was just peeking over the hills, sending knife-like spears through the still dark leaves of the pine trees. She edged closer to the window and watched the tamarack's leaves just beginning to turn red gold in morning's light. 'It's time,' she groaned. 'You can do this, Kate. Nothing to worry about, just get up and do it.' She groaned again, more painfully than the last time, and rolled to bury her head in the pillow. 'What were you thinking? You're not a teacher. What do you know about teaching? When will you stop saying, "Sure, I can do that," to everyone about everything?'

She was still muttering to herself as she quickly threw a wrap around her shoulders against the morning chill and headed for the kitchen basin to wash away traces of the night's dreams. This morning, it was harder to leave her loft. It was safe. She could lie as still as a summer night and roam far into the world of her fantasies. In the world of her mind, she didn't have to battle practicality with desire, solidity with excitement, the expected with the unexpected. She was free and unfettered by the 'shoulds' of the world. "You should do this, Kate. You should do that, Kate." It made her want to scream. But she was doing the 'should' now – getting ready to teach her first class.

It was September fifth, and morning promised a warm, sunny day, the first day of school. She was apprehensive, yet excited to be on the other side of the classroom. Some of her students had been fellow classmates just two years before. As she dressed, she was remembering the harassment a couple of the most aggressive boys had put the last teacher, Mr. Stinson, through.

Kate wondered how she would handle it if they did it again. Toads in the lunch boxes, poison ivy in the wood stove. As the inevitable smoke filtered through the room, the itching and sneezing began until they had all been forced to leave school for the day. But the worst, and the funniest – to Kate, at the time anyway – had been the use of old Mrs. Hale's cure for constipation, a condition she repeatedly complained of to anyone who said "How are you?"

Mrs. Hale, who appeared to be at least ninety, had been taught by her mother to gather medicinal herbs in the forest. Most people in town had at one time or another sought her healing herbs when the doctor couldn't fix their ills. She had taught herself to bake certain herbs in brownies. "It keeps you regular," she said. "Cleanses the body, and you take your medicine in something you like to eat."

Mrs. Hale's constipation brownies had found their way to the school house and into Mr. Stinson's stomach. His appetite for sweets was well known to the students and verified by his girth. He had greedily munched the brownies under the watchful eyes of the two boys who had brought the unexpected gift. Shortly thereafter, he had headed for the outhouse and hadn't returned to the school for two days.

At the time, although she had felt a certain empathy for the teacher, she couldn't quite bring herself to ignore the humor in his shocked expression, his exclamation of horror as he recognized his predicament and fled the room.

Kate pondered as she briskly walked through Jackson's woods to the school. Her back was straight, head held high – teacher style – she thought. That's who I am now. The teacher.

She had just reached the edge of the woods, where sunlight colored the foliage gold, when Mel's buggy pulled up. Hardly waiting for the rig to stop, he jumped down, grabbed her arm and squeezed. His face was lit in anticipation; eager, wide eyed delight danced in his eyes.

"I went by your house. Thought I'd give you a ride on your first day," he said.

Kate's face didn't show nervousness; she would never allow it to show, but the stiffness of her back and neck gave her away. Mel put both hands on her shoulders, gave her a little shake and said, "Come on, Kate, you're going to be the best darn teacher this county ever had . . . the prettiest, too," he added softly.

With a quick, stolen kiss on her lips, he swung her easily up and into the buggy.

"Did you cut a hickory switch?" he asked. "I've heard that you can't teach without one."

"Darn, I knew I'd forgotten something."

Mel leaned back in the seat and looked at Kate. "Ah," he crooned. "What a beautiful morning. Tell me, Kate. Has there ever been a teacher who played hooky on the first day of school?"

She laughed, feeling a bit more relaxed. "Not that I know of."

"Do you want to be the first? We could go sit on the Muskegon River and fish. I'll show you my secret spot. I don't give away my special place to just anyone you know. Or we could fly a kite. I haven't done that in a coon's age." He held his finger into the wind and said, "From the west. It'll be a good kite flying day."

Mel's unusual banter continued until Kate's back settled against the seat. It was more words than Mel had strung together in all the years Kate had known him. By the time they reached the school, Kate was at ease and laughing, worries put aside by Mel's gentle wisdom. He had an uncanny ability to know immediately what was important and what was not, what was worth worrying about and what couldn't be solved by worry. Some things just were, to Mel. They just existed as part of life. They had to be accepted, and you moved on.

"Thank you, Mel. You're good to me."

Mel didn't speak, just nodded.

"I feel like I could handle a hundred students, a hundred frog-toting, poison ivy-spreading, prune juice brownie-baking maniacs."

Mel jumped from the buggy and went around to help Kate down. His eyes were gentle and spoke love and pride as he left her at the door of the school house. Kate walked in knowing she could handle the job. She was going to be great.

She settled her books and slates on the desk, and then heard a soft knock on the door. She opened it to find Mel standing there like an errant school boy with his hand behind his back.

"I wanted to bring you flowers, but couldn't find any close by. Anyway, this might be more useful," he said grinning. He reached for Kate's hand, placed a three foot long slender branch in it and left her. She looked at the switch in her hand. It had been carefully stripped of branches and bark. It was cool to the touch. She flicked it through the air, and the end whipped back and forth whistling in the air. Kate smiled. Much better than flowers, she thought. She was still grinning as she placed her gift next to her and deliberately in front of where the older students sat.

For the rest of the day, whenever she felt her confidence slipping, she looked at the switch resting against her table. Her back straightened, and her eyes took on a look saying 'Don't mess with me. I have a switch and I'm willing to use it.' Even Peter Nestor backed down, and he thought he ruled the schoolroom like the family ruled the town. Today, however, he wasn't quite sure, and they all eyed Kate with new reserve. They didn't quite trust the look in her eyes and the hickory stick so near her hand.

'I can do it!' she silently shouted to the walls of the empty schoolroom. 'I scared the hell out of that Nestor bully! Oh, Kate, don't say hell, even in your mind. Someone will surely hear you thinking cuss words. They'll read it in your eyes.' "Damn these eyes," she said out loud, grinning, then added, "Sorry."

She took the long way home, wandering aimlessly through town. She didn't want the day to be done. She felt too good and was restless. She noticed many townsmen standing in doorways, gathering in Nestor's store and in all of the saloons. Shouts came from the Landmark office, and she saw men with angry faces waving dollar bills in their outstretched hands.

Kate stopped to stare and wonder at the anger. It appeared the men had finally been paid their wages, and hope surged inside her. Maybe Mark had returned and their suspicions had all been wrong.

She had tried not to think about Mark. She knew two things: they had been looking for him without success, and the payroll had never shown up. Everyone knew Mark had left the train and the sheriff along with a couple of Landmark men were following his trail. According to the news in town, they were always just days behind Mark as they followed him from town to town. It had seemed to the authorities at first as if Mark wanted to be found, but lately he had become more and more elusive.

Kate edged closer to Landmark's office. A portly man in a tailored blue suit was introducing himself to a group of plaid shirted men. His watch chain stretched across a well-fed belly and glittered in the sun, an insult to the men around him who had been stretching potatoes and milk gravy for their families the last several weeks. Two huge rings ignited angry sparks in the eyes of the men surrounding him.

"Brent Cole," he said, his pale skin growing red as he noted the men forming a circle around him. "Part owner of Landmark."

"Matt Keller, foreman of your crew."

"Seems like we got a little trouble with your men," Cole said, eyeing the men pointedly. "I'm going to check in at the hotel and wash up. Meet me in the dining room in half an hour. I'm sure we can figure a way to get the men back to work, talk some sense into these jacks. I'm counting on your help, Matt."

With orders given, he rolled on the balls of his feet and bounced away. His short, stubby arms stuck out from his sides as if the tight stretch of his shiny suit coat wouldn't allow them to hang down and swing freely.

Matt watched him go, concern clouding his face. He looked around him and saw all the men – the 'jacks' according to Cole – eyeing his retreating back. He thought about the man's foolish words. He was figuring he could talk his way around the men, make things happen with smooth talk, a penny on the dollar, and the thin shell of his handshake. Matt was already sure Cole's mouth was going to get him into trouble. He didn't know these men, but Matt did, and he knew they sure as hell weren't going to take a handshake home to feed their families.

Crude remarks followed Cole, remarks made deliberately loud enough for him to hear. His neck flushed red, but he made no concession to having heard and bounced his way through the hotel door.

When he was gone, they gathered around Matt, demanding answers he couldn't give, each man blurting out a question before the next finished.

"What's he really like? Is he as womanly as he looks . . .?"

"Is he gonna pay us what he owes?"

"Let's see him in the woods. Why, he couldn't chop down a little dandelion. Did you see those pudgy little white hands?"

"Come on, boys," Matt tried. "Give the man a chance."

"He's a girl, Matt," John Altman shouted.

"John, Brent Cole could be on your side. He could be here to settle things," Matt said trying to soothe tempers. He didn't really think so, but he did want to give him every opportunity to smooth things over with the crew. He needed to get back to work, too.

Matt left the group to go meet the owner, listening carefully to the voices rising in volume as he walked away.

"Did ya see his coat and pants? I'd like to see him in the woods with that pretty outfit on."

"And those rings. Hell, I could buy a farm."

"He couldn't swing an axe. He'd chop off half that belly on the down stroke."

"Hell, he'd never make it that far. He'd brain himself with his axe on the up swing." Altman went on, liking the sound of his own story and embellishing. "His arm would catch on his belly, you know," he said, pantomiming the action and sticking his stomach out as far as his lean body would allow. "He'd lose his grip, drop the axe on that bald, shiny head, and it'd all be over. Hey, that's a thought," he said stopping to think for a moment. "Let's invite him to a friendly tree felling contest. We'd get rid of him, and no court in the country could fault us for it, cause he did it to himself."

John slapped his neighbor on the back, enjoying his own joke. In fact, he enjoyed everything. As long as he wasn't stuck in his father's clothing business chained to a desk and forty sewing machine operators, he was happy. But to a man, the others weren't.

Cole wasn't in the dining room yet, so Matt sat down and waited, going over what he had to say to the man when he got there.

Fifteen minutes later, a voice at his back said briskly, "How bout a drink? I don't know 'bout you, but I'm parched."

He turned to find Cole looking refreshed and out of place in another three-pieced suit. The Hersey Hotel rarely saw such finery. Although clean and well tended, the wooden tables and chairs gave note to its nature. The lumber baron's fastidious dress stood in marked contrast, a stark reminder of the differences in backgrounds and stations in life.

"That train was rolling up enough dust to choke a man," Cole barked and called sharply to the bartender for a scotch.

He downed the drink with one tip of his head, slammed the glass on the table and said to Matt, "Now, what are we gonna do to get the jacks back to the woods?"

"Well," Matt said slowly, thinking about his words. "They want daily pay. They need reassurance that pay is coming to them when it's due."

"We can't do that," Brent scoffed. "Our budget isn't set up that way. You know we can't." He leaned into Matt as if Matt was a partner and part of the 'we.' "With the little payroll problem we recently had and tying up funds in land acquisition, we're tight."

He circled a finger in the air, signaling another drink from the barman.

"They're spoiled, Matt. They think they can dictate when they'll work and when they won't. Hell, we can get men who want work from anywhere."

"I understand, Sir, but truthfully, I have to look at it from the men's point." Matt sipped his beer slowly trying to avoid an uncomfortable thought, scabs from other camps. He knew that was what Cole was thinking about, and he was trying to figure out how this man would accept opposition. To Matt, he didn't look like the sort who would take kindly to having his errors pointed out to him.

"These men work hard all week, expecting pay at the end. When they have to go home empty handed, it doesn't settle very well with them."

"They'll get their pay," Cole grunted angrily. "Eventually, they'll get their damn money."

"Eventually doesn't work for them, Mr. Cole," Matt countered. "First off, you don't know lumberjacks. They're a different sort, from all kinds of backgrounds that don't much lead to trusting. And they can't or just plain don't save anything for a rainy day. What's in their pocket gets spent."

Cole thought a moment, twirling a huge diamond ring around and around a thick white finger.

"How about setting up a meeting for me with the men? I'll talk with them myself and see if I can convince them that they'll get paid as soon as Landmark has the ready money."

Matt watched him, still playing with his ring, and knew he was nervous. About talking with the men? About Landmark? Matt wasn't sure. "Won't work," he said.

"Set it up," Cole demanded.

Matt shook his head slowly, eyeing Cole and seeing stupid determination. He had to hand it to him. The man met obstacles head on. But he didn't know lumberjack pride, and he didn't know determination until he had seen it in mass at a lumber camp.

"Okay," Matt said. "Tomorrow morning, eight o'clock." And rose, knowing it was folly.

Outside, a huddle of booted, plaid shirted men were waiting for him. They gathered around Matt as soon as he came out of the door, asking questions, blustering out comments, and making demands, all at the same time. Even the quiet men, those who watched and listened, were close by, in the background giving silent support.

"Hold it," Matt bellowed. "I can only answer one man at a time. Just listen and I'll tell you all I know."

Sam Prichard, a burly tow headed man who had come from another camp the year before, spoke loudest. "Is that fancy pants afraid to talk to us hisself?"

"No, in fact, that is exactly what he wants to do, but he wants all of the men, so I'm counting on you men to round up the rest."

"Where?" one of the Thompson boys shouted.

"Well, I forgot to ask," Matt said, a little embarrassed by his omission. "Probably at the office here in town."

"There ain't room for all of us in there," Pritchard bellowed. "How about out at camp, in our kind of territory?" With an explosive laugh, he continued. "I'd kinda like to see him out there in the woods, all duded up in his suit and hat, tiptoeing around the snakes in his pointy shoes. I can see him now." Pritchard pantomimed for them. "Ooh . . . I don't like dirt, and sawdust plugs up my nose and gets all over my nice trousers."

There was a great burst of raucous laughter at the picture Pritchard had painted in their minds.

"Alright," Matt said smiling and trying to calm what looked like might lead to a riot. "Have your fun, but when you come to that meeting tomorrow, come with an open mind."

"What do ya mean by that?"

Matt stared at the man who had spoken, a man fairly new to the camp. "Nothing, just don't judge the man before you meet him. And I don't care how much of a drunk you put on tonight, I don't care what time you get home or even if you don't get home at all, just be at camp tomorrow by eight with just breakfast in your bellies."

Again, the new man said, "What do ya mean by that?"

"Sober," Matt said sharply, and threaded his way through the crowd.

Kate awoke to a damp, chilly day and knew immediately she was late. The sun was already up, and so were Willie and Ruthie. She could hear them downstairs arguing, and Kate usually left for school before they were even out of bed. She jumped up, tugged her long flannel gown down around her goose pimpled legs, and splashed cold water on her face from the pitcher beside her bed. She dressed quickly and flew from the house. Eight o'clock. The kids would be there in fifteen minutes. Kate took the shortest route through the woods, marveling at the stillness. Everything was so damp and quiet the smallest sounds could be heard. The sigh of a mournful loon drifted to her from its home at the river bank. Nuthatch and the tiny tufted titmouse voiced early morning complaints to their neighbors, in the silence, their noise seeming much larger than one could imagine their tiny bodies ever producing.

Enjoying the sounds, she still hurried as quickly as she could down the shadowed path when an angry voice stopped her. For a moment, she had thought it was directed at her, it had sounded so close. But looking around, she realized it was really quite far away. She stood still, listening. It was many voices, many angry shouting voices, and it was coming from the lumber camp. The sounds were ugly, to Kate, and threatening. She stood still for another moment, her mind battling indecision. She needed to find out what was happening to cause such anger in the lumber men.

For several moments, she fought with herself, then – decision made – she left the path and headed through the woods for the camp. Brambles caught at her dress, but she didn't care. The voices were getting louder and uglier. A few minutes later, she crested the hill, just in time to see several men, menacing in their anger, close in on a short, stocky man dressed, as far as she could tell, in a suit. She stopped, surprised at the sight and taken back by the incongruous picture it made. Why would a man in a dress suit be at the camp? What was going on? But she didn't have time to dwell on the questions in her mind. The lumberjacks looked like they were about to tear the suited one apart. Matt and a couple others appeared to be trying to calm them, but they were outnumbered and the mob seemed riled to the point of insanity.

Kate was immobilized by the sight, and the sound of their rage made her heart pound. But Matt was in trouble. He was one against many, and it seemed the stocky man, whoever he was, was in worse trouble. She turned and ran for some kind, any kind of help. Town was too far away. She'd never make it in time, so she headed for Mel's farm. He'd know what to do, and he had a horse to ride for more men if he thought it necessary. She hiked her skirt around her waist and ran like the wind. Branches tore at her, scratching her face and legs. Blonde hair once tied neatly at the nape of her neck, fell down her back and flew into her eyes.

She arrived exhausted and disheveled at Mel's, found him in the barn where she knew he would be tending to the milking, and collapsed in a pile of straw. Mel just stared at her, obvious surprise in his eyes at her appearance. She looked so beautiful in her tousled state it was difficult to concentrate on what she was trying to say even though he knew it had to be really important. In between labored breaths, she tried to explain what was happening at the camp.

Mel collected himself, threw a saddle on his mare, and gave Kate quick orders.

"Stay put here," he commanded. "I'll send someone to tend the school til I can get back for you." He finished tightening the cinch and turned back to Kate. "I mean it, Kate. Stay away from the camp, and town, too. Go on in the house and get Ma to give you some tea or something."

"Alright," she groaned, still sprawled in the straw. "I can't even move a toe right now anyway."

Mel stared at her. She truly didn't know how beautiful she looked. Artlessness was part of her beauty, and he wanted desperately to forget the camp, shut out the problems, and join Kate in her straw bed. With an exasperated sigh, he lifted Kate from the straw, turned her by the shoulders in the direction of the house, gave her a little shove and he was gone.

Mel raced toward town, gathered as many men as he could find quickly, and started back to camp. The sides of his mare were heaving and foam was dripping from her muzzle when he reined her to a stop at the top of the hill. Below was a shambles, a full scale brawl. In a brief instant, he took in the sight.

Matt Keller ran from one man to another, pushed and pulled at them, yelling for them to stop. A punch landed against his nose which was already bleeding profusely, and one eye was purple and swollen. The two Thompson boys were on the ground out cold. Always ones for a good fight, they had been some of the first to join the fracas. It appeared they hadn't fared well. Jack Bay, the Boston lawyer-turned-lumberjack, was swinging a tree limb in a half circle, fending off anyone close enough to get in the way. It didn't matter which side they were on, he didn't want a fist on his face. He had always liked it just the way it was.

In the middle of it all sat Cole, hiding his head in his arms. Mel couldn't help the small grin playing around the corner of his lips when he saw him, and he tried to suppress it. His suit must have really gotten under their skin, he thought, because it hung in shreds over his back, showing pink skin through the rips in the shirt underneath the tattered coat.

Mel and his men waded through the tangle of lumberjacks to Cole and pulled him out of the mess. When he was safely away, they began pulling out one man after another. Some needed a little forceful persuasion, but eventually, they were all sitting or lying off to the side, nursing wounds and staring savagely at Cole.

After checking on the Thompson boys and a couple of others who were lying on the ground just to make sure they weren't as dead as they looked, Mel turned back to Cole.

"What in hell happened here?"

"Arrest these men!" Cole demanded, his bravado back with the return of safety.

"I'm not the sheriff, Mister." Turning to Matt, he asked again. "What's going on, Matt?"

"Well," Matt wavered, rubbing his jaw and wincing. "We were having a little meeting with Mr. Cole here, and I guess the men didn't quite agree with what he was saying."

"That was it? They didn't quite agree? What the hell is wrong with all of you?" Mel glared, standing tall, his shoulders broad and thrown back. His face questioned the sanity of the whole lot. Looking at the huge man with his fists planted squarely on his hips, no one wanted to venture an explanation likely to invite Mel's anger. He could toss anyone of them aside with one hand, but they weren't comfortable with his silent glare, either.

He had been gentle with the wounded, lifting them easily from the fracas and placing them safely in the soft grass, even folding his jacket to place beneath a bleeding head. Now, however, when they were safely settled down, his stare made them feel like bad children, still angry, but foolish, too.

"So you thought a friendly little fight would fix things?"

"Friendly?" Cole groaned, trying to stand but falling back against a tree stump. "I've seen friendlier snakes, and I didn't trust them either." Again he grabbed his chest and wheezed in the effort.

Matt kneeled beside him, feeling a bit responsible for the whole mess. He had known the men couldn't talk sense with Cole, especially in their own territory – their woods. But he'd been foolishly hoping for the best. "Maybe we ought to get you to a doctor," he said quietly.

"I'm not going anywhere," he said with as much bluster as he could manage through the wheezing. "Not til these men say they're going back to work."

Mel looked around at the men, confusion on his face. "I thought that's what you men wanted?" he asked.

"You've been sitting in Sadie's complaining about not working."

Sam Prichard spoke from his seat on a tree stump. "Yeah, we want to work, but we want to get paid, too. I've worked in other camps, and I know how it goes. If you let 'em push you around once, they figure they can keep it up. They own you," he growled. "And nobody ever owned Sam Prichard."

He sat there glaring at Cole, running a huge, dirty thumb down the edge of an axe as if testing for sharpness. His jaw bulged from a wad of chewing tobacco. Brown liquid seeped at the corners of his mouth and into creases formed by the ever present grimace he wore.

"And I don't ever aim to let that happen," Prichard said softly, the menace evident and incongruous with the volume of his voice.

"I told you, mister," Cole sputtered, growing redder in the face. He knew Pritchard's type. He was a trouble maker and needed to be dealt with. "You either go back to work now and get paid at the end of the week, or you don't go back at all. You'll get your back pay"

The men began talking all at once, and the anger evident in the voices said it was threatening to turn into another brawl.

"There's other men waiting for your job," Cole stupidly threatened.

"Matt," Mel said pulling him off to the side. "We gotta get that fool out of here. He's gonna get himself killed if he doesn't shut his mouth."

Matt kicked the ground in front of him, dust rising at the toe of his boots. "I'll try, Mel, but he's as bull headed as they come. And none too bright."

"Go on to the cook shack," he told the men. "Cool off and get some coffee." Then he and Mel walked over to Cole to try to talk some sense into him. Matt knew the man didn't understand lumberjack temperament. They were good men, but inclined to get easily riled and take action. They understood action. Too many lively skirmishes had landed many of them in lumber camps far from their homes. Some were not welcome in their home towns and were facing some jail time for prior actions they had been unable to contain. They knew their own minds and understood one path – theirs. They weren't bad men. Many were the kind you could trust with your life. But they used muscle at work, after work, and to make a point. It was hard to guide them to a point of view different from their own. Especially a view belonging to a man in a suit.

"Mr. Cole," Matt said quietly. "I thought you were going to reason with the men, explain Landmark's situation."

Cole puffed up, groaned and spouted. "That's exactly what I did."

"I gotta tell you, Sir, you can't handle these men by coming out here with threats to give their jobs away. They won't take it lying down."

Cole bridled and squinted his eyes at Matt. "Listen here, Mister. Don't tell me how to run my business. I've handled hundreds of men from Detroit to New York, men a lot smarter than these yokels."

Matt stood, hands clenched at his sides, and glared at Cole. "I doubt it," he spat calmly. "Bullied maybe, but you can't do that to this crew." Matt bent down to Cole and spoke softly, but grimly, into his ear. "These aren't your dressed up dudes from your city offices, Mister. Maybe you can twist them around to get what you want, give them a little pat on the back so they'll smile and obey, or maybe give them a penny from your money bag. This is the longest chat we'll have, Cole, and I'm going to give you a little piece of advice, so listen good. These men don't give a damn how they look, and some don't give a damn what they do, so watch how you talk. And if you can't do that, watch your back. One of them is likely to bust an axe handle over your skull next time, and I'm beginning not to give a damn if they do."

Cole watched as Matt strode angrily over to the cook shack. He looked around, recognized he was alone, except for the giant man standing a few feet from him, and it dawned on him what his foreman said was true. He almost felt the crunch of his skull as an axe handle thudded into it. His scalp prickled as he watched the men milling around the cook shack. He saw the red, blue and green combinations of plaid stretched tightly over bulky, muscled shoulders and arms; khakis covering, but not hiding strong thighs; thick necks corded with tendons taut with anger. Cole felt unaccustomed discomfort and looked around him for an ally.

"You're one of the men who stopped the fight, aren't you?"

"Yes," Mel answered, not offering more. He didn't like the man.

Cole stammered a little, not used to having to ask for anything. He gave orders. He didn't ask. "I need to get back to town," he stated.

"I thought you were staying here til the men went back to work?"

"Well, I can't sit here all day and night, now, can I?"

I should just walk off and leave this idiot, Mel thought. He deserved whatever he got. But he couldn't. He spotted Jack Bay off to the side of the group and motioned him over. "Give me a hand here, Jack."

"Sure," he grinned. "With what?"

"Cole."

"Sure, again. What do you want to do to him?"

"Jack," Mel groaned, appreciating Jack's sense of humor. "He wants to get back to town. I need help getting him up on my horse."

"Ahhh," he said drawing it out and nodding. "I guess I can help with that. Say," Jack added, turning his grin at Cole. "Sure hope I didn't hurt you with that limb I was throwing around. Just trying to keep my pretty face intact. I wouldn't look good to the girls with my nose all over my face."

"No," Cole admitted. "I was too far away."

Right, Jack thought. He was too far away, hiding his head under his arms and running from a punch.

"Glad to hear it. I was just keeping away from the boys until I caught my breath. Didn't want to hurt anyone."

"Come on, Mr. Cole, Jack. Let's get going," Mel said, intervening in Jack's bit of fun with the bruised man.

With one man on either side, they practically carried Cole to the horse and lifted him on. Before they left, Cole turned to Jack. "Aren't you one of them?" he asked.

"Sure am. Why?" he answered.

"You don't sound as crazy as the rest."

"Well, Cole, I'll tell you. It isn't worth stewing over. I'll stick with what the rest decide, but it doesn't really matter. If I don't work here, I'll work somewhere else. Move on. A lot of others will, too."

Mel started to lead the horse away, hearing its rider grunt with each step. Jack smiled at the sound and followed a bit.

"Cole," he said. "Let me give you some free advice, man to man."

"Do it fast." Cole said. "This isn't a parlor chair I'm sitting on."

"If some of these men are forced to move their families on, they'll make sure every lumberjack in the state knows the score in these hills."

"So what," Cole spouted wearily. "I don't give a damn what they think."

"Figured that, but you will," Jack said, grinning at Cole. "You might get other men to work in these woods, but they won't be jacks. You remember that."

Cole tried to sit a little straighter in the saddle, wincing as he stiffened his back and tried to put some bluster into his voice. "Is that a threat?"

Watching the exchange, Mel admired him just a little for his attempt at bravado, but pitied him his lack of real bravery. It was all bluster.

"No, sir. That's not a threat. I already told you," Jack smiled, his white teeth gleaming against the dark brown of his weathered face. Even after the fight, Jack's shirt and trousers were immaculate, shirt tucked neatly into the belt, pant legs tucked neatly into his shiny boots. His hair was combed back at the sides without one brown lock finding a wayward way out of line. His face was shining and looked like he had just stepped from the barber's chair after a hot water shave. But Jack would look immaculate at nine in the morning or nine at night after a full day's work. The men marveled at how he could swing an axe all day and not sweat. It just didn't seem right not to sweat, or not to grow whiskers in the daytime. He had a sort of compact elegance even in a coarse flannel shirt.

Jack considered Cole's question. "Like I said, I don't much give a damn."

Cole watched him warily as Jack turned away, grinning as he neared the men who were lying or sitting on the ground by the cook shack. He had a word or two to say to most of them, and most of them groaned and grinned back, making crude comments about Jack's unharmed state.

"God, Jack," Sam Pritchard said as he passed by. "Don't you still look pretty? And you stink like women's perfume," he said, goading Jack.

"I like my smell a hell of a lot better than yours, Pritchard. When's your next bath? End of the month?"

On the path through the woods, out of sight of the camp, Cole let himself go and slumped over, hanging on to the horse's mane to keep from falling. Mel didn't like the arrogant fool, but he didn't want him to fall off. It was a long trip into town going at such a slow pace. Every once in a while, Cole would start to slide, and Mel had to stop and shove him back on. He considered tying him to the saddle more than once. They didn't talk. It took all Cole had left in him just to cling to his mount, and Mel wasn't one for chatter at any time, let alone with a man he had grown to dislike in the short space of time he had known him.

In town, he half carried Cole into the doctor's one-room office and sat to rest. It had been a harrying morning.

Doc Cheston, a feisty little man of about five foot five, checked Cole out. He poked and prodded; peering at Cole through glasses so thick they made his eyes look as big as silver dollars. "What in the hell happened to you?"

"A friendly little fight, so I'm told," Cole said scowling.

"God, I'd hate to have your friends mad at me. You look about half dead. How do you feel, almost dead or just a little bit?"

When Cole didn't answer, Doc prodded at a spot and Cole yelped. Doc chuckled loudly. "Ah, so you can feel. Broken ribs," he said. "Knew it, just didn't know which ones. No more bumpy rides for awhile. Arm's okay, though. Just a sprain. You got a hard head. That's good, pretty normal, too," he chuckled again.

Mel fidgeted, knowing when Doc had a new audience, he liked to milk the opportunity. He was the town joker with a stethoscope. It felt like they had been there forever, and he was chafing to get back to Kate. He hadn't forgotten she was waiting at the farm. Finally, he dropped Cole off at his hotel room, telegraphed Wisconsin, as Cole had requested, asking for news of the payroll theft and letting them know Cole would remain in Hersey for the next few weeks.

My God, Mel thought on the way home, what fools some men are. Even more disturbing was the thought that such fools could own companies and control the lives of so many people. How does it happen? Where was justice, the reward for hard work and kindness, when men like Cole could turn the world upside down on a whim or for their own greed?

He shook his head, glad he worked with cows and crops instead of people. At least their whims were guided by nature, and while they weren't predictable, they were more understandable than pipsqueaks like Cole. Nature, he could admire, and deep down he believed nature's whims were not really whims at all, but parts of a plan too large and awesome to be fully understood by mere men. He was still speculating on men, nature, and the laws of both as he turned onto the path to the barn.

He halted his horse and sat listening to the sound of milk squirting with a familiar whoosh into the bucket Kate was bent over. She sat on his short milk stool, knees spread, and her bare arms rhythmically moved in front of her. Her forehead was pressed into the side of the cow, and her back was straight. Kate heard him ride up and knew he was watching her, but absorption and the cadence of her work kept her from acknowledging him. She was lost in another world of musty hide and fresh milk smells, of contentment and the warmth of the beast she rested her face against.

She came out of it as easily as she had fallen under its spell. "All finished." She picked up the bucket and patted the cow. "That's the last, and everybody's been fed. What pigs chickens are." And she laughed gaily at her own wit.

"You shouldn't have done that, Kate. I told you to sit and rest. Drink tea."

"I did. How long can a body just sit? I got bored, and it was fun."

Mel took the bucket from her and led the way to the house. "Come on in. We'll have some lunch, and then I'll take you to school."

"I need to get going, Mel. I'm really late."

"Hang on, Kate," Mel said. "Ed Miller said he'd send his wife over. No rush. She'll love being in charge for a while. You know it isn't often she gets a chance to be in control of anything."

Mel grinned his slow grin, thinking of poor Helen Miller in the school room trying to raise all thirty children to be good upstanding bankers, carbon copies of

Ed Miller, all in one morning. Kate read his train of thought and pictured the chubby woman with starched blue hair bustling around the room, straightening shirt-tails, tightening pigtails, and pursing her tiny mouth in disdain as the errant shirttails flopped out again and pigtails flew.

"All right, what's the scoop? I'm dying to know what was happening at the camp. Tell."

"In good time my sweet friend. In good time. First, lunch."

And they were good friends, Kate thought. The best. She felt so comfortable with Mel. He was strong, both physically and in the most important inner ways. Mel couldn't be rushed. He moved firmly through whatever needed to be done. He carefully considered actions and their consequences, and then did what he knew to be right. Kate watched Mel as they walked to the house and pondered her friend. How could anyone just know what was right? Mel always considered others in his deci-sions. Their needs were perhaps more important to him than his own. But Mel just knew right. Kate wished for the hundredth time she could be more like him, could just refuse to be confused about life and its choices.

"Ma, where's lunch," Mel yelled as they entered the kitchen. "I'm starved."

Kate pulled on his arm, trying to turn him toward her. "Well? Tell me. What happened?"

"Not much. Just a fight."

"What do you mean, not much? Who was the man they looked like they were about to kill?"

Mel shook his head and grinned. "Not on an empty stomach."

Kate stomped her foot and glared at him, knowing all the while nothing would move Mel unless he wanted to be moved. At the moment, he didn't. He was enjoying too much just keeping her near him and in attentive suspense.

When they had eaten lunch and were in the buggy, Mel told her what had happened.

"You mean they still won't go back to work?" she asked.

"That's what they're saying."

"Pa's mill. What's going to happen to it?"

"Tom and Will might have to tighten their belts and wait it out, just like the men are doing. It won't be his first time, Kate." Mel spoke calmly, but inside he still pondered the stubborn stupidity of men, the simple foolishness. Some things you had to fight for; principles were one, and maybe this was principle. But according to Mel, the fight was an extreme last resort, something to be avoided unless the cost was loss of oneself.

"The camp won't close, will it?" Kate asked. "They will go back to work, won't they?"

"Sure, but if what Jack Bay says is true, Cole is going to have to give a little or have a camp full of men who don't know a tree from a pussy willow. Probably some fighting to boot. The crew isn't willing to give up completely. They're a stubborn lot, and they're not going to let a bunch of strangers take their jobs. Don't know what will happen then."

Kate sat, quietly thinking of what it meant to her father, and to the whole family. No money coming in, again. Except hers. Now she could help. Her mother's face came before her, and Kate saw the look she knew would be directed toward Will –the 'you've failed again' look.

Mel glanced at Kate, saw the concern on her face, and regretted telling her what he knew. He reached his hand to her and lifted her chin so he could look her directly in the eyes.

"Hey, maybe it's not all that bad. Maybe I got things all mixed up. I'm pretty good at that. You know how dense I can be."

Kate looked directly back into his eyes and read them. She knew, alright. Mel was never dense. He saw most things with immense clarity, exactly as they were.

"My salary will tide us over, Mel, but Ma . . . I'm afraid she will take this out on my father. He doesn't deserve it, not this time. It isn't his fault."

"She won't blame Will for this, Kate. She's a fair woman."

"You don't understand. Ma is fair, but she has been through so many of his dreams. Pa never seems to wear down. He's sort of . . . young. You know what I mean?"

Mel nodded, knowing what Kate said was true. Will had eternal youth.

"But Ma has always been the one to worry about food on the table and shoes on her children's feet," Kate continued. "It's taken a toll on her, and she seems to get so much older . . . and angrier. I don't like it for Pa or her."

Kate had surprised herself, shocked she had said these things about her parents, even to Mel, but it had felt good to be able to. Saying it out loud made it not seem so terrible.

Mel didn't respond. He merely put his huge hand on hers, covering it completely and making her feel small and cherished. Her fingers barely came to the knuckles of his hand. He curled his fingers over hers softly, yet firmly. She felt the calluses press against her soft skin. They spoke maleness, strength, security. Kate moved her hand in his to search out the strength of those calluses against the back of her hand where the skin is fragile, and the veins flowed with life and stirred under his palm. The sensation both comforted and excited her. She looked at him, and Mel wondered at the odd mixture of emotions plainly written on her face. It was a blend he had come to know as thoroughly Kate, a face alive with clearly spoken thoughts even though her lips had not said a word.

CHAPTER FIVE

Autumn's gold turned to brown and whirled to the ground on sudden gusts of wind. Warm, sunny days changed in an instant to cold and damp, then back again as only Michigan falls can do. Every once in a while, the air would fill with the awkward song of geese heading for their southern homes, and the earth would momentarily darken in the shadow of their flight.

For Kate, time was at a standstill, and her inability to make things happen chafed. Change happens all around me, Kate thought, as she waited impatiently for news of the lumber camp and Mark.

As fall progressed, she had watched Ruthie, in her first girlish crush, bake cupcakes, slip away from Ellen's watchful eye, and rush them to some secret destination before they cooled. She envied Ruthie's innocent, care-free attachment to some nice, available young man.

She saw her brother, Willie, grow in his new job at Nestor's General Store, from a little boy to a swaggering young teen, jingling hard earned change in his pockets and reflecting the promise of manhood on his face. They were artless and free from care. Kate reflected on their innocence and wondered where hers had gone. Had she ever been as young? She was beginning to think there was something wrong with her, and she was unnaturally possessed. By Mark.

Will went to see Mr. Cole just about every day since the fight at camp. He came home a bit quieter each time, the tilt of his head a little less proud, his smile a little more forced. He never volunteered any information, just sat quietly through meals, keeping up the farce that all was well.

Kate finally decided to meet it head on and asked her father for news. She found the opportunity one evening when Ellen, Ruthie and Willie had gone to church meeting, and Kate was cleaning up the dinner dishes. Will sat sipping his coffee while Kate fussed at the dinner table, moving the salt and pepper shakers, brushing nonexistent crumbs.

"Did you see Mr. Cole today?" Kate asked, as nonchalantly as possible.

"Yes, but I don't think that it does any good."

"Well, what does he say? Is he going to make it right with the men and get them back to work?"

Will just shook his head slowly back and forth, a disgusted look on his face.

"He doesn't understand the lumberjack. Never will. His dollars and cents are on paper. Never really had to check his pocket before he ordered his dinner." Will stared at his hands clenched together on the worn wooden table, fine boned, calloused, hands with both strength and grace in finely shaped fingers and clean, white nails.

Kate stopped fussing with the dishes and looked long and hard at her pa. She would give anything to make life go well for him, give him the success he dreamed of and in which Ellen no longer believed. He had such great dreams. It was what kindled the light in his eyes, what made him. But fear had replaced the light, fear for his wife and family, and another failure.

"Cole has the means to wait it out. The men don't," he finally said, "and neither do I." He moved to leave the room.

"Wait, Pa," Kate blurted out. She could no longer keep still. "Has Mr. Cole heard anything about the payroll and . . . Mark Ramey?"

Will tilted his head and looked steadily at Kate, searching for some clue to the daughter who was so special to him, so much a part of him.

"Kate, why are you so interested in this payroll business?"

She squirmed under Will's gaze, feeling as though he could see through to her heart, her foolish, willful heart.

"Well, we know him. That's all. He seemed so nice, he just couldn't have . . . I mean . . . it doesn't seem like he would steal. I guess I'm just concerned. That's all."

Will walked over to where Kate was standing, twisting a dish towel into knots, took the towel from her and, with her hands in his, led her to the table. After sitting down, he raised her hand and stared at it. He saw a woman's hand where once had been a chubby child's. It startled him. She wasn't a little girl any longer, and if what he suspected was true, what Kate was feeling wasn't a little girl crush as he had thought. For once, Will was at a loss for words. His usual glib tongue failed him, and the wrench at his heart felt too strong to bear. Very softly, words came.

"Are you a bit taken with this man, Kate?"

"He was nice," she lied, trying desperately to sound casual and to still the telltale shaking of her hands in his. She watched her pa look back and forth from the hands he held in his to the face which couldn't lie. But Kate's words hadn't matched the nervous agony of her eyes, and Will knew it.

"When did we start telling each other fibs, Kate? That's not for you and me."

Minutes of silence passed before Kate spoke.

"Alright," Kate admitted, unable to test an untruth under her father's gaze. With Will's blue eyes just inches from hers, holding her with his intensity, she lost her desire to keep her affections a secret. She wanted to share at least some of it with her father. He would understand, she knew.

"I was fascinated by him," she said. "His face just keeps popping into my mind when I least expect it. I don't know why."

Will released her hands now the pathway had been opened, leaned back in his chair and studied his daughter. A slight smile played around his lips and removed years from his face, gave it the roguish charm most people found irresistible.

"I don't want to pry, Kate, and if I'm overstepping bounds, you just say so, but it's just that you've been pretty quiet since that payroll deal and just a little too interested for it to go unnoticed."

This startled Kate. She had thought her feelings were well hidden.

"Has Ma noticed? Has she said anything?"

"No, she hasn't brought it up, but I've seen her watching you and getting a bit agitated whenever Mark's name is mentioned. She has her sights set on Mel being your husband some day. You know that."

Kate shook her head, and Will understood there would be no marriage between those two with Mark even remotely in the picture. He knew what love could do, how it could drive a person and make the heart sing. The security Mel could offer Kate would override all else in Ellen's mind and he appreciated his wife's concern. He didn't blame Ellen for wanting more for her children, more than she had gotten from him.

"Hey." Will reached out and gently tapped under Kate's chin, forcing her head up and her eyes to meet his. "We can talk, you know. Maybe it's better when your ma isn't around, though. Then you might not get so jumpy every time his name is mentioned."

Kate stood and put her arms around him, smothered his face against her stomach, and kissed the top of his head. What a pa, she thought. Could any other girl have a pa like hers? He knew her inside and out. But his knowing wasn't the best part. He understood and accepted all of her, unconditionally. His love was always there, for the good parts and the bad. Kate thought approval was what it was all about, not having to hide parts of yourself from the people who loved you. Not having to fear censure.

Will spoke through the maze of Kate's arms. "Kate, I just want to mention one thing. I won't tell you not to care for Mark; no one can. Just don't get so wrapped up in a dream you can't see anyone or anything else and you fool yourself."

He took Kate's arms from around him and looked her squarely in the face. "Mel is an awfully good man, and if I'm not too old to see clearly, I'd say he's in love with you. Always has been."

Kate's elation at being so well understood abruptly fled at the mention of Mel's affection. She stood like a chastised child, staring at her feet.

"Hey, did I say the wrong thing? What's so bad about being loved?"

"Nothing, if you can return it."

"I thought you had a great deal of affection for Mel," Will said.

"I do, Pa. It's something I can't explain, even to myself. The only thing I can tell you is before I met Mark, I thought someday Mel and I would be married. Now, I find myself comparing the two of them. I hate myself when it happens, but it just does. And unconsciously, when I'm with Mel, I find myself looking for the butterflies that were inside me when Mark was near. I hate it! I hate myself! And I feel stupid and mean, and . . ." Kate stopped for a moment and then said softly, "I want those butterflies, Pa."

Kate broke off, looked at Will, desperately hoping to see understanding written on his face, and did.

Will ruffled her hair like he had when she was a little girl, and with a sad smile said, "Don't feel so bad, Kate. You can't feel on command. Don't ever let anyone try to force you to. I've always followed my butterflies. Perhaps I shouldn't have, but I don't regret any of it. You'll sort it out. Maybe when you see Mark again, you'll find you've built up feelings that don't really exist except in your imagination, which isn't so bad, by the way. Remember you were just sixteen when you met him and were pretty impressionable. It's a great age for some of the biggest butterflies in the world."

Kate hugged her pa again and went to her loft to sort out the next day's school work, but more to sort out the things they had talked about. Will went out into the chilly night to sit on the porch swing and think about his little girl grown into a woman. He identified with Kate's passions and hoped she could hold onto them, not let them become lost in the living of each day, the routines of life. He smiled to himself at the butterflies Kate had described because he knew those same beautiful creatures. They still lurked inside of him. Not as often as they once had when dreams came easily and he still had the confidence to pursue them, but they were still there. Butterflies were what made the living of each day special if you didn't let the weight of living chase them off.

The week went better for Kate after having confided in her father. She was able to give full concentration to her students, and it seemed half of her troubles were over. She knew he didn't judge her, perhaps even applauded a little capriciousness in a woman. Kate knew that to her pa some errors in judgment and a bit of a wayward spirit were natural parts of growing, not to be hidden or even completely controlled. And if you learn to view them from a spectator's position, you can even laugh at yourself, shake your head at your own foolishness and move on. They were a necessary part of life.

Several times during the next week, Will met Kate at the school house in time to walk her home. On the way, he filled her in on the news of Mark's whereabouts, learned through telegrams to Cole from Landmark. So far, the news was not good. He was running, but was getting less and less careful about hiding his trail. It certainly looked like he was guilty of the theft. He'd taken the money.

But Kate would not believe it. The day before, Cole had told Will his men were only a couple of days behind Mark, and it had been getting easier each day to track him. Mark's picture had been sent to all the area sheriff's offices, and it seemed only a matter of time before he would be picked up.

"Pa," Kate said suddenly. "Something just struck me. What about the lady they said he boarded the train with?"

"Didn't I tell you? The same thought struck me a couple of days ago. I asked Cole about it, and they haven't seen a trace of her."

Kate was indignant. "Well, they spend all this time looking for Mark and don't pay any attention to her. That doesn't make any sense!"

"I think so too," he said. "But by the time they thought they might have to look for just her, it was too late to pick up her trail, and they were already too close to finding Mark to back track."

"Didn't they even try?"

"Well, they found out that she left the train before Mark. Now they think it could have been a set up, just to confuse anyone looking for them."

Kate kicked at a stone on the road, angry at what she thought was a gross negligence. Will threw back his head and laughed at her as she dropped her books, grabbed her toe and hobbled around on one foot, yelling. She hopped over to the grass and sat down, nursing her wounded toe.

"I must be out of practice," she grumbled. "I used to be able to kick one stone all the way home, never lose it and never hurt my toes."

Will sat down beside her. "That's old age creeping up on you. Now, Ruthie or Willie would never miss."

"Do you know where Mark is right now, Pa?" Kate asked quietly, her voice almost a whisper on the afternoon wind.

"Well, honey, as far as they know right now, he's somewhere in southern Illinois. That's about as close as I can tell you."

"Come on," she said, rallying and trying to put it behind her. "I'll show you who old age is creeping up on. I'll race you the rest of the way home."

When they got there, winded and red with exertion, they both hit the door at the same time and burst into the house laughing. Mel was there with Ellen, and they just stood there shaking their heads at them. Mel took Kate's books from her and pulled out a chair. She collapsed on it and grinned up at Will.

"Tie, right?"

"Right," he said and fell into the chair next to her.

"Good to see you again," he said to Mel when he could get his breath. "You've been a stranger around here."

"I've been busy with the farm," Mel said. "I saw Kate's mother in town today, and she invited me to dinner."

Mel glanced at Kate as he spoke, as if he had to explain his presence, almost apologizing.

"I'm glad," Kate said, trying to put him at ease. "You need a break from work once in a while."

From her chair, Kate studied Ellen who was obviously avoiding Kate's eyes. The dishes rattled loudly as she tried to look completely absorbed in her cooking. Kate knew her mother was doing her best to push Mel and her together, and she had to chuckle at her all too evident scheming. She knew, also, Ellen truly thought it was the best for her daughter. Kate grinned and couldn't help letting her mother know she was onto her scheming.

"Are you meeting Mel on the sly, Ma? Making secret, decadent trysts?"

That brought Ellen around. She turned, blushed and started stammering.

"Why . . . of all the . . . well, I never . . ." was all she could get out. Ellen's ability to be teased was limited lately, but couple teasing with sexual innuendo, and Ellen's pure soul baulked; her poise crumbled. She creased her brow in a much too deliberate scowl and mumbled something about being doomed to purgatory for our wicked thoughts.

But, somewhere deep behind the façade, Kate knew Ellen was secretly pleased. She was a woman, the kind of woman who would fall hard in love with a man like Will, and women, no matter what the age, like to be thought desirable, worthy of a secret assignation.

"Sorry, Ma," Kate whispered loud enough for all to hear. "I should have known you would not want to talk about it in front of Pa. He's slender, but if he's riled enough he might be able to whip Mel," she teased and turned to see Will grinning and beginning to get into the act himself.

"You always told me I was the love of your life, Ellen. Don't leave me for this whippersnapper." He playfully got down on one knee and pleaded, making Ellen feel more foolish by the moment. "What about the children; they need you. I need you. Don't leave us."

Will was grasping at Ellen's apron, pulling downward with each word, until the apron came untied at the back and left Will in a heap on the floor with the apron in his hands. Will was still playing the wounded husband in between mournful sighs and uncontrolled giggles, and by this time, Ellen was thoroughly embarrassed.

"Get up, Will," she half whispered in a groan. "Mel will think we're all fools."

They laughed, open, clear laughter, Will with his head back and mouth wide, Mel with a deep rumble, his broad chest heaving with each breath, and Ellen, now smiling, looking from one to the other questioningly, as if she was wondering who these people were and how she had gotten caught in the middle of all the foolishness. Kate felt better than she had for a very long time.

Supper was gay, with Ruthie and Willie joining in the light-hearted banter. Willie told Mel all about his Saturday job and how he was going to be rich one day. He regaled everyone with stories about the customers he saw in the store and mimicked old Mrs. Wellington.

She was a tall, thin woman, with sparse sprigs of grey hair sticking through a dark brown net. When she walked to town, as she did every day, you could hear her coming before you saw her. She chewed constantly and loudly, smacking her lips as she chewed, and she talked to herself as she walked, bent forward at the waist. Willie scrunched up his face, folded his lips in to appear toothless, jutted his chin as she did, and in a high, screechy voice said, "God damned men . . . screw, screw, screw . . . that's all they want . . . screw, screw, screw . . ." They roared in laughter at his impression of her until Ellen, who was momentarily too stunned to speak, stopped them.

"Willie, the Lord's name. What in the world has gotten into you, and we don't talk about . . ." She couldn't say the word, but a small grin played around the corners of her mouth and belied the pretended frown.

The next day, Mark was caught. Will found Kate hanging clothes on the line, the wind whipping her hair and the linens she was trying desperately to attach to the line. When he told her, he was not prepared for the impact those words would have on Kate. Color left her face, and her hands remained frozen on the line, turning as white as the sheet she was holding. Will took the sheet from her and dropped it into the basket at her feet. He didn't know what to do, how to help her. The blankness of her face scared him, so he just talked, quietly, slowly, giving her time to collect herself.

"They're bringing him here for identification by Cole. We'll be able to see him, at least. He won't have to run anymore. That's something, Kate. Now he can stop and get to the bottom of what really happened." Will rambled on and on, not even knowing what he was saying, just buying time for Kate.

"It'll be tough tracking down what happened from jail, but he'll . . ."

"Jail?" Kate screeched. The word brought her out of her suspended state.

"Sweet girl, he's suspected of robbery. Of course they'll keep him in jail. He probably won't be there very long. Just long enough to be properly identified and sent back to Wisconsin."

"Do you think Ma will let me go see him?"

Will began picking the linens from the basket at his feet and started hanging them up.

"Let's just wait and see, okay?"

For a time they both worked silently. The wind bit at their damp fingers, turning them red, and the fresh wet sheets slapped at their faces. The smell of burning leaves drifted their way occasionally, and automatically, Kate thought how the wash would smell of smoke when it was brought in. Odd, she thought, how the mind works, clinging to daily trivialities when all she wanted to do was scream. Holler loudly at the unfairness of it all. Punch Cole and all his kind, and cry.

Will took Kate's arm when they were finished and walked toward the house.

"He didn't do it, you know," she said firmly.

To Kate, it seemed Sunday was a month long. Through church, while legs went to sleep from sitting on hard benches and minds traveled in as many directions as there were people, Kate's mind could only focus on Mark. She heard not one word of Reverend Haven's sermon, which didn't bother her anyway because he usually talked about evil, not good, fury not love. Kate had never believed in his kind of God, the fire and damnation kind. Hers was one of forgiveness and kindness, and no amount of preaching at her would change her vision of the Lord. She had made up her mind.

Throughout supper, Will tried to cheer and distract her, Ellen glancing skeptically at both of them out of the corner of her eye. When it came to her family, Ellen never missed a thing, not a slight change in mood, not a change in appetite, not a misplaced hair. She didn't always try to do anything about it; she couldn't, but any difference was obvious to her, and she worried.

Ellen watched them both and knew they were trying too hard at normalcy. They were avoiding each other's glance, and when their eyes did meet, it was with meaning, an understanding which excluded the rest of the family.

The long evening and even longer night had left Kate exhausted. She lay in her loft sorting out the mixture of dread and excitement in the possibility of seeing Mark again, even if it had to be in jail. If a cell was where he was, she was going there. No one, not even her mother could stop her. And then she felt stupid, thought herself a fool, and drew horrible pictures of Mark not even remembering who she was.

Monday came, and school tried its best to take over, occupy Kate's mind. Frantically, Kate tried to think of a logical excuse to see Mark, some fairly innocuous reason for her to be at the jail. When school was over and she still had not come up with a plan, she walked out the door, determined to go anyway.

She hadn't gone ten feet when a buggy drove into the school yard. School children were still hanging about, their cries of laughter ringing in the sharp fall air. Their mirth mingled with the honk of mallards finding watery stopping places on their way south, and the crisp swish of brown leaves moving to the rhythm of the wind. Kate stopped, more grateful for her father than she could express, and for a long moment she took in the sights and sounds around her, then walked with forced calm to her father's buggy.

"Pa, I'm so glad to see you."

"Thought you might be," he said smiling. "I also thought since I had an errand in town, and just happened to hear about Mark, that we would stop in at the jail to see an old friend. You're just along for a ride home."

"You are a sneak," Kate said, giggling at him. "And I don't know what I'd ever do without you."

Kate was so excited and nervous she could hardly sit still. The day was suddenly beautiful. The sounds were not the everyday noises of autumn; they were somehow more poignant, more symphonic.

"I've spent all day trying to invent a reason to go there," she said. "I couldn't find one."

Will settled back and let the horses, Penny and Jill, amble along in their own good time. It was comforting there in the buggy, the two of them together, no words needed, the familiar sounds of the aged work horses' hooves thudding against the packed dirt road. Kate rested against the wooden back of the buggy seat, feeling release from the day's tension. She watched the back ends of the Hughes' family pets who had served them in all capacities; work horse, harness animal, saddle horse, and Kate drew comfort from their solidity and loyalty. When the farm had been sold to start the mill, Penny and Jill had been taken from the fields. Now they served by carting the Hughes family around. Kate looked around contentedly as their huge, hairy feet hit the dirt road with solid thuds and watched the sway of their bulky backs.

They stopped directly in front of the jail, and Will leaped down. He turned to help Kate, but she was already off and heading for the door. She suddenly stopped, her hand raised to grasp the doorknob but not touching it, and turned to Will. Her face wore a look of fear and excitement Will knew as thoroughly, comically Kate.

For a brief moment, Will mentally cursed Mark for having caused even the smallest pain in his little girl; yet, in the next moment, as the alternating flickers of joy turned up the corners of her mouth and set her eyes alight with blue ice, he would rather Kate have these intense feelings, in all their forms, than not know passion at all.

Insecurity gripped her, and Kate faced her father.

"I was thinking last night, Pa. Maybe he won't even remember us."

Will grinned and puffed out his chest. "How could he forget us? We're special. Don't you know that?" He lifted a tendril of Kate's blonde hair which had come loose from the rest of the heavy mass tied loosely at the nape of her neck. It looked like pale honey in the sunlight and was soft and silky to touch. The blue print dress she had so carefully chosen that morning was crisp, yet flowed smoothly around her full hips from a yellow sash which cinched her small waist. Kate's cheeks were pink from the chilly ride and added to the beauty of her grey-blue eyes – eyes reflecting all of Kate's thoughts, eyes which couldn't hide.

"Look at you, my beauty," he said with formal Will Hughes elegance. "How could anyone forget you?" Will paused for a moment lost in thought, then glanced back to Kate, grinning. "Maybe your ma has been right all along. I guess I haven't really seen you in quite some time. You truly are a sight, Kate. Perhaps we should keep you under lock and key before you drive all the Hersey boys mad, and one of them snatches you and runs off."

"We just going to stand here all day talking?" Kate said, blushing at her father's words.

"Jake," Will said as he opened the door. "We're here to see Mr. Ramey."

Jake was the jailor, a large burly man with a belly hanging well over his belt. His reddish hair stuck out over large fuzzy ears, and his nose was wide and bumpy. He made people smile just to look at him, and Kate had to wonder why now, when her stomach was churning in anticipation and fear, she would notice Jake's comical appeal. She watched his stubby hands pick up the keys and followed when he nodded his head, red curls flopping, for them to follow.

Mark didn't hear their approach, and Kate used the time to search every aspect of his appearance, feeling like an intruder as she watched him sitting on the bare cot, his head bent, and his slender fingers threading through his hair. He had lost weight, Kate saw, and the clothes she had so admired were torn and dirty. The part of his face she could see, once a beautiful bronze, was brown and weathered. In the seconds before he noticed them, she poured over his body, building a mental picture of his departure from the train up to the time of his capture. His boots were caked with mud. The jacket which once had hung elegantly from his wide shoulders, now hung in long folds, exaggerating his gauntness. All this Kate saw from between the bars of his cell.

As Jake set the key in the lock, Mark heard and lifted his head to see them standing there.

"Mark, how are you?" Will said.

The growing confusion on his face made it clear Mark did not remember them, and Will tried to cover the long pause, hoping to spare Kate's feelings and lessen Mark's obvious embarrassment.

"Will Hughes," he said, "from the mill in town. Just stopped by to see if we could be of any help." Another short pause while Mark stared at him, questions in his eyes. "Not much of an accommodation here," Will added, filling space. "Are they feeding you properly?"

All this, occurring in a matter of moments, seemed hours long to Kate. She felt like running out of the room, but stood firmly rooted, her legs unable to move, her mouth unable to speak.

Mark stood slowly and automatically tried to smooth his tangled hair. Kate could see his continuing confusion, then his eyes moved to Kate, and recognition dawned. He smiled and Kate's butterflies soared.

"Of course, I remember you." He instinctively wiped his hand on the pocket of his jacket and reached his hand through the bars to shake Will's. "And this is the birthday girl who plays piano and sings like the angels."

Kate couldn't speak with Mark looking at her. She nodded dumbly, staring at him and hearing the jangle of keys as Jake finally unlocked and opened the cell door. No one spoke as they entered the small room and Jake left, locking them in.

Mark broke the silence.

"I'm glad to see you, Will," he said, and then turned to Kate. "And you, Miss Kate, look even lovelier than before." He picked up Kate's hand which hung with dead weight at her side and, like before, so many years ago, bowed low and brushed the back of it with his lips. She felt at once as stiff as a statue on the outside, yet melting and liquid on the inside, with fire and butterflies all mixed together.

Still, Kate was mute, but Mark and Will seemed not to notice, or deliberately ignored it. Looking embarrassed, he waved his hand at the single cot.

"I'm afraid this is all I have to offer in the way of seats, but please . . ."

Will grasped her hand and moved her to sit somewhat gingerly on the wooden cot, her back primly straight, like that old string had been tied to her head again and was now attached to the ceiling, not the sky, but was keeping her firmly erect.

Mark squatted nearby. Silence again commanded the cell and seemed to roar through Kate's head. Odd, she thought to herself. How can silence be so damned loud? Damn, I wish I knew for sure if I spoke to myself or out loud. I'm always doing that. What's the matter with me? Should I apologize?

"Are you being treated alright?" Will asked again, smiling and trying to make casual conversation.

"Sure," Mark answered with a sardonic grin. He made a circle of the cell with a sweeping motion of his hand. "All of the comforts of home. Here we have the master bedroom, where you're sitting, and I'm in the dining room. Of course, I just arrived, and the furniture has been delayed a bit, but when it comes . . ."

He stopped mid-sentence, hand suspended in the air and stared into space. The naked face Kate had seen on Mark when she had played piano for him was once again revealed. It was only a moment, but it seemed much longer to Kate as she sat watching despondency play across his face and come pouring from his eyes.

Will shuffled his feet on the uneven boards of the floor, making a soft noise and breaking gently and as unobtrusively as possible into Mark's musing.

Very softly, concern evident in his voice, Will spoke. "What can we do to help, Mark? Anything, anything at all. Just tell us." He, too, had seen Mark's hell, and felt the weight of his suffering.

Mark turned slowly, loathe to come out of his brooding, and stammered, "I don't know. I just don't know . . . I thought . . . If I could just have found her . . . it." His broken sentences, the inability to express his thoughts, was so unlike Mark. Kate cried, terrible silent tears that couldn't be shed.

Neither Will nor Kate understood what it was Mark was trying to tell them. They only saw his anguish and confusion. The silence lengthened, filling the cell with defeat and suffering. Mark's fingers, the nails broken and dirt filled, pulled involuntarily at the frayed edge of his jacket, thumb and forefinger rubbing back and forth in jerking movements. Throughout the broken statements, he had been staring at the barren walls of the cell. He seemed slowly to become aware of Kate and Will again and turned to them.

Mark fought with himself, wondering why they had come. To see a real criminal up close? To hear all the sordid details first hand? He stared at Will, trying to read the answers in his eyes. He no longer trusted, but what the hell, he thought. Give them what they want.

"Well," he said slowly. "I'll tell you what happened, and you can believe it or not."

Kate stopped him, more sharply than she intended. "You don't need to explain anything, Mark. We know you are innocent, and that's enough."

Mark looked intently at her, trying to believe her words, but finding difficulty accepting them at face value. It seemed forever ago since he had believed in others, even in himself. Then he thought of Ginny, the woman he'd met who had openly invited him into her home, into her life for a brief moment. There was an honest woman, he thought, one who knew herself and accepted him. So, perhaps, there were some left in the world, just not many.

"Kate, here," Will interjected, "has said from the very first it was all a mistake. In fact, heaven help anyone who said otherwise. And she has a darn sharp tongue when she gets on her high horse about things like innocent until proven guilty and all that stuff." Will grinned as he spoke, lightening the atmosphere in the small, chilly room.

You could hear the gust of a sigh escape Mark's lips, a sigh of surrender.

"That's kind of you Kate," he said softly, "especially since you know so little about me. I guess I owe you some kind of explanation, some evidence to support your trust."

"Only if you want to, Mark," Will said. "If you do, go ahead. Perhaps we can think of some way to get you out of here."

Mark paced the cell, back and forth, back and forth. He reached his hand up in a reflexive action Kate was to recall years later, to smooth back his shaggy brown hair, then to run a hand over his face as he thought how to begin.

"You know," he said as he paced, "what you say is true. I didn't steal that payroll. I might just as well have for all it will be believed."

Kate was listening intently, watching Mark, taking in every movement, every line at the corners of his eyes, each curl of hair escaping his effort to brush it back and finding its way back over his forehead.

"Well, after we had picked up the payroll, we were going to my parents to pick up the kids . . . my wife and me . . ."

That was all Kate heard other than bits and pieces in between calling herself all kinds of names: fool, child, hussy – lusting after a married man. Even Ellen couldn't have been harder on her than she was on herself. If Mark had noticed her at all, it was probably as an amusing anecdote to tell at the club. Little country girl falls for older city man. The old story. Only this time, it was her. Kate wanted to sink through the floor. Would have if it was possible. Instead, she straightened her back, lifted her chin, and determined to remain his advocate. It wasn't his fault she had fallen in love with him. He wasn't the bad one here. She was. He had merely been kind to a foolish young girl.

How long she had been lost in her own thoughts, how much of Mark's tale Kate had missed, she never knew. She became aware of her surroundings while Mark was telling about waiting in their train compartment for Lorraine to return, becoming aware it wasn't going to happen, and then beginning his search for her.

"Do you mean to say," Will interrupted, "that your wife took the money?"

A look of disgust passed over Mark's face, followed closely by anger. Kate was afraid for a moment it was directed at Will for calling Mark's wife a thief. Mark squatted back down on the floor, closer to them than before, and Kate knew he was about to say something he had never talked about before, something painful, close to his heart. She didn't know why he felt the need to confide in them; she simply knew he did. Mark didn't know why either; but he wanted to, he must.

"Lorraine – my wife," he said harshly, cutting each word off sharply, "is a heartless, spoiled child. At the risk of sounding like I'm making excuses, I married her when we were both too young to know what we were doing. She was, and is still, a very beautiful woman and can be charming when it is to her advantage. It soon became clear to me her charm was skin deep and devious. Anyway, that's beside the point. I never made enough money to suit her, no matter what I did or how much it was. She apparently took it upon herself to see she got enough." Mark stopped, suddenly weary.

"Do you have any clue as to where she would go?" Will asked.

"I was following her trail as fast as I could, but the sheriff found me too soon. I thought if I found her, I could get the money back to Landmark and keep her name out of it."

Mark paused, giving Kate time to wonder why he would take responsibility just to clear Lorraine. She didn't understand his need to protect this woman. She had stolen money. She was not a good woman, even if she was his wife. Kate was growing furious with this unknown woman for treating Mark so horribly when he obviously cared for her. When Mark continued, she understood.

"I could care less what happens to Lorraine right now," Mark said, "but I have two beautiful children I do care about. How can I let them be branded by having a mother in prison?

"What will you do now?" Kate asked. "You can't go to prison for her. Your children will need you," she ventured tentatively.

"I've thought about nothing else, and I've decided I will not sit in jail and let her raise my children. They won't turn out to be spoiled rotten adults, and I will not have them neglected. If she can't give them love, I can. I will. On my own."

"Well, then," Will said, sounding like all had been settled and the world was in fine shape. "We have two choices, find Lorraine or prove you didn't take that damned payroll." Will looked at them both as if for approval, rubbing his hands together in mounting excitement at the challenge. "Have you told the sheriff your story?"

"No, I wanted to think it out first to make sure I was doing the right thing. But I know now. My kids need me. Me . . ." he said more softly.

Will stood and, like Mark had done, paced the cell as he planned. Mark took his place on the cot beside Kate. He touched the back of her hand for a moment, lightly, just to get her attention, and Kate shivered.

"Kate," he said quietly, "thank you so much for coming here and for your faith in me. I know you didn't really have any reason for it. That makes it all the more valuable. Faith" he said more to himself than to her, "is rare . . . worth more than diamonds. The only thing worth having."

Kate sat mutely, unable to respond. She looked at Mark, looked down at the hands lying still on her lap, and then watched her father still pacing.

"Here's what we'll do," Will said suddenly, standing in front of the two on the cot and pounding his fist into his other hand. "The quickest way to get you out of here is to find your wife. So, we'll hire one of those investigating people. There must be lots of them in Grand Rapids. They'll be able to pick up her trail where you left off. How far ahead of you do you think she was?"

"I can't be sure, but I was traveling faster than she most likely was after I finally backtracked to where she got off the train. Probably a couple of days at the most." Mark showed the first little bit of life Kate had seen in him since they had walked in. A positive plan and allies had given him back a little bit of the pride which was such a part of him. "But, Will, I have nothing to pay an investigator, and I'm sure they will want their money – in advance."

Will ignored him and turned to Kate. "Jack Bay!" he said grinning his thoroughly boy-grin. "You know him, Kate. He's one of the lumberjacks. Used to be a lawyer back east somewhere. Got disgruntled. Hates cities and rules and good women, so I hear. Not that he cares a bunch for the others either, for more than a night, that is – oh, that's not for you to hear, is it, Kate?" He raised his arms in the air as if to say well, you're a big girl and this is your Pa talking.

"Yes," Kate said, "I know him, but what about him?"

Will continued his pacing then stopped to explain to Mark about the camp fight, the men not working and not getting paid for what they'd already done.

"That man, Jack, would do a crackerjack job, and I don't think he really needs money right now. He's not working now, anyway. If he needs funds, we'll work it out."

Will was excited, and Mark and Kate caught his enthusiasm. It seemed at the moment it could work, and Mark could be free to go on with his life. He called to Jake to let them out, and while they were waiting, Mark thanked them each warmly. Kate saw at least a little of the humor and grace which was Mark and had been missing when they first entered.

"Will you be back, Kate," he asked, "when your father comes by?"

"Not if he comes during the day. I teach school now. Maybe if he comes later in the day. Can I bring anything if I do?"

"I do need some things," he said, his eyes glowing new fire. "I haven't changed my . . . things in forever." He stopped, stared at Kate who had begun to blush and was looking at her father for help. Mark was enjoying the tiny moment of fun.

Kate, not to be made sport of, turned to face him. "If you mean to say you need underclothes, I think I can handle that, Sir. Make a list of your needs." Kate was sure Mark had deliberately set her up, and she chided herself for the blush. Silly school girl! Little country girl!

"I think Will can take care of it for me," he said smiling at Kate.

When they were again in the jail office, Will gave instructions concerning the comfort of Jake's prisoner. He threatened Jake's fuzzy red hair would be hanging on the jail wall if clean blankets weren't on Mark's cot by nighttime. The door leading to the cell was to be left open so that heat could get into the cell. Decent meals were to be prepared and coffee when Mark wanted it.

Jake's mouth hung open while he tried to absorb everything Will had said, a somewhat difficult task for Jake who plodded through life just managing to put one foot in front of the other without stumbling. Will went over it again, more slowly and less threateningly, and Jake nodded his head in understanding.

"Sure, Will. I'll take care of everything. You'll see."

Outside, the day was just turning to dusk. Will was chuckling over his talk with Jake. Jake did his job well as long as no complications arose, and his size was enough of a deterrent for most problems, like late night saloon discussions turned heated. Sadie's was where Jake was most often needed. He had pulled old George Simms out of enough would-be-brawls to have been classified his personal body guard.

Will looked at the sun starting to drift behind the trees and hustled Kate along. "I didn't mean to stay so long. Ma's going to wonder where we are."

"She's going to be mad, isn't she?"

"Well, probably, and I won't lie to her, Kate, about you being there. But I won't mention it either if she doesn't come right out and ask. I just picked you up from school and stopped off at the jail."

"She can't blame us for wanting to help him, can she? That's the Christian thing to do. She can't deny that."

"Naw," he said, putting his arms around her and swinging her off the ground and into the buggy. "Now you put it that way, I guess she can't."

On the way home, Will chattered happily, going on about Jack Bay, Jake, and whatever else came into his mind. Kate hadn't seen him so light hearted in weeks.

She listened dreamily for awhile, and then drifted into her own thoughts, back in the cell with Mark. She went over everything they'd said and done, mentally piecing together the parts she had missed. The fact Mark had a wife had shocked Kate, but it didn't erase her feelings for him. She had hoped, although faintly, seeing him again, she would find her memories had been built on some childhood infatuation.

As the buggy bumped along the road, her imagination jogged up pictures of Mark's wife. Kate saw her in harsh beauty with a wicked leer and her smile a red smear across her face. She envisioned soft, white hands with long painted nails turned under on the tips, fairy-tale witch-like. Everything comprising her beauty, Kate exaggerated to look ugly. When she realized what she had been doing, she giggled at herself and the pictures she was conjuring out of envy. But she kept it up and loved it, keeping the joy of her discovery to herself.

Will heard Kate's chuckles and peered through the growing darkness at her, a questioning look in his eyes.

"Did I miss the joke?"

"No," Kate said, pausing to wonder if she really wanted to share this evil little side of herself. "I was just trying to picture Mark's wife. He said she was beautiful."

"Is that funny?"

"Well," Kate admitted, giggling. "There's more. In my mind, I created a beautiful woman who looks a bit too much like a malevolent witch."

"That was a little rough on you, wasn't it? Still feel the same?"

Kate couldn't answer. Couldn't take tenderness right now or she'd end up crying like a homeless puppy. She just nodded and stared straight ahead, wide-eyed and willing the tears to stay away.

Will saw and asked no more questions. The rest of the ride home was filled with the sounds of the night. When they arrived, he kept the rest of the family occupied with harmless chatter while Kate slipped off unnoticed to her loft.

Kate didn't go back to see him for many days, and it was Will who took some clothes to Mark. She tried to forget he was nearby, but trying seemed only to keep him in her mind. His face appeared unexpectedly and with sharp jolts of feelings. She felt unpredictable dampness seep into the corners of her eyes at the strangest moments and stomped her foot in anger at her silliness.

"You don't cry, Kate. What's the matter with you?" She shouted at the empty schoolroom walls. "And he wasn't toying with you. That was in your own mind, you stupid girl. Damn, damn, damn! Yes, that's right! I swore, damn it!" But then she peered guiltily out the open window to make sure there were no loitering students who could have heard her tirade. "Sorry," she said, and then laughed out loud at herself and felt momentarily better. Swearing works, she thought. I'll have to remember that.

Kate drifted through those days in a work frenzied fog, sleeping fitfully at night and trying not to snap at her students during the day. She tormented herself for staying away from the jail. Mark needed friends who cared. She also suspected most of her thoughts were irrational, knew she had become obsessed with a need to know all there was to know about what was going on.

When she could be alone with Will, he gave her the latest reports on the progress with Jack Bay and the search for Lorraine. Jack Bay had taken an immediate liking to Mark and had agreed to pick up the search for Lorraine where Mark had left off. They had spent a couple of hours going over the territory Mark had covered, and Mark gave him as accurate a description of Lorraine as he could given his anger with her. It was hard to remember her beauty because it was covered by her greed and his knowing her too well.

Will had described to Kate the difficulty Mark had in talking about her. On the one hand, she was the mother of his adored children. On the other, Jack needed to understand her deceptive nature in the guise of an angel.

"She'll buffalo you," Mark told him. "If you aren't on your toes, you'll come back here thinking I stole the payroll and dumped her off in some little hick town. That is, if you come back at all. She's good."

Jack had laughed, his slender face crinkling just slightly and giving him a somewhat elfish look. He was enjoying himself and always liked a battle of wits and wills. He also knew no woman could outwit him. Not again. Not anymore.

"She might just try to keep you with her, if she thinks you can do her any good," Mark added.

"One wool hood was enough for me," Jack drawled, grinning. "More than enough for any man. I don't think she can work her magic on this non-believer."

The jailor, Jake, had also come to like Mark – almost adoringly. He jumped to the slightest suggestion Mark made as if it had been a command. So Mark's cell had as many amenities as was possible given it was still a cell, and the wooden door dividing the cell from the main room was left open to allow the heat through.

Mark had told his story to the sheriff, but as he knew would happen, he wasn't believed. Talk around town was bad. It was a set up, they said. Mark and his wife had deliberately separated to confuse the law. Many of the men were unhappy, out of work, and broke. Their wives were fearful. Mark was the scapegoat, the easiest target for their anger, but their plight didn't make it any easier for Kate to hear them maligning Mark.

She overheard one man in Nestor's store talking about what a dandy Mark was with his fancy clothes and always putting on airs, and he wasn't the only one talking. When she heard Sam Prichard going on and on, describing and mimicking Mark disparagingly, she couldn't help herself. She turned to him, drew herself up tall and straight.

"You might consider lessons from him, Mr. Prichard," and she looked him up and down, from muddy boots to torn dirty flannel, disdain evident in her eyes. "I'm sure Mrs. Prichard would appreciate it."

She left Nestor's and managed to hold her stiff demeanor until she reached the sidewalk. Hoots of hilarity from the men around Prichard who had enjoyed Kate's short speech followed her out the door. She also heard some things about her she wasn't sure she liked, something about her father having his hands full. As she opened the door, she took the opportunity to glance their way.

Nestor was grinning at her, shaking his head and saying, "You're right about that. Poor Will . . . That sprig of a girl surely is a determined handful." But she saw admiration in his eyes, too. She gave a little skip, and turned her face to the bright sky and chilly air.

Late in autumn, the trial was set. In Hersey. Everyone knew it wouldn't be a fair trial if it was held there. The men were too angry, felt too much pain from tightening their belts so much there were no notches left. Men who can't put food on the table for their families will find someone to blame, someone to take responsibility for the haunted looks on the faces of their children. Angry grumbles sprung up on every corner.

In the stables, Mace, the smithy, listened with a stern set to his jaw, and knew it was all wrong. In once friendly places, where good will was the norm, hostility and antagonism were bred, and revenge was the root of conversation. While the forests surrounding town were quiet in the stark absence of lumberjacks, voices rang loudly in Sadie's Saloon and around Nestor's pot bellied stove.

Mark would pay for their resentment if the trial remained in Hersey, and Kate feared there would be a lynching, men would be out to wash their troubles away in Mark's blood. Cole knew it, but claimed he was unable to travel due to the injuries that had not yet healed, and he was a necessary witness in the prosecution.

Once, when Will was telling Kate about Jack Bay and what was being done to prove Mark's innocence, keeping her up to date as much as possible, he appeared to grow inwardly pensive and away from her. She watched, curious about her father's expressions and growing concerned it was not going well for Mark.

"What is it, Pa? Are you not telling me something? Where are you?" she finally asked.

Will came back to her, back from somewhere else, some place where people go when they are not really where they want to be. Will had the uncanny ability to connect with people, and sometimes, to his own detriment, he felt their needs and hurts by relating them to himself. He felt their pain.

At the moment he was being Jack Bay and was feeling loss and anger. He knew Jack wore a false front and showed only what he wanted people to see. The soft places, the tender inside ones that tore so easily were under guard, protected by an insulation of easy smiles, laughs which came too readily and left just as quickly.

"I'm here, sweet girl. Just a little tired, that's all."

"Since when do we tell fibs to each other," Kate asked.

"Seems like I've heard that line before," Will answered, grinning.

"Well, you've used it enough on me that I figured it was time to turn the tables. So, what's the matter?"

"Nothing. Truly. I was just thinking about life and people. You never really know what some have had to go through, what makes them the way they are. I guess sometimes we get so wrapped up in our own little worlds with all our own little problems we forget others might have it worse, or had it worse at some time."

Kate's concern grew as she listened, thinking Will was talking about Mark, about his case, and worried it had grown worse.

"No one would guess," Will continued, "that Jack had any concerns at all, more than what he wanted for breakfast, anyway. He gives that impression. It seems that the world is a fine glass of wine for him till you look behind his eyes and easy laugh. But Jack's been burned," Will said softly. "Real badly. I guess I always wondered why a hot shot lawyer would give it all up to cut trees in a burg like Hersey. Didn't make sense before. Friends that weren't really friends, just men to have a drink and a game of cards with."

"What are you saying, Pa? I don't think I understand."

"Not much, Kate. Just that once you've been hurt so deep, you tend to protect that part of you. I suspect Jack has been there and is damned determined not to be there again, so he keeps people far enough away he can't really care for them. They can't touch the part of him that can hurt."

"I guess I never really saw Jack that way. He always seems so carefree, so happy."

"Sometimes we do that, Kate. Sometimes we play games with ourselves so long, we fool ourselves, too. It's easier."

Kate was thoughtfully quiet for awhile, questioning. Had she been fooling herself, hiding from herself? And Mel. Had he been in pain while she pretended her affection for him would grow into the kind of love she knew could exist?

She thought about her pa. Did he play games, too? Were his sorrows too deep? Did he hide behind his swagger and easy laugh? And her mother, was Ellen hiding? Was she the same woman she was before her own disappointments? Probably not, Kate thought, because every once in a while, the guileless Ellen peeked out, unchecked, and Kate saw the woman who had captivated her father.

Kate liked illusion better, much better. She wanted to be a girl again, to escape her mother's watchful eye and run into the woods to watch deer graze and squirrels scamper through the trees. She remembered that girl, the one who coyly flirted with the lumberjacks in town and sneaked near the camp to listen to their songs and then play them on the piano when her mother wasn't nearby.

The world was a much happier place then, and it seemed such a short time ago. What had happened?

It was a clear, chilly day. Kate saw her breath misting in the air and the breath of the horses as they lifted their heads to snort and stretch their necks. The trees looked stark and angular against the white of the sky, complementing Kate's feelings.

She had not been back to see Mark since the first time, and a mixture of emotions held rational thought in check. She felt guilty, like she had abandoned him when he needed friends. She wanted badly to see him, and at the same time she wanted never to see him again.

His trial was set for the following week. Jack had hardly had time to get started in his search for Lorraine. He had eagerly agreed to the job, anxious to keep busy while the camp was down, but there was no longer any time for him to complete it.

Will had arranged for a lawyer who would ask for a postponement, but whether or not the local judge would grant it was another matter. The longer the men in Hersey were out of work, the angrier the cries were against Mark.

"What do you think his chances are, Pa?"

Kate watched Will try to formulate an answer, and she knew. If it had been positive, the words would have come readily, but Will stared ahead, put the reins from one hand to the other, warming the one in his pocket before reversing the process and taking the chill from the other. Biding time.

"It's not fair," she blurted. "He's innocent. Why should he pay for her crime?

"Kate, you just have to accept what you can't change. Mark may go to prison for awhile, but we'll keep Jack on the job until he finds her and brings her back with whatever evidence is left."

Kate growled something unintelligible and pounded her fist on her knee.

"I hate it! How can this happen? It's so wrong!"

Will patted her knee, knew her frustration in not being able to effect change, and just nodded his head.

"Poor Mark," she finally said. "I don't know how he ever got mixed up with someone like her."

Will straightened his back and looked at her.

"Don't pity, Kate. It's not worthy of you or kind to the recipient of your pity. Save it for wounded animals," Will continued. "You know, we're all foolish at times, and we pay for it. Believe me, I know. I'm often foolish, and like always happens, payment comes due. The trick is to pay the debt in as good a humor as possible. Chalk it up to a moment of bad judgment. Pity sucks dignity, leaves a shell. Don't drain a person of what is theirs."

He turned to Kate and grinned, softening his words a little. It wasn't often he lectured her, and when he did, it was necessary and meant a lot to him. It wasn't about some trifle she had done.

"Maybe that's why I'm foolish so often," he said. "I've learned to pay my dues so well that I'm getting pretty good at it. It makes being foolish a lot easier in the long run. Though I'm not advocating it for you."

Kate felt a little chastised, but as they rode she thought about what he had said and knew he was right. Understanding isn't the same as pity, she thought, but she still felt so badly for him. Was sorrow a bad thing?

She was so wrapped up in thought she didn't notice the buggy had stopped and Will was waiting to help her down. She no longer felt nervous about seeing Mark, and for the first time looked around at the tiny office of the jail.

It had been built when Hersey had found need of a place to put drunk or unmanageable townsmen and lumberjacks. Prior to building the jail, Hersey had found other means of dealing with the occasional unruly man, usually by hauling them off to their homes and passing them into the care of their wives or mothers – a punishment much more constructive and practical than sleeping it off in a cell. Depending on the man, public embarrassment might, or might not work, but the town women's gossip network worked quickly and served to chastise most errant family men. But that was when Hersey was a sleepy little farming town, before the lumber boom. As Hersey grew, so did the need for a jail.

Kate noted the unpainted walls which still showed faint boot marks put there when the slabs of wood still lay in the muddy street waiting to be nailed together and made into walls. Over the single window hung brown checked curtains grown dusty and faded from the sun. A black wood burner stood in one corner with a granite coffee pot on top. Another corner braced up a shotgun and a broom, both of which you could tell from the collection of dust had not been touched for quite a while.

Jake got up from his makeshift desk when they entered and automatically took the keys from a nail on the wall behind him.

"Hey, Will," he said, and nodded respectfully to Kate. "Would you want to take some coffee back with you?"

"That would be nice, Jake," Kate answered for them both.

Jake helped with the cups and pot, and as they entered, Kate smiled to see the door leading to the cell area was open to let in the heat as Will had asked.

Mark was sitting in a real chair, instead of on the cot, reading and smiled when he saw them. After Jake had left, he came forward and took Kate's hand in his.

"Kate, I'm so glad you came. I was beginning to think I had somehow offended you."

"Oh, no, Mark. It's just been really hectic at school and there just hasn't been the time to get away," Kate lied, feeling foolish at the small deception, but not knowing what else to say. The larger lie was she would have liked to say a great deal, but it was not possible and would never be.

Mark, momentarily silent but smiling, looked around his cell. Two chairs and a small table had been added, plus a woven rug, thread bare, but colorful, nevertheless. A small lamp glowed on the table next to a book Mark had been reading and a well used pad of paper. Mark waved his hand in a grand gesture, indicating the additions to the room.

"I told you my furniture was due to arrive any day. Thanks to Will, we have a parlor. Please, have a seat, both of you."

They sat, somewhat uneasily, but not nearly as much as Kate had imagined or expected. Kate felt like she had done this before, this same exact scene. It was eerie, but comforting, as if she already knew the conversation they would have.

"Kate, I didn't have a chance to ask you last week about your work. How do you like being a school teacher?"

"I like it a lot," she answered eagerly. "After I got over being afraid I didn't know enough to teach others . . . and of the would-be-bullies, I really started to enjoy it."

"You afraid? I can't believe that."

"Well, I have a hickory switch by my desk that is highly respected." Kate laughed as she thought about Mel bringing it to her and told Mark how she had acquired it. He seemed genuinely interested in what she did, and they chatted lightly from one topic to another, forgetting his problems for the time. Only when he asked if Mel wasn't the name of the boy who had his cap set for Kate's hand was there a small moment of unease, and the discomfort was in Kate only.

"Hasn't that young man asked you to marry him yet?" Mark asked teasingly. "What on God's good earth is the matter with him?"

Kate, not knowing how to respond, just stammered something about time and not being ready and work, none of it making any real sense and knowing it was all lies.

Mark sensed he had stumbled into something distressful and quickly tried to move away from the uncomfortable moment.

"I have a strange visitor every day," he said with seriousness. "She comes to my window every morning just to swear at me."

Kate giggled, knowing exactly who his visitor was by the brief description, but she wanted to bate him just a little.

"Come on now, Mark. A strange lady just stops by to swear at you?"

"Well, not just at me, at men, all men. Do you know of a woman like that? She has grey hair, chews like a cow with a cud, and cusses like a drunken sailor."

"You must know her, Mark. A person wouldn't cuss at you for just no reason at all. Is she a woman scorned by you?" Kate teased.

"No!" Mark blurted out. "I don't know her."

"Well, what does she actually say?" Kate asked with pretended innocence, knowing what the woman says every day to everyone she sees.

"I . . . she chews a lot."

By this time, Will was chuckling loudly at Mark's obvious discomfort. "Well, Mark, I'm with Kate on this one. What's the scoop with this lady? Does she have a fancy for you?"

"Good God, no." Mark said explosively. "She hates men. Thinks all they want is to scre. . . Oh, God. I'm so sorry, Kate. You just . . ." He stopped mid-sentence, thoroughly embarrassed and looked pleadingly at Will.

Will was doubled over laughing at Mark's stammering. He pictured his understandable confusion as old Mrs. Wellington came to his window to harp at him about the wicked ways of men.

Kate joined her pa until tears ran down her cheeks and she began to feel a little sorry for Mark who was smiling, but not knowing why.

"That has to be Winnie Wellington," Kate told him, still trying to control the giggles. "She's the town character and really a nice old lady, but a little . . . uh, embittered, I guess you'd say, by the loss of her husband."

"Her husband died?" Mark asked.

"No, that might have been easier on Mrs. Wellington; no, definitely easier," Kate said, beginning to blush just a bit. "Her husband was sort of a . . . man about town. Well known at Sadie's. One day, he just up and left with one of Sadie's ladies; Mattie, they said. I don't really know who for sure."

Mark looked a little saddened by Kate's story, and it was obvious he was feeling badly for Mrs. Wellington. "Has she been odd like this since?"

"It gets worse with the years. Time and the kids teasing her every time she walks to town."

They talked quietly for some time about the old woman, and Kate saw a part of Mark she had only glimpsed in rare moments he had been lost in another place. He felt sympathy for Mrs. Wellington, appeared to care she had been so hurt and abandoned by her husband. His steel grey eyes softened to the color of a cloud long after the rain has passed.

They forgot Will, who was unusually quiet, consciously absent, but watching and listening. It was unsettling looking at them. They don't know the beauty of how they look together. And Kate doesn't know how beautiful and inviting she is, he thought. And if Mark can't see she loves him, he's blind. If I'm not mistaken, he doesn't see Kate as a kid sister, an interesting, but young sweet girl. He just doesn't know what he sees, yet. It hasn't occurred to him, and he's no rogue, even if he once was. Probably doesn't know that either. Will's heart broke for his daughter because he knew Kate did not love lightly.

The drive home was outwardly tranquil. Kate rested her head against her father's shoulder, and he let her ride in peace. No questions. No admonitions. It was too

soon to speak about their visit, about what he had
learned as he watched them. Yes, Kate had told him
about her feelings, but now he had seen it for himself.
He needed to think about what he had seen.

Kate was thinking the same. It was too soon. She
had also learned . . . Mark was respectful and caring; he
was not just a gallant rogue and she just a foolish girl,
romanticizing and fantasizing. She grinned a bit and
tried out some pretending.

'You jump around all over the place, Kate,' she said
to herself. 'By tomorrow morning, you'll probably have
forgotten his name.' Then, under her breath, she said,
"No, Kate. You'll painfully always know him. But that's
alright."

CHAPTER SIX

I n the week between Kate's visit with Mark and the original date for his trial, snow fell in giant drifting flakes and clung to the branches in stark contrast to the deep green of the pines. Looking across the valley, you could see the rolling hills covered in pure white with only the small homes and barns dotting the countryside with color. It was the kind of snow that created elaborate flower-work designs on window panes, like 'Sunday best' table cloths or intricately forged ironworks.

It seemed everything slowed down with the first snowfall. Most of the heavy farm work had ended, except for the daily care of the animals or small repairs lazily done by lamplight. A kind of sleepy quiet settled over, and like huge, hulking bears, townsfolk moved around slowly in the valley seeking a resting place for the winter.

Nestor's General Store was the place for activity, and discussion was of the trial. There, at Sadie's, or one of the other six saloons, men passed the time of day or a jug. At Nestor's, home brew in a brown jug sat by the stove, just close enough to warm and not explode. When the jug was passed from hand to hand, it was ceremonial, a ritual of manhood and winter. It caused a harsh clearing of throats and reddening of faces. The smell of damp, steaming wool greeted customers at the door, along with a warm blast of smoky air. When the jug was lifted while they waited for the trial to begin, it was accompanied by cynical toasts to Mark's conviction.

After the first real snowfall, men had time. Squatting close to the blackened stove to warm their chapped hands, they lit pipes and cigars, or rolled cigarettes, carefully tamping the tobacco from leather pouches onto paper, scowling with concentration, and enjoying the small effort of rolling, sealing and twisting the ends to perfection prior to lighting. On these cold and blustery days, the air eventually turned blue with the smoke of many men who sought warmth and companionship there. The women, whose daily chores did not end with the coming of snow, avoided the circle around the stove, and some were happy to see their husbands squatting near that stove, out from under foot in their kitchens, and not at Sadie's.

During the last few weeks, winter snow brought more than the usual quiet to Hersey. The axes from Landmark lumber camp were emphatically at rest, and their silence was louder than ever over the snow muffled hills.

Kate recalled it was during winter she could best hear the voices of the men working in the woods as if she were right there in the camp, so distinct were the sounds. They carried across the snow crusted hills, curiously enhancing and at the same time muting the sharp thwack of axes meeting wood, the harsh scrape of saws biting through bark, and the crack of branches as they crashed through still upright trees.

The men were restless with waiting. If the days were unusually quiet, the nights were not. As dusk wore towards dawn, there was some ruckus every night as the discontented men blew off steam, almost always in one of the seven saloons. Resentment against Landmark, Cole and Mark could be heard everywhere in angry whispers that turned later in the night to angry shouts.

It wasn't just the lumberjacks who felt the impact of the camp closing. The merchants, who had expanded operations with the lumber boom, were seeing their goods sit on the shelves, unsold. And much of what they did sell was not for cash, but on tab. Store owners were overextended, and the tabs they were running for the out of work men went unpaid. The farmers weren't buying with the coming of winter, and the lumberjacks had no money. No one was content, and the air in town was tense.

Kate could feel it. It was like waiting for dynamite to blast after the fuse had been lit, she thought as she walked to the makeshift courtroom. Who in this town has not been impacted by the theft of Landmark's payroll, she mused, and could think of no one. Not one person and the thought scared her.

The last week before the trial had not gone well for Mark. The trial had not been moved to another – more objective – town, and news from Jack Bay still wasn't good. A wire from him said he was about in the same position Mark had been when he was arrested; about two days behind her, as far as Jack could tell. They were all amazed she could move from place to place so quickly, without being spotted and picked up. The only way she could move about undetected so easily was she had help and she was good, like Mark said. And she was smart. She used her feminine wiles to get what she wanted.

Kate thought Lorraine probably pretended to need protection from the bad, mean husband she was running from. She hated pretense in anyone, but most especially in Lorraine. And some men fell for it, happily, when it came from a beautiful woman.

Kate was determined to be at Mark's trial, no matter what, if only so he could see a friendly face in the crowd. Someone who believed him. She had told her mother her intention, and then quickly left the house before Ellen could speak. It no longer mattered what her mother thought or said. Kate would be there for him, even if there was nothing she could actually do. On the way out the door, she heard Ellen mumbling about Kate being willful, her father's daughter and ruining her chances and her reputation. Kate was glad she could not hear the rest.

After two postponements, Mark's trial was finally beginning, and the town hall, now makeshift courtroom, was packed with men from the camp, frustrated merchants, and just busybodies wanting to know everything, the newsmongers wanting to see firsthand. They filled every seat and stood leaning against the walls, all eager to witness the fall of the Landmark agent.

Kate had threaded her way through them, ignoring their crude comments until she gained the place saved for her by Mark, behind the defense table. He and his lawyer sat just in front and, as he turned, his face lit in a smile. She could feel the tension in the room drawn to the breaking point and hoped he didn't feel as she did, that it was pointed directly at them.

As she sat, waiting for it to begin, Kate thought about Ellen's words to her as she had left the house and knew the townsfolk agreed with Ellen. Some avoided her, but glared when she looked them directly in the eyes and defied them to say anything about Mark. In the packed room, an odd circle of space surrounded Kate and Will who had joined her.

Will nodded his head to acquaintances, ignoring their outraged looks, and Kate admired his composure, his self-possession. She lifted her head a bit higher and imitated his actions, actually smiling as she nodded. She silently thanked her father for his lesson in dignity.

She didn't know the judge. He wasn't from Hersey, but had come from Big Rapids for the trial. She stared at him, trying to see through the exterior and into the real man. Was he fair? Logical? Would he be swayed by things he was sure to have heard? She couldn't see his eyes from where she sat and wished she could go up and talk with him on some pretext or another, assess him up close.

His dress was conservative, a dark blue suit. He was thin, to the point of gaunt, and his hands shook as he fussed at papers on the table. A full head of hair, graying just along the sides, belied the impression of old age the rest of his appearance implied. As he lifted his mallet to bring the court to order, bulging blue veins streaked his hand.

Kate looked at Mark to assess how he was viewing the judge. His back was straight as he leaned against the back of the bench, one leg crossed at the ankle over his knee. His hair had been trimmed and only one brown curl defied combing and had escaped and hung over his forehead.

His suit had been cleaned and pressed and, though worn, from a distance looked almost as elegant as it had long ago with the white cuffs of his linen shirt just peeking out of his jacket sleeves. He gave the impression of relaxed confidence. His demeanor alone should have told anyone who wasn't blind, Kate thought, how wrong they were in accusing him of any crime. Mark appeared assured, certain of acquittal, but Kate saw as she peered around him, his hands were held together so tightly the knuckles were white.

The prosecution's work was quick. Their witness explained Mark had been given the money. Others said they had seen him board the train, and still others said he had left. If he had not taken it, then where was the money? The lawyer for the prosecution was sharp in his incriminations and added very little else because little else was needed. The defense had no way to cast doubt on these simple facts because they were true, so cross examination was brief, and the prosecution rested.

The judge said, "Present your case," to the defense.

Dobbs, Mark's lawyer, stood to ask for a recess until the next day when their witnesses would be arriving to testify in Mark's behalf.

"They're on their way here now, Your Honor."

"Is their testimony pertinent, Mr. Dobbs?" the judge asked.

"Yes, Sir. The conductor will show, beyond doubt, Mr. Ramey knew nothing of his wife's departure from the train. He and Mr. Ramey searched the train thoroughly for her when she was found to be missing."

"The conductor will be accompanied by the station attendant who can attest Mr. Ramey did, in fact, have to search for her whereabouts after she left the train. These facts prove no plan was made for a common destination for meeting after the theft was accomplished.

"Does the prosecution have an objection?"

"No, your honor, we do not."

"Alright, Mr. Dobbs, we'll recess until tomorrow at 10:00," he said wearily. "Court is adjourned," and banged his gavel loudly on the table.

There was an angry rumbling in the room at the judge's decision. Kate knew their resentment boiled at having to wait for the guilty decision with a long prison term attached. They had counted on a conviction that day and frustration was high.

But a delay was inconsequential; they might just as well kill Mark, she thought, because being incarcerated in prison would do the same.

The saloons were stocked up on victory whiskey, as the owners had planned on a night of celebration and congratulations. Kate could already hear it. "We got him . . . knew it was him all along . . . I could tell by his eyes. I can read a face, you know, his face and those pretty, white shirts." Hersey would not be a good place for a stranger to pass through this night. The saloons would be full of impatient men, men full of whiskey, frustration and disappointment.

Kate watched Jake lead Mark, looking assured and serene to all who didn't know him well, back to the jail. As soon as they could weave their way through the crowd, she and Will followed. As they passed by his small window, Kate peeked through and saw Mark collapsed on a chair. His pride and strength had held him erect throughout the testimony but were now absent. With no one to see, his shoulders bent, and he held his head in hands weaving fingers angrily though his thick hair.

Kate's heart broke. A sharp, gnawing pain wrenched her deep inside where wounds did not readily heal, and a sob rose to her throat. She would not let it escape, would not give in to weeping! Then rage took over. This can't happen! He is innocent and good, and you are all morons, she said to herself. You are idiots! Not half the man he is!

She stomped her feet in the doorway of the jail, banging her boots on the floor much longer than getting rid of the snow required and enjoying the angry movements. "We're here, Jake," she said. "Please let Mr. Ramey know we'd like to see him."

Will watched her, heard the fury in her voice, and felt her sorrow. He wanted to hold her like he had when she was a little girl, but now was not the time and he knew it wouldn't help her.

Jake jumped from his chair, startled at the imperious command, and did what she had asked. He returned looking down at his boots and mumbled "Mr. Ramey said you should go home."

"What? Are you crazy, Jake?"

"No, Kate," he pleaded. "Mr. Ramey said just that."

Kate easily pushed Jake aside and strode through the door, leaving Jake just staring after her. Will followed, nodding his head back and forth.

"You can't stop her when she's riled, Jake. It's okay, though. He'll want to see us."

By the time they entered Mark's cell, he had heard them, was standing and had collected himself.

"Kate," he said, "I told Jake to send you home. You shouldn't have gone to the trial."

"And why not, Mr. Ramey?" Imperiousness still tinted her tone, but it was intentional now. She was trying to lighten the mood.

"You know why. I saw a hundred eyes staring holes through me today. Angry eyes. They would have dragged me out of there and strung me up if they could have. And they might, Kate. They're not men when they're like that. They're a mob and not to be trusted."

"You think I can't handle those fools? Do you think I care?" She said with a grin, her hands on her hips and feet planted wide. "Besides, Pa's with me. He'll look out for me."

"Just the same," Mark answered, looking at Kate with warm liquid eyes. "I don't want you at the trial tomorrow. Kate, did you see the way they all looked at you? They're thinking things I wouldn't even tell you."

Mark turned to Will for help. "Come on, Will. You must have seen it, heard some of the whispers. They are linking Kate with me . . . and in ways that . . . Will, damn it. Help me."

"Kate's got a mind of her own, Mark. I wouldn't have her any other way," he said a bit sadly, but grinning at Kate as he looked at her. His words buoyed her, let her know Will understood, cared about her feelings, and most of all, he admired her strength of conviction.

Kate didn't respond except to take Mark's hand in both of hers; stroke the back of his, feel the gentleness and strength, and he relented. Her hands and her eyes said it all. She would be there, no matter what. No matter what anyone said; no matter what anyone did, it wouldn't make any difference.

Mark's lawyer, Dobbs, soon joined them, and after a few pleasantries, Kate and Will said their goodbyes. They all agreed, in what was a futile attempt at bravado, to celebrate in the Hughes kitchen over a cup of Will's famous hot toddies. Kate knew it was a fruitless effort to believe in a 'not guilty' verdict. Will knew it. Mark knew it, and knowing was painful.

When they left Mark and Dobbs, they were quiet, each wrapped in their own thoughts. In the buggy on the way home, Will sat very close to Kate, every now and then tucking the lap robe around her legs, straightening wrinkles that weren't there, closing gaps to the wind. It didn't matter; she didn't feel the cold. The ride was silent, but comfort was given through the continual fussing over the robe, the woolen warmth that couldn't take the chill from Kate's bones no matter how many blankets she had been wrapped in. Will knew he couldn't fix anything for Kate, but didn't know any other way to comfort her. Not now. The pain was too big, and words wouldn't help.

Dinner was on the table when they arrived, and the spicy odor of pork roast, heavily salted and baked fast in a hot oven, greeted them and was a welcome smell. It smelled like home, like nothing could touch or harm you. The kitchen was warm from the cook stove, and Ruthie and Willie were laughing and talking in the corner. Probably about their respective boy and girl friends, Kate thought with good hearted envy.

They rushed at Kate and Will, both asking questions about the trial at the same time. Will held up his hands in surrender at the onslaught and looked at Ellen's frowning face as she stirred gravy in a heavy black skillet.

"Well, alright, Will. Get it over with so we can sit down to a peaceful dinner," she said grudgingly.

Will told them about the trial, leaving parts out and filling in certain areas in hilarious detail. Ruth and Willie were eager and intent listeners, questioning everything from the color of the judge's suit to where he and Kate had sat.

Kate listened, as if from a distance, as if it was a crazy story about someone she didn't know or care about. She helped put the finishing touches on the dinner table. The warmth they had greeted eagerly when they had first entered the room seemed stifling now, and prickly heat rose from her back up to her face, flushing her neck and cheeks, and lending a falsely healthy glow. Space diminished before her and the clatter of dishes and chatter of the others seemed to close in around her until she felt she would choke or scream. She screamed.

"For God's sake, can't you talk about something else?"

The room was abruptly silent while strange faces peered at her. Minutes stretched into hours, into days, as only vaguely familiar eyes bored into Kate's, trying to fathom if the voice they'd heard was actually their sister's voice, their daughter's. From a distance, Kate watched as Ellen approached. It was as though she stood outside her own body, an impartial observer, and she watched as Ellen scolded some poor distraught girl who was in a distant way related to herself.

She looked at the strange woman's grim face as she spoke, and then looked down at the toe of her black boot, musing over the deep scratch at the tip. It looked like a cane, she thought, maybe the striped kind you hang from a Christmas tree. She could still hear the woman scolding, but it was distant, and she didn't feel the need to intrude. The other girl might want to pay attention, but Kate was finding more pictures on her boots. The left one had dirt streaks from the snow and could look like a floppy eared dog if you looked from the right angle. She'd like to point out the pictures to the others, but it somehow didn't seem like a good time.

Ellen's hand shaking her shoulder brought the room back into focus. "In this house, Kate, we do not cuss, nor do we speak in that tone of voice to members of this family . . . or to anyone else, for that matter. Your apology is expected."

"I am sorry," Kate said softly, and in the following silence whispered, "Can we please talk about something else, anything else."

Ellen did not understand Kate's pain and only saw a need to guide her eldest child, the most unruly and difficult, as she had always known.

"Although I agree it's a dreadful subject, you were interested enough to go to the trial, while your brother and sister did not. If your father sees fit to relate the events to them, you are in no position to argue the matter."

Ellen looked at Kate, searching for some sign of comprehension, some indication the young woman Ellen had tried so hard to rear was inside the girl in front of her.

"You are clearly out of place, young lady."

Kate was beginning to boil with frustration. Her hands clenched into fists at her sides. She wanted to pound the table, anything. She wanted to lash out at everyone in the room, at the very walls closing in on her . . . and confining him. At the moment, her mother's goodness, her fairness, seemed pious and pompous. Her rational world, where people just went from day to day, doing the right thing, aggravated and disgusted Kate. For the first time in her life, she wanted to strike her mother, to smash the wall of spiritual fortitude holding Ellen upright, giving her strength. Ellen's staunch forbearance, what made her the strong woman she was, was the monument that Kate wanted to see come tumbling down. At that moment, she wanted to see her mother weep, to wail out her woes, to complain to the world that it had not treated her fairly, not given her all she had been promised.

"Don't you ever let go and just scream?" She shouted at Ellen. "Doesn't your good, Christian virtue ever burst . . . like a . . . dam in a flood?" Kate rambled on while Ellen stood, shocked by the outburst. "Don't you ever feel things? Happy, sad, what ever?" Her words trailed off, the emotion spent. The feelings had been released in a flood of angry words. Kate knew regret, but was too empty to feel it deeply. She heard her father from a distance.

"Leave her alone, Ellen."

"I will not, Will. You have encouraged her to act like a renegade, and if she continues, that is exactly what everyone in this town will think of her. Kate must learn . . ."

"Ellen!" Will did not speak loudly, but his voice reverberated throughout the room. The depth and the intent in his voice stopped Ellen's words as surely as if he had clapped a hand over her mouth. Will did not assert himself frequently, but when he did, not many argued.

"Leave her alone," he said softly. "Do as I ask, please. Put the food on the table and start eating. We'll be back in ten minutes. Kate, get your coat."

Through a haze, Kate saw her mother standing with her hands on her rounded hips, mouth open and staring at them as they left the house. Ruth and Willie had said nothing at all and were, Kate supposed, in shock over the episode. Disagreements between their mother and father, other than what was done in a half-teasing manner, either took place when no one was around or they never happened at all. It was a shock to see open anger on the faces of two people you had always assumed to be in at least some accord.

Well, Kate knew perfect accord was not real and knew, too, her parents had lived more in placid acceptance, but never had she seen harsh open disagreement. She was stunned and felt guilty for having been the cause.

Once outside, Will took her hand in his and they walked for moments before he said anything.

"You looked awful white in there, Kate. I thought for a moment you were going to faint on us."

"I'm not the fainting kind. You know that," she said softly, not sure of herself, her feelings, or what her pa would have to say about her outburst.

"Well, that's what I always thought, but for awhile, you sort of drifted away from us."

Will paused, deep in thought wondering how best to smooth over the rift between two of the three women he loved most in the world.

"Don't be too hard on your mother, Kate. She doesn't understand what you're feeling. You haven't confided in her, I think. Am I right?"

"I . . . couldn't. You know that."

"Well, I guess I knew that, but she's your mother, Kate, and she wants the best for you."

Kate held firmly to Will's arm, stopping their slow walk, and turned him to face her. "Pa, she's so . . . unyielding. Did Ma ever just bend with the wind, or cry just because she felt like it . . . or laugh out loud for the sheer joy of it?" Kate's eyes were shafts boring into her father's, searching for answers to things she knew, but needing his words anyway, a confirmation of her own knowledge. "Has Ma always been so . . . separated?"

"I'm not sure what you mean, Kate."

"You know, so . . . contained?"

Will's sigh could have been heard by a thousand distant angels, so deep was his sorrow. Kate heard and knew it was regret speaking, from deep within, from years of having been someone he had promised not to be, from years of wanting to be something or someone else for Ellen. He took a deep breath.

"Your mother is a good woman. I haven't made her life easy, Kate, and I'm not the best of husbands, but she never complains. She'd have to be half saint just to put up with my shenanigans all these years."

"That's just it!" Kate cried. "It's the saint part that sometimes gets to me. Just once I'd like to hear her scream or stomp her foot so that it rattles her precious pots and pans, or throw something big and hard and loud! It's not human to hold everything in so much."

"Kate," her pa soothed. "I didn't bring you out here to get all riled up over your mother, although I have to agree it can be a little frustrating now and then. We're out here letting our dinner get cold so you can get your heart set back in its proper place in your chest and not hanging out, waving about on your finger tips. Now you just hear what I have to say."

Will took another deep breath after his rather long speech and looked around him at the deepening night. The wind was beginning to pick up, and their breath blew quickly from them, making light passages of white frost in short wisps in front of them. Their steps were quick and close together for warmth, their arms wrapped tightly together forming a unit out of two. He took one last long breath, held it for a moment, and then spit it out.

"Kate, I think you better reconcile yourself to the fact that Mark is going to jail, for awhile, anyway," he added quickly after glimpsing the look on Kate's face.

Kate instantly pictured Mark in manacles or pinned to a dungeon wall, with water seeping in about his feet, fed daily on bread and water. She shook her head to banish the nightmare and saw him on a chain gang, tied to hardened criminals, murderers, and breaking rocks with a hammer bigger than himself. She knew her thoughts were foolish; dungeons didn't really exist; it was only in fiction horrors occurred. But for those few moments, the pictures invaded her mind. It was impossible for her to imagine someone like Mark in prison, and . . . impossible, also, to imagine him coming out of prison in one piece, body, mind and spirit.

"Kate!" her father said sharply. "Did you hear what I've been saying?"

"Sure," she mumbled. "You said get used to the fact that he is going to jail."

"You were wandering, Kate. I also said we'd get him out as soon as possible, as soon as Jack gets back with Lorraine. That's what I want you to remember tomorrow if things go as I suspect they will. And tonight, remember it, too, and take it easy on your mother. You upset her to begin with just by going to the trial. Not that I don't hold with your going," he added.

Kate was contrite, knowing how easily she could make Ellen start calling on all of the saints to help her with Kate and her willful ways. She just couldn't be Ellen, didn't really want to be.

"I'll try to be a little easier on her, Pa. I will."

Will patted her arm, gave it a little squeeze, and his step became noticeably lighter. The light in his eyes, Kate could see in the rising moon, was full of concern and love, and she wondered how her mother could ever have been hardened by life with this tender man.

"Come on," he said in a voice that was husky and thickened by his feelings for the girl-woman by his side.

"Let's get some dinner before those two siblings of yours eat every last morsel. I'm suddenly starved."

"Don't call them mine," Kate chirped back. "They're your children. I didn't have anything to do with it . . . can't claim them. You have that privilege." She giggled, feeling almost good for the first time that day. Her arm woven tightly through Will's, feeling his warmth and the special knowledge that he understood her so well made the events of the day more bearable.

"I only claim them when they're angels like their Pa," he chuckled.

Kate stopped him just outside the door and looked at him, deep into his sparkling grey eyes.

"You are you know."

"I am what?"

She stood on tiptoes and kissed him on the tip of his nose.

"An angel," she said. "You are my angel, and I don't ever want to be without you. Couldn't," she added and left him standing on the steps as she reentered the kitchen, fresh and feeling, if not good, at least resigned and more confident. Everything would work out. And she had her pa. To ask for more would be testing the gods.

The last day of the trial arrived. Kate went early to avoid the throngs of men she had been forced to weave through before, and especially to avoid the crude comments. The room was only half full, and she was, like before, the only woman present. She had time to look around her and wonder how it was this same room during town meetings could feel like such a friendly place, so homey and comfortable.

Now, when Mark's freedom was at stake, when his future would be determined by a few words from a jury made up of men who had been in some manner impacted by the lumber camp closure, the hall looked sinister and sterile. As Kate looked around her, she saw the jury platform had not been swept and was cluttered with left over garbage from the day before. Chairs were

cocked at odd angles where the men had left them, eager
to be released from their day of jury duty.The haphaz-
ardness formed a picture in Kate's mind; of pieces being
thrown together like a painting she had seen in one of
her text books, a painting with no apparent logic, no
symmetry, and no warmth. Even the walls and bare
windows emitted sinister waves of chill and looked as
cold and forbidding as the winter they held out.

Smoke curled out of the stove in the corner, seeping
from some hidden crevice and filling the air with the acrid odor of lichen covered wood which had been hidden
too long under years of damp, decomposing leaves and
discovered too late to be of any worth – except to wrinkle the nostrils of those nearby. Kate shook her head and
wondered angrily why someone wouldn't have had the
foresight to bring in some clean hard oak. Is that too
much to ask?

Will had gone to see if the day's two witnesses had
arrived as planned, and Kate felt strangely abandoned
sitting in a room quickly filling with men she had
known all her life. Yet, they looked like strangers. She
listened to their raucous laughter, heard the back slapping and bravado. Heard her name mentioned several
times and stiffened her back.

"Let them talk to the back of my head," she said softly
to herself. "I will not turn to acknowledge what I hear!"

A dog barked in the distance, and out on the street
buggies creaked by and voices carried on as if this was
just any day, as if nothing earth shattering was happening in the town hall. How could it be? She thought of the
next week when they would decorate the Christmas tree
in front of the church and sent up a prayer for Mark to
still be near to help with the highest lights, to sing the
tenor parts in the carols.

The room was stifling with noise, voices growing
louder, shouting to be heard over the clamor. Kate's
heart pounded, and her breath came in short gasps. God,
she wanted to run from this place! She hated them all,

every damn one of them! Yes, she thought, that's me, swearing again. I'm incorrigible. Goody for me. Damn, damn, damn them!

Boots thudded against the wood floor right next to her, startling her from her thoughts. She turned in time to keep some men from taking the seat beside her, managing with a glare and a couple of well aimed barbs to save the place for her father. She put her hand on the seat of Will's chair, and looked up.

"This seat is taken." When they leered and moved to sit anyway, she said firmly, "If you take that seat, you're going to have to do it sitting on my hand."

"You should be at home where you belong, Kate, with the pots and pans," one said with an unfriendly smirk. "But I hear that's not all you're good for."

"And you should be in the barn with the rest of the animals," Kate retorted. "You're not getting this seat."

Finally, she heard a voice bellow. Mark and Dobbs were on their way from the jail. Her throat grew thick, and her stomach heaved in anxiety. It was happening. In a little while they would know. She couldn't stand the suspense of the unknown, and yet she didn't want the moment to come.

Kate didn't turn to watch, but the heavy rumble of voices following them down the center aisle told her they were approaching. Mark took his seat, and then turned to Kate.

"I asked you not to come here today, Kate."

"Yes, you did. Sorry I couldn't honor your request."

He looked away from her, his eyes scanning the crowded room, then back to her.

"You're a stubborn woman, Kate, and you shouldn't he here, but I'm glad to see a friendly face. I think it's the only one in the room. Is Will coming?"

"He brought me here then left to see about the witnesses. They are here, aren't they?"

"They're here," he said in a grin it was clear he didn't really feel.

Kate mentally added what Mark didn't say, but thought; they're here, but they might just as well have stayed home for all the good they'll do.

The judge entered, and Mark turned to face the bench as the gavel banged for order. Will slipped into his seat beside Kate and nodded to Mark, whispering his good wishes. It didn't take long for the room to grow stifling with heat and the musty odor of damp, un-washed wool.

The judge looked even paler than before. Dark circles under his eyes were accentuated by the ashen color of his face. He looked worn, as though he hadn't slept well for a very long while. Kate wondered if he had been troubled by the obvious prejudice of the jury. He was so thin he appeared to struggle to remain erect. With apparent effort and dignity, the judge straightened himself and called the first witness to the stand.

The train conductor told in detail how he and Mark had searched the train for Lorraine until it had become evident she was no longer aboard. His testimony was convincing, and Kate could see at least a few members of the jury thought his words may be true. Her spirits rose, and for the first time since the trial began, she had some hope.

It was short lived. The prosecutor examined his testimony and turned it against Mark. He asked why they hadn't wired from the next stop for the law to hold Lorraine.

"It is apparent that both you and Mr. Ramey knew exactly when Mrs. Ramey had gotten off the train, especially since Mr. Ramey went directly there after he got off."

"I offered to do just that," he said, "but Mr. Ramey refused my help with a wire."

The prosecutor turned to nod knowingly at the jury members. Kate could see the thoughts behind the eyes. The brief moment of indecision was gone, and they had convicted him. Voices grew heated, bitterness clear in barely suppressed outrage.

The judge called for order with the banging of his gavel against the wooden table. Kate watched Mark in front of her. She could just see the back of his broad shoulders and a partial side view of his face, but it was obvious he was strained in the effort to just sit there quietly, not responding to the things they were saying. She knew there must have been a reason, some logic in his decision not to send the wire. But Mark had not yet had the opportunity to explain why, and at this point, who would believe him except her and her father?

The conductor stepped down, and the station attendant was called. Kate in one glance dismissed his credibility. Even though it was still morning, the man wobbled to the witness chair, and his voice slurred as he gave his testimony. She heard sporadic chuckling around the room as they watched Mark's last chance drown in the liquor the attendant had consumed earlier. His story was short, and the prosecutor didn't even bother with any detailed cross examination. He knew, as Kate did, it wasn't needed.

When his lawyer called Mark to the stand, he ignored the angry sounds erupting again and turned to nod to Will and Kate, and then walked slowly, with head held high. After he was sworn in, his lawyer asked a few questions, and ugly voices resounded throughout the room each time he responded. Then Dobbs asked Mark to tell the courtroom what had happened, in his own words. While he talked, Kate looked around the room, assessing how his words were being received. Here and there, an occasional face seemed to consider what Mark was telling them. Some wore doubtful expressions clearly saying 'you can't fool me, mister.' Most faces, however, wore fury. They leaned forward on the edge of their seats, fists clenched, ready.

God, Kate thought, they're out to kill. As she looked around, fear grew, and she knew no matter the outcome of the trial, Mark would need to flee Hersey. The town had suffered as a result of Lorraine's crime, and someone was going to pay. The men in the courtroom who had been feeding their families on potatoes were out for blood. The merchants who'd had prosperity ripped from their grasp were just as angry and ready to see him pay.

Mark, looking weary but serene, told his story. He explained how he had discovered the payroll was missing, why he had not wired from the station, how he was trying to protect his children. He wanted to get the money back to its rightful place for the men. Then he finished his story, telling them all how he had been arrested when he was just getting close to finding Lorraine and the payroll. He sat tall in the witness stand; his broad shoulders thrust back, and looked directly at all the people who wanted to see him in jail. Kate admired his composure, the outward appearance of tranquility.

When the prosecution finished cross examination, any sympathy Mark had gained was gone. The simple truth of the events took over. The money was gone. It had been in Mark's care.

The judge excused Mark and asked if there were any other witnesses for the defense. If not, he would ask the jury to come to a decision.

It was over. The judge instructed the jury in their duties and sent them to the back room to make a decision. He allowed himself to slump in his chair to wait for a verdict.

Order left the room with the jury. Acrid comments were shouted back and forth across the aisles. Some dealt with Mark's fate in prison; some with Kate. Though they clearly wanted Mark to hear and respond, he did not give them their satisfaction. He ignored the rest of the room and turned to talk with Kate and Will. His face was composed, if sad, and Kate wanted to reach out and just touch his cheek, to smooth away the tiny lines around his eyes.

"We're not done yet, Mark," Will said. "Jack's not a quitter. He'll find her, and when he does . . . she'll take the beating you're getting right now."

A smile crinkled around Mark's eyes, and he reached over to grasp Will's hand. He held it for a moment, as if loathe to release the hand of friendship.

"Will," he said haltingly, his voice breaking slightly with the rise of feelings. "I've never thanked you for all you've done for me. I don't know another man who would have gone to all the trouble you have for me. I'll see Jack Bay gets paid for all he's done as soon as I'm able."

Will waved his hand as if whisking away the idea he had done much.

"I was happy to help. I guess I kind of go along with Kate, here. No one can convince me you took the payroll. You're not the guilty person, no matter what the jury might say."

Mark's eyes grew cloudy and watered. He squinted, and then widened his eyes, keeping wetness at bay. "There's one more thing I want to ask of you, Will."

Kate saw he was as close to tears as possible without actually releasing them. But he struggled. He took a deep breath, pulled back his shoulders, and Kate desperately tried to check her own tears as she watched. It was so damn hard to see pain in those you cared about, and that was about the only thing that made her cry – someone else's tears – shed or unshed.

"My children are with my parents here in Michigan," Mark explained. "Grand Rapids is a pretty good sized town now, and they have a telegraph service. They live just outside a small city called Marne, right next to Grand Rapids. If you could wire my parents a couple of times to see how the kids are, or maybe if you know someone headed in that direction they could stop in to see them and let you know . . . I'd . . . well, I'd sleep a little better just knowing you were in touch with them." He went on, "My parents are getting a little on in years, and you never know . . ."

His words trailed off, and he covered his face with shaking hands, his self-imposed composure lost in worry over his children. Grief and defeat replaced his proud bearing, and Will looked away, unwilling to intrude where Mark would want privacy, where what was precious remained safe and untouched.

Kate couldn't turn away. She could not abandon him in his grief. With a giant wet streak staining her face, she squarely faced Mark and reached out her hand. She softly pressed it against the side of his face, over his own hand, and let it remain there, unmoving. He didn't turn to her or acknowledge the contact, just remained motionless. Minutes passed and soon his other hand moved to cover hers, pressing it into his. It was a recognition of something. Kate didn't know what, nor did she care. She felt more than words could have said. She begged whatever gods prevailed to allow her to take some of his pain and was rewarded. Sorrow coursed through his body in a deep shudder, through their hands, and came into her heart. She felt the physical power of his sadness, and it left no room within her for anything but his pain and her happiness in being able to share it.

Stillness came over him, and the strain in his neck muscles eased just a bit. His shoulders once more drew back, even if only slightly. He removed his hands from his face and looked at Kate. Sadness was still there, but the torment was gone, the agony less intolerable. His eyes were wet, but he didn't hide from her. Kate was to remember these moments much later and know their combined strength was powerful.

Mark continued to press her hand in his, moved his hardened palm against it, imprinting the feel of her skin, unconsciously loathe to let go. The strain of rampant emotions, Mark's eyes staring steadily into hers, and the feel of his hands moving over hers began to confuse her, and the sensation brought a slight flush to her face. Gently she removed her hand, trying not to reveal her feelings and yet leave the comfort and strength her touch had seemed to give him. He straightened, breathed deeply and turned from Kate to Will who was looking intently around him at the boisterously chattering men in the room. Will seemed to be surveying the room and listening to predictions of Mark's fate which was being shouted from man to man. Mark ignored them and spoke to Will.

"I'm sorry. For the watery eyes," he said.

"Nothing to be sorry for, man, and if those kids of yours should have to stay with their grandparents for awhile, well, they'll just have to take me on as another Grandpapa. I'll be keeping in touch with them as much as I can. Besides, aren't you jumpin the gun just a bit? You aren't convicted yet."

Mark nodded slowly, knowing Will was just trying to make light of the situation. He knew, as well as Mark, conviction and a prison sentence were coming. He let it go, though, unwilling to speak the truth. Will was a dreamer, so let him dream for them all for just a few more minutes.

Mark wrote out the address of his parents and talked about his children, his son Jamie who hated his brown unruly curls.

"He thinks he was cursed at birth by some fairytale witch." Mark continued, his memories flowing into words, "He thinks they're unmanly, silly boy. He's beautiful, and his eyes . . . they're big and round, and they fog over when he's sad, mist over like a Scottish highland at dawn."

Both Kate and Will were silent, enraptured by Mark's description. Love and beauty filled his words and the visions he created. Flossie, his baby girl, was a garden of different exotic flowers.

"You should see her," he said. "She's a sunflower, fresh and pure, and in the next moment, she's a saucy daffodil, vying with the snow for first position in the sun." He was clearly smitten with her dark beauty and eyes of black fire. Obviously, no girl, young or old, could compare with her grace of feature and mind.

Kate smiled and knew if he'd had ten children, they would all be exceptional in his mind. Well, she thought, if they came from his loins, she'd have to agree they'd be extraordinary.

He was deep within the memory of his children when the jury filed their way back into the room. Chill crept from Kate's toes up to the back of her neck as she searched the faces of the men for a clue to their verdict. It did not seem possible that she who cared so much about this man could be ignorant of his fate, and they not only knew, but held it in their hands. All but two wore hardened looks of satisfaction. Mark's back was to the jury. Kate nodded.

"They're here," she said, "and so am I."

He lifted his chin and turned to face them. I am not guilty, he thought, except for the crime of being foolish. For this I am going to jail.

He heard the judge's gavel sounding like an iron hammer against metal, echoing within the room and ringing over and over in his head.

"Have you reached a verdict?" the judge asked.

The jury foreman stood, large fists clenched at his sides.

"We have your honor." His shaggy head lifted high, chin jutted forward, jaw muscles twitching.

"How do you find the defendant, Mark Ramey?"

Indistinct rumbles began at the back of the room and slowly moved in waves to the front. Before the man's answer could be completed, the rumbles had turned to roars. Boots stomped the floor and back slaps resounded throughout the room.

". . . guilty." Mark saw the word. He couldn't hear it. Didn't need to hear it to know what had been said. The others in the room had either heard or had known in advance. The applause was deafening, and the room spun with noise and fear, unnamed kinds of regret for what he could have been and hadn't.

Kate hadn't heard either. She just sat there, too tired and drained to move and watched Mark's back as he sat motionless. He never once turned his head to acknowledge the remarks flying around the room. Not once did his head bow in defeat or his shoulders sag from the weight of the conviction of his errors.

Jake, the jailor who had become Mark's friend, stood and motioned Mark to rise. He did and his elegance was complete. He tugged the white cuffs of his shirt so they peeked out from the sleeves of his grey suit, pushed the knot of his tie to tighten it correctly, and straightened his collar. After buttoning his jacket over the silk vest, he turned to Jake and held out his hands.

Kate admired his poise, his grace, and knew his innate elegance had partially been responsible for his conviction. He had something the rest of the men in town would never have, and the women wanted in a different way. He was different, and his style could not be learned or bought. It was integral to who he was. Jake put the cuffs around Mark's wrists. Mark turned to Kate and Will and mouthed a silent "Thank you."

She watched them leave the room and damned the woman who had made this happen.

CHAPTER SEVEN

S everal springs came and left, bursting forth in brilliant arrays of color made more noticeable by the stark change from winter's grays and whites. Robins, the harbinger of Michigan springs, brought songs in praise of the sun to the northern hills. Lady's slippers, in muted shades of deep and pastel purple, blanketed the banks of the Hersey and Muskegon rivers and flourished beneath the craggy tamarack trees which sheltered the flower's delicate growth. Where ironwood and poplar trees were the giants of the woods, violets covered the forest floors, competing with jack-in-the pulpits, tiger lilies, and the much coveted trout lilies.

Kate walked slowly, going through the woods to get to town so she could look for mushrooms on the way, the prized morels with their brown, sponge like caps, and elephant ears with their outlandish distorted shape. She knew they would somehow manage to find their way from beneath the damp spring leaves of darkened oak woods to sprout almost instantly. Mushrooms, with their musty tanginess, were considered treasures and were used to enhance breakfast omelets and dinner stews alike. It sometimes seemed the entire village of Hersey crawled through the undergrowth to search for these woodland jewels, and later the bragging around

Nestor's stove grew into mushroom tales that could match any wild fish story.

Kate was, however, as much involved with the wild flowers catching her attention, and she was saddened by the changes that had come with the felling of the forest trees. The trout lilies were few, as they required deep shade for their tender leaves. The flower, itself, hid under wide leaves, guarded from the sun by the thick covering of its own leaf. With the lumber boom and subsequent removal of a wide expanse of thick, leafy shelter, the forest floor burned too warm for many wild flowers. They, like the mushrooms, hid under short growth seeking cool, moist earth and a canopy of shade.

"So stupid," she said out loud to the wildlife around her. She laughed at herself and thought it sounded more like the barking of a dog, instead a laugh.

"I've turned into a dog," she said, again out loud. "An ornery dog with its foot in a trap. And I feel like one."

The woods grew sparser with each spring, when you could clearly see the work of the Landmark lumberjacks. Hundreds of tree stumps cluttered patches of barren ground where towering pines once formed a natural green sunshade. Where tall forests had towered over moist wooded land, the sun now parched large tracts, and naked earth washed into the rivers with each rain. The sight of this devastation drowned the joy of a new spring, and Kate knew she had been right to join the reforestation meeting she was on her way to attend.

Kate's loyalty to her father and his mill battled with her desire to preserve the land and the forests which were quickly disappearing from Osceola County. Neither she nor many of the committee members wanted to interfere with the lumber business. They merely wanted the cutting of the trees done in a way that didn't scorch the earth. Kate wanted them to consider the effect of what they were doing and work with the earth, not abuse it. She wanted them to be selective in their cutting and to replant trees for the future. A hundred years of growth should not be felled without thought.

But the grasp for lumber and the resulting cash had become a fever. Fighting over land boundaries erupted frequently as lumber companies crept from leased properties over onto the privately owned acreage belonging to some neighboring farmer. The air had become tense with watching behind your back, and men were quick to accuse. Kate thought she understood. It seemed the opportunity to make money was fleeting, and if you turned your head for a moment, it would be gone. It wasn't so farfetched, she thought. Things could disappear, anything could, and in a whisper of time. It had taken a century to grow some of those trees, and they had disappeared overnight. Barren ground stared back in reproach.

She stood in a lone clump of blue spruce trees, her hand upon the rough needles, feeling the sting of their spiny ends, reflecting on yesterday and the days before, and the years before the yesterdays. It was hard to realize the 1800's were gone forever. So many changes had occurred. Yet nothing at all was different. And still, the twentieth century sounded foreign to her, a number that should be far off into the future, not a new year to be celebrated in her own lifetime.

Twenty-three, she thought, and laughed a wry, cynical sound that tormented her mother. She was a pitiful thing, an old maid, the school teacher spinster. She knew Hersey folks pitied her. Wasn't the goal of every woman to find a husband, get married, and have children? Why shouldn't they pity her? She had not succeeded in their goals. Kate could understand their wonder and undeserved pity, but could not join their ranks, not when other memories kept intruding on her thoughts.

Each year Kate saw new faces in her classroom and was continually startled when the older girls left her school and appeared in what seemed moments later with a baby and a husband in tow. She had to admit, to herself only, it made her a bit sad, and she had wondered at times if she could, and would, forever keep Mel at just enough of a distance to forestall the question of marriage. She wanted a family, but somehow the time was just not right. Yet, she knew time was not the issue, and a proposal had finally been spoken.

Two years before, the last of Mel's sisters had married, leaving just the youngest brother at home to be cared for. Mel had finally felt free to ask Kate to be his wife. What should have been a joyful moment had been so painful for them both.

Kate cared deeply for Mel, even loved him, and he was such a huge part of her contentment, her life. She also had great respect for him, as a person and as a man, but a voice deep inside her rose to the surface, telling her she couldn't lie to Mel with a commitment she didn't intensely feel. He had been good to her in the last many years, not pushing their friendship beyond the point where she could be comfortable, letting her silences go unquestioned and leaving her privacy intact.

Mel knew Kate had attended Mark's trial and had visited him in jail. It would have been impossible for Mel not to have heard all the talk about town. It had been risqué, juicy news in Hersey, and the scandal of her behavior had almost rivaled the excitement engendered by Mr. Wellington's running off with the saloon girl.

A young, single girl should not have been involved with a married scoundrel. And to top it off, one who was sitting in jail for theft. Kate had ignored it all, and since she never spoke of it, Mel had not mentioned it either. She almost wished he would question her about Mark, about why she had felt the need to be near him, so she would have been forced to explain her thoughts and feelings. But he hadn't, and too much time had passed to try to explain now. It would have been awkward and difficult. It seemed so long ago, and yet Mel's proposal was as clear as if it had been yesterday.

In Mel's quiet, enduring way, he had patiently waited, and then finally he had asked for Kate's hand in marriage. She had become so accustomed to Mel's friendship it came as a surprise when it actually happened.

They had arrived at the Hughes' house after Sunday evening church before the rest of the family and were sitting on the porch swing taking in the last of the night's warm breeze. Kate knew something was on Mel's mind by the way he kept fidgeting with his hands, a behavior so unfitting his normal composed attitude. While never flamboyant with arrogance, Mel's confidence was displayed by solid assurance. Kate thought of him as rocklike with the mountain's innate knowledge found only with quiet watching, listening, and knowing. She always admired the stillness in Mel and only briefly wondered what could have ruffled him so much he uncharacteristically fidgeted.

Mel finally sat back in the swing beside her and rested his arm on the back. Kate lay her head on his shoulder to look up at the sky, hoping, selfishly she knew, whatever was on his mind, he would forget for the moment and just relax to enjoy the beautiful night. She heard the crickets chirping in the grass nearby and could smell the apple blossoms on the craggy trees screening the house from the road.

She felt Mel's shoulder tense beneath her head and felt the tension building in him as he sat trying to voice his thoughts. So close had they become that sensing each other's feelings had become natural, and they no longer thought it unusual to know what hadn't been said. Kate waited, expecting he would tell her his problem when he was ready.

Mel suddenly laid his hand on Kate's, his fingers curling around and pressing into her palm. She heard his intake of ragged breath.

"Kate, will you marry me!" he said, breathing a sigh of relief in a quick explosion of anxiety, glad to have finally said it. Mel had been staring deliberately out in the direction of the apple trees while he spoke, and Kate watched from her sidelong glance as he slowly turned his head to look at her, waiting for some reaction.

Kate was stunned into silence. She had always known this day would come, but she had been expecting it for so long the actuality had been pushed from her mind. A myriad of thoughts and words crashed through her brain, climbing over one another, none settling long enough for a coherent response. Some were gentle refusals she had actually practiced, loving comments about time and friendship; none would be the words Mel needed to hear.

She had, at times, even mouthed an acceptance, trying it on to see how she might feel engaged to Mel. All the rehearsed lines bounced around in her head, and none seemed right now the moment was here. None would spare the man she really did love, but not enough to marry. But that wasn't true, and she knew it. She loved him more than enough, just not in the way she was selfish enough to want. And she loved him too much to cheat him by marrying him anyway. Mel deserved more. So did she, and it was unfortunate she knew it.

His first proposal had been almost two years ago. Somehow Kate had managed to refuse him as a husband and keep him as a friend, even more than a simple friend. Mel's staunch integrity would not allow him to be angry with her. Their continuing relationship, Kate knew, was most certainly not due to her ability to explain her reasons, but to Mel's deep loyalty and, yes, stubbornness. She also knew how deeply hurt he had been. His back had straightened, and he had turned his head away from her to hide the anguish which poured from his face.

Kate wondered briefly if she had accepted, would he have shared his joy; was he just unwilling to share his pain? Mel had never given her the chance to share his burdens and sorrows, but buried them instead under his pride – and his unwillingness to cause her distress. She had pondered this about him before, thinking it was his way of protecting himself, or it was a part of his male image, or perhaps it was merely his way of distancing himself from her. What ever it was, it pained her to know he was alone in both his sorrows and joys.

Mel's fortitude showed. He hadn't given up on the idea of marriage with Kate and asked each year at about the same time, making a joke of it by relating it to the seasons. "Just like you can't stop the coming of spring," he'd say grinning, "it's me again, asking the same old question. You going to give in this year? Is this getting boring for you, Kate?" He teased and made jokes of it, hiding from his emotions, but she knew, also, it was Mel's way to quietly fight for what he wanted, a proud but stubborn man.

Signs of his determination bloomed in every corner of his farm. He forced it to produce even in bad years when every other farmer had failing crops and ailing cattle. The size of Mel's holding had almost doubled since he took over after his father's death, and new paint on the house and barns were evidence of his hard work and prosperity. If you passed his place late at night during the spring, summer and fall, you would surely hear his machinery hard at work when other farmers had long since gone to bed. In the winter, lights in the barn and sheds would reveal Mel bent over a thrasher with a look of concentrated resolution on his face.

Mel was a fine mix of gentleness and strength. In all the years she had known him, the only time Kate could remember seeing harshness in Mel's eyes was when she had badgered him about the hours he worked and accused him of being too hungry for a dollar. He didn't even look at her, but intently glared somewhere off in a land of his own.

"Why not?" he growled back with something close to bitterness in his voice.

Kate knew much had been said and left unsaid in those two words. She knew, too, it had to do with her and dropped the matter. But she did worry he worked too many hours and enjoyed himself too little. And she was somehow at fault. He took brief time out to escort Kate to the occasional town dances and a few other social functions, but according to his mother, Mel did nothing else except tend the farm.

The Hughes family had come home while Kate and Mel sat silently on the porch swing. Their lazy chatter was a balm to wounded spirits, yet had put a rein on what would or could have been said. Will sat down on the steps, pushed the errant hair from his brow and caressed the sky with his soft blue eyes.

"Did you ever see a night like this before?" he mused. No answer came. None was expected. "It's like a woman's touch just before you think the sparks might burn you."

"Pa," Kate said softly. "You're getting poetic again. What's got you tonight? Did Reverend Havens try to send you to hell again after church got over? Did he catch you in the entry and try to redeem your wayward soul?"

"No, just thinking about young love, Willie and his nice girl, Mary. She's going to make him a good wife, but it's hard to think of Willie as a man, old enough to marry and then have babies, too. God, I'll be a grandpa," Will said groaning a little.

Kate felt Mel stiffen at her side. Will's poetic comments about love and marriage could not have been more ill timed. Silence took over, all of them deep in their own different thoughts.

Mel was seeing himself, in love and married to his girl – this woman by his side. Kate saw her little brother, a younger version of Will, with Will's easy sense of humor. Excitement about what ever came his way lit Willie's eyes just like his father. He seemed never to take anything seriously, but Kate knew that wasn't true. He was serious about his Mary and was the love in his mother's life. He couldn't be a flibberty gidget, Ellen's term for those who did not take life seriously enough, because Ellen would not hear of it.

"Ma will really miss him when he gets married and moves out," Kate said, knowing her brother was still on Will's mind and something more he wouldn't come right out and say.

"Well, she still has Ruthie to hold on to," Will said a bit sadly.

Kate let the silence settle for awhile, waiting for her father to say whatever was on his mind. He stared at the sky for awhile, rubbing his smooth shaven chin as if it had whiskers which could be bristled back and forth. But his cheeks were always clean shaven, as smooth as the cheeks of an infant. Yet it seemed to soothe him to make the movement, and it prompted thought and speech. Kate saw the signs and waited.

"Willie will be just fine," he finally said, "but I'm wondering a bit about our Ruthie. Have either of you noticed?" he said, including Mel in the conversation. "She used to be sort of . . . a dandelion on the wind, not crazy or bad, just alive and happily blowing with the breeze. What's happening?"

"Well, Pa, Ruthie's growing up. Haven't you noticed?"

"That doesn't mean she needs to be so stern and frowning all the time," he said.

"I know," Kate responded, "She's growing more . . . like Ma," she finished, whispering the last words.

"Kate," Will said, beginning to admonish her for her disrespect, but let silence fold over what he had been about to say.

Kate left Mel alone on the swing to sit by her father on the steps. She listened to her mother and sister moving about inside the kitchen and understood her father's concerns.

"Ruthie will be fine, Pa. She's just at that age when she's trying hard to be an adult, and she thinks being like Ma is being grown up. She'll get over it," Kate soothed.

"That's crazy. What about laughing once in a while just because it feels good. What about some fun while she's young? I feel like I am responsible for this change in her."

"Now that's crazy!" Kate cried. "What on earth do you mean?" Kate saw her mother's frowns and compared them to Will's dancing eyes and easy laughter. She gently slapped his hand in protest. "Why," she said coyly in a fake southern drawl, "that's just plain silly, you old fool. Don't you agree, Mel?"

"Sorry for this melancholy, Mel," Will said looking up at the man listening on the swing. "But you're like family, so you see it too, I think." He leaned against the rail post and tilted his head back to look at the sky. "It's the night," he said, "the night and the preaching and the look of young Willie's face when it lights on his Mary. Those two," he mused. "It's beautiful and what every young person, old too I guess, should be feeling on a warm spring night." He paused for a moment.

"We felt that way once. It's my doing she doesn't laugh much anymore. I've made it kind of hard on her. I had my dreams, and they were often selfish. Because I'm an old geezer, I can preach to you and you have to sit there and take it," Will said grinning. "Keep your dreams, young ones, but don't be selfish. Don't take other's dreams away when you're searching for yours."

"Pa," Kate said. "If anyone has been hard on Ma, it's me."

"You, Kate? What have you done?"

"Mostly whatever I wanted, whenever I wanted. I couldn't be who she wanted me to be. I'm a spinster. I was the talk of Hersey when I insisted on going to the jail and Mark's trial. You know what everyone said about me. Ma hasn't forgiven me for creating the biggest scandal since old Wellington escaped his wife."

"She loves you, Kate. You know that. She just has different rules to live by than some of us. Or maybe you and I have different rules than others." Will paused. "Speaking of Mark, I hear his time is about done. I wish we could have been more help in clearing his name."

The porch swing momentarily stopped its rhythmic swinging and creaked under Mel's weight. Will noticed and cursed himself for a fool for mentioning Mark with Mel right there. Kate noticed, too, and did not turn to look at Mel who was watching Kate's face, searching for answers to questions he hadn't asked. Kate tried desperately to control her joy, hoping to spare Mel, knowing her life without Mel in the last five years would have been dismal – knowing, too, he deserved more from her than pain.

Later, as Kate was tossing under her quilt, trying to make herself quit thinking of Mark and go to sleep, she saw a strange glow in the night sky creeping through the loft window. Slipping into her robe, she tiptoed lightly to the window and tried to figure out what was coloring the sky such an inky peach hue.

She wasn't sure how long she had stood there. Her thoughts ranged as far as the sky was wide. She was just about to turn back to the warmth of her bed when the glow in the sky turned red. It looked like the flame of a candle reflected in a dark pool. In an instant, she knew it was a fire, over the hill about half a mile away.

Kate ran down to her parent's room. "Pa, Ma," she screamed. "Wake up. There's another fire. Looks like it's at the Tate's place."

Will was up and awake in an instant, as if he'd never been asleep. While he donned his clothes, Ellen was gathering things they would need.

"Get your brother up, Kate. He can help."

When Kate returned to the kitchen, she saw Ellen had gathered sheets, burlap sacks, buckets, and a huge pile of other things they'd need. She had to marvel at Ellen's clarity of mind and her strength. No fussing. Just do what had to be done. Will brought around the wagon and was loading the supplies when Willie appeared, somewhat disheveled, but ready to go.

"I'll follow just as soon as I can dress, Will, with as much food and coffee as Kate and I can carry. You'd better get going." She stopped Will just as he was about to climb up onto the wagon, her hand on his shoulder. "Please be careful," she said.

Kate watched the exchange. Noticed there was no emotion, no "I love you," no farewell kiss. She was to wonder about that brief comment – "Please be careful."

Kate and Ellen dressed quickly and roused Ruthie to prepare more things at home while they were gone, things they knew they would need.

They worked in silence, gathering food and drinks. There was, thankfully, leftover chicken, roast beef, loaves of bread baked the day before, plus current pie and coffee to haul out for the fire fighters to refresh themselves with. Kate poured freshly brewed coffee into a stout metal container they used to take drinks to the field, and they were ready.

They were almost out the door when Ellen stopped Kate. "Where's your scarf?" she said sharply. "You'll catch a chill."

"Mother, I'm almost . . . never mind. I'll get it."

When she came back with her scarf, Ellen had already set out, and Kate had to hurry to catch up with her. As they neared Tate's, Kate's breath caught in her chest. The house was engulfed in flame, and the heat was so intense it burned her cheeks even at a distance. She stood motionless, still holding her burdens, and stared at the men as they fought the flame's destruction. She caught sight of Willie racing toward the flames, throwing the contents of one bucket of water while reaching back simultaneously for another. Mel was on the fire truck, pumping frantically up and down on the compression handle, trying in a futile effort to create enough force of water to reach the roof and have some effect on the flames. She seemed planted in place, unable to move, a single motionless object in a sea of frantic motion.

"It's hopeless," she said. "There is no house left." Then she saw the flames, not at the Tate's, but at the back edge of the section, almost a mile away. She screamed and pointed, but couldn't be heard over the noise of the workers and crackling of the fire.

Kate ran to Mel on the fire truck, pounded on his foot until he responded. She just pointed. And he saw. His shoulders sagged. How many more? How much can we take before we're too tired to do any more? Mel shouted at Jack, pointing at the new fire. When Jack got to him, they quickly made a plan and divided the men so half could be dispatched to the neighboring farm.

Wagons rolled down the road, loaded with tools, food and coffee. Will stayed behind to direct the work at the Tate's; Kate and her mother went along. Mel made a last effort with the truck water, and then raced off behind them.

Kate followed her mother's lead. She watched her mother setting up makeshift tables, hefting huge planks and setting them on saw horses some distance from the fire. She was incredible in her strength and determination. Kate hustled over and began to help. There was no need for talk. Ellen directed the work in monosyllables, and Kate responded.

In a few minutes, they were once again set up and an occasional man rushed over to gulp a cup of lukewarm coffee or glass of water. Later, when the fire had begun to burn itself out and the barns were no longer in danger, more of the firefighters wandered over to grab some food.

Almost every able man and woman had raced to help, bringing tools, food and energy, but they were defeated before they had begun. The fires were out, but they had burned the homes to the ground. People stood in small groups, huddled together against disaster, talking, comforting the stricken families, and beginning to plan for rebuilding.

The ashes of the fire were still glowing embers, and the sun threatening to rise when Mel left in his wagon to gather the tools for rebuilding the house. Will had taken the wagon to the mill to get what lumber was already cut. Jack Bay's job was to gather funds or supplies, and he began collecting promises as soon as he had washed the soot from his face and arms. Ellen walked Mrs. Tate and her two children back to the Hughes house and made temporary beds for them in the loft. Kate began the repacking of the food containers and wondered how she would find the energy to cart it all back to the house.

She finished packing and sat on the grass under a maple tree. A bucket was still attached to a spout stuck into the bark, and maple sap leaked in a steady drip into the bucket. Kate mindlessly counted the drops as they splashed into the sweet liquid. It was comforting. The sun glowed faintly in the eastern sky. The smell of soot and damp ash filled her nostrils. One, two – one, two, three, she counted, too tired to begin the haul home.

Two feet were suddenly in front of her, feet she hadn't heard approach. Then a man was sitting next to her, and his arms were around her. Kate nestled into his arms and wrapped hers around his chest. She sobbed just a little, and tears crept slowly down her cheeks, streaking through the dirt as they slid.

"Thank you, Mel. Oh, thank you."

"Just rest here a minute, honey. Then I'll drive you home."

He was so safe, so sane, and she was so tired. "Thank you," she said again, and closed her eyes for just a moment of peace.

For many families, the year was spent rebuilding. Barn raisings became common events as more and more fires raged. Drought and barren forest lands were the enemies which no one knew how to battle. But people grew closer. Neighbors helped neighbors, friends depended on each other, and almost no one refused to help.

Kate continued to admire her mother's untiring spirit of giving. Ellen took non-paying boarders into their home, cooked for the homeless families, and asked for nothing in return. She made clothes from whatever material was available for those who had lost all of theirs. In her stalwart way, she just shoved the garments at them.

"These might do," she said, "till you can find something better." When grateful tears threatened the eyes of Mrs. Tate, Ellen just waved her hand. "They're not much . . . but they'll cover your young ones."

Will carted lumber where it was needed, unloaded it with a handshake for payment. "You'll pay when you can, Tate. I know you will. Just get back on your feet," he said, and turned his back before Tate would feel he had to give a response.

Tom Reeves, Matt Keller, the Thompson boys, Jake the jailor, even tight fisted Nestor did what they could to help those families who had lost everything. Hersey folks came together – and they seemed to be the better for it. They had smiles for one another, and the bickering over land and lumber seemed to stand still for a time.

Kate watched her father's quick step and easy smile grow as he darted around town making things happen. It was what he loved. He even sneaked a hug from Ellen now and then, and Kate saw her mother didn't push him away. Perhaps conquering disaster brings loving out into the open, like spring or fireflies. Or, perhaps, being so close to the death of dreams, as happens when a family home goes up in flames, makes people more aware that in each moment there is the possibility of losing what is precious.

Kate wondered about the changes she saw in the people around her. She wondered, too, about her feelings for Mel. He had worked tirelessly to help the families in need and continue to keep up the work at his farm. Yet, he still found time to stop by the school to drive Kate home once in a while or visit the Hughes porch for a short time on a warm night. He always smiled in his slow, easy way and had a gentle word for all the Hughes, but always a special one for her.

Kate was thinking about Mel when she woke. It was summer, so there was no school to rush off to, but she still rose early to enjoy the cool of the day. It was green and lush along the river bank, and weeping willow trees growing by the river's edge provided shade and privacy Kate loved. The long sweeping arms of the willows spread from the bank and out over the water, making a filtered canopy of their branches. They trailed their leafy fingers in the swift current, catching errant leaves and water bugs, their long legs glued to the water's surface.

Kate watched the sun making patterns in the eddies, playing kaleidoscope games with the river's deep purples and blues. She took off her shoes and socks and crept out on a heavy branch that lay out over the river to dangle her feet in the cool water. She felt alive and glorious in the willow shade with water splashing against her legs. Kate hiked up her skirt in decidedly unladylike fashion and shoved her legs further into the river, leaned back to balance herself, and then heard a sound behind her. When she turned to spot the intruder, she started to slide, grabbed the limb with both hands, and found herself hanging, her fingers fighting for purchase on the branch.

"Damn it!" she yelled as she fell into the water. As she was fighting to the surface and gasping for air, she once again admonished herself. 'Kate, when will you learn not to swear? Well, not now,' she thought, and then shouted, "Damn you, Mel. Give a girl a warning, will you?"

Mel stood on the bank grinning, a fake look of concern on his face, while she fought the current and came up choking.

"I don't see the humor in my predicament," she said between bouts of laughter. "I'm drowning and totally soaked!"

"I can see that," he shouted and ducked the water she splashed at him as he backed away and out of reach. Mel changed his mind after a moment and began to wade in after her, but Kate kicked water at him and splashed until he backed away again.

"Get away from me, you devil!" she shouted. "It's all you're fault that I'm here."

"I was just coming to help you out," Mel said, grinning at Kate and liking the way she looked. "You probably weigh a ton with all those wet clothes, and you're gonna sink any minute."

"I don't want out. In fact, I think I'll just stay here the rest of the summer. The water feels like heaven. Here," she said, sending a spray of water at him with the side of her hand. "Try a little."

Kate stood quietly for a few moments, and then waded toward the bank, looking subdued and innocent until she got within reach of him. Then she ducked, grabbed an ankle and pulled as hard as she could. He hit the bank with a groan, then slid into the water, and came up grabbing at Kate.

"You little brat," he sputtered and finding Kate's head, shoved it under the water. They tousled, laughing like kids and loving the sheer joy of splashing about in the water on a hot summer day. Mel dunked her under again, and Kate took advantage of her position to pull his leg out from under him once more and send him sprawling.

Kate climbed the bank, grabbed a branch of the willow tree and swung out across the water and back again, gaining momentum with each swing and trailing a foot in the current to splash Mel as she went by. He stood watching her antics and ran his hand over his hair to squeeze out the water, then reached out his other hand to catch her as she swung by. Kate dropped into the water in front of him, her hands on her hips, defiant and smiling, daring him to dunk her again.

The laughter left his face. Mel held her at arms distance, just taking in the sight. Her soaked cotton dress clung to her body; her hair, loose from its ties, hung in wet strands over her shoulders, and droplets made her eyelashes thick and shiny.

Kate saw his eyes straying over her, and she suddenly shivered, unable to speak or move. Her throat tightened in her chest and a prickling sensation crawled down her spine, a feeling she didn't understand, but didn't want to end. Mel's hands tightened on her arms, and Kate was glad she couldn't move her hands to touch the dark hair glistening where his shirt had opened. She saw his chest heave as his breath grew more rapid, and she felt she should leave the water, but couldn't.

In an instant, Mel pulled her roughly to him and pressed his lips to hers almost angrily. His lips traveled to her throat, covering it hungrily, and his arms held her so tight Kate could hardly breathe. The pulsing of her heart was so rapid she thought it would burst. Just when her legs felt so weak they couldn't hold her upright for another moment, Mel slipped an arm under them and carried her to the bank.

He sat under the willow tree, still holding her. With branches touching the ground all around them, they were in a private haven, the sun above soft and filtered by a leafy canopy. His lips touched hers again, more softly this time, and he slowly laid her on the ground, sliding down next to her, and pressing his body to hers. She pulled him closer, melted into him, the fever in her body drowning rational thought, not comprehending anything.

Mel drew an arm from under her head to lean over her and smother her neck with soft kisses. Then pulling the front of her dress open, he pressed his lips to her still glistening skin. He found her breast and nuzzled it with his lips.

"God, you're beautiful, Kate . . . so beautiful," he groaned. Kate's intake of breath every time his lips found new skin kept her from speech. Her head was spinning and the need to draw Mel even closer to her was demanding.

When his fingers fumbled with more buttons on her dress, Kate's eyes flew open to see Mel's mouth covering her naked breast. Reality hit her, and her hands suddenly pushed at his shoulders and brought him up in wonder. They stared at each other, passion and confusion mixing and erupting from their faces. Mel's gaze drifted to Kate's open dress, and his brown eyes darkened. His gaze stayed there a moment, and then with an explosion of breath, he abruptly stood and turned away from her.

He paced with his back to her while she rebuttoned her front and tried to rearrange her soggy dress. She brushed the twigs from her as well as she could and tried to retie her hair, taking time to sort out what had just happened. She didn't feel wicked. In fact, she felt something close to glorious, but she also knew she should feel wicked. Nice girls simply don't behave in the way she had just done. She walked to where Mel was standing and tried to formulate the words to make it all okay, but she couldn't find them. She put her hand on his back with a caress not meant to be passionate.

"Mel, I don't know what to say. I don't know what just happened."

When he didn't turn around, she thought he was angry with her. "I'm sorry," she repeated. "I shouldn't have let that happen. I don't know what I was thinking. I guess I wasn't," she mumbled, fearful she had changed in his eyes.

Mel turned with a sudden jerk and grabbed her shoulders, his fingers biting into her skin. His eyes were such a mixture of emotions they would have melted the soul of the devil.

"You're sorry!" he moaned. "I'm the one who's sorry! I wouldn't hurt you for anything, not the whole damn world. I just couldn't keep my hands off you, you looked so . . . I mean, your dress was clinging to you and your body was so beautiful." His eyes wandered from her face, down to where the damp dress still clung to her breasts.

She crossed her arms in front of her, suddenly embarrassed. Mel continued to stare, watching her discomfort. After several deep breaths, he was once again composed, and Mel's eyes lit his face in a grin.

"Give it up, Kate. I already know how beautiful you are. I've seen you."

An uncomfortable blush rose to Kate's face, and she tried to cover it by threatening to shove him into the water again.

"Mel. I don't know what just happened, and I don't hold you responsible, but I can't do that anymore. I . . . really . . . liked it," she stammered, "but, well . . . do you know what I mean?"

"You could if you would marry me."

Kate looked up to see if he was teasing her again, but his face was serious, and his jaw was set. He looked out across the river, squinted his brown eyes at the glare of sun on the water. Creases formed around his eyes in the weathered tan of his skin, but the rest of his face was clear and smooth. Kate wanted to reach out and trace the lines, wipe away the sadness and worry. She felt so deeply for this man. As if he had read her mind, Mel spoke, still staring at the sparkles of sun on the water.

"Kate, you do love me, don't you?"

"Yes," she answered, not able to explain further.

"Then I won't ask why you won't marry me. I have a pretty good idea, but that's your business, and I won't pry. I have to say this, though." He picked up her hand with both of his and touched it lightly to his lips. Then he looked at it like it was something he had never seen before or would ever see again. Kate heard a sigh quiver through his body, and he caressed the side of her face softly with the knuckles of his hand.

"I love you, Kate, but I won't be coming by anymore," he said sadly.

Kate stiffened as if she had been slapped and searched his face for signs of a joke, some reason for him to have said what he had. Mel saw the pain and confusion on her face and quickly gave his reasons.

"Kate, I have to. Don't you understand? I've thought so before, but I just couldn't do it. Today makes it necessary."

"But why, Mel? I don't understand."

"I know you don't, but I can't explain, or I won't," he said, "because you wouldn't understand. You don't feel that way, but I do."

Confusion grew and mixed in with indignation and frustration.

"What? Am I too dull to absorb complicated matters?" she demanded, abruptly drawing back her hand. "I realize I am only a woman, but I have a mind!"

Mel was stunned and stepped back from her anger, but she could not be contained.

"If you think I'll just accept your decision to stop seeing me after all our years of friendship, without some explanation, you're dead wrong!" she shouted.

"Kate," he said in frustration, "you don't want to hear this, and I can't talk about these things with you."

"Well, I'm not moving until you try."

Mel sat down, silent, exasperated by her stubbornness. It seemed even the sounds of nature were quieted, waiting for him to speak. He reached for a blade of grass with trembling fingers and slid it between his teeth. Thoughtfully, he chewed the grass and turned his gaze once again to the river. He watched it splash against the rocks, felt his heart being similarly beaten, and wished he could float away in its current to unknown places where a woman named Kate did not exist.

"Kate, sit down," he commanded. "If you were the kind of woman I could find it easy to say this to, I wouldn't need to say it," he said in chopped words. "There would be no need." He turned to face her squarely. "For that matter, if you were that kind of woman, there would be no need for me to stay away from you."

Light dawned in Kate's eyes, and she blushed thinking of Sadie's girls. She knew about them. In fact she kind of admired them.

"Do you mean to say, Mel, that if I hadn't stopped us a few moments ago, you would still be my friend? Still see me? Is that what you're trying to say?"

It was Mel's turn to blush, and he quickly tried to backtrack.

"No, Kate, don't ever get the idea that I would want you to . . . I mean, I would never . . . not with you, Kate. Not without marriage."

"Then if it's not what just happened, I certainly don't understand. You don't want me to be one kind of woman, but you stop seeing me because I am the kind of woman you want me to be . . ."

Mel held up his hand in surrender. His mouth turned up at the corners in a grin that was as sad as it was joyful. He shook his head at her in confused wonder.

"Stop, you're confusing me! If you keep on, even I won't know what I'm talking about."

"So explain it to me, and I'll shut up."

"Kate, this idea has not just occurred to me today. I've thought about it for some time now. I love you, Kate, but I am afraid for us, afraid I will hurt you." Mel looked her straight in the eyes as he talked and his voice was strained with emotion. He stopped for a moment to gather his next words, but his eyes never left her face. They probed for understanding, and he reached out for courage to continue. He paused long enough that Kate prompted him.

"How will you hurt me?" she asked, her question a whisper on the wind.

When he finally spoke, the words came flowing like a dam had burst.

"I know you, Kate. You are an innocent, but also a passionate one. I love you. As my friend and companion, as the mother of children I'd like to have with you, but mostly as my wife. My lover, Kate. Don't you understand? I want you for my lover, Kate. All of you." The fountain had been turned on, and Mel continued, broken sentences, feelings he had kept hidden for years, pressure that had building for so long. "I loved you when you were a girl with no shape but that of a boy and watched you grow into a woman with everything that a woman should have. When you filled out, so did my need of you, until . . . damn it, Kate! Being near you drives me crazy! I work to forget it, then come running to see you when I just have to and can't help it anymore!"

Mel had grasped her arms in a painful grip, and Kate just stood there watching and wondering.

"Kate, I have kissed other girls, looking for some way to love another, to feel what I feel when I kiss you. All I end up feeling is how much better it is when I am near you, how you fit me." He kissed her softly, holding her away from him, a tender kiss that said goodbye.

"There is a shadow around you, Kate, and it's hard. I know you love me, but that shadow gets in the way, like a fence that either keeps the horses in or the predators out. It keeps you inside yourself and me out." Mel walked away, but turned back briefly. "If you ever truly need me, Kate, I will be there, no matter the circumstance."

Kate sat on the bank and watched the river passing by and wondered if life had just passed her by. She had let it happen, had been the reason for it. She felt empty, lost. She would no longer have Mel in her life, and it was unthinkable, even terrifying. What was the matter with her? Why could she not marry this wonderful man, one she loved deeply? What was she waiting for? But she didn't have the answers to her own questions, and she wanted nothing more than to curl up in a ball and go to sleep for a long, long time.

She picked up her shoes, tied the laces together and carried them toward home. Dust clung to the damp edges of her dress and turned quickly to mud. It slapped against her legs with each step. The sun had dried parts of her clothing, but still wet places felt cool in contrast to the dry heat rising from the road.

Kate's mind wandered over the events of the morning, backwards from the end when Mel had said goodbye and walked away. She remembered the caresses, the touch of his lips on her bare skin, and grew warm with the memory. She hadn't felt wicked. She had felt glorious, and wondered what was wrong with her. Was she just basically a bad woman, the woman her mother had always said she would be? Should she feel bad?

"Well, damn it," she said to the road in front of her. "I don't feel wicked and I don't care if I said damn it. I'm just sad and already lonely. And, damn it again, I'm angry."

As Kate neared home, she wanted more than anything to turn and run, not to meet Ellen's eyes as she took in her disheveled appearance. She didn't expect her mother to say much, but it was the eyes she didn't want to see. She didn't deliberately do things to disappoint Ellen, but it seemed she frequently did, and that, too, made her sad – and angry.

"You were out early," Ellen said from behind a shirt she was hanging on the line.

"Yes, I went for a cool morning walk," she responded, "and an unexpected dip in the river." Kate's sad smile puzzled Ellen, and it was the strange smile that stopped Ellen from questioning.

Kate changed and began Saturday's chores. Nothing else was said about the morning, and in between brief comments from the rest of the family, she was left alone to think.

Dusk buried each day in its blanket of darkness and morning rose in a starched linen sky, and Kate marched through the summer, orderly, dutiful, bored and unreasonably irritated. The heat was intense and threat of fire constant. Grass fires had engulfed some fields and crops, but they had been fortunate lately; no more homes had been destroyed. Still, the heat made everyone tense, and the threat of fire, never far from anyone's mind, increased the tension.

Evening had not brought the usual respite from the heat. A thick haze hovered over the sky, forcing the air into a stifling stillness. Will rose from the dinner table with slow deliberate movements, shoulders slightly bent, arms hanging at his sides. Ellen and Ruthie were at the sink, silently rinsing dishes. Kate suddenly couldn't stand the silence.

"What's the matter with all of us?" she snapped. "Look at us."

All eyes were riveted on Kate, wondering what she was talking about.

"Can't we laugh anymore? Has the heat melted our tongues?" She turned to lash out at her father for no other reason than because he was there and what she saw pained her. He looked old and tired, and the gleam in his eyes had been missing for a long while.

"What's going on, Pa? Why are you so . . . you know what I mean," she said irritably.

Will just stared at her, curious about what had sparked the outburst from his daughter, but not responding to her question. Not really understanding the question at all.

"What are you going on about, Kate?" Ellen said sharply from her place by the sink. "Why do you say something is the matter with us?"

"Well just look at us. We go to work, we eat, and we sleep. We don't even talk, and God forbid we smile or laugh." Kate's voice was rising as she spoke, and the others stared, open mouthed. She could not seem to stop ranting, wasn't even sure what she was so angry about. She just knew she was, and once started, the hurt and restlessness came pouring out.

"God does not forbid us laughter, Kate. But there's more to life than laughing, and work is honorable. You should be grateful you have work."

"Why, Ma? Because I don't have a husband? I should be happy I have work to do? Is that what you're saying? I'll never have a family to work for because I'm a spinster schoolteacher? Go ahead! Say it!" Kate's voice kept rising and her hands clenched at her sides. Ellen strode firmly to her daughter, as angry as she had ever been.

"Stop this instant!" Ellen's voice was a low growl, and her face was white, red blotches staining her neck and cheeks.

"Why, because you don't want to hear the truth?"

"No, because you are being disrespectful to this family."

"I am only speaking the truth. Look around you. Have you even looked at your husband lately? Does he even look like the same man you married? He's miserable. Can't you see it? Do you even know why or care?" Kate raised her arm and pointed a shaking finger at her father, turned to Will and felt the sting of her mother's hand on her cheek.

Stunned silence hung in the room. Kate lowered her arm and turned her face to Ellen. Her hand was still raised, poised in the aftershock of the slap and appearing ready to strike again. But she didn't. She saw the red growing on her daughter's face, and she was abhorred by what she had done. She didn't understand what had happened, and thought she would never understand her older daughter. She didn't even know how to begin.

Kate turned to face away from Ellen and said cruelly, "I'm turning the other cheek, Mother. Isn't that what you preach?"

Kate heard a long groan from across the room and turned to see her father slumped in a chair, his hands over his face. He hadn't said a word during the entire argument, and the sound of anguish coming from him stilled both mother and daughter.

"Are you happy that you have finally changed him, Ma? Well, I'm not. I can't stand to see it, and I'll be looking for a teaching post in another town. I need to be away from here."

Kate moved to kneel by her father, grief bending her shoulders and filling her heart.

"You're not happy, Pa. Why won't you do something about it?"

"You won't understand, Kate. I'm not young anymore."

"That's just not true, Pa. You are young enough to do anything you want to do, and you are dead bored with the mill. It's not fun anymore and it's killing you."

Will looked across the room at his wife and saw the woman he had married, the one he had fallen in love with so long ago and still loved. It showed on his face, and Kate saw it and understood. More than anything else, he hated hurting Ellen; more than settling down, more than not following new dreams, more than being stuck in one place, he hated making Ellen unhappy. And he had done so much of that. He couldn't take back the moves and the failures and couldn't give back the years, but he could make the rest of them peaceful for her. They had food on the table, a home, and a thriving business. It was Ellen's turn to get her dream. He was paying his dues. Maybe she would love him again, and maybe she would smile.

"Not true, sweetie. But thanks for telling me how I've been behaving. I needed it, and I have a new dream that will be occupying my time."

"What? Tell me."

"Nope. My secret."

Kate stood and saw a small gleam in her father's eyes.

"Well, Pa, I need to find a teaching post away from Hersey. I need to do something other than just drift from day to day."

Will struggled with himself to find the right response. Kate brought sunshine into his life and every day he saw himself as a young man in this willful daughter.

"I don't want you to go, but . . ."

"Your father's right," Ellen interrupted softly. "Going off by yourself, an unmarried woman . . ." She stopped, fearing what she was about to say might start Kate off on another tirade.

"I hadn't finished, Ellen. I was about to say that she should try it. It's only selfishness on my part that wants to keep her here. It might be just what Kate needs. She knows how to take care of herself."

He took her hand and, like Mark had done so long ago, kissed the back of it.

"Go honey, follow a dream."

Will got up from his chair, walked over to his wife, took her hand and softly caressed the calloused palm. Then, turning it over, he kissed the back of it as he had Kate's, but lingered there for a time, then left the house. Ellen stood speechless, a slow blush rising up her neck.

A long silence followed Will. Then Kate went to her mother, honesty forcing her. "Ma, I had that coming," Kate said quietly. "I am so sorry." Ellen knew what she meant and was grateful for her daughter's honesty.

All she could say was "I know," and hope that Kate knew what she meant. She couldn't talk about what had happened. Maybe later, but not yet. Her sorrow was too great, and words did not come easy to her.

Kate sent off letters to several of the nearby townships asking for teaching posts. Replies came back negative. Most had teachers who had been there forever and would likely be there until they died. Kate pictured them slumped over their desks, their hickory switches still clutched in their hands, cobwebs growing over their backs, and the students still sitting in their seats waiting for class to begin. That could be me, she thought. Most likely will be. She continued to send out the letters, going further and further from Hersey, but nothing could be found, so she waited . . . and waited.

She saw the cabin from a distance, weathered boards peeking out of thick vines hanging from the branches of trees surrounding it. Vines draped over the roof and hung over the walls, almost completely hiding the cabin. Kate could not recall seeing it before and approached it cautiously, calling out, "Anyone here? Hello, anybody home?"

She had walked a long distance, wandering further than her usual hike through the woods. No one answered her call. "Strange, spooky place . . ." she said to the foliage. "But I like it."

She pushed the vines apart and moved toward the cabin. The undergrowth and thorny brambles caught at her hair and clothes as she made her way to a door hanging from a single hinge, cocked at an angle that made entry easy. It creaked loudly when she pulled it open, startling her in the heavy silence.

"Hello," she said again even knowing the cabin was empty. The scurry of feet and wings greeted her, and she ducked, covering her head and leaping aside as bats and forest rodents fled through the door she had just opened.

"Damn! Sorry! I didn't mean to invade your space. Well . . . yes, I guess I did, cause I'm here, aren't I? Sorry about the cussing, too. Shouldn't do that," she said, recently becoming certain she needed to reform her habits. As her eyes adjusted to the darkness inside the cabin, she began to see what was left of someone's home.

At first glance, it appeared to be one room. A small bed filled one side; a wooden table sat in the center with two chairs at either end. A dry sink and a stove occupied the space opposite the bed. On the stove was a black kettle and above it hung a large iron skillet. A stone fireplace filled the back wall and held logs placed ready to light. Ashes had been swept from the hearth.

"Neat man, aren't you," Kate whispered. On the front wall, next to the strangely angled door, hung a pair of black trousers turned grey with dust and an equally dusty black hat. A matching coat and once white shirt hung on a peg next to them.

"Odd," Kate said. "Seems out of place here," fingering the fabric of the coat and sending dust into the air. Other than the dust, the room was neat. Everything was put away on shelves or hanging on pegs.

Kate looked around, imagining the person who had called this cabin home. She saw him lying in bed at night, listening to the creek as it spoke softly from a few yards away. She saw him carefully tending the stove so the stew he had made didn't burn.

"Probably squirrel stew or rabbit," she said to the chinked walls. "I'll bet there's a small garden nearby with carrots and potatoes in it. Okay, they were there at one time. Maybe it's a she. Could be a she – why not?"

Kate brushed away cobwebs as she probed into the nooks and crannies of the room, feeling like an intruder, but knowing whoever had called this home was gone long ago. Without acknowledging or even understanding what she was doing, she grabbed a broom standing in the corner and started sweeping. Dirt swirled and eddied around her, settled on her until she was as filthy as the cabin had been, and she kept sweeping until the wooden floor was visible and the walls were free of dust and cobwebs.

Outside, she found a battered bucket and filled it with water from the creek. She found some lye near the dry sink, some rags hanging over it, and she began scrubbing. The table was clean, a beautiful, smooth oak plank; the stove was black and glistening in the light coming in through two newly washed windows. She took the quilt from the bed to the river, hiked up her skirt, and waded out deep enough to let the current wash away the accumulation of dust. She stood knee deep in the water, feeling the coolness against her legs and the heavy pull of the wet quilt against her arms. It felt glorious. Her arms ached and her back burned, but she felt great. She threw the soggy quilt over some branches so it could dry and sat at the edge of the river, smiling.

Turning to look at her cabin, she made plans. "Tomorrow," she said to the brambles surrounding the cabin, "I'll bring some cutting tools, and you will have to go. Yes," she said. "I'm talking to you. You scratched my face and tore at my hair, damn it!"

I'm talking to weeds, now. No wonder the whole world thinks I'm a bit daft. I need a dog. I could talk to a dog, or at least people would think I was talking to the dog when I'm having conversations with weeds and trees and water bugs. Not some little, yappy thing, but a real one – big, and one that likes to walk in the woods.

That decided, Kate took a last tour of her cabin, nodded to the walls but not talking to them, and walked out wondering where she could find a dog and how she was going to talk her mother into letting her keep it.

'Look what followed me home, Ma. Can I keep it?'

Kate went back to her cabin several times each week throughout the rest of the summer and fall. It began to feel like home, and it looked like Kate. She had brought some of her things with her each time, and now an apron hung next to the man's clothes, freshly washed in the creek, dried and hung back on their pegs. For some reason, it didn't seem right to get rid of his things. The cabin was his, too. Well, actually, it was his cabin – only. He was just sharing it with her.

An old table cloth she had found in her mother's closet now covered the table, and on it sat a jar with dried flowers and weeds. She had haphazardly made two blue checked curtains and tacked them to the sides of the windows on one of her trips, leaving the panes open to the sunshine. A colorful rag rug covered the floor in front of the hearth. On the rug was a small pillow where the dog laid his head when they were there.

He groaned a small sigh of contentment, and his eyes followed Kate as she moved around the room.

Kate had asked about a dog around town, checking in with Nestor who saw everyone when they came to the store for supplies or just to sit and sip a jug. No one knew of a litter of pups or even a grown dog they just couldn't keep anymore. She had begun to give up the idea of having a conversational partner when one just showed up at the Hughes house.

About two weeks after finding the cabin Kate went home after school to find a good sized, red haired animal lounging on the porch. It sat up when she approached, cocked his head, and rolled huge brown eyes at her. She sat down on the steps and held out her hand to him. He ambled over, laid his chin in her upturned palm, and stared at her.

"Where on earth did you come from?" she asked him. "You are beautiful. Can you talk?"

"I don't think he talks, Kate. It's a dog." Ellen stood at the other side of the screen door, a dish towel in her hands. "And I don't know about beautiful. He's kind of shaggy with all the hair hanging down his legs and chest."

"Well, where did he come from? He didn't just show up all of a sudden."

"No, Mel brought him by. Said you needed some protection if you're going to wander the woods at all hours of the day and night."

"And you said okay?" Kate asked, stunned her mother had agreed.

"What could I say?" she answered. "Mel brought it, and said you needed it, and it needed a home. He stays outside," she added, "and you take care of it."

"I love him," Kate said. "That was really kind of Mel."

"Kate, Mel is a kind man. I couldn't refuse his gift to you."

Ellen turned back to her kitchen, and Kate put her face into the fur at his neck. He smelled fresh, like the river after a rain. Mel had bathed him, Kate thought. And he was smart to bring the dog to Ellen when Kate wasn't home. He knew the chances were much better Kate would be allowed to keep the dog if he approached Ellen with it.

Kate smiled. Smart, stubborn Mel would always find ways to do what needed to be done. How did he even know she wanted a dog? Mr. Nestor, she thought, and smiled again – her champion. Some people were wonderful. She stood, untied the leash from the porch rail, and ran down the steps with her new conversation partner.

"Well," she said to him, "You need a new name, one you will have to show me. Do you like the woods? Do you like to play in the river? Will you care if I say damn and talk to trees?"

Bug gave himself his name within the first week. They had walked to the river, as they did everyday after school. Water Bug, his full name, leaped from the bank, spread eagled into the river, and his long fringe seemed to float on the water just like the water bugs Kate loved. Bug floated down a ways, then paddled back, floated down and paddled back, his brown eyes never leaving Kate's face. He climbed the bank, shook, his long fringe flying, and covered Kate with spray.

"Damn," she said. "I'm wetter than you are now."

Bug sat on his haunches, looking contrite, but Kate was sure he was grinning.

"You really are a water bug, aren't you?" Kate nuzzled his wet mane and said, "That's you. Water Bug. Bug for short. Let's go home, Bug."

Between working on the cabin, taking long walks with Bug, and teaching, Kate kept busy. Summer fled into fall, and autumn slid quietly into winter. Then Willie and Mary's wedding occupied her, and shortly after, helping to get ready for the coming of their baby. She spent a lot of time at Willie and Mary's house. They were always happy to have Kate and Bug there, and the playful banter filling their home was refreshing.

"I'll bet the baby will have freckles," Mary said. "Although I hope not. I always hated mine."

"Well, I want this kid to have freckles on his nose, just like his mother's," Willie always said. "They're cute."

Kate was sure the baby would have the famous Hughes twinkle and strut. "I can just see him now. At two this baby will be swaggering all over town – owning everybody he looks at."

"What makes you think it's a boy?" Willie said. "I think it's going to be a gorgeous girl, just like Mary."

Mary had a knack for turning their small house into a cheery and comfortable home. Chintz curtains pulled back from the window panes let in the last of the sunset and framed the trees in their front yard. The pine table in the kitchen, made by Willie and his father at the mill, was scrubbed to a satiny sheen, like the counter and the floor. The few pieces of furniture had been made by Willie with love. Mary had even found a mat for Bug to lie on. It was always there for him when they visited. Kate felt good in their home and hoped what Willie and Mary had between them would last as long as they did.

Motherhood sat well on Mary. She wore the expansion of her belly with pride. Kate spent quite a bit of time with her since Willie worked long hours at the lumber camp. Hard labor sat well on him, broadening his shoulders and hardening his belly. On his day off, he worked at Nestor's, earning extra money in preparation for the baby.

Kate watched through the months as Mary sewed the tiny nightdresses and hand stitched edges on flannel for the diapers. Her lips would turn up at the edges and her eyes took on a dreamy look as she worked. Kate saw and every now and then felt a tinge of envy creep in. She loved Mary as a sister and wanted her happiness, but occasionally she wished for some of what Mary had for herself and wondered if she should have accepted Mel's proposal. She could be sitting in his beautiful house sewing for a baby of her own instead of living vicariously through her brother and his wife. Was it wrong to wish for what someone else had? Was she evil for just wishing?

"Damn it, Kate. You're turning into a vicious old spinster. Just like they all said you would. You're going to start chewing like a cow and swearing at men soon. And don't say damn in front of the baby."

"Did you say something, Kate?" Mary asked.

She shook herself and looked guiltily at Mary. "I don't know . . . did I?"

"Probably not. I just thought I heard something."

"Maybe the baby kicked. Is he moving?" Kate asked, changing the subject.

"No, he's quiet," Mary said looking at Kate a bit suspiciously.

"What are you wearing to the Christmas eve ball?" Kate asked, sidestepping the questions.

"Well, we're probably not going," Mary said.

"Why on earth not?"

"As you can see, I'm not fitting into my clothes too well these days."

Mary stood and turned sideways, her stomach drawing all attention from her small frame and stretching the cloth of her dress tautly. She grinned to show she didn't really mind and was quite proud of her girth.

"I guess I didn't really think about it, but I'll bet we can remake one of my dresses to fit you. I'm bigger, but that's perfect. I'll bring a couple by tomorrow."

Mary clapped her hands like a little girl and sat down. "Do you think we could?"

"Sure, we'll just take the shoulders up a little and lift the hem, put a little extra in the waistline, and we're all set."

"Oh, Kate, you're an angel. I really did want to go." She sat for a moment, smiling and thinking how happy Willie would be, and then hesitated. "You're going, aren't you?"

"No, I don't think so this year," Kate said as nonchalantly as possible. True to his word, Mel had not been to see Kate since the river bank episode. She kept waiting, hoping he would reconsider, but he had made up his mind, and he always kept his word. She missed him desperately.

"Kate, it's none of my business, but why doesn't Mel ask you to these things anymore?"

Trying not to sound hurt, Kate said briskly, "Well, he just doesn't. Maybe he has a girl," and laughed to show she didn't really care.

"Kate, you can tell me to shut up and butt out if you want to, but I'm going to ask this anyway. It doesn't seem like you are as happy as you could be – or should be."

"Nonsense, I'm fine. I've got my very own private nephew coming soon – or niece. I can love him – or her – as much as I want and not have to wash diapers. And I have Bug to love. What more could a girl want? A dog and a nephew!"

Mary sat silently just looking at her friend. Suddenly, with determination, she said, "Why won't you marry him?"

Kate was startled into unaccustomed silence and couldn't come up with an answer. How could Mary know Mel had even asked? She thought about jesting her way out of this private conversation, but decided on a point blank approach.

"I just can't, Mary."

"I don't understand."

"I just can't. It's not something I can explain."

"Just one more thing, Kate, and then I'll let it go. You seemed happiest when you were together. It seemed you loved each other."

"Yes, that's true. We do, or did. It's a long story, and not one I am sure I want to try to explain, or that I even can. I'm sorry." How could she explain to this sweet girl she had known a very special love, and it was for a married man, a man who was most likely still in prison many miles away, didn't even know she loved him, and certainly didn't return it? How could she say this love had spoiled her and would, it seemed, continue to haunt her? It could not be replaced by anything short of what it was. She couldn't explain, and didn't even know if she understood it herself. It just was.

"It obviously bothers you a lot," Mary answered.

"Yes, I miss Mel terribly, but you would not give a broken gift to someone you cared about would you?"

"No, of course not, but what if that person would rather have a gift that was a bit broken rather than not have it at all? Especially if he had wanted that gift his entire life? Would that make a difference?"

Kate silently pondered Mary's logic and knew she was at least somewhat right in what she was saying. But after thinking about it, she came to the conclusion there was something wrong with the reasoning. In the beginning, it might work, but she knew after awhile Mel would resent her because he wasn't first in her heart, and she would understand. You needed to be first in line when you love someone and they love you, not second to anything. As much as Kate wished for it, Mark would not leave her heart, and thoughts of him plagued her with butterflies. Even if she might find contentment in Mel's love, she would not do that to him.

Mary thought of her love for Willie, and let it go.

Kate left, and in the following days, she tried to be content with her life. She was fairly successful, especially when she could find serenity in the woods.

Snow blanketed the ground and continued to fall. Branches laden with white leaned to the earth and cracked when the weight was too much, snapping loudly in the muffled quiet the snow brought.

"Come on, Bug. Let's go," she said. He perked his ears and leaped up, his front paws on Kate's shoulders and his nose inches from hers. Then he ran to the door, waiting.

'Come on; get your coat. Mine's already on,' he said with his eyes.

Snow swirled in when she opened the door, and she quickly slammed it shut.

"Need boots, too, it seems." She grabbed her galoshes, wrapped a scarf around her head and they were off.

Bug leaped into snow already piling in drifts, shoved his face in, and took big mouthfuls, looking at Kate with each bite as if to say, 'Try it. It's good.' He spun, took a giant leap at her as if to drive home his point. She tipped backwards, fell, and he was immediately standing over her, licking her face. 'You meant to play in the snow, didn't you? It's fun, right?'

"Right, Bug. Don't look at me all innocent," she said, laughing and picked up a handful of snow and threw it at him. She made angels in the snow, her arms making wide wings. He responded by racing around her in circles until she caught him and rolled him in the snow.

"Damn it, Bug. I'm thoroughly wet, and it's your fault. People are always getting me wet. And, no, I'm not going to apologize to you for cussing. Get used to it. It's you and me, boy. Just you and me, and you have to like me just as I am. It's a law of some sort."

Bug nodded; sat and watched her as she brushed off the snow and rearranged her scarf.

'I'm patient,' his eyes said, 'but are you ready now?'

The sun was shining, and the snowflakes clung to her wet face and settled on her shoulders. It was a long walk to the cabin, but they kept moving and were finally there. She heard the ripple of the creek before she actually saw the cabin and felt like she had come home.

Inside, she held a match to the already prepared logs in the fireplace. It caught quickly and sweet smelling smoke filled the room. She pulled on the damper chain, and flame leaped up the chimney flue, sucking the smoke with it. She hung her wet coat and scarf on a peg next to the man's coat and hat and turned to savor her room. Bug had already curled up on his rug in front of the hearth, and steam had begun to rise from his wet fur. His head rested on his front feet and he looked asleep, but Kate knew his eyes followed her every step. She lit a fire in the cook stove and put some leftover soup on to simmer. Its aroma completed her contentment.

Snow coated the window panes, the depth rising with each gust. Kate cocked her head, listening to the wind. It seemed to be louder than before, but she was warm and safe. She sat by Bug near the warmth of the fire and stroked his head.

"What do you think, Bug? You like it here, too, don't you? We're as snug as a bug on a rug," she said giggling.

Bug nodded, rolled his eyes saying, 'of course, you silly woman. It's warm, quiet, and I know you're gonna share your soup.'

When Kate awoke, it was to the sound of howling. Bug was standing, the hair on his back was raised, and a low growl came from his throat. He glared at the door and then at each window as if some prowler was about to enter. Kate registered the sounds and immediately knew they were in trouble.

The prowler was a winter storm, and it was blasting them full force. Wind rattled the panes in the windows, shook the door she had carefully hung back on its rusty hinges, and blew in through the cracks in the chinked log walls.

"Well, Bug, I think we shouldn't have taken a nap. I'm not sure we should hike home through the woods right now. What do you think?"

Bug agreed, and since Kate was awake and on guard, he settled back down on his rug but kept his eyes open and alert to dangers he might feel compelled to attack. Kate added logs to the fire, fixed two bowls of soup, and they both settled in to wait out the storm. After two hours of listening to the wind howl, Kate's concern was escalating. It wasn't letting up. If anything, the wind howled louder, and the snow was piling faster.

She wiped a small spot at the top of the window pane and could only see white.

Several small logs were left in the wood box by the fireplace, but she knew they wouldn't last long, and she'd need to bring some in from the wood pile the owner of the coat had left. She put on her own coat, wrapped the scarf around her head, and opened the door to a blast of snow and wind.

"Come on, Bug. Let's go play in the snow."

Bug looked up at her, his eyes wide and mournful. 'You've got to be kidding. It's warm in here. Did you see that snow?' He stretched, dragging out the time he had left in the warm cabin, saying 'I don't like it, but well . . . you're my Kate. I'm sure there are bad things out there, so I have to protect you,' and ambled to the door.

Outside, the wind beat at the trees, bent branches, and blew snow so violently she couldn't see. It bit at her hands and face and stung her eyes. She felt the cold immediately seeping through her jacket, and for the first time, she was afraid.

"Damn it, no one knows where we are," she mumbled. "I'm such an idiot."

Kate felt along the wall of the cabin, guiding herself to the woodpile she knew was at the back corner. Bug hugged her legs, moving only when she did. She grabbed several pieces of wood, piling as many as she could hold on her arms, and retraced her steps to the cabin door. Three more times they trekked to the woodpile and brought in as much wood as they could carry. The stock pile was getting low.

"That's it, Bug. We should be okay tonight, anyway. The storm can't last long." Bug agreed, thought it was a good thing to be out of the cold. After hanging her wet things next to the man's, she added a log to the fire and sat down on his rug. He moved over to give her some room and laid his soggy head in her lap. Kate was pretty sure his eyes rolled to the soup kettle, but she was too tired to respond.

"Later, Bug. More soup later, Okay?"

Darkness fell and the snow continued to fall, piling in huge drifts as the wind blew it across the ground. Ellen had put dinner on the table, but watched out the windows while she worked. She had no idea where her daughter was, and her concern overshadowed her irritation in not knowing.

"I don't understand, Will. Where could she be on this kind of day?"

Will rubbed his hands through his hair and over his face, brushing against the absent whiskers.

"I just don't know. She likes to walk in the woods with Bug. But she wouldn't get lost. She knows these woods better than anyone." He, too, looked at the windows, then at the door, willing Kate to walk in, with Bug in tow and a gust of snow following them.

Ruthie looked from one parent to the other not knowing what she should do. She saw the fear in her mother's eyes and the helpless despair in her father's. She went to the window and looked out at the storm. Her sister could be stranded out there in the blizzard. But how could she give away Kate's special place? She was not even supposed to know about it; had only found out through Mr. Nestor and then later, Mel.

Ruthie had never told Kate she knew about the cabin. She didn't know why. She only knew she loved her sister, her sister was sad, and she needed this place for herself. And she didn't want to intrude. But now, she had a decision to make.

"She should have known better than to go walking in this weather. She's not a child," Ellen said, fear grinding out the words.

"These storms come up unexpected, Ellen. The best of us get surprised by them."

"Well, now see what comes from such foolishness. Here we are worrying about her, and . . ." Ellen stopped, her eyes round and wide with trying to stave off the tears she so hated. She slammed down the pan she had been holding and walked to the window. Her fingers rubbed a small circle in the frost on the pane. She placed her forehead on the cold glass above it and stared out at the solid wall of white. Longing gripped her; for her child out in the snow, for her inability to understand this child she had born, for her own weaknesses that reared their ugly heads in anger at this child. Her throat tightened, and she released a deep breath.

"I'm going for a walk in the woods," she said in a voice that invited no discussion.

"Wait," Ruthie whispered in an explosion of breath she seemed to have held in forever. "I know where she is."

Will and Ellen stared at her, blank expressions on their faces that turned in a speck of time to hope and then disbelief.

"How could you know where Kate is?" Ellen asked.

"Because I know she has a cabin in the woods. Mr. Nestor told me, and I've talked with Mel. She's taken all kinds of stuff there to fix it up. I've seen her do it. Like rugs, and curtains, and leftover food and stuff." Ruthie looked worried to be telling on her sister, but she was determined they believe her. "Mel knows about it. We talked one day in town," she said looking tentatively at her mother.

"Where is this cabin?" Will asked much more calmly than he felt.

"I don't know. I just know that she has one, and it's in the woods, a long walk from here."

"I'm taking one of the horses. Too much snow for the rig. If I know Mel, he'll know where this cabin is. I'll check with him first. If he doesn't know, then Nestor."

"Will, get Willie to go with you. You don't want to be out there alone."

"I'll saddle both then and pick him up on the way."

It was past bedtime by the time Will got to his son's house, but Willie dragged himself from the comfort of his quilt without asking a single question. From there, they plodded through the blizzard to Mel's farm. It took several minutes of banging on the door before Mel heard them, the wind was so loud and the snow muffled their efforts. When Mel opened the door, they stomped their way into the entry trying not to leave mountains of snow as they went.

"Do you know about this cabin of Kate's?" Will barked without explanation.

Mel finished belting a long terrycloth robe around his huge frame and considered his reply. Was Will mad at him because Kate had found a cabin she liked to visit? Was this his doing? Why does he care whose fault it is now, in the middle of a blizzard? Mel had known for a long time about Kate's visits to the cabin, and he understood her desire to be there.

"Yes, I know Kate has a place she visits. Why?"

"Because she is not home! She is out in this blizzard somewhere, God only knows where, with just Bug for help if she needs it. That's why." Will was angry and knew he was taking it out on Mel, but he couldn't help it. He was afraid, and he didn't like feeling fear.

"Saddle my mare while I dress," Mel said, and he ran up the stairs.

Mel knew exactly how to find the cabin. It took a long time to get there because of the blizzard, but he knew every turn, every snow covered tree that marked a turning place. When they spotted a faint light through the frosted window of the cabin, Will released a long-held breath. He knew just by looking at the place it was Kate's.

They tied their reins to nearby trees, patted their horses gently, knowing they were leaving them out in weather they really wanted to escape, and banged on Kate's door. It rattled on its rusty hinges, and they heard the low growl of Kate's Bug. They didn't wait for Kate to open the door. When they burst through, Bug lunged at Mel, grabbed his arm and held it. He had to stand on his hind legs to do it, but he held on, not biting down, just staring Mel in the eyes and daring him to move another inch.

"Can you call him off?" he said, looking at Kate calmly.

Kate snapped her fingers. "Bug," she said.

The dog gave one more glare at Mel, said 'Don't move an inch,' and released his hold. He turned to walk toward Kate, staring behind him all the way as he went to sit at Kate's feet.

"I can see you have a protector," Mel said, rubbing his arm.

"I didn't know it before, but I do now." An uncomfortable pause filled the room.

"Want some soup?"

Will looked around at his daughter's place, took in the feel of it and wanted to stay.

"I'd love to, Kate, but your mother is really worried about you."

"Another time then," she said. The reality of how afraid she had really been hit her and she hugged her father, but only a little. "I was alright, you know. We would have been fine, but I feel bad Mom was worried. Can I carry Bug on the horse with you? The snow is really too high for him to walk."

Mel watched her, instantly and irrationally angry she could evoke such feelings in him.

"Get your things, Kate. It's a long way back, and your mother is worried." But he looked around and wished he could stay here with her. Right here! Damn her! He looked at the man's garments hanging on the wall and again irrationality took over.

"Who do those belong to?"

"The man who lived here, or still does, I guess," she said.

"And that is?"

"The owner," she said. "I'm just a squatter here, but I don't think he minds. I'm keeping it up for him. Doesn't it look nice?" she asked, begging for understanding.

Willie broke the silence. "It is homey," he said. "I wouldn't mind living here if it wasn't for the baby coming." He looked over at the stove. "The soup smells good."

"Let's go," Mel interrupted. "The snow is getting higher."

Kate put ashes on the fire, closed the damper just enough to let the smoke escape as the fire died, put the leftover soup in a bowl outside to freeze for their next visit, and donned her coat and scarf. She looked around her before closing the door and wished she could stay. It was home to her and Bug. Mel took her arm and hoisted her onto the front of his saddle.

"My mare can take two people best," he said to Will and Willie. To Kate he added, "It will still be there when you come back," he said a bit gruffly. "Hang on. I'll get Bug for your dad to carry." He lifted Bug and placed him in front of Will who steadied the dog as he tried to get comfortable.

"It's okay, Bug," Kate said. "Pa will hang on to you. You just enjoy the ride."

"That was a damned foolish thing to do," he growled in her ear after easily throwing his leg over the horse to sit behind her.

"Sorry," Kate responded, feeling like a child being reprimanded by a parent. "I didn't mean to get snowed in."

"You could have been on your way home when this storm hit, stranded in the woods, not able to see a foot in front of you! We never would have found you! You could have died out there, Kate!"

"Look, damn it, I appreciate the rescue, but I don't need to be spoken to like I'm some kind of nitwit. I would have been alright in the cabin until the blizzard let up. I'm not a fool when it comes to the woods," she barked back, and then whispered to herself, "just about everything else, and I can say damn if you can."

They rode slowly through the deep snow, bent forward to keep the wind and flakes from stinging their faces. Much later, Kate turned her face to Mel.

"Thank you for coming," she said contritely, "and thanks for Bug. I love him."

"I know," he said quietly in her ear. His elbows squeezed against her sides, an awkward but heartfelt hug. "Sorry I growled at you. I was just so afraid you were lost in the woods."

"I know," she said, and she did.

They moved down Main Street slowly, singing the familiar carols and feeling the snow fall lightly on their faces. Families were clustered together, arms linked or wrapped around the shoulders of their mates and children. The blizzard had gone, and in its wake the beauty of winter came. There was no wind, just giant flakes drifting lightly, piling in soft mounds around them. Their goal was the huge spruce tree at the end of the street. It was there they planted the star at the top, and on the ground underneath, they placed baby Jesus and the rest of the nativity scene.

Kate walked with Willie and Mary. Ruthie was by her side. She held her sister's arm, squeezed it with love; family was everything.

"Sing harmony with me, Ruthie," she said. "You take the high part with your beautiful soprano. I'll come in with the bass – okay alto – but mine is more like a bass." When other carolers on the street paused in song, Ruthie began singing in her smooth soprano, high, sweet and pure. "Oh, night of holy light" . . ." Kate looked up at the stars, catching snowflakes on her lashes, and began the harmony. "It was the light of God," she sang softly against the melody. Ruthie's voice rang out in the still night, an honor to beauty and all gifts from God. It was so pure it hurt to hear. Kate let long phrases go by before joining her because the splendor of Ruthie's voice could not be intruded upon. Willie moved closer to them, and after a few phrases, his mellow tenor joined in. "Angels on high, angels on high," he sang, taking over the melody. "Oh hear the angel voices." Then all three came together, and the night was silent except for their song. "Oh light oh angels' holy light, On this God's special night."

Ellen watched her children as she walked, and her throat caught with the wonder of them. Three siblings stood together, arms holding each other close, and she gave thanks they loved so much. Kate looked around, noting the peace on the faces around her. A small knife gnawed at her as she thought about the fact that Mel wasn't there enjoying the Christmas festivities, and a similar knife sliced through her heart when she thought of Mark in his jail cell. 'Where is God?' she said to herself. 'How can he let this happen?'

As they continued down Main Street, more and more people joined, and lanterns filled the night. When they reached the end of the street, each family carefully placed an ornament on the tree. Each child was given a small bag of goodies; an orange, some walnuts, a pair of mittens made by the town mothers.

A small tear slid from the corner of Kate's eye and down her face.

"Don't cry, Kate," Ruthie said, looking at her sister, not understanding the tears, and her own eyes watered.

"I'm not sad," she lied to Ruthie. "These are tears of joy. I'm just uplifted by the beauty of this night." But she was horribly sad. In some weird way, she felt apart from everything, and she didn't want to be. She wanted to embrace it fully, to grasp the person next to her and hold on tightly with all of her heart, to give herself completely to the feeling of the night and the glory of it all.

They chose Willie to place their ornament on the tree, and Willie pulled Mary along with him. He placed it as high as he could reach and turned to Mary.

"Look okay there? You're the artistic one. Should I move it to a different branch?"

"It looks just right, Willie. Just perfect."

Will slipped an arm around Ellen's waist, snuggled her a little closer.

"You are more beautiful than that Christmas tree," he whispered in her ear.

Ellen stiffened but stayed in his one-armed embrace, warm inside and out. She couldn't think how to respond to her husband, what she should say, so she didn't. But her eyes glowed brighter than the stars in the sky, and an almost imperceptible sigh escaped her lips. Will saw and smiled. Recognizing that particular grin, Ellen gently slapped his hand.

"You have always been incorrigible, Will."

"Yes, I have."

CHAPTER EIGHT

W inter passed. The depression threatening the nation was kept at bay by the winter snows which forced most people to stay close their homes and warm hearths. It seemed the hills surrounding Hersey also sheltered it from the outside world. Money was tighter, and Christmas gifts were fewer, but it had never been an extravagant time for the folks in Hersey anyway. That year's deep snow helped them bury their heads until spring, and the Reed City Pioneer kept them informed about world events; however, it felt far, far away. The Farmer's Almanac was more avidly read by candle light than the newspaper.

Spring came with the usual mud and crocuses, bringing people back into town; farmers buying seed, lumberjacks looking for people who didn't wear plaid or swing an axe, and folks just needing to see faces other than the ones they had been looking at all winter.

At Nestor's, reality hit. Bills from winter supplies had been put on tab there because drought-killed fall crops had not provided enough to see many through the winter. They now needed seed and had no means of getting it. Nestor typically allowed seed to be paid for in the fall when crops were sold, but that was before, when they had not started the growing season already owing money. The effect of carrying so many families on credit was to jeopardize his store. He would not allow his store to fail, but he felt for these people, not mentioning their debts when they came into the store, respecting their pride. He knew they would pay when and if they could. He just wasn't sure when. The haunted looks on their faces said it all; they were two steps away from poverty, and fear of losing their farms made them turn their faces away from the people they owed money to.

Will's mill still ran, but it had slowed down considerably, and they had found it necessary to lay off two of their men. Will took only a portion of his salary, trying to leave Tom and the two men who were left with full pay. Kate contributed to their family household with her salary, and Will knew they could handle the cut better than the others.

The lumber camp was scheduled to bring all its men back and begin moving logs full scale next week, and everyone hoped the economy would be stimulated by the flurry of activity at the camp and the whine of the mill's saw.

Willie and Mary had felt the sting of winter at its worst. With the camp running just a skeleton crew, he had no work. Willie had finally swallowed his pride and approached his father. Will, with Tom's agreement, took him on at the mill, and that had tided them over. But it hurt, in the heart and belly where pride lived. Will had laid off two men and then given his son a job, but what else could he have done? Mary was very pregnant, and Willie was to be a father any day.

"I'm soon to be grandpa," he said to no one. "What in hell do I think about that?"

Kate kept a close eye on the melting snow, waiting for confirmation winter was gone, and she could hike through the woods to her cabin. She worried about it – perhaps somewhat selfishly.

What if the man with the coat had returned? What if it had collapsed under the weight of snow since no one had been there to clear it from the roof? What if . . . what if all of the things that could happen had happened? She made herself go to school each day, but her mind was in the woods.

Ellen watched her restless daughter, concern creasing her brow. Ellen had become contented during the winter when they were together as a family, sitting around the lantern, mending, doing winter kinds of chores. That was life to her, what she loved. The only thing missing was her son. Ruthie and Kate had grown even closer, and since the Christmas walk, they had sung together more often. Ellen often stopped her work, tilted her head toward the loft, and listened to the sweet harmony her daughters made. Pride smiled on her face, and love softened her heart.

"I should be singing with them," she said to herself. "Why can't I do that? What hardness in me prevents it? I'll have to think about that," she said, answering her own question. "You must, Ellen Hughes."

He jumped, curled into a ball, and rolled down the bank like a tumble weed on the prairie. There was nothing special about it. Men without the price of a ticket rode the trains on flatbeds or in the baggage cars where they were out of the rain or snow. They slipped in quickly, just as the train began to roll and jumped off before it stopped in order to avoid the conductors' eyes. Most were well aware they had nonpaying passengers, but kindly and conveniently grew nearsighted. What did it hurt? The trains were going where the men wanted to be, for whatever reason.

He stood, looked around and watched an old man throw a package from a flatbed and then follow it, leaping and rolling as Mark had done. He picked up his own bag and waited to be sure the other man had survived his fall with all limbs intact, then turned toward the river he knew was nearby.

"Hey," the man shouted. "Wait and I'll walk a space with you."

Mark pretended not to hear. He didn't want company, just solitude. He was filthy, hadn't shaved in days, and wasn't in the mood to talk.

"Mister, wait up a minute," the old man repeated, yelling louder now.

'You can just walk away, Mark,' he told himself. 'Oh, hell, give the old man a few minutes of your time. That's about all you've got to give anyone.' Mark finally stopped, looked back at the man and waited.

"Harley," he said as he limped up to Mark and held out his hand. "Harley Benton and you are?"

"Mark Ramey. Did you hurt yourself jumping off the train?"

"No, I always limp. Old injury. Nothing new. Where you off to, young man? Looking for work?"

Harley looked as if water hadn't touched him in months. His long hair stuck out at every angle from his head and was the color of dirty straw. Suspenders held up a pair of trousers so worn and grimy they no longer had color. He threw the rolled ball of his possessions over his shoulder, hiked up his pants.

"Let's roll, son."

Mark moved off toward the river.

"Well?" Harley said, as they began walking down the road.

"Well, what?"

"I asked you a question. You looking for work?"

Mark looked at him and didn't immediately respond, didn't want to get into a personal conversation with this strange man. Didn't really want any conversation.

"Young man, you don't hear real well, do you?" he added before Mark could form a reply.

"Yes," Mark finally answered. "I am."

"Work is a good thing," the man went on. "Something most folks should do. Now me, I don't like work. I've worked, but it's too confining. Takes most of the day, you know. Keeps folks from doing what they want to do, what God put them here for." The man droned on and on.

Mark only listened with half an ear, responding with a nod now and then when he thought it was expected or Harley demanded. His thoughts were elsewhere. When they came to the river, Mark stopped.

"I'm going to clean up some," he said. "I'm pretty grubby."

"I'll wait for ya. Got no where to get to fast," he said.

Mark stared at him, not believing Harley would just sit there and wait while he bathed.

"I wouldn't mind a little privacy. I'm going to take a bath, Harley."

"Well, hell. A bit prissy, aren't you? I'll walk off a little then."

When Harley left, Mark sat heavily, removed his shoes, socks and clothes, and dove out into the water. He paddled against the current, turned over on his back and stared at the sky. The water felt wonderful and washed away some of his weariness. He was thinner than he had ever been, and grey etched the hair at the sides of his face and sprinkled his four-day growth of beard. He scrubbed at his hair and body, let the river wash away days of dust and rail soot. Refreshed, he paddled to the shore, sat on a rock and shaved while the sun dried him. He pulled clean clothes from his bag, stuffed the dirty ones in and checked his reflection in the water.

'A bit haggard,' his image said to him. 'Well, you walk the streets for a year and see how you look,' he said back. He picked up his bag and called out to Harley. "I'm done, Harley. You ready?"

When Harley saw him, he whistled. "Well don't you look fine, now. You got a date? Some pretty little thing waiting for you in town?"

Mark just smiled and tolerated the man's chatter.

"You don't talk much, do you?" he asked.

"I'm not much in a talking mood," Mark answered. "I've got some things on my mind."

"Maybe I could help, if you want to tell me about it. I'm pretty smart, you know. I've been helping people all over the nation, from Oregon to Maine. People just tell me their problems, and I figure them out. Like magic." Harley went on and on, nonstop, about his magical powers of solving problems until Mark thought he would like to punch the old man.

Just to shut him up, Mark finally said, "Look, I need work, and I have a prison record. There you are."

"Well, what the hell," Harley said, stopping in the middle of the road to stare at Mark. "What'd you do? Rob a bank? Kill a man over some woman? You're a pretty good looking feller. Bet the ladies are after you. A bit on the scrawny side though. Embezzled!" he said, pounding his fist into his dirty hand and smiling. "Bet that's it."

Mark held up his hands, palms out as if warding off further onslaught of words.

"None of those," he said. "I am guilty of nothing except stupidity."

"Well, Mr. Ramey, being stupid is not a good thing, but I didn't know they could put you in jail for it. Lot's of other things, but not for being stupid, and a whole lot of people are stupid at least some of the time."

"Mr. Benton, they can and did," he said, warming to this strange, overbearing man. "I've been out for a year now, did time for something I did not do, and now I can't find work. People don't want to hire a man who has spent time in prison. There are plenty of men looking for work without time."

"Well, that's simple. Told you I could fix things. Don't tell em about it. Just leave that little fact out of your story. See how easy it is? Told you I was a problem solver."

Mark slumped a little and ran his fingers through his hair. The old man watched, for the first time silent, if only for a moment.

"Mister, I finally tried that, even though I hated every minute of it. It's dishonest," he said.

"Well, didn't it work? It should've if they didn't know about the time. What they don't know can't hurt em."

"No, in a short while, they found out and fired me. I was almost happy they did."

"You're a strange man, Mr. Ramey. So why are you heading wherever you're heading? Know people here?"

"Yes, I do, a man who befriended me once before. I'm hoping he will again. I don't know what else to do." Mark thought twice was asking a lot, and his pride had kept him from coming earlier. He thought of Hersey with a mixture of emotions, some good and some bad. It had seemed a peaceful town to him, and he surely needed some peace. Yet, some of the people there most likely still hated and resented him. Small towns are harsh in their judgments, but if he could work for Will, he would send for his children, and they would have a home – with him. These thoughts ran through his mind, flitting in between Harley's nonstop chatter. Mark had ceased to listen and only heard a word now and then, enough to be able to respond when necessary. It didn't need to make much sense because Harley didn't care. He just wanted to talk.

Harley stopped walking and grabbed Mark's arm.

"You sure you ain't hard of hearing? How old are you, anyway."

"What? No, I can hear just fine. Thirty-eight, why?"

"Well, I'm sixty-two, and I been around a bit. I'm thinking you don't really want to ask this man for work because you're too proud. Think you should be able to do everything on your own. That's stupid, and that's why they put you in jail in the first place. Want to go to jail again for being stupid?"

Mark shook his head, looking ahead at a man who was working on a fence surrounding a plowed field.

"No, Harley, I don't."

When they came abreast of the man at the fence, Mark knew he'd seen him before, and then recognized Mel, the young man Mrs. Hughes had chosen for Kate. He wondered if they were married now, had kids. Probably, he thought, and something akin to sorrow washed over him, a small ache started in his stomach and rose to his throat. He was glad for them, but the ache was there nonetheless.

"Hello," Mark said, stopping a distance away.

Mel looked up from his work, greeted the two men casually, not recognizing Mark.

"Mark Ramey. We met when I was in Hersey a few years ago," Mark said, seeing the blank look on Mel's face. Recognition dawned in Mel, and something close to fury flashed briefly in his eyes. Mark saw the anger and didn't understand. Had he done something to this man?

"This is Harley Benton. He came off the train with me. Good looking field you have," he said, filling the gap.

"Best there is," Mel responded, wondering what Mark was doing back in Hersey.

"I don't want to keep you," Mark said, uncomfortable with what he had seen in Mel. Perhaps this was how everyone would greet him. He had known his arrival wouldn't be met with open arms, but this first taste of it didn't settle well.

After the shock of seeing Mark, Mel stepped back a bit and looked at the man who had stood in his way for years. What he saw startled him. He was thin to the point of gauntness. His hair showed flecks of gray, and his face bore the signs of age. Lines were etched around his eyes, and his clothes, while clean, were threadbare. There were nicks on his face from shaving in the icy river water, and his hair grew over his collar at the back of his neck. This is not the same man, he said to himself, and a touch of remorse for his resentment crept in. He hated feeling sorrow for this man, but he did.

"You in town for a visit?" he asked.

"No, I'm looking for work." He grimaced and said, "Thought I might see Will about it. How is the Hughes family and yours?"

"All fine," Mel said, leaving it there, not wanting to get into that conversation. "And you, Mr. Benton? Are you looking for work, too?"

Harley had stood silent, watching the play of words, and knew there was an undercurrent going on he couldn't pinpoint.

"No, son. I'm just looking around the country. It appears you have a fine field here. You have a large holding? Big family, Sunday dinners, the good life?"

"Enough," Mel said.

Mark grasped Harley's arm, hearing the start of another long diatribe from him beginning to build.

"Sorry we've taken your time, Mel. Good to see you again," he said and began to steer Harley away from Mel and down the road.

As they walked from Mel's place to the Hughes' home, Mark ignored Harley's chatter and rehearsed what he would say to Will. He thought about the first time he had seen the Hughes family. He'd been there to contract for Landmark's lumber to be sawed at Will's new mill. It had also been Kate's sixteenth birthday and a lovely evening at the Hughes' house. He'd been a different man then; sure of himself, confident in his future and the thought that there was nothing he couldn't make happen. What a rude awakening he'd had over the past many years.

He thought about the last time he had seen them, at the trial. Will had been a friend to him when luck and his own powers had deserted him. Kate, too. For whatever reason, she had befriended him and brought him some peace. It was intolerable he had to turn to them again, and if he'd had another choice, he would have taken it. His stomach churned at the thought. Begging did not come easily to him.

Near the Hughes home, the road and the river came together briefly, and the water was still. It rested there, reflecting cotton clouds overhead. Purple images of tamarack trees merged with the white puffs. Mark stopped there, dampened his handkerchief, wiped his face and rinsed his hands. He peered at his reflection once more and grimaced, then swiped at the dust on his shoes and stuffed the cloth into his bag. When he turned away from the water, Harley was staring at him, a grin on his face, his arms folded over his round belly.

"You surely must have a woman waiting," he said, his lopsided grin expanding.

Mark was too anxious to take Harley's jabs well and barked at him.

"I'm looking for a job. The least I can do is look presentable when I go begging! You might consider that yourself!"

"I got no one to impress," Harley said, the grin still in place. "And let old Harley give you some advice, free. You let life tie your insides in knots, the only kind of knot you get is a hangman's noose, and you're the one who stuck your neck into it. Just you, boy. Only you and nobody else."

Mark just nodded, feeling a little contrite for lashing out at Harley and remembering another man who had told him something similar when he'd been searching for his wife.

"And let me tell you something else. You gotta laugh at what life hands you, cause it hasn't handed you death yet, has it? Has it come knocking at your door yet?" When Mark didn't respond, he added, "Well, then," as if his point had been made and agreed upon.

The Hughes' home came into view, and it looked much like he'd remembered it. Smoke curled from the chimney and snaked out in soft grey puffs. It seemed homey and comfortable. The gardens had been hoed into nice, neat rows, and early orange and white crocuses bloomed beside the porch.

"Would you mind waiting out here?" he asked Harley.

"It would be my pleasure."

Mark knocked at the door and heard, "Come in, the door's open." He did and was greeted by the woman he remembered as Ellen, Will's wife, and a big red dog. She had her arms in a tub of soap and spoke to him without turning.

"I'll be right with you," she said. The dog backed up to the hearth, lowered his head, rolled his eyes upwards at Mark and didn't say anything.

Mark stood at the door and took in the room. The rugs scattered around were bright; so were the curtains at the windows. The furniture was in good repair, and the painted walls looked fresh and shining. 'They're doing well,' he thought to himself and was glad for Will. His hope grew. Then as quickly as the thought entered his mind, he was remorseful. 'What have I become that I enter a man's home and assess it for my benefit?' He was still castigating himself when Ellen turned, wiped her hands on her apron, and saw Mark standing at her door. She stiffened, her mouth opened in preparation for a greeting but seemingly fixed, unable to close. Several uncomfortable moments lapsed while both struggled to find appropriate words, and then Mark found his tongue.

"Hello, Mrs. Hughes. I'm Mark Ramey. Do you remember me?"

Ellen moved a step back, stopped, and frantically worked in her mind to find a civilized way to greet this man. She was sure he was responsible for her daughter's strange behavior, for refusing to marry the best young man in Hersey, one who loved her dearly, and because of that Ellen found it difficult to be kind to him. However, she was a civilized woman. She prided herself on being charitable and a Christian. She would be hospitable. She held out her hand to him.

"Yes, Mr. Ramey. I remember you."

"I'm here to see Will," he said. "Is he at the mill?"

"Mr. Hughes comes and goes. I'm not sure where he might be at the moment."

"Would it be alright if I waited for him," Mark asked.

Ellen pointed to a chair, told him to have a seat, and turned back to her wash.

"I'll wait outside," Mark said. "Mr. Benton walked with me and is outside, so I'll just sit with him."

"Oh, for heaven's sake," Ellen said, once more drying her hands. "Bring him in and I'll get you some lemonade."

Harley bowed low at the waist when he was introduced. Ellen just stared, wondering how and why this filthy man was in her kitchen.

"My dear lady," he said. "You are Florence Nightingale to me. I would dearly love to quench my thirst with your offer of lemonade. Although I am already refreshed by your loveliness, I graciously accept."

Ellen continued to stare, unable to move. Bug finally rose from his bed by the fireplace and glided over to sniff at Harley.

"I can see, now, why Mr. Ramey was so intent on cleansing himself at the river," he continued, his hand held out, palm up, to Bug who had already decided Harley wasn't growling material. He licked Harley's hand, rolled his eyes once more at Mark, and retreated to his rug.

"Mr. Benton," Ellen started.

"Harley," Mark blurted.

"I'll just get the glasses," she said and turned away, a slight blush on her cheeks.

Mark followed her. "I'm so sorry, Mrs. Hughes. He's a bit daft, but he doesn't mean any harm. He just sort of followed me here after I left the train, and I didn't know what to do with him. Is that how you got Big Red over there?"

Ellen brought three glasses, filled them with lemonade, and joined them at the table.

"That's Kate's Bug, a gift from Mr. Bronson."

Ellen seemed interested in what Harley had to say as he regaled them with whatever came into his brain at the moment. Because of him, they were actually laughing when Ruthie came in, surprised to find two strangers sitting in her mother's kitchen. After reintroducing himself and introducing Harley, he turned to Ruthie again.

"You don't remember me, do you?"

Ruthie thought he looked vaguely familiar, but didn't know why or how.

"I was here for your sister's sixteenth birthday," he said. "She played the piano and sang beautiful hymns."

"Oh! That Mark!" she said, her hand going over her mouth in shock. "Yes, I remember you." She was thinking robber, criminal, and the one who gave Kate such a bad reputation. She watched him carefully while they talked, and again, Harley's crazy mind and mouth helped them through the uncomfortable moments until they were once more laughing.

"You don't seem the same," Ruthie finally said. "You were a bit of a dandy back then. . . Oh!" she said, and again her hand went over her mouth. "I didn't mean anything, I just . . . well; you know . . ." words would not come to her aid.

He patted her hand, seeing her blush prettily when she realized what she had said and feeling her discomfort.

"Yes I do, Ruthie, and you are right. I was entirely too frivolous then, and fanciful, too. I have grown up," he said. "And so have you. You have turned into a lovely young lady." Ruthie blushed again and looked at her mother for help. How should she respond to this compliment?

"Don't fill her head with flattery, Mr. Ramey. Vanity is not something the Lord likes to see."

"My dear Ellen . . . may I call you that?" Harley asked, but went on before she could answer. "Would you have the lovely rose hide its beautiful bloom, or should it raise its head proudly knowing that God had blessed it with beauty?" His voice rose and he opened his arms like he was embracing the world and all its creatures. "Would you turn away from God's beautiful sunset, or would you openly praise it? I ask you. Is it sinful to recognize beauty? To be thankful for it?"

Mark rubbed his hands over his face and through his hair, groaning, knowing another of Harley's lectures was about to begin.

"Harley, stop" he said in a warning voice.

"No, I will not. You need to understand," Harley said. "Look at me. Really!" he said, stomping his foot on the floor and grinning. "Look at me!"

They all did, staring and waiting to learn the reason they all needed to look at Harley. Even Bug raised his head to stare at Harley.

"Don't I have beautiful eyes?" he said softly after he had all their attention. "I love my eyes."

There was deafening silence while they looked at his eyes. Then laughter erupted in response to Harley's words, laughter so deep it was painful. They held their stomachs and groaned; water filled their eyes and ran down their cheeks. Harley just sat with a wide grin on his face, his two beautiful eyes sparkling.

Will walked up to the door in time to see his wife and daughter with two strangers, all bent over the table in laughter. One would catch a breath momentarily and then erupt in laughter again when they looked at Harley's beautiful eyes, and it would infect all the others. He stood in the doorway watching in disbelief. A smile lit his face and his heart was lighter than it had been in a very long time. Then he recognized one of the strangers.

"Mark!" he shouted. "Well, I'll be damned. How are you?" he said and flung open the screen door. He took two long steps, grabbed Mark's hand, and then wrapped an arm around his back in a big hug.

Mark alternately shook Will's hand and slapped his back, more happy to see his friend than he had imagined, and relieved to know Will was glad to see him.

When they stopped the handshaking and back slapping, Mark introduced Harley.

"Will, I'd like you to meet Harley Benton. Harley, this is my friend, Will."

Will grasped Harley's hand in both of his, shaking and smiling.

"A friend of Mark's is mine, too," he said.

"Well, Mr. Hughes, I can't lie," Harley said. "I just met Mr. Ramey today, so I can't claim we're really friends, but he seems like a nice enough man. Although he's a bit edgy, you know what I mean? A bit tied up in knots sometimes, and those knots are gonna choke him some day. Needs to relax and just take life as it comes."

Mark groaned again, said "Harley, just say hello, nice to meet you, like normal folks, okay?"

Harley looked around at all the faces watching him. Moments passed in silence as everyone waited for his response. He savored the moments, made the most of their rapt attention, and looked from one face to another.

"I do have beautiful eyes, don't I?" he said. "You all just can't take your eyes off mine, can you? Praise God for beautiful eyes."

Everyone bent in laughter once more. Ellen wiped the tears from her face again and again. Ruthie held her sides and complained her stomach hurt. Mark slapped his knees and gasped, trying to get breath. Harley giggled and smiled. Will stood there with a blank look on his face not understanding the joke but loving the feel of his house.

When Ellen had caught her breath, Will kissed her on the cheek and said, "Mrs. Hughes, would you please fetch the jug. This is a celebration. Our friend has returned to the fold."

But Will was celebrating the laughter in his house, the joy in seeing his wife and daughter with tears of laughter on their faces, and he wondered about the man who had brought this to his family.

Ellen brought the jug, even though she did not approve of whiskey. A smile even flitted across her face as she did it. She felt like a girl again, and hummed a tune while she started dinner. Ruthie joined her in the preparations, leaving the men at the table to sip at the jug and talk.

Mark told Will what he had been doing for the last year, about spending coveted time with his children who were staying with Mark's parents, but not yet getting to the part about being stone, cold broke. For once, Harley just listened, watching the interplay of Mark and Will's conversation. Will had time to take in Mark's appearance while they talked and understood more from the way Mark looked than what his words said. Will saw the dark circles under his eyes, his thin body, and the lines on his face that hadn't come from laughter. Nor, Will thought, had it all come from prison. He would have been well fed there. Will knew without being told Mark was here for help and it had taken him a long time to bury his pride and do it. It would have been a last resort for a man as capable and strong willed as Mark.

"Where are you staying?" Will asked, "because if you haven't had time to get a room, yet, you can just forget it. You're staying here. Willie's gotten himself married, so his room is just sitting there."

"I couldn't impose, Will. That's not fair to Mrs. Hughes," Mark said, all the while thinking of clean sheets and a roof over his head.

"Nonsense," Will was quick to respond. "And Mr. Benton?"

"It's Harley, Will," Harley interrupted. "I'm just pretty eyes Harley."

Will laughed, feeling good about this strange man.

"Well, Pretty Eyes, if you don't mind the smell of hay and horses, there's a perfectly good room in the barn, and it's yours if you want it."

"Will," Mark said, uncomfortable with barging into the Hughes home, "I don't think I can do that. It is too much to ask, but if we could talk a bit, privately, I'd appreciate it. Then I'll be on my way. I do thank you, though, for the offer. You have been good to me."

"See what I mean, Will?" Harley said, interrupting the conversation. "The man is tied up. He's gonna choke soon." Harley leaned forward in his chair and looked back and forth from Mark to Will and back again. "Let me tell you something, son. If a friend gives you a gift, you don't throw it back in his face. The man wants to give you something and what do you do? You pitch it back to him like it's a worthless thing."

"Harley, don't start lecturing again," Mark said, trying to stop him before he got on a roll.

"Well, as I see it, you need a bit of a lecture. Will has a bed and you need one; so do I," he said turning to Will. "Mr. Hughes, I accept your offer with great pleasure and gratitude. I will delightfully lay with the horses tonight, and I thank you for your kindness. Now, when Mr. Mark Ramey grows up and learns to appreciate the world around him, learns how not to be prideful, he will agree that it is the kind thing to do to accept your offer of a bed. He'll learn not to do battle with the world that is just there because it is there."

Mark was groaning again, trying to tell Harley, in a kind way, to just shut up, but Harley was not getting it and went on. Will was grinning, enamored of this strange man and liking him more and more. He had knowledge of humans hidden under his rough exterior, and the more Will watched and listened to him, the more he believed Harley had an uncommon sense of people. He liked this bizarre person.

"It is my pleasure to offer it to you Harley, and I am sure Mark will gain your wisdom some day," he said, grinning at both Mark and Harley. "Let's go see what provisions are needed out there."

They went to the barn and found everything Harley would need was already in the small room where he would sleep. After shaking the blankets and beating the pillow to rid it of dust, Harley said he would lie down and take a short nap if the two of them wouldn't mind being on their own for a while.

Mark breathed a sigh of relief and quickly left the room with Will close behind.

"He's quite a man," Will said. "I don't think I've met anyone quite like him before."

"Yes, he is. I really didn't know what to do with him. He's like a puppy that follows you home and has no where else to go."

"Well, he's welcome to stay as long as he wants or needs," Will said, "but I think that Harley finds what he needs when and where he needs it. Let's take a little walk."

When they were well away from the barn, Will came quickly to the point of what he believed was the reason for Mark's visit, trying to spare him the pain of having to find the words.

"I don't have a place for you at the mill, Mark. I've cut my own salary, and even worse, I've had to lay off two good men." He saw Mark's shoulders sag and hated what he had to say, but knew it was best not to beat around the bush. "I'm really sorry. Wish I had something to offer."

They walked down the road in silence, the sweet smell of new spring in the air, each man alone in his thoughts. Will thought about Kate and what she would think about having Mark near by. How would she feel if Will could do nothing to help this man? But Mark wasn't the same man now. Maybe her feelings would change. He didn't know if this would be a good thing or not.

Mark's mind was a flood of thoughts, none of them good. This was his last hope, and he didn't know what to do anymore.

"It's alright, Will. I understand, and I shouldn't have come. I just thought . . . I just didn't know where to turn."

"Listen, just stay awhile and let me think."

"I can't," Mark said, "I appreciate the offer, but I've got to find work, get my kids a home – with me. I've tried desperately to find work near Grand Rapids where they're staying with my parents, where I've been, too. But it's hopeless around there, just about anywhere, it seems, with my history."

"Give me a couple of days. I've been thinking about a change lately, and you might just be the nudge I've needed. Please, just a couple of day."

"How is Mrs. Hughes going to feel about this? I don't think she was very happy to see me at the door."

"She'll be fine. She's a charitable woman."

"I don't want charity, Will," Mark said, his pride rumbling forward.

"I didn't mean that," Will said quickly, aware he had unintentionally ruffled some feathers. "What I meant was that she has a good heart. She has welcomed lots of people into our home. It's her way."

Mark thought about that for a moment, then asked about what he really was thinking.

"Does she not like me for a particular reason? Other than the prison sentence, I mean. But I can understand that."

As carefully as he could, Will explained about Kate and what the Hersey people had to say about her during and after Mark's trial.

"It upset Ellen to hear folks say things about Kate that weren't true. But you know how people are. Sometimes they're damn mean. Anyway, Ellen doesn't hate you; she just wants the best for Kate and you sort of got in the way, according to her."

"God, I'm sorry. I didn't realize. Now I know I shouldn't stay. I should have insisted Kate stay away from the trial."

Mark looked so remorseful Will wished he hadn't said anything, but he'd thought it would help him understand Ellen's coolness to him. Yet, she had looked so happy when he stood at the door and watched them he had not known anything else had transpired. Well, Ellen would just have to accept it and get over it. Mark was staying, and that was that.

"You're staying," Will said, throwing his arm around Mark's shoulder. "And a mountain of your insisting Kate stay away wouldn't have made a difference. She'd have nodded her head like she understood and then done what she was going to do in the first place."

Silence stretched as they walked back to the house.

"We're going to figure something out. Between the both of us, we'll figure something out," Will said, hoping he was right and it wouldn't take longer than a few days.

Mark was tired, both physically and mentally, the only thing he could do was accept Will's strength at the moment. He was incredibly grateful to have a shoulder to lean on, and wanted desperately not to think, not to worry for a while. A long, slow breath escaped his chest and he felt the muscles at his neck and back release. For the first time in a very long time, he felt like he could sleep. He knew his troubles weren't over, but for the moment there was peace. He had shared his trouble with a friend, and it felt good.

"As the great and all-knowing Pretty Eyes Harley once said, I accept your offer with gratitude and pleasure. Thank you, Will."

Will smiled and looked closely at Mark, his head tilted in thought. "That man Harley has something. I'm not sure what – but he has something."

"Yeah, a love of talking," Mark said, grinning back.

"Well, that too. But there's some wisdom in his words. I think I'll listen. I just might learn something. We'd better head back. Dinner will be soon, and we don't want to let Ellen's food go cold."

They walked into the kitchen at the same time Kate was coming down from the loft after changing out of her school clothes. She stopped midway down the stairs, her eyes wide and her mouth frozen open following a sharp intake of breath. One hand clutched the rail, and the other was gripping her chest. Bug was beside her and sat on his haunches when she stopped.

"I guess your mother didn't tell you we had guests," Will said, filling the silence.

"I'm sure you remember Mark Ramey, Kate. He'll be staying with us for a few days."

Kate nodded, and then nodded again, still perched on the step where she had been when they entered. Her eyes continued to be huge round globes, but she had managed to close her mouth.

"Come on down, Kate," Will said, looking her in the eyes and trying to speak to her with his. "Say hello to Mark and help your sister set the table."

Kate moved forward, stumbled off the stairs, tripped on the hem of her skirt and lurched headlong into Mark. He caught her before she fell to the floor, his forearm high on her chest, her fist frantically clutching his jacket as she fell, and hanging on for dear life. In a matter of seconds, they were both in a tangled heap on the floor, Mark on his back, Kate's head on his stomach. Bug stood with his front feet on Mark's shoulders, his shaggy head poised over Mark's face and his wet nose against Mark's nose.

Kate didn't move; she couldn't.

'If I just close my eyes and pretend I'm not here, this will never have happened,' she thought. 'Maybe I can just sink through the floor boards, live in the crawlspace with the mice and raccoons, for ever and ever. Am I talking out loud?'

"Kate," Will said, concerned because she wasn't moving, just lying there motionless. "Are you alright? Mark, are you okay? Bug, get off Mark."

Kate still didn't move. Neither did Bug. Kate was busy sinking through the floor, trying to disappear, and Bug was busy checking out Mark's pupils. Harley picked that moment to knock at the screen door.

"Damn," she said softly. "I'm no good at sliding through the floor. Sorry."

"Come on in, Mr. Benton," Ellen called out.

Harley opened the door, saw them on the floor, and moved closer for a better look. "Looks like I'm missing out on the games. What are you all playing?" While they were untangling themselves from each other, he said, "I like games. I'm pretty good, too."

"Don't be sorry," Mark whispered to Kate. "I should have caught you. Would you mind asking your dog to move?"

"No. Not that. Yes, you should have. Never mind. He's pretty ferocious. Trained to protect, so be careful." Kate was stammering, but couldn't stop.

"He's slobbering on my face."

"He must like you. Go lie down, Bug."

Bug reluctantly released his hold on Mark and moved with a conqueror's stroll over to his rug, turned three times and laid down where he could keep his eyes on the man still on the floor with his Kate. Mark took her hand to help her up and introduced her to Harley.

"Well, aren't you a lovely young woman," Harley said. "These Hughes ladies are surely some of nature's best blossoms. You are fortunate, Mr. Hughes, to be surrounded by such beauty every single day, just like a sunrise," he said, still staring at Kate who had yet to regain her composure. "I can see now why Mr. Ramey was so intent on sprucing up before he got here, and why he came here in the first place."

She just stared back at this odd man and wondered what he was doing in their kitchen. But her mind was still in the sinking through the floor stage. She knew a response was expected, but didn't know quite what it should be.

"I . . . thank you."

"No, don't thank me," Harley exclaimed loudly. "It is I, a scruffy old man who thanks you for the vision."

Kate finally looked around the room at Mark and her family, unmistakable questions pouring from her eyes. 'Help,' she was saying. But they had all had a little time to get used to Harley and were enjoying Kate's discomfort just a little. It wasn't often they had a chance to see it.

Kate looked Harley up and down. What could she say that was polite and nice in return for the compliments he had given? Nothing jumped out at her. He had a round little belly that seemed to stick straight out in front of him. His hair and clothes were filthy and ragged. Who knew what was growing in his beard?

"And you, Mr. Benton . . . um . . . have nice eyes," she said.

After about three full seconds of stunned silence, howls of laughter shook the room. Kate had found just the right nice thing to say in return for his compliment. Ellen and Ruthie giggled into each others' shoulders and held the other up after quickly dropping the plates to safety on the table. Mark had fallen back down to the floor and was holding his head in his hands. His back and shoulders heaved in laughter. Will's head was tilted back, his mouth was wide open and huge guffaws erupted from it. Harley was slapping Mark's back, saying "I told you so, told you so," in between fits of laughter.

Kate just stood and stared. "Damn," was all she could say, looking around her at the strange hilarity in the Hughes house. No one scolded her, so maybe no one heard. Maybe she hadn't said it out loud.

"Harley," Will said after catching his breath. "I don't know how or why, but you certainly are a tonic."

"Yes, sir, I am," he said, a mile wide smile on his face. He stuck his thumbs in the waist band of his trousers and pushed his shoulders back and his belly out. "I'm definitely a tonic."

Mel was not having fun. His heart was sore, and his mood foul. After Mark and Harley left him mending the fence, Mel finished his task and headed for the barn. He hitched his horses to the plow and stayed in his fields for the rest of the day, pushing his horses harder than he had ever done. He scowled and cursed stones he turned over with his plow.

"You'd think after all these years of picking stones, you damn things would be gone by now. You're just here to plague me!" Anyone passing by would wonder what possessed the normally quiet, peaceful man.

When the sun began to set, he put the horses away and strode into the kitchen, his heavy boots thudding against the floor.

"Ma, I'm going into town. I'll get something to eat there," he shouted into the kitchen.

His mother peered around the door, wondering at the harsh sound of her son's voice.

"Are you okay, son? Is everything alright?" she asked quietly.

"I'm just fine. Don't wait up," he said, slamming the door as he went out.

All day long, with each bump of the plow, Mel's usually sensible head had carried far-fetched and implausible pictures of the man he met again today just stepping in to carry off his Kate.

"She's not yours, Mel. Never was, never will be," he said disgustedly to himself.

To Mel, it was unthinkable that Mark, with nothing to call his own but the shirt on his back, had been the mountain between himself and Kate. This crook was the unspoken barrier he had always felt being shoved between them. For years, Mel could sense his presence in Kate, could see him in her eyes as they drifted lazily, looking but not seeing. He had always known, but he never asked because he hadn't wanted to hear the words.

Now the ghost was here, looking for work. He'll most likely stay, why not? Mel came as close to hating as was possible for him. In anger he slapped his mare on her rump with the end of the rein. She reared up on her hind legs and emitted a screeching whinny. Mel almost fell, but he grabbed her mane and held on, lying low on her neck and whispering to her.

"I'm so sorry. I know you don't understand. I'm sorry," he whispered over and over.

His eyes watered, for the mare who had never been struck by him, for Kate who deserved so much more than a penniless life with a man just out of prison, and for himself. Once more, he almost hated the man who had let Kate love him when he had no way of returning it. A married man, no less.

Mel tied his mare to the rail outside of Sadie's, spoke a few more gentle words, nuzzled her face with his own, and stepped into the saloon. He was greeted by a welcoming crowd of men with slanted grins and good natured jeers about Mel's 'all work and no play' policy.

The light inside was glaring after the darkness and showed the muddy, unpainted floor and dusty curtains. It smelled of old beer, whiskey and too many cigars. Sadie grinned at him from behind the bar and waddled around to bring him a glass of beer.

"On the house, handsome," she said throwing two flabby arms around his head and smothering him between her huge breasts. "I figure if I give you a free beer and let you cuddle these, you'll come around more often," she said putting her hands under her enormous breasts and lifting them as high as they would go. "Why are you such a stranger? Young buck like you should be out and about all the time."

Time had not been kind to Sadie. Her frizzy hair was streaked with earthy brown and gray. Her more than triple chin waved as she talked. But she was loved by the men who visited her saloon. Her puffy, cherubic face dimpled when a mischievous grin lit her eyes, and

Sadie was free with hugs and motherly advice. Although, many of the wives and girlfriends in town didn't always agree with Sadie's wisdom.

"I've got too much work, Sadie," Mel answered. "Otherwise I'd visit you every day, just for the hug."

"You're a sweet talker, but keep it coming."

Mel sipped his beer, looked around the room at the men, and a few women, in various states of sobriety. They appeared to be having fun, laughing, joking with each other, or just talking quietly. A small sigh escaped, unnoticed. He sipped some more and looked at Sadie who had taken the chair next to him.

"What's with Mel Bronson tonight?" she whispered, leaning closer to him.

"Nothing, Sadie. It's just been a hard day."

"They're all hard, sweetie, if you let 'em be hard. I don't see you doing that cause you're not cut from that cloth." She left him to go around the bar and pour a few drinks for the paying customers and then brought another back for him. "Third one you buy," she said grinning.

"Sadie, just what kind of cloth am I cut from?" he asked her, grinning and teasing but serious, too.

"Why, you're the kind that should be a husband and father. You'd be the best at both," she said, a thoughtful look on her face. "In fact, I hear all the talk in town, and I know many a young lady who would just die if you would give them the time of day. But it seems they all know you've set your cap on only one woman."

"Well," he said sadly, "that isn't going to happen, Sadie."

"Then look around you, Mel. There's more fish, you know."

"Nope, there isn't, Sadie. But I thank you for your wisdom – and the beer. I promise to buy my own next time," he said, and got up to leave before Sadie could smother him in another suffocating hug. "Oh," he said, turning back for a moment. "Has Will Hughes been in tonight?"

"No, sweetie, he hasn't."

Mel stopped to pat his mare and apologize again for his behavior to her earlier. He told her he'd only be a few more minutes and left for Nestor's store. He knew Will often spent time there talking by the stove, especially on a chilly spring night.

Nestor's was as muddy and cluttered as Sadie's. The stove was burning to take out the damp chill of the night, and boots steamed as wet clay dried on the soles. Mel walked in to hear Jacob Harper listing his views on the falling crop market. The room was quiet except for a few grunts of assent and his deep voice. Jacob was young, but his assurance leant authority to his words. Every man present had a stake in what Jacob was saying, so they listened carefully, weighing what his words might mean to them personally.

When Jacob finished, all heads turned to welcome the newcomer, and a chair was pushed forward for him along with the ever present jug of home brew. Mel tipped it up, swallowed, and choked, much to the delight of the rest. He passed off the jug, held his chest and coughed. His throat felt seared all the way down to his belly, and his eyes watered, spilling down his cheeks.

"Damn, what is that stuff, kerosene?"

The rest found great humor in Mel's reaction to the home brew.

"You need a little more practice, Mel," Ed Miller, the banker, said, looking like he'd sipped quite a few times and had practiced a lot. Ashes from his pipe had dropped onto his vest, and Mel couldn't help thinking Mrs. Miller would give him a lashing when he staggered home.

Gordon Tilmann, standing at the edge of the group spoke up.

"Welcome, Mr. Bronson," he said in his officious way. "It isn't often you grace us with your presence. What is the occasion?"

Tilmann was as commanding in his advanced years as he had ever been. His hawk-like face and lion's mane of hair were impressive.

"Just out for a bit of air, Gordon," Mel responded. "I thought I'd just get out a bit. It's been a long day" he said again.

"Well, as long as you're here, what are your thoughts on the dismal crop prices? You're a man of substance, and growing more so by the year, I might add. What do you have to say about our future?"

"I just tend my farm, Mr. Tilmann; make it grow the best that I can. That's all I can handle. I do what needs to be done."

"You see," Gordon said to the rest. "That was spoken like a real man, not a scared little girl. If you don't like where you are today, make something else out of yourself. That's all there is to it."

Gordon had said many times if he lost all his land and money, he'd just make it happen again, and that comment rubbed a lot of men the wrong way. They had tried, and many had failed. What makes him so different? He owns thousands of acres planted, sowed and reaped by hired hands, and in the last year or so the sale of crops has not even paid their wages. Sooner or later, he might be forced to sell acreage, but Tilmann's head never droops. He never shows fear seen on the faces of many. He persevered. He wasn't afraid of work.

Mel passed up the third passing of the jug, much to the jocularity of the rest, and pretended to cough at just the idea of nipping again.

"I kind of favor lemonade," he said, helping them with their jokes. "It doesn't burn when it goes down. Not much of a man's man, huh?"

"Nope, and from what I hear around town, the ladies kind of like that in you," Jacob said, a wide grin on his face. "Guess that makes you a lady's man."

"I can't see that," Mel answered. "By the way, has Will been in tonight?"

No one had seen Will, and Mel came to the conclusion his questions would go unanswered, at least for the night. He said goodbye to the group, stood up carefully, and made his way to the door.

His head buzzed from the beer at Sadie's and the nip of home brew at Nestor's. He wasn't used to alcohol, and he struggled to make sure one foot was in front of the other on the way to his mare. He rubbed his face trying to clear his confused thoughts.

"Can't figure out why people drink that stuff," he told his mare, caressing her muzzle. "You wouldn't like it," he told her. "Can you find the way home without my help?" he asked her. "I'm just going to sit here and hang on, if that's alright with you." He was sure the horse nodded assent, and Mel thanked her, apologizing once more for his earlier behavior.

He put the mare in her stall and wobbled to the house, hitting the sides of the door on his way in. Once in bed, he fell immediately to sleep which was at least part of his goal that night. His mother was awake, listening for his return. Mel's earlier behavior had been so unusual she'd been concerned. She tiptoed to his room, saw him sprawled on the bed fully clothed and snoring. Her heart broke for her son. She knew the reason for his solitary existence but wouldn't ask him about it, wouldn't pry. He was too private and proud. But her heart still broke, and she wished he would talk to her, let her help.

She wanted to shake some sense into Kate, tell her what she was missing out on. In her mind, there wasn't a better, smarter, more caring man in the world, and Kate was just plain foolish.

She stood still, thinking and watching Mel sleep. She had known her son was taken with Kate from the moment he saw her when the Hughes had first moved to Hersey. Kate had been just a girl. At the time, Mel's mother had grinned about his infatuation and thought he was certainly old enough to be interested in girls. She thought he would get over it and move on. She should have known better. Mel never rushed into anything, and when he made up his mind, he rarely ever changed it. Her son deserved a family, should have one. There wasn't much chance he would unless Kate was in the picture.

She quietly got a spare blanket from the closet and covered him, then pushed the hair from his forehead and left a gentle kiss, something she'd never do when he was awake. She wished he was a baby again so she could hold him in her arms and soothe away his troubles with a lullaby.

For the millionth time, she missed her husband. He would know how to help. A man could talk to his son, and a son could talk to his father in a different way than he could to his mother. As she had done many times before, she walked outside, found a long tree branch lying under a maple tree far from the house and smashed it against the tree. Her anger at circumstance slashed against the bark, broke the limb over and over until there was nothing left but a short stick left in her hands.

"After all these years, I'm still angry at you, Jacob Bronson, for leaving us! I need you! I miss you," she whispered, then thrust her shoulders back and walked to the house. "We'll cope, but I don't have to like it."

CHAPTER NINE

M ark reveled in the clean sheets, the good and plentiful food. He had been there for two days, rose early, before the sun was up, and watched it rise from the porch. Bug joined him, but kept his eyes on the man just so he would remember who the boss was. Every once in a while he would stroll over and stick his wet nose against Mark's cheek just to cement the point.

Mark made coffee and had it ready for Ellen and Kate who were the next to rise. Ellen was shocked someone besides her brewed coffee and pleased beyond words she could drink her coffee while getting breakfast ready. 'Such a silly little thing,' she thought to herself, 'but it means a lot to me. Don't know why.'

He did some minor repairs on the house, fixed a hinge or two, replaced a couple of boards on the porch, but most of their day he and Will scoured town, talking to people, trying to figure out what work was available. They spent the evenings sitting on the porch taking in the cool breeze drifting across on the scent of lilacs.

Harley made himself useful in the barn, cleaning the stalls and taking care of the horses. He seemed to love it there and came to feel proprietary about the barn and horses. Once when Will was heading out to saddle up the mare, Harley stopped him cold.

"She's not ready," he said proprietarily to Will. "She hasn't been brushed yet, and she can't go without it. Give me ten minutes," he ordered. Will just stared at him, shrugged his shoulders and smiled.

"Guess I could do that, Harley. I don't have much to do around here with you two around. Not that I'm complaining." He settled back in his seat to wait the required ten minutes.

Ellen had somehow gotten Harley to bathe. At least, that was what both Mark and Will thought because on the second day, Harley's clothes were hanging on the line, and Harley was wandering around in a sheet. Mark and Will had come back from town for lunch to find Harley sitting on the porch step wrapped in white. A scowl was on his face, and he looked different. Will looked from Harley to the clothes line and back to Harley. He leaned over and sniffed at his hair, then stepped back and stared.

"Damn, do you smell sweet," he said. "Is that lavender I smell? Did you roll in a flower bed?"

"Are you courting a woman?" Mark chimed in. "Seems you think that's the only reason to get clean."

"I just thought it was time," Harley answered, his fuzzy head held high. Now it was clean, his hair curled and glistened in the sunlight.

"I didn't know you had such pretty hair," Mark said. "It's downright fit for a girl."

Harley finally grinned, liking all the attention his bath had brought.

"Guess its not just pretty eyes I've got, huh?"

Just about then, Ellen came out of the screen door and headed for the line. She returned with Harley's clothes.

"I think they're dry now, Mr. Benton. I'm pleased you felt free to ask me to wash them. I'd be happy to do them every few days." She placed the folded pile by him on the porch and left before he could close his mouth or respond.

They grinned and watched Harley walk to the barn with his fresh clothes held gingerly so they wouldn't wrinkle.

"Damn, she's good," Mark said. "I never would have believed it."

"She is, Mark. That she is."

They had lunch, teased Harley about his good looks and Ellen about the dangers in being left alone with such a handsome man around. Ellen scoffed good naturedly at their jibes and told them to eat and get out.

"I have work to do," she said, a phony scowl on her face.

Will stared at his wife, marveling at the change in her. She smiled more often and blushed, too, when they teased her. What had happened to make this wonderful change? He didn't know, but he wanted to keep Harley forever if he was the cause.

"You just remember, Mr. Benton, Ellen is spoken for," Will said, his gray eyes twinkling. "Mark and I are heading back to town. We have some business to do, so behave yourselves."

In town, Mark was less content. People there remembered him as the robber of the payroll, a womanizing dandy. He heard whispers behind his back, and while it usually didn't bother him, some of it made him want to respond with a fist; when it included remarks about Kate. The rest rolled off his back, and he typically greeted whispered comments with a smile, daring them to continue while he grinned at them. When they included Kate, however, his ire flared.

Two stout women in Nestor's spoke in voices they knew would be overheard.

"She's no better than he is," one said. "He's married, you know."

"Guess she figures she's an old maid anyway. What does it matter who she cavorts with?"

"Well, I say she's a disgrace, no better than any of Sadie's girls. Poor Mrs. Hughes."

Mark turned to flay the old biddies with a few well chosen words when he felt Will pull at his arm.

"She doesn't need defending, Mark. She's done nothing wrong."

Mark's breath came out fire, but he backed off.

"Old bitches," he said. "Don't they have anything better to do?" But he walked over to the women, smiled at them and said, "Good afternoon ladies. I hope you are having a wonderful day." He tipped his hat in salute and turned from them, but watched their mouths form identical O shapes that stayed there until he and Will left the store.

They laughed once they were outside, but the anger still simmered in Mark. He thought about Kate; her hair, golden and flowing down her back; her walk, free and swinging like nothing could or ever would get in her way; the pure honesty in blue eyes that slanted when she laughed; her unfettered warmth. Her scrutiny was scathing and wise; her strength resolute, and her actions sometimes foolish but sweet. How did he know all of this? He didn't understand how or why, he just knew; he had learned it by watching at her sixteenth birthday and by being near her before and during the trial. She wouldn't have liked being defended from the filthy mouths of the old biddies. She probably would have said nothing herself. She would have merely held her held high and smiled. He was glad that was what he had done.

He heard Will talking, but only caught it mid-sentence he was so caught up in his thoughts.

"Sorry, Will. I was wool gathering. I didn't catch what you said."

"Don't worry about Kate," Will said. "I told you, she can take care of herself. Always has. Anyway, I was saying that I think I have the answer to our problems. Interested in hearing?"

"Yes! What?"

"Let me preface this by saying that the mill doesn't need me, can't even use me, as a matter of fact. So, I've wanted something else to occupy my hands and mind. I know what it is. The smithy."

"What are you talking about?"

"The smith shop. It's Yager's Smith Shop, on the edge of town across from the elevator. The old man died a couple of years back. Mrs. Yager has been running it with a hired man, but it's not doing well, and neither is she."

"So what are you thinking, Will," Mark asked, "that she hire me instead?"

"No, I'm thinking of making an offer for the shop. She could really use the money with those two youngsters she has. She can put it into something that she can do instead of having to hire help to make it work."

Mark stopped dead in the street.

"Will, you can't buy a smith shop so I have someplace to work."

Will put a hand on Mark's arm, watched the sorrow cross his face. "I told you, in the preface," he said. "I've wanted something else to do. I get restless when I do the same thing over and over, and the mill doesn't really need me anymore. It will continue to run just fine with just Tom, and I want something to do. I'm thinking I can borrow a bit from the Mill for a small down payment and pay her the rest monthly. It will give her an income each month."

Will was growing more excited as he talked. His eyes twinkled, and his hands waved in the air as he described the shop and what they would do to it.

"It even has a small living space in the back. You could live there until you saved enough to build a place of your own. Not that you aren't welcome in the Hughes house," he added. "But I know that eventually you will want a space to call your own. Any man would."

"It feels like I would be taking away from your family, Will. That doesn't feel too good," Mark said, his face somber, his hands clenching and unclenching in the excitement of possibility. "How can I do that?"

"You can't if you let your pride get in the way. Talk to your friend Harley about that, and he'll explain pride and its disease. You can do it if you believe that you would be doing a favor to me. And you would. Look," Will said, gripping Mark's arm tighter, "every time I get the wanderlust, Ellen is scared we will be packing up and moving. I won't do that to her anymore. The rest of my years here on Earth will be spent making up for the years I made her a vagabond. With this smith shop, I can get my fingers into something new and stay put while I do it." He paused for a few moments; let his words sink in, watched Mark think. "Well, what do you think?"

Mark looked around him at the muddy streets, still showing the signs of spring's thaw. He watched people going into the shops and coming out, brown wrapped packages in their arms. They had places to go, things to do, and lives to live. He saw them nod to each other and heard them shout greetings. He'd like to be a part of what he saw.

"I'm feeling that knot that Harley talks about," he said. "Is my pride turning it into a noose?" he said smiling. "He'd surely have something more to say about that."

"Well, don't stick your own neck into it," Will said, smiling back. "Let's do this together, Mark."

Mark turned to Will, put his hand out in friendship and partnership.

"One thing," he said, still holding Will's hand, "when the shop makes money, I pay you for half of what the selling price is." He paused for a moment, knowing he had to have Will's understanding about something else. "You have to know I'll be making frequent trips to be with my children until I can make a place for them here. I'll make the rides at night so it'll be just Sundays I won't be working. Will that be a problem for you?"

"You know better than that. Of course it's fine. It's a deal then," Will said, squeezing Mark's hand in a bargain sealed.

"Done, let's go see it and see the Widow Yager." A few steps down the street, Mark said, "I can't thank you enough, Will."

"Then don't."

In a matter of days, the deal was settled. The shop belonged to them, and they began the long process of setting things to right. It had not been well taken care of since Yager died, and many of the tools needed repair. They mended, cleaned the work benches and floors, put in rows of nails where they hung the mended tools. They hauled a huge supply of wood, mill leftovers, and worked until they were both exhausted and filthy.

They had sore muscles, were covered with soot, and had solved most of the world's problems while they worked. They joked kindly about Mrs. Wellington and other town characters and sorrowed with her and them. They heard silence and liked that too. It was a comfortable environment, and both of the men grew in it.

Will had a sparkle in his eyes, and Mark exuded some of the confidence that had fled with all the payroll troubles and his futile efforts to earn a living. They both grew muscles with the activity, and they both laughed a lot. They had just about completed the repairs and cleaning. They would have been swaggering on the walk home if either of them had had the energy.

"We've done it, Will," Mark said. "It's ready to go."

"That it is, Mark. We need to let people know we're ready for business. Any ideas?"

"Signs," Mark said. "We need some fancy signs. Do you think Kate and Ruthie would help make them?"

"All we need to do is ask," Will answered, knowing his daughters.

When they got home, they burst through the door, both wanting to tell the news at once. "You should see it, Ellen," Will said. "It's clean. You will love it."

"It doesn't look like the same place, Mrs. Hughes, but look who did the work," he said grinning and sticking out his chest. "Although, I think poor old Will, here, is a bit worse for wear now. He just can't take it like a younger man."

"Well, excuse me Mr. Whipper Snapper who is not that much younger than I am. Who is it who needed a break this afternoon? Huh? Tell me the answer to that one."

Ellen just continued her dinner preparations, nodding every now and then, liking the sound of their gentle banter.

"Mr. Benton finished fixing up the barn roof today," she said, still working at the sink. "I don't know what else to have him do, but he is determined to do something. Do you know?"

"Benton!" Will cried. "We need Harley for this special day. Go get him, will you, Ruthie?"

Ruthie fairly skipped out of the house and came back with Harley in tow. He was still clean; his hair was still curly and shiny.

"What's going on? Miss Ruthie seems about to burst."

"We're celebrating, Harley. The shop is ready to go. We'll be open as soon as we put out the sign," Will said, his chest puffed out and his face lit like the fourth of July.

Ellen slipped quietly to the pantry and pulled out the jug and three small glasses. She slid them in front of Will silently, and he looked up at her, an unasked question in his eyes. 'Why did you do this?' he wanted to ask. 'I didn't even ask for it, and you brought it to me. I love you,' were his silent words.

'I know,' was her unspoken reply.

Will poured, lifted his glass.

"To the success of the Ramey, Hughes Smith Shop," he said loudly and with pride.

They drank, and Harley, peering around Bug who had as much of his body as would fit on Harley's lap, lifted his glass again.

"To the success of life and happiness," he said, and when they lifted their glasses to drink, he added, "Wait, don't drink yet. I'm not done."

Mark groaned, rubbed his free hand over his hair.

"Harley, how long is this toast gonna take?"

"Just a few moments. A good toast takes time, you know. It's a thoughtful work of art, something not just anyone can do properly. You don't want to just rush in and say the wrong thing."

"You'd know – about the wrong thing, that is," Mark said grinning at him.

"As I was saying – life and happiness, and cutting ropes that tie knots in your innards. Looks like you've done that young man, cutting the ropes, I mean. My work may be done," he finished, and touched his glass to both of theirs.

"Whoa, Harley," Will said, suddenly afraid Harley would be leaving. "Your work isn't done here. I've got a lot of stuff that I can't get to. I need you – if you're willing to stay, that is," he slowly added, suddenly concerned his alarm had shown. Will's thoughts were on Ellen's face, the light in her eyes, the almost ready smile. He didn't want to lose the woman he knew and loved. But it had taken Harley to bring it out in her. He'd do a lot to keep Harley with them, just for her – for her smile.

Kate was not much different from Ellen. Harley made her laugh. She was free with her sardonic banter when he was around, much like she used to be. Kate had long ago ceased to be quick to tease in the heart of the family. The atmosphere had been just too uncomfortable since her reputation had been smeared by the town's guardians of morality, and Ellen had taken it so much to heart. But Harley had brought her out of her shell, brought out the devil in her, the devil Will loved – the kind and loving devil he had deliberately reared her to be. Kate was nobody's mouse. Will had made sure no cat would play, in the wicked way they sometimes do, with his little girl. But she loved, loved deeply, and sometimes that can make you think and do odd things, he thought to himself as he watched the interplay around the table.

And Ruthie . . . he was no longer worried she was growing into a woman who couldn't laugh. She had become the kitchen clown around the dinner table. Will's heart warmed when he watched her bait Harley and Mark.

"So, who are you going to bathe for today, Harley?" she had asked. "You still got your eye on Mama? I'm thinking Pa's going to fight you for her."

"I've got tricks up my sleeve little one. Some I haven't even tried, some I don't even know yet," he responded, eyes glittering in fun.

"I'm thinking Mrs. Wellington," Ruthie said coyly. "She's been missing her man for a long time, and you might just be the one to make her happy – if you're looking, that is, and since you're all spruced up with shiny curls on your head . . . who knows?"

Mark stifled a groan, already hearing the discourse that might come from Harley. He remembered the woman at the window who came by daily to swear at him and all men in general when he was in the Hersey jail.

"I'm not sure that's the right mix, Ruthie," he said. "They'd probably talk each other to death."

"Hey, she just needs a little loving." Will said, getting into the fun of the evening. "Say, what about christening the new shop tomorrow? We'll get some lemonade and whiskey and do it up right. Tomorrow after Kate gets off work. Can you come straight from school tomorrow, Kate, or do you have parents coming in to beg for their kids?"

"I'll make it happen, Pa. Although they've caught spring fever and are trying everything they can think of to make my life miserable, I'll be careful not to mete out punishments because they usually happen after school is out for the day."

Harley piped up. "They just want to be around the beautiful school teacher as long as they can," he said. "Who wouldn't?"

"Well," Kate said, "their time is spent writing on the board: I won't do this; I won't do that; I won't do the other thing. I don't think they're having much fun."

"I can't imagine you trying to outdo spring fever," Mark said. "That's pretty strong."

"Well, you should be there to see what goes on. I caught that little runt Billie Wells in the classroom during recess. Do you know what he was doing?"

"No," Mark answered. "I can't imagine. What was he doing?"

"Hiding everyone's lunch. We ended up finding them in the rafters, under the porch where the cotton rats had nibbled on the sacks, and in my desk. I think the kids thought I had put them there to eat."

"What else does the poor defenseless teacher have to put up with?" Mark asked, amused at the picture she created.

"Let me see," Kate said, a finger aside of her temple in thoughtful repose. "The list goes on and on. One day last week, I got to the school at the usual time, but the Wells boys were there waiting for me to open the door. That's a rarity in itself. They were unusually polite . . . for them. I found out why later."

"Well, what happened, Kate?" Will asked.

She straightened her shoulders, steeled her eyes. "Did you ever hear fifteen bull frogs croaking in unison? I think they were harmonizing – three part. They hadn't figured out the four part stuff yet, but they're young. They'll get it."

They all pictured the bullfrog scene, each seeing a different sight. Harley said bullfrogs are the harbingers of great things and they bring great luck to those they deem to visit.

"Obviously, Kate, they like you and will bring you good fortune. Listen to their croaks because they are sweet pieces of information you can use to make good decisions."

They all looked at Harley like he was a crazy man, but they had gotten so used to his strange ways they listened to his words with at least some sense they could just possibly be true.

"What were they singing?" Will asked. "School days, school days, dear old golden rule days?"

"It could have been, but it sounded like fifteen Willies when his voice was changing."

"Where did you find them?" Ellen asked quietly, her face stark given the prospect of coming upon a bunch of frogs when you weren't expecting it.

"In my desk," she answered. "I opened it and all but a couple came leaping out at me. The others stayed snug in the corners until I fished them out."

"What'd you do?" Mark asked.

Kate grinned, relishing the end of the tale. She had been shocked at the discovery of the frogs, but it hadn't taken her long to get control. She grabbed them from her desk as they jumped out, and holding up the hem of her skirt just far enough to create a large depository for the frogs, she piled them in. With thirteen frogs in her skirt, she walked around the room and gave every student a frog. Two were frogless, but she didn't mind because she knew they had not been part of the game. When most of them had frogs in their hands, and Kate had warned them about harming the creatures, she began a lesson on amphibians. They looked at the wonderful muscles and jumping capacity of their hind legs and compared them to how far humans can jump; they wondered about their bulging eyes and their unbelievable throats that could bulge outward and make such thunderous sounds.

"I thanked whoever had brought the frogs," she said, "and asked how they could have known that I had prepared a lesson comparing frogs to humans."

"You are a great teacher," Harley said in between bouts of laughter. "I wish I had been in school with you. Wish you had been my teacher. I might have liked school."

"Yeah," Kate said, loving his smile and grinning back. "You would have been the boy with the frogs. I would have had to get out the old hickory switch for you."

"You really like teaching, don't you?" Mark asked. "It seems to suit you, and you like your little delinquents?" It was more a statement of fact than a question because it was obvious Kate found humor in her students' pranks.

She really did enjoy them most when they were spirited and a bit unruly. Perhaps they reminded her of herself and the things she might have done more of had she been willing to take Ellen's admonishments.

"Yes, I guess I do," she said. "And I guess I like them best at this time of year when they leap out of the natures that have been drilled into them, and they try something new. They don't behave like cattle lined up at the corral for slaughter. They're all different, and I like that. They are originals, every one of them. But that's not saying it's easy."

"Well, Kate, try to go easy on them tomorrow so you can get there around 3:30. We'll be christening the shop. Harley, will you escort Ellen and Ruthie to the shop? You can bring that mangy horse on your lap, too, if you want. Mark and I will be waiting with refreshments."

"What a silly question," Harley said. "I deem it an honor and a delightful responsibility to safely escort my two beautiful ladies and my Bug."

"Excuse me, Mr. Benton," Kate piped up. "You can claim my mother and sister, but not my dog," she said grinning. "You keep trying to steal him and I'll be inviting Mrs. Wellington to visit you in the barn! I'll tell her you saw her in town, fell immediately in love and have been pining away," she crooned, her hand theatrically over her heart.

Kate was excited about the shop christening. All during class the next day, she wondered what she could do special for their great day.

'Damn – curtains!' she said, and again wondered if she had said it out loud. She looked around the room, didn't see any shocked faces, so she assumed her words had been silent. 'I need to be careful of that,' she admonished herself. 'But it's such a good word . . . and it works so well for me.'

She let school out early, much to the delight of the spring-fevered students, and ran home. In an old trunk, she found a curtain she could make fit the one window in their shop. It was a bit faded, but the gay red and brown print would liven up their shop, and it was something she could do for them. She quickly pressed the material while Ellen watched with curious eyes.

"It's for the shop, Ma."

Ellen just nodded, a small glimmer in her eyes.

"That will be nice, Kate," she said. "Where are your students?"

"Off terrorizing someone else I hope."

"Need help?" Ellen asked.

"Nope, just a stick and a couple of nails. I'll take Bug with me. Tell Harley I didn't trust him with my dog," she said laughing.

Kate walked back to the shop hoping to find it empty, and it was. She looked at the window, assessed her needs, and pulled up a chair. It wobbled a bit, but she steadied herself by hanging onto the wall while she hammered a nail into the sill beside the window pane. She had one nail in, the curtain hanging from the stick she had attached to the nail, and was ready to pound in the second when she heard a sound behind her. She turned to ascertain the source of the noise, saw Mark, wobbled on her chair, and grabbed the wall for support.

"You weren't supposed to be here," she said, a slight blush creeping into her cheeks.

"Curtains," Mark said, leaning against the door frame and taking in the view of Kate stretching to work on their window. "Nice touch. That's very sweet of you."

Bug just rolled his eyes like he knew Mark had planned it all along.

"Well, it's not much," she said, and turned back to hammer in the last nail. When she did, the chair wobbled again; she gave a little yelp. Mark leaped across the room and held the chair steady with one hand. His other arm circled around her waist like a burning sash. Warmth spread from her middle to her chest, tightening around her throat and making words impossible. She moved to the side away from his heat, heard the snap of a chair leg and tilted, clawing the wall with one hand and grasping Mark's shoulder with the other. He fell backwards in a heap on the floor with her on top of him.

Once again, they were on the floor with Kate's face on his chest. Bug had been ready this time and in an instant had pinned Mark's shoulders to the floor with his huge front feet, his nose once again pressed against Mark's.

How many times would she wish to slip through the floor boards and become one with the rodents? she wondered. How many times would she be this close to Mark and have it be an accident? "Get up Kate," she said to herself. "I don't want to. I just want to stay here, just like this. Or slip through the floor, Kate, you can do it. You love critters. Damn!"

"Well, then just stay, or slip through the floor if you can, but I think we'll be having company soon," he said. "And would you mind calling Bug off?"

"Did I say all that out loud?" she whispered, praying the answer was no.

"The wanting to stay?" he asked.

"Well, thinking out loud is a concern, but it's mostly the damn. I keep saying it, knowing I shouldn't, but I do it anyway. Sorry."

"Yeah, you said all of it. You said damn and that you wanted to stay here, just like this – or slip through the floor, whatever you meant by that. Do you have a thing about rodents?"

'Damn, I said it out loud again.' Kate stiffened; her thoughts lingered on all of their entangled body parts and wondered how to end this odd embrace, her face tucked into his stomach, his arms around her back.

"Off, Bug – for now," she added.

Mark ended her dilemma by pulling her up to face him. "Are we destined to always end up on the floor in a tangle? Am I a klutz or is it you?" he asked grinning, his thumbs caressing her cheeks.

His eyes searched her face, and then his lips melted into hers. Kate responded by sliding further up on his chest, her breasts pressed against him, and her lips responded to his. Her breath seared through him with a sigh of long held passion.

"Kate," he groaned. "Kate," was all he could say.

"Don't Kate me," she breathed against his lips. "You caught me when I fell. I'm your responsibility now," and she kissed him again, more thoroughly this time.

When he had breath again, he put his hands at the sides of her face and looked at her.

"Do you know what you're doing girl?"

She didn't speak. She just gazed at him with many years of pent up love and a half smile dimpling one cheek.

"I am fully aware that I am almost lying on top of you and kissing you."

"I'm not sure that you do, know what you're really doing, I mean."

"I think I know what I am doing," she said and wrapped her arms around his neck, nuzzling his face as she did so.

"Kate, please. We need to get up. Your family will be here soon."

Kate's response was a long, slow kiss that enflamed him. He crushed her with his arms, pulling her into him in an embrace that consumed both of them. A groan escaped him, but it was not the same as the one he gave to Harley. It was one of love and agony, passion and caring, hope and despair. It said everything Kate wanted to hear. A huge smile crossed her face and she snuggled deeper into Mark's embrace.

"Is this another game that I've missed? You two play a lot," Harley said at the entrance of the door. "I can't believe you would play games without me again . . ., and you should probably know your family is just a step or two behind me."

"You might want to slip through the floor now, or get up before your family gets here," Mark said to Kate, grinning just inches from her face. He rolled, grabbed her hand, and pulled her to her feet. Her face was flushed and her eyes were sparkling. A cat's grin was plastered on her lips.

"I'm up. Fun game, Mark. We'll have to play it again some time," she said looking at Harley and trying to appear composed, although it was obvious she was more than a bit distracted. Her face was flushed with a rosy hue, her lips were swollen and wet, and her breath came in gasps.

"The next time you want to hang curtains," Mark said, "find a chair that won't tumble you to the floor."

"I would have been fine if you hadn't interrupted me," she bantered. "I know how to use a chair and a hammer. Harley, this man keeps throwing me to the floor. I'm just standing there, doing my work, and all of a sudden I'm in a heap on the floor. What would you do?"

"I guess I'd just kiss his pretty face," Harley said, smiling at the two of them. "And here is the co-owner and his family. Let's do some celebrating!"

Will saw the pink glow on his daughter's face the moment he walked through the door. It left no doubt in his mind about things, and he was of two minds about it. One, his Kate loved this man and had since the moment she met him. Two, the man was married and penniless. But she loved him. What else is there?

"Kate, take the jug and set up the glasses," he said, trying to distract attention from her glowing face when Ellen and Ruthie walked in. Perhaps a little time might tone down the obvious.

"Nice curtains by the way, but aren't they supposed to hang across the window instead of down one side?"

"They were playing a game," Harley said. "They got started before we were here to play with them. I'm always the last man left when it comes to games."

"Mark's fault," she quipped. "He thinks he knows something about home decorating. He doesn't. I'll fix your glasses and finish what I started," she said.

"Not sure you should do that right now, Kate. Your mom and sister are due here in a few minutes," Will said, teasing his daughter. "And make five, Jack Bay's joining us for this celebration. Although I'm not sure Harley needs a drink. His tongue is always as loose as the proverbial goose."

Kate only heard the first part – not sure she should finish what she had started. Did he know her so well? She looked him in the eyes and knew the answer to her question.

"The curtain, Pa. I'll finish putting the curtain at the window like I started to do when I was rudely interrupted."

"Oh, my apologies for the mistake. Thought . . . well, something else," he said with the Hughes twinkle in his eyes.

"Is Willie coming – and Mary?" Kate asked, filling small glasses with the home brew Will had brought and trying to change the subject.

"Yeah, Willie and Mary are coming like Joseph and Mary," he said, then suddenly glanced around to see if Ellen had heard his blasphemy. Seeing Ellen had not come in yet, he continued. "He's leading their old nag as slowly as she can go with Mary sitting on top and wincing at every step. I swear she's going to have that young one at any moment."

"Willie, get her down this minute," they heard from the open door. "She shouldn't be up there. Look at her!"

"She wanted to come, Ma," Willie pleaded. "She wanted to be here for this."

"Well, you should have more sense, look at her," Ellen yelled.

"Mom, it's alright. I wanted to come," Mary whispered. "Help me down, please, Willie."

Jack arrived just as Mary was turning herself around in the saddle preparing to be lifted down. Between Jack and Willie, they hoisted her off the mare and carried her as if she was sitting in an armchair into the smith shop.

"Get a chair!" Jack shouted. "We'll not let our precious cargo touch this scurvy floor!"

"Scurvy!" Will shouted back, laughing, while Mark dragged one of the only two chairs in the place over to Mary. "I'll have you know we scrubbed this floor with lye. It is fit for queens, and other royalty," he continued, bowing low to Mary and winking at her.

"My God," Harley said, then "so sorry for the Lord's name, but it's not in vain, Mrs. Hughes. I am praising our Lord for the beauty in this family. Not only do you procreate it, you go out and find it. I am Harley Benton, at your service, young Mrs. Hughes, lovely procreator."

Mary squirmed in her chair, unsure as most people were just how to respond to Harley. She lifted her hand to shake his and he just held it.

"I am unable to release you so quickly, Miss Mary. May I call you that?"

Mary just nodded and looked at Willie for help. So Harley continued to hold her hand, and she let him.

Ellen stared at Harley. Mark shook his head and groaned a little, but smiled. Jack nodded his head, liking the quick tongue of the stranger. Willie moved from foot to foot, not sure if he was supposed to rescue his wife or not. Kate grinned; glad the focus was not on her for the moment. Will finally stepped in to break Harley's spell.

"It's time for the christening of the Ramey, Hughes Smith Shop, not the baby," he said in an aside to Mary. "We'll do that after you've given birth." He gathered the lemonade for the ladies and the whiskey-filled glasses and passed them around. They had just raised their glasses high, and Will had turned to Mark for a silent, private salute when Mary screamed and grabbed her stomach.

Every face in the small room went white, especially Willie's.

"Will, go fetch Doc Preston," Ellen commanded. "Kate, find some clean rags, somewhere, anywhere, even if you have to go begging at houses. Jack, start a fire and get a kettle going."

"Already there, Mrs. Hughes." He had rekindled the hot coals in the forge and had a kettle on almost before Ellen had even begun issuing orders.

Ellen yanked the curtains down from their hanging perch on one side of the window and placed them on the clean workbench in the center of the room. She knew the curtains were clean. She had washed them herself. When she turned to Mary, what she saw gave her pause. Harley was squatted in front of her, Mary's legs on either side of him. His hands were on Mary's swollen belly, her dress was lifted to just below her breasts, and his face was nestled into Mary's naked stomach. He was crooning to Mary's abdomen and Mary was half sitting, half lying in the chair, no longer screaming.

"I'm breathing for you Miss Mary," he said. "Listen to my breath. I'm calm and peaceful. This is just a natural part of life, and you can be peaceful, too."

Mary seemed to calm with his words, then a contraction would wrench her, and she would contort in pain again. Willie stood at the back of her chair wringing his hands, not knowing what he should be doing, not knowing what he could do.

When Harley saw the tightening of her abdomen, he crooned again softly, in a chant Ellen didn't recognize and couldn't place. He seemed to get the rhythm of her contractions and anticipated when they would come and worked to make her peaceful before the pains began. "Let old Harley have some of your pain, Mary. I want to help you with your work." He caressed her abdomen in a way that made Ellen uncomfortable, but she saw it was helping her daughter-in-law, so she said nothing. 'What a strange, man,' she thought, already for more times than she could count.

"Ready," Jack shouted from the other room. "Fire's hot, and I have rags in boiling. They should be sterile soon."

By the time Kate and Will returned, Mary was on the table on the clean curtains, Harley was at her side soothing the child inside of her with his voice just inches from her abdomen, Jack was still tending the fire, and Ellen was holding her daughter-in-law's hand watching as Jack and Harley took over.

"Doc Preston is on another call," Will said breathlessly. "Don't know when he'll be back. What are we going to do?"

Kate burst through the door at the same time and shoved towels and sheets at Ellen. "From neighbors," she said. "What should we do now?"

"Now we wait, possibly for a very long time. First babies are like that," Ellen said.

"It won't be all that long, Mrs. Hughes," Harley said with his ear on Mary's belly. "Our baby is going to move eagerly and lovingly into this world."

Will and Kate took in the scene, especially Harley at Mary's belly. They saw Jack calmly stoking the fire and bringing out boiled cloths, wringing and hanging them for future use. "You can wait outside," Ellen said. "Take Willie with you. We're doing just fine in here."

Kate took Willie's hand and led him out the door. Bug, Ruthie, Mark and Will followed. They sat on the steps in the waning sunshine. Robins still chirped the coming of spring. Tree toads still heralded dusk. Lilacs still scented the warm spring night, but none of them heard or smelled what was around them. They listened intently for sounds coming from the smith shop, and none of the surrounding sounds and smells could break through their thoughts. Their ears were trained for the voices from inside. But they only heard silence from there, and the quiet worried them even more than the screams they expected to hear.

"Jack, I need a couple of large logs wrapped in several layers of cloth," Harley said. "Place them behind her when I raise her shoulders."

Harley lifted Mary, and Jack placed the cushioned logs behind her back. Then Harley positioned her feet next to her thighs and placed himself between Mary's knees. Ellen watched, still uncomfortable with what she saw. Harley would be seeing what no man should, and it disturbed her.

"Mr. Benton, I don't think . . ." she said hesitantly.

"Mrs. Hughes," he interrupted, "with respect, I will smooth this child's way into the world. It need not be as traumatic as most make it out to be." And he leaned between Mary's legs, caressed his face against her belly, and crooned the lullaby, the same one Ellen had only heard for the first time a few minutes ago. Mary's legs relaxed as they parted, and the pain on her face seemed to dissipate. Within minutes, Harley was cradling a small head in his hands, his lips breathed life into the newborn's mouth, and then arms and legs appeared. Jack was instantly beside him with a clean sheet, and the child was born. There was no screaming, no pain that could not be borne in silence, and no sound at all until the child uttered her first gasp of delight. She didn't even yell. She crooned – like Harley.

"If you and Jack will take our baby girl and give us a few minutes, Mary and I will finish this up," Harley said. "You know, there's afterbirth that needs to happen and all that."

Ellen was so stunned at what Harley had done she just nodded, eager to comply with his apparent knowledge. Jack knew his work was completed and led Ellen by one arm into the living area of the shop. Her other arm was holding the baby.

"She's beautiful, isn't she, Mr. Bay?"

"Yes, she certainly is. It's a great way to christen the new shop, don't you think, Mrs. Hughes?"

Outside, no one even knew the ordeal was over until Harley had completed his work and went outside to tell them. There had been no screams, no mother's cry, no baby's cry, no need for a traumatic entrance into the world – or even for trauma while you're in the world, according to Harley. As he had been known to say – there was no need for knots.

"There's another beautiful Hughes lady," Harley said when he faced the trio on the steps. "I must say I am impressed at what you produce. How about that whiskey now? Oh, I almost forgot. Mr. Willie, since we have a new beautiful Hughes girl and you are somewhat responsible, you are welcome to introduce yourself now."

They all raced to the door, each fighting to be the first but finally recognizing Willie had the right and backed off. They went through the birthing room and finally into the living space. Jack was holding the new Hughes girl. Ellen was removing the sheet from her just enough to inspect all the parts. They were all there. Fingers, toes, two eyes, one nose, and a mass of black hair sticking out at all of the angles one could imagine.

Willie walked in tentatively, saw Mary sitting in the chair where she had first felt the birth pain, and he kissed her. All the while he watched Jack with his child. He went to him and held out his arms. Reluctantly, it seemed, Jack gave her up. Willie placed their child in Mary's arms and surrounded them both with his.

Mark watched them with a sad smile, and his gray eyes clouded with longing for his own babies. It didn't seem so very long ago Flossie had been born – and then Jamie. What he was seeing intensified his yearning for his children. It was always there – a deep, sick ache, and he tried to push it aside for the moment. He'd been able to get back to visit with them briefly since he'd been in Hersey, but it wasn't the same as being with them every day, watching them grow and tucking them in each night. "I'm doing everything I can, little ones," he whispered to himself.

"I'm still waiting for that celebration drink," Harley said. "Babies are born every single day, but a new smith shop is not! You folks really know how to play games," he said. "Every day there's a new one. I'm kind of liking being around here. What's next?"

Jack retrieved the glasses and passed them around. "To the new Ramey, Hughes Smith Shop," he said. "And to the newest beauty in the Hughes family," and he raised his glass to Mary and the baby. "May you both be healthy and strong."

Ellen raised her lemonade to Jack's glass. He saw the stress and fatigue in her face and drew the only other chair for her.

"Sit, Mrs. Hughes. You've earned it."

"We need to get Mary into a bed," she said. "And she needs to see Doc Preston to make sure she and the baby are in good health."

"They are, and that will happen, Mrs. Hughes. In good time. He'll be back soon. You just take a moment's rest," he said, and he refilled her glass with lemonade and a little bit of home brew, for medicinal purposes.

Ellen gratefully took the chair and sank into it. 'What a strange group,' she thought. 'We just brought a baby into the world, with an odd lumberjack and a railway hobo as midwives. I don't understand all of this, but it seems peaceful and right.' She drained her drink and asked Jack if he would pour more.

"What do I know?" she asked out loud. "Not sure that I know anything anymore."

"You know much," Harley said to her. "You put us all in the places where we would do the most good. You are my heroine," he said kneeling in front of Ellen and grasping her hands.

"No," she said, feeling the effects of the home brew mixed in her lemonade. "You're my hero, Harley."

Ellen drank her lemonade and then looked around at the people in the room.

"We need a wagon for Mary," she said as she sat and sipped her drink. "Where's Ruthie?" suddenly aware her other daughter had disappeared. "Where is Ruthie?"

Every face in the room looked at the others and wondered what had happened to Ruthie. She had come into the room with Ellen who had been organizing Mary's entrance. Since then she had not been seen, and no one had even noticed. Every heart in the room felt shame at not noticing her absence, but so much had been happening each of them tried to make excuses for their lack.

"I'll go look around," Jack said.

Harley moved in his path, indicating he was determined to be a part of the search. "Me, too," he said as he led their way outdoors.

"She's probably just outside, wanting to be away from the ruckus," Jack volunteered when he turned and saw the alarm on Ellen's face. "We'll bring her in for a toast. It's alright, Ellen."

Jack and Harley found her standing in front of Sadie's Saloon. She had wiped a small circle of dust from the window and was peering in. They stood on the wooden boards that served as a sidewalk for a few moments just watching her, and when she didn't move from her spot, they walked up and stood on either side of her.

"What'cha doing sweetie?" Jack whispered in her ear, knowing deep in his heart something was bothering this young woman.

"Nothing, just looking," she said. "I couldn't do anything in there to help, so I just walked."

"Well, sometimes knowing when to walk is a good thing," Jack said, his voice honey and caring. "You don't feel bad about walking, do you?"

"I guess. Yeah, I guess I do."

Harley stood back and let Jack do his work. He figured Jack was doing just fine, soothing voice, caring heart. 'Jack's okay,' Harley thought. 'Wonder where he comes from?'

"Well, Ruthie," Jack said to her, "you're a step ahead of most people who don't know when to walk away. It's not the same thing as running away. That's pretty smart of you. Everybody has a place. And you shouldn't feel badly about birthing not being your place, if that's what's bothering you. You've never done it, and some of us have." He spoke softly and then paused for a few moments before he added, "You have a beautiful niece."

Ruthie continued to stare into the clean space she had made in the window. It appeared she was intent on whatever was happening in there. She didn't respond to Jack's sympathetic words. Long minutes went by and both Jack and Harley were wondering what they should be doing and saying that they hadn't.

Harley finally took the bull by the horns. 'This is a young woman who needs me,' he thought to himself. 'Harley's going to do his thing,' and he took Ruthie's elbow and steered her away from the window and down the street to the Smith Shop.

"You know," he said softly, "if you tie yourself up just thinking about things, you're not going to be any good as an aunt. And you're an aunt now. She's going to need you. You don't want knots twisting you up when you're taking care of your niece, do you?"

"No," Ruthie gasped, "of course not."

"Well, then. She's in need of an aunt, and you're gonna be it. Yeah, Kate's there, but she's gonna need you too. You're younger and are gonna understand her better. Know what I mean?"

Ruthie nodded, grasped Harley's arm more tightly and lifted her chin.

"Yes, she's going to need me," she whispered, her eyes alight with new purpose.

Jack followed behind looking at Ruthie in a new light. 'A nice young woman,' he thought. 'But she's been a bit left behind the Hughes family fires – doesn't know who she's supposed to be and a bit confused. Been there,' Jack thought. 'Been there a lot, and it's not a good place to be.'

When they reached the shop, Doc Preston was pulling up. He looked like he had spent the last twenty-four hours on the road, but he slid off his horse and ran into the shop after throwing his reins to Jack who tied the mare to the post and followed.

Harley marshaled Ruthie into the room and whispered in her ear.

"Doc is going to need to see Mary, so just take the baby and hold it until he wants her, okay?"

Ruthie nodded and did what she'd been told. She walked over to Mary, held out her arms, and Mary placed her child in Ruthie's arms.

"Thank you," Mary said. "I'm sure I won't be long."

"Don't worry. I'll take care of her," Ruthie said looking into Mary's eyes, and meaning it. She took the baby and walked into the other room, inspected her niece beneath the sheet covering her, and admired the new Hughes female. The rest just watched her as she confidently took the child and left them. Ellen nodded at Harley, and Will did the same to Jack. Kate and Mark smiled covertly at each other, and Willie just looked bewildered. His baby and his wife had just left his care, but he didn't know what to do about it – and it still felt okay.

It was Sunday. The sun had just crested the eastern hills, and it was a perfect day for roosters to crow their loudest. Mark was due to be at the Hughes house soon. Kate stretched, but didn't stay long to enjoy being snug in her bed. Today she was going to show Mark her cabin, and she was excited.

She'd been back only once since the long winter and deep snow had kept her away, and she had worried all the way through the woods. But she found it just as she had left it. The roof hadn't fallen in from the heavy snow she had worried about. Rodents hadn't taken over completely, and the man's coat and trousers still hung where he had left them. She swept, cleaned away the winter cobwebs and her cabin was as tidy and snug as she remembered. She prepared the fireplace so it could be lit and provide warmth quickly when she returned. She couldn't wait to show it all to Mark.

"Get up you lazy critter," she said nudging Bug off the bed. "If Ma knew you slept on my bed, she'd ban you to the outdoors, you bed bug." Kate grinned at the peaked ceiling and felt warm all over. "We're going to the woods, Bug" she whispered, and he showed his excitement by stretching out on his back so Kate could rub his stomach. "And be nice to Mark. You can roll your eyes at him, keep him on his toes, but try not to stand on him anymore, okay?" Kate was pretty sure Bug nodded, but she was also sure sometimes he lied to her.

Kate dressed quickly, ran downstairs and out to the pantry where she grabbed the basket she had packed the night before. Everything except the coffee was ready. She stoked the fire, set the pot to perk, waited for it to brew, and carefully poured it into containers they could carry. Then she and Bug sat on the porch steps and watched the sun finish rising. They heard his footfall in the silent morning before they saw him.

"Lazy bones," she said rising from her seat on the steps. Bug just laid his head on his front feet but rolled his eyes up in greeting.

"We've been up for hours," she said, "just sitting here waiting for you."

"Oh? Is that why I see sleep creases still on your fair cheeks?" he said grinning and running a finger down the side of her face. "And Bug looks like he's not even awake. He hasn't attacked or even slobbered on me yet." Mark scratched behind his ear, and Bug pretended not to notice.

"I kind of miss having you in the Hughes house," she said. "But I'm guessing you like having your own place, huh?"

"Yes, it's not fancy and it's attached to the shop, which gets kind of grimy, but it's private. Not that I didn't love being here, but you know how it is, Kate."

"I do. I do understand. That's why you're going to love my cabin," she cried eagerly. "Let's go."

"Ready if you are. Come on Bug," he said, still scratching his ear.

Kate handed Mark the large basket and picked up a smaller one to carry. Bug stretched deliberately, rose and went around to the side of Kate where Mark wasn't.

"You don't like me much, do you Bug?" Mark asked.

Bug peered around Kate and rolled his eyes.

Kate patted them both. "Don't be jealous, boys. I love you both."

Mark squeezed Kate's arm, happy to be out in the beautiful day, and happy to be with her.

"He'll learn to love me, just like you did."

"I didn't learn that, Mark. It just hit me – like a big club."

"Did it hurt?" he asked, grinning at the world.

"Just when you weren't nearby. And, if you'd stop throwing me down to the floor, Bug might like you a little more."

"Me?" he asked with an exaggerated look of pain on his face. "I seem to recall a certain woman throwing herself at me both of the times we were tangled on the floor."

"You kicked the chair out from under me. Who do you think you are kidding?" she said smugly. "It was intentional, and Bug knew it. That's why he stood on you."

"Yeah? Is that also why he always rolls his eyes at me and slobbers all over my face?" he asked laughing at the memory.

"Yep. That's his defense mechanism. Be wary of my protector because he'll slobber you to death. Unless he likes you. He likes Harley, you know."

They bantered comfortably as they walked, and were at the cabin long before Kate thought they should be. Time had flown. The sun was up, and the cabin looked cool nestled in the trees. Kate grabbed Mark's arm and stopped.

"There it is. Isn't it wonderful?"

Mark stared at the cabin. It did look wonderful. It was a little space of serene heaven in the woods.

"It's beautiful, Kate. I love it."

"Then let me introduce you," she said and led the way down the small path she had cleared. She opened the door – no lock – she wouldn't try to keep the man with the clothes from his own home, and stepped in.

Mark followed and then was quiet. Kate didn't know what she had expected, but she was waiting for some response, any response. Mark just looked around, his face a blank.

She waited silently, her happiness overshadowed by fear he had expected something more grand.

"You don't like it," she whispered sadly, and put her basket on the table.

Mark placed his basket next to hers and slowly turned. Three times he turned in place, his eyes taking in the space that was Kate's. He saw the neatly laid fireplace, all ready to be lit. He saw the scrubbed counter and table, the floor with its cheery rag rugs, the garments hung on pegs, the shelves with carefully aligned dishware, pots and pans. The whole room reeked of his gentle, spirited Kate.

Then he looked at her. A tear was forming at the corner of her eye, and he knew she had been waiting.

"Oh, Kate, it is perfect. It is beautiful. It is you," he said and folded her in his arms, cradling her head at his chest. "I love it."

"You were so silent. I thought you didn't like it."

"I was silent because it is so perfect. I am in awe."

She tipped her head back to look at him, and Bug took that as a sign. His Kate didn't sound happy, Bug thought, so it was time to do something, like stand on this man once again. He came up at their sides, stood on his hind legs, placed his front paws on Mark's shoulder and his nose in Mark's face. His eyes stared directly into Mark's.

Kate began laughing and couldn't stop.

"Down, Bug," she gasped.

Bug slobbered a bit before he got down, just for good measure, and went to his rug in front of the hearth. He circled three times, lay down and rolled his eyes, but kept them open.

"Where did you get this creature?" Mark asked laughing and wiping his face with his handkerchief.

"Oh, wait," he said, remembering Ellen telling him Mel had given the dog to Kate. "I understand, now."

"What do you understand? You need an excuse for Bug not to fall in love with you?"

"No, I remember now that your mother told me he came from Mel."

"Yes, he did," Kate said with a satisfied grin on her face. "Mel thought I needed protection. And Bug is protecting me – from you."

"Well, I think that Mel had it planned from the beginning. I think he had a little talk with Bug about me – maybe about any man who is not your father or brother."

"Then why does he like Harley so much?" Kate fired back.

Mark thought for a moment. "Cause Harley's just another fearsome animal?" he said laughing.

"Light the fire, Mark. It's all set to go. If you're not afraid of stepping over Bug, that is, and don't call Bug an animal. He doesn't like it"

"Witch woman," he said playfully. "I fear nothing – except you."

The fire quickly took the damp chill out of the cabin, and they were snug and warm. Kate took care of the food in the baskets and poured them both some coffee. They moved the two chairs to face the fire and sat sipping their coffee. They talked about the shop, Willie and Mary's baby, and whatever came to mind. They were serene, contented and happy in each other's company.

"How is business?" Kate asked.

"Picking up," he answered. "Not that I'm turning business away yet, but it's coming along better than I expected."

"I'm so glad, Mark. Pa seems to be happy helping out there. He needs to be busy – and needed. I'm sure before long you'll be so busy you'll have to hire help."

Mark squeezed her arm and smiled at her.

"You're such a sweet optimist."

"Hungry?" she asked.

"A little. What can I do to help?"

They walked a few yards to the stream, filled a bucket with icy cold water, and took it back to the cabin. They picked wild flowers, and Mark arranged them in a jar for the table.

"Wow, that's beautiful, Mark," she told him. "You have quite a creative talent with flowers."

"I have many hidden talents," he said, grinning. "I just don't want to spring them on you all at once. It's too overwhelming."

Kate laid out their lunch; cold chicken, cheese, green beans spiced with dill, and peach pie for dessert. They moved their chairs back to the table and ate with relish, talking between mouthfuls over the top of the wildflowers.

"Bug! I forgot Bug," Kate exclaimed.

"Let me get it, Kate," Mark asked. "What can he have, a little of everything?"

"Yup, he's a bit of a pig. And I think you're trying to win him over with food."

Mark fixed a good sized plate and took it over to him.

"Here you go, boy. Dig in. See, I'm not so bad."

Bug looked at Mark as if to say, 'Okay, I'll eat your food, but I'm not licking your hand, so don't get any ideas.'

Mark had filled the hearth kettle with water from the stream. It was hot when they were done eating, and together they washed and dried the dishes. They walked in the woods, held hands, searched for trout lilies, trilliums, elephant ears and morels. When they found a spot where the mushrooms were abundant, they ran back to the cabin for a basket and were able to almost fill it with the tender, juicy morsels.

"Ma is going to be so happy to get these," Kate said. "She especially loves the elephant ears."

"Let's take her some wild flowers, too," he said.

"Are you trying to curry her favor, Mr. Ramey?"

"Well, it wouldn't hurt. She doesn't care much for us being together."

"It's only because you're still married, Mark. It's not you. And Jack is going to take care of that. It will happen soon," she said, wrapping her arms around him and nuzzling his neck with her lips.

Mark put down the basket he was holding and wrapped his arms around her. He tilted her face to his and kissed her deeply and slowly, tenderly. She responded, her breath seeming to leave her body. She was melting and on fire at the same time, weak and dazed, yet fully aware of her senses.

Mark's hands explored her back, pulling her against him, feeling her breasts crush against his chest. He licked at her lips, and Kate's mouth opened to receive the thrust of his tongue. An explosion of breath escaped her. She began to discover his mouth with her own tongue and his breath erupted, warm, moist and eager.

"Kate," he whispered harshly. "Kate, you are driving me wild." His hands moved lower to the rise of her hips then up to where soft breasts swelled. She felt his growing manhood pressed against her and was not afraid. She felt need and warmth deep inside her. "Kate," he said again, but this time he held her arms, held her away from him.

"What?" she asked breathlessly, confusion on her face.

"I love you. It's not the time." His words were mere breaths, but they were firm.

She just nodded. "When?"

"When I am free," he said, resolution, need and sorrow etching his face but clear in the low rasp of his voice.

"And what if that never happens? What if Lorraine is never found so she can set you free? What then?"

"Then . . . I don't know. Then . . . Kate, I can't just let you throw yourself away because my life is so messed up. Let's do this right so you don't get hurt in the crossfire of my problems."

Kate's breathing had returned to semi-normal, and she considered what Mark had said. She didn't like it, but she understood what he was saying. She also knew she would be his wife with or without a paper, with or without permission from Lorraine and the legal system.

"Do you love me, Mark?" she asked.

"Kate," he whispered, "I love you more than I ever knew it was possible to love."

"Then I will grant your wish," she whispered, the beginning of a twinkle lighting her eyes, "but only for a time. If Jack cannot get your divorce by the end of a stipulated time, I will be your wife anyway, in every way – honorably – with joy, and with your last name whether it is legal or not."

It was Mark's turn to just nod. This was a stubborn, willful woman he held in his arms and heart. She would not be swayed by what the world might say or think about her. Will had tried to tell him, and now he saw it firsthand. He loved the fire in her, and he loved the fire lighting her eyes and the tenderness he felt in her touch. She was everything he imagined a woman should or could be. He reached for her again and was stopped by huge hairy paws on his shoulders and a wet nose against his cheek.

"It's alright, Bug," he said. "I love Kate, too." He ignored the wet nose and scratched Bug's head.

Kate laughed, scratched the other side of Bug's face and was happy.

"We're a family already," she said, giggles erupting from her lips. "Mom, Dad, and Water Bug!"

The sharp blade of memory twisted in Mark's gut as a vision of his family passed swiftly through his mind. He saw Flossie and Jamie in the woods with them, laughing and happy. He struggled to push the scene away, to keep his sudden sadness from Kate. She didn't need the moment spoiled by his pain.

He shook his head to clear it and groaned playfully. "Wait just a minute. I have a canine son?" he asked.

"Shhh . . . He doesn't know."

"That I'm now his dad?"

"No, silly, that he's canine."

They took their time getting back to the cabin, and they were slow in packing things up. Neither one wanted to leave.

"It's kind of hard to go. I really like it here," he drawled slowly, then looked sideways at Kate, his head tilted and his eyes questioning. "By the way, who belongs to the man's clothes?"

"The owner," she told him, sounding surprised he wouldn't have assumed that fact. "I cleaned them the best I could and then put them back where I found them -- just in case he comes back."

"You don't think he's going to mind that we're here . . . using his home?"

"No," she said with certainty Mark couldn't understand. "He won't mind. He'll like it that I've taken care of the place."

Mark just looked at her, speculation on his face. She was so sure about the man with the coat and trousers.

"I'm not even going to question it," he said. "For some reason, you just know it, and that's good enough for me."

"Good," she said, her head cocked to one side and a cat's satisfied look on her face.

They checked the fireplace for glowing embers, piled ashes on them, gathered the baskets, one empty and one full of mushrooms and flowers for Ellen and said farewell to Kate's special place.

"I have to keep reminding myself that I can come back when I want to, otherwise I get all teary-eyed when I leave," she said as they closed the door. "I don't know why."

"I suspect it's because the place is your own, Kate," he said softly. "And that's important. It's also very much you. I love it too."

They walked home hand in hand, each carrying a basket, and each in their own thoughts. When they neared the Hughes' house, Kate said "Thank you for going with me. Here, you take the mushrooms and flowers in to Ma."

Mark just grinned. "Yes, I'd like that – curry some points in my favor."

When he handed Ellen the basket and she peeked through the flowers to find mushrooms, her face lit up.

"Just look at these," she said beaming at Mark. "They're huge, and I'm making pork roast right now they will be just perfect with." She turned back to her dinner, eager to clean the mushrooms and put them in the pot.

"There's nothing Ellen likes better than mushrooms," Will said, a knowing grin spreading across his face. "And flowers," he added, glancing sideways at Ellen. "She'll do almost anything for a pretty bouquet."

"Mark's a good mushroom finder," Kate said, looking quizzically at her mother and father feeling they were passing a secret joke to one another. "And he really knows how to arrange flowers. You want him to fix a vase for the table, Ma?"

"Well, sure. I can't get to them right now anyway."

Mark took the wildflowers from her and began fixing them in a tall vase Ellen found in the pantry. When he was finished, he placed them on the counter near Ellen, and asked her if they were presentable. She gave them a quick look, and then a second one.

"Kate was right," she said. "You fixed those better than I could. Have a seat. You'll be here for supper, right? Taste your own mushrooms?"

Mark smiled, wondering at Ellen's seeming change of heart, nodded, and went over to sit on the hearth by

Bug, gave him a little scratch on the head. 'Okay,' he thought. 'I feel pretty good right now.'

Ruthie, hearing the voices, came down from the loft and inspected both the mushrooms and the flowers. She had put on a pretty blue, print dress, and her hair had been pinned back from her face with two coral combs. It flowed down her back in shiny curls, and she looked beautiful. Will and Kate both stared at her for a moment, wanting to ask why she had dressed so carefully for Sunday dinner, but they both decided silence was best at the moment.

Ellen brought their curiosity to an end by asking Ruthie and Kate to set the table for seven.

"Seven?" Kate asked. "Who are we expecting? I only count six."

"Well," she said slowly, drawing it out and making a point of Kate and Will skipping Sunday services, "after Ruthie and I left church this morning, we ran into Mr. Bay. He was so helpful with Willie and Mary's baby I invited him to supper tonight."

"Oh," both Will and Kate said together, nodding, comprehension dawning. Ruthie had dressed for Jack.

Kate and Ruthie set the table and completed it with wildflowers in the center. Then Ruthie volunteered to fetch Harley, who with one glance sensed contentment in the atmosphere and smiled. They were relaxed and chatting comfortably when Jack knocked on the screen door. Ruthie leaped to open it, and Will and Kate exchanged more knowing glances. Harley slanted his eyes at Jack and then watched Ruthie whose face showed a slight blush from neck to forehead. Mark ran his hand through his hair and didn't know whether to groan or smile. Ellen told him to come on in, her back to the rest, tending supper. Bug actually sat up in greeting, cocked his head and Mark was sure he smiled. 'Damn dog,' he thought, ". . . likes everyone but me.'

"Thanks for inviting me Mrs. Hughes, Ruthie. It will be a real pleasure to have some home cooked food."

"It's our pleasure, Mr. Bay," Ellen said, turning a bit to greet him. "Especially after all you did for us and the baby. Find a chair. Supper will be soon."

"We're going to have to build a bigger kitchen," Will said, grinning around the room and loving all the noise and chatter.

Jack asked about the baby, and Ellen was soon happily engaged in telling him almost –true-tales about the miracle of the most recent Hughes. He smiled, nodding at the appropriate times and asked the correct questions. Ellen was hooked. In her mind, Jack Bay was a good man. He had wanted to know about a baby. What else could say more?

At supper, Kate was reminded of when Mark had first come to dine with them. She watched as Ruthie stumbled through the meal, looking at everyone except Jack – unless he was looking away from her. Then she watched him intently under her dark lashes. Kate remembered it so well, and knew her sister was in the first stages of love – or infatuation – or whatever it is that captures one person's heart. She also remembered feeling like a silly, awkward school girl, and her heart went out to Ruthie.

Ruthie moved the food around on her plate, picked at a bite or two, knocked her glass of water over and watched it splash on Jack's shirt. Her hand went to her mouth which only partially covered her cry of horror. Jack quickly scooted his chair back and started sopping up the water with his napkin.

"I'm so sorry," she groaned. "I'm so – such a klutz. Sorry."

"It's just water, Ruthie. I'm sure it needed to be washed anyway."

"No, no, you're always so clean and neat. I'm sure it didn't," she sputtered. Her face was red and her eyes had gathered water of their own in the corners. If I could just fade away right now, she thought, even if I never came back, I would gladly go – fade into somewhere else, anywhere else.

Kate's heart broke for Ruthie. At least she hadn't dumped water on Mark. She might have though. As nervous as she had been it wouldn't have surprised her to dump the whole table on him, and then tumbled him to the floor in the process. She'd had enough of her own silliness lately. Kate found her sister's hand under the table and squeezed it. She leaned close to Ruthie and whispered in her ear.

"Don't even think about sinking through the floor right now. It won't help. There are rodents in the crawl space. I've been there."

Ruthie just looked at her sister, tears threatening to spill. She nodded, eyes wide trying to hold back the flood.

Bug chose that moment to climb half-way onto Ruthie's lap. He lapped at her face and stared around the room looking for the culprit who had saddened Ruthie. She cradled his head and said, "Get down, Bug. You have to get down now." Bug looked around the table, rolled his eyes at Mark, and went back to his rug. He turned three times and lay down, his eyes on the table looking for the bad guy, almost certain it was Mark.

Jack pulled his chair back up to the table, and Mark, trying to smooth things over, asked, "How are the mushrooms, Mrs. Hughes?"

"They are sweet and tender, Mark. You found them at the perfect time. Don't you agree Mr. Bay?"

"I do, Mrs. Hughes. They are sweet and tender, just like the Hughes ladies."

"Here, here," Harley exclaimed. "You have spoken truly, Jack. You're a man of my own inclinations."

After supper, the men stood, groaning with exclamations of being overstuffed, each vying to stick his stomach out furthest as proof. Harley won, of course, and since he'd won, he claimed the right to kiss the cheek of the cook – and then the table setters. Ellen blushed with the attention, Kate gave him her cheek for a similar kiss, and Ruthie kissed him back – just for being Harley. Ruthie loved the old man, and Will did not want to see the day Harley would return to his wandering life. They would all miss him if – when it happened.

After dishes were washed and put away, the ladies joined the men on the porch. It was a warm, scented spring night, and the lazy conversation hardly competed with the evening sounds of crickets and cicadas.

"How about a song, girls?" Will asked. "This reminds me so much of the first night Mark was here; I'd like to complete the memory."

"You should hear Kate play piano and sing, Jack," Mark added. "And I hear tell Ruthie adds a mean soprano." Mark looked at Kate who was groaning mildly. "Please, Kate?"

"Only if we can just sit here and sing," she said. "I don't want to leave this beautiful night – and only if Ma will add a third part."

"Nonsense," Ellen protested. "I haven't done that in years."

"Not true, Ma. I hear your alto all the way to the loft when Ruthie and I are singing. You've been caught. You don't sing – we don't."

Ellen flushed, but nodded her head. They sang all of the hymns they had known for years, and Ellen slowly gained confidence to be heard. Her sweet alto blended with the others so well the three were like one voice. Will leaned his head against the back of his chair, a smile of contentment on his face, and looked from Ellen to Kate to Ruthie and then back again to his still beautiful wife. He couldn't imagine how he got so lucky. At some point, Will joined in, and then Mark's tenor and Jack's baritone added to the depth of the music.

Harley leaned against the porch rail, his eyes watching first one then another of the Hughes and their guests. His face had turned almost angelic in its serenity. His curly hair was a halo in the dusk. Will glanced at

Harley, and it occurred to him it was possible they had been entertaining an angel – unaware. A very strange one, but an angel nevertheless.

As evenings must do, their night came to an end with many thanks for the good food and as much for the company. Ellen even extracted a promise from Jack to return and provide his baritone for other Sundays on the porch.

"I can't pass up great home cooking, Mrs. Hughes, and such beautiful music." He shook hands all around, kissed the ladies, and whispered in Ruthie's ear.

"You're the most beautiful woman in the room. Never doubt it." Then he put his finger over his lips to shush her response and winked.

"You want to walk them down the road a ways, Ruthie?" Kate asked. "I need to walk off some of that dinner. Come on Bug. Let's go Ruthie," she said, and grabbed her hand before she could respond – if she could have.

Spring turned to summer which fled too quickly and was showing signs of being gone soon. Trees were turning red and gold, and the days' warmth dissipated as soon as dusk enveloped the earth. Mark had the back room of the shop almost ready to bring his children to live with him. He'd hoped to be able to provide a better home for them, but a mansion wasn't in the cards, so he spent almost all his free time cleaning the single room and building beds for the three of them.

He partitioned off part of the large room so Jamie and Flossie would have small separate spaces, and he would sleep wherever his blanket hit the floor. It really didn't matter as long as they were together. It wasn't much, but he just couldn't be without them any longer, and he hoped to give them much better in time. 'I will,' he thought. 'I just have to.'

The Hughes family had spent many of the summer nights on the porch, with Mark, Harley and Jack who had become a Sunday regular. Ruthie had become less

nervous as the weeks passed, but obviously more infatuated, and it seemed Jack paid a little more attention
to her than the others. Kate didn't know if he returned
her affections a bit, or if he was just a really nice man
who saw Ruthie could use some special attention. She
had asked Mark about it, but he was noncommittal.

"Can't say, Kate. Jack's a private kind of man, so I
don't know."

"But you can see Ruthie is head over heels, can't
you?" she said, hoping for more information.

"That's pretty clear, but I still don't know. I do
know I like Jack a lot – trust him more than almost anyone, but Jack's an enigma. I don't know where he's going or where he's been. I just think he's a good man."

One day in their loft, Ruthie approached Kate with a
question. "How much older is Mark than you are Kate?"

"I think it's nine years," Kate responded. "Why?"

"I just wondered. Does it matter to you or Mark?"

"No. It just is what it is. Why should it matter?" she
said, looking at her sister intently. "Is this about Jack?"
she asked.

"Maybe," Ruthie said carefully. Then after a few
moments, she gulped and words came gushing out. "I'm
just not sure if he treats me so nice because he likes me
or he thinks I'm just a little girl. He winks at me, but
people wink at little kids because they think they're cute
kids. I just don't know, and I'm not a little girl. I'm
eighteen now! I'm a woman!" She threw the pillow
she'd been holding onto the floor and grabbed another
one and punched it a couple of times. Bug, who had
been lying at the end of the bed, crawled on his belly
over to Ruthie, laid his head on her lap and rolled his
eyes at her. 'What – who is making you sad?' his big
brown eyes questioned. 'Let me at them. I'll stand on
them until they quit.'

"Ruthie, if it bothers you so much, why don't you
just ask him?"

"What, just say – Hey, Jack, do you like me as a woman or are you just being nice to a little girl?"

"Well, that's a start. Maybe you could take the bull by the horns. You just take his hand one Sunday night when we walk them down the road a ways. See how he responds, or you could simply tell him how you feel. Maybe he returns your affections."

"That's you, Kate. You can do that because you're brave. I'm not."

"Come on. Look what you do with Harley. You tease him, make over him. You're not afraid of him."

"Yeah, but I'm not in love with Harley. I just love him. It's different."

"I understand, Ruthie. I truly do. Just have a little talk with Jack. Give it a try."

Ruthie didn't have the chance to talk with Jack because the next morning, Mark pounded on the Hughes door in a panic. The beginnings of autumn were in the air and a chill came into the kitchen with Mark.

"I'm sorry to barge in, Mrs. Hughes, but I need to see Will – and Kate, if that's alright."

"Sit down, Mark. Breakfast is on its way."

"I need to go – quickly," he said. "I'm so sorry."

"No need to go without breakfast," she said in her quiet, matter-of-fact way. "Will and Kate will be here momentarily, so just sit yourself down and drink some coffee."

He could do nothing else but obey Ellen's commands, so he sat and gulped the hot coffee.

Ellen turned back to the stove and moved the sizzling bacon around the frying pan.

"What's wrong, Mark?" she asked, her back still to him.

Mark raked his hand through his hair, his elbow on the table. A small groan escaped his lips.

"It's my children," he said. "The telegram said she's taken them."

"What do you mean, she's taken them?"

"I mean, she went to my parent's house with a sheriff and took them. They tried to stop her, but she had the sheriff there, and they couldn't do anything about it. She took them, that crazy, selfish bitch" he spat angrily, his fists clenched in front of him on the table. Then he heard his own words coming back to him, and his face literally fell. "Oh, my God, I'm so sorry, Mrs. Hughes."

Mark felt a hand on his shoulder and silence filled the room. He stiffened, wondering if he had gone too far with Ellen, and he sat with his forehead in his hand, tears filling the corners of his eyes. He was suddenly so tired that moving on, doing what needed to be done felt impossible. Then he felt her hand on his head. She was quietly stroking back the hair he had mussed with his own hand.

She thought about all of the times she had stroked the heads of her own children; when they were sick, when they had dirt and tear streaked faces. Her hand caressing their messy heads had always calmed them, made them feel better, and she had loved and been grateful for her ability to ease their pain.

"Children are the only people who can truly break your heart, Mark. I understand. What can we do?"

Mark looked up at her standing at his side and the seed of beginning to know this woman filled him.

"You are an amazing woman, Mrs. Hughes. Thank you."

"Drink your coffee," she said to him and then turned toward the loft and the back bedroom, "Kate, Will, come to the kitchen now, please."

Mark explained the reason for his early visit, and both Kate and Will understood his anxiety.

"I need to go. I need to find them," he said.

"Well sure you do. No question." Will agreed to run the smith shop during Mark's absence and offered any other help he might need.

"I should have brought them here before, no matter if they had to live in the shop." He rubbed his face again.

"I just thought they were better off temporarily at my parent's home. Fresh air, a real home – not just a sooty room behind a smith shop."

"Mark, we understand. Just find them, okay?" Kate said. Then, "Why not take Jack with you? He's a lawyer. He can help. You need him."

"I couldn't ask that of him, Kate."

"Well you sure can. He'd do it, too."

A small knock on the door sounded and it opened. Harley walked in.

"Couldn't help but think I might be needed," he said. "Something just wasn't right in my mind."

"Have some coffee, Harley," Ellen said. "Sit down."

Will briefly explained Mark's situation and Harley just nodded. Kate added she thought Mark should ask Jack to go with him, but he was hesitant to ask him, thought it was imposing.

"Of course he would," Harley said. "That's our Mark."

"Well, convince him otherwise," Kate spouted. "That's what you do. Do your stuff."

Harley grinned at her, but his eyes were sad.

"Our Mark doesn't know how to say thank you yet, or please. Thought he was learning, but he's got a ways to go."

"Jack has other things to do than to go gallivanting across the country with me," Mark spit, a bit miffed he was being dissected by Harley right in front of his face.

Harley leaned forward, his arms on the table, and he stared into Mark's eyes.

"Young man," he said. "Let me ask you a question. If a man could help your children, would you turn that man away because you have pride that needs to be kept intact, because you can't say 'please help me'? Would you hurt others for your pride? Is it so much a part of you it comes before your babies?"

Mark groaned. A deep sigh came from his belly. It was partly because Harley was lecturing again, but part of it was because he knew at least some of what he said was right.

"How do you know Jack would even do it?" Mark asked.

"I don't know, but I know Jack Bay, and you will never know if you don't ask," Harley said calmly. "Bend your back, Mark, when the wind blows hard. Then you won't break, and you won't get blown away in a storm."

From her place at the stove, Ellen heard Harley's words and took them to heart. I too have been standing stiff in the wind, she thought. I have been breaking because my back has been too rigid. I'll not do that any more. I'll bend.

"Thank you, Harley," she whispered to herself. "I think you have been an angel sent to us. Thank you."

Kate and Will walked Mark down the road a ways. They talked quietly in the growing dawn and Mark agreed to ask Jack to go with him on his search. Then Will assured him the shop would be well taken care of, and he turned back and left them alone.

"God speed, Mark. Come back to us soon," Will called as he walked away.

When Mark turned to Kate, he folded her in his arms and stood there silently. She felt his breath as deep, raspy groans in his chest. She felt his heart beat against her, and all she could do was to hold him, try to give him strength and love. Finally, she whispered in the folds of his shirt.

"Find them, Mark. Bring them back. They could even stay at our place until you build your house. You know Ma would love the opportunity to mother them. That's who she is – a mother."

"Yes, I understand that about her. She is a nurturer – an amazing, unselfish nurturer. But I'm settled thinking they'll just stay with me at the shop. It's not perfect, but we'll make do."

"I love you, Mark."

"I truly know that, Kate, although for the life of me I don't know why, but I am grateful, and I love you so much."

She watched as he sprinted toward town. His shabby coat flapped in the breeze and the wind tousled his hair.

"He doesn't deserve this," she said to the morning air. "He deserves better." She watched until she could no longer see him and then raced back to the house. She was late getting ready for school. They'd probably burn the place down if she wasn't there to stop them.

Mark went back to the shop, and threw some traveling things into a bag. He was locking the door when Will rode up and tossed the reins of one of his mares over the post. A small buggy was attached.

"It's a bit slower, but both you and Jack will easily fit. The kids can ride in the back when you find them. It will save trains or trying to find a rig when you get there – or if you have to track them down."

Mark cocked his head sideways at Will, then looked down at his boots. 'Think,' he said to himself. 'Just say thank you and take the reins.' So he did.

Will nodded and smiled. "Harley would be proud. Be safe," he said, and went into the shop to start his day.

CHAPTER TEN

They were gone for many days. Fall dropped its chill into the air, and the nights grew white frost on the grass. Jack, of course, had agreed to make the trip with Mark. In fact, he demanded, had even seemed eager to do it. He had been told a lot about Lorraine long ago when he'd been hired to track her after the payroll theft, and he'd always felt badly about his lack of success. He didn't like what he'd heard about her, and his own past had mixed with Mark's bad luck and circumstances -- with a bad woman. He wanted to be a part of making it right.

Their ride was comfortable, if bumpy and cold. Talk was sporadic at first, and then both men found some ease with each other and an empathetic ear.

"I was such a stupid fool," Mark said. "I can't imagine, now, how I found her so sweet, how I could have loved her."

He gripped the reins hard in his hands, and the mare looked back at him, confused by the tight feel of the reins pulling against her. He took a harsh breath and sputtered, "I thought she was an injured young woman. What a fool. She was a user and abuser. I just didn't know it until too late." He paused and silence filled the air as daylight gave way to dusk.

Jack was deep in his own thought. The similarities were strong, and his own pain found its way back into his chest. He'd thought he had beaten it, but it was back. He'd run from it, but it had chased him all the way to Hersey, Michigan. He slapped at his leg, trying to drive it away, but it was still there.

"You're gonna bruise yourself," Mark said. "Want to talk about it?"

"Doesn't do any good," Jack said. "It doesn't go away."

"Did you ever try? Talking, I mean."

"Nope. Not much for talking about myself."

"That's your choice," Mark said. "Just know that I can hear."

Jack turned his head from side to side and then around like he was working kinks out of his neck. The night grew darker and quiet enfolded them. Mark tried to hum one of the hymns they had sung on the porch just a few weeks past, but it seemed ages ago he'd felt any kind of peace. Finally Jack blurted out pieces of his own story, and Mark filled in the missing parts.

"I was married once, too," Jack said. "She didn't want children right then, and I did, but that didn't matter for awhile."

Mark considered what he'd heard and knew there was much more Jack hadn't said. He mulled over the possibilities then just asked. "What happened?"

"I found her in bed with my brother. In our bed."

"Damn, that's hard to take," Mark told him, more shocked than he wanted to seem at Jack's words, but he was familiar with flighty woman, knew their infidelities, but your own brother? Trees became dark silhouettes against the sky as the moon rose, and several passed by in the long minutes of silence until Jack took a deep breath and continued.

"I had to leave – couldn't look at her again – Brian either or I would have killed him.

Mark let Jack's words roam his brain and settle in. His hands let the reins go slack and the horse slowed but kept moving down the road, heading them steadily on toward Marne and his own family.

Finally, Mark spoke. "You're sure – about what you saw?"

"No doubt," he said, shaking his head, his words clipped and harsh. "My little brother . . . the one I looked out for like he was my own kid. That's the hell of it," he added more softly.

Jack looked at the field they were passing. Short stalks of corn glowed in the light of the moon. He heard the rustle of night critters move through the stalks and a coyote bay at the moon. He finally heard Mark's voice, low and gravelly next to him.

"A real wrong was done to you," Mark said. "I don't know that you ever really get over it."

Jack waved his hand, as if to say 'Never mind. It is what it is,' and Mark continued. "Maybe you just learn how to live with it until the hurt doesn't infect every part of your life . . . until you can smile around it, and it feels alright."

They talked on into the night and rode in silence, deep in their own thoughts, and each learned about the man next to him.

The next morning, they neared the outskirts of Marne. Mark explained his parents had a small home close to town, but not actually in it.

"It's nice," he said. "Lots of places to explore in the woods near the house. Lots of other kids nearby. I had a good life with great parents. My kids deserve the kind of life I had."

"Well, that's why we're here," Jack said matter-of-factly. "You're going to give them that."

His parents met them on the front porch. Both looked drained and fearful, and Mark saw they had aged years in the months since he had last seen them, when he had visited his children after prison, left to find work, and they had all been full of hope. The children had been there for the five years he'd been incarcerated.

It seemed Lorraine was comfortable letting them shoulder the responsibility for them while he was gone. She had only taken them when she learned Mark was out and could care for them himself.

His mother was a small woman, coming only to her husband's shoulders. White hair framed her face, and lines of sorrow etched her once creamy skin. She stood on tiptoes to hug Mark, and even then, he had to stoop for her to reach.

"Mom," he said after returning her embrace. "I'd like you to meet a friend of mine, Jack Bay. Jack, this is my beautiful mother."

Jack reached out a hand to shake hers, but she pushed it aside and reached up to circle his neck with a hug.

"A friend of my boy's has to be hugged," she said. "It's very nice to meet you. I wish it was for better reasons. This is my husband, Mr. Ramey."

Mark's father was tall, over six feet and with a massive shock of wavy, graying hair. His shoulders were wide and tapered to narrow hips. Jack saw an older Mark standing in front of him. His hand was strong in Jack's, but the set of his shoulders and his cloudy eyes spoke of grief.

"Come on in the house," he said, running a hand through his thick hair and over his drawn face. Again Jack saw Mark. He had seen him repeat that same mannerism so many times when he was troubled.

"We can't stay but a few minutes," Mark said quickly. "We just need to know a few particulars about them taking Jamie and Flossie."

"In good time, Son. Coffee first and a brief sit," his father commanded kindly. Jack saw uncomplicated, easy strength in the aging man, and a yearning to see his own father crept out from under the heavy, inside rock where he had buried it with all the rest of the memories that had brought him so much torment.

Mark's mother brought coffee and apple pie to the table and served them silently. Small wet marks glistened in the creases of her cheeks.

"It's going to be okay, Mom. We'll find them," Mark said seeing her tears and struggle for composure.

"Yes," she whispered, unable to speak further without releasing the sobs that had built into a malignant growth in her chest and throat.

The older man folded his arms on the table, leaned forward intently, and cleared his own throat. "See the sheriff in Grand Rapids," he said gruffly, "the downtown office. That was the name on the paper. She had to get help from there because no Marne sheriff would have done what she wanted. A Marne officer would have found a way out of it."

"What did the paper say?" Mark asked.

"It gave her custody of the children due to abandonment and the fact that you, their father, had a prison record. It said something about you being an unfit parent, unfit to be a guardian of children."

Mark ran a hand through his hair, then down over his face. His father repeated the movement. Their thick waves overlapped, crisscrossing and flopping in curls down over their foreheads and ears. They looked like two boys would after rising from a night of restless dreams when they slayed dragons; weary, sorrowful, but still strong.

Shaking his head at his fancifulness, Jack broke the silence. "Do you have a copy of the papers, Mr. Ramey?" he asked firmly. "By law, they should have left a copy with you."

"We do, and it's Mark," he said, "not Mr. Ramey."

Jack smiled, thinking it appropriate they would have the same names, they were so alike.

"Mark it is then. Is it big Mark and little Mark?" he teased quietly, wanting to break the gloom angst and worry had engendered. "Or is it Mark and Markie? I was Jackie for a long time. So I figure . . ."

"Don't go there, Jack," Mark interrupted, but he was looking affectionately at his mother. "I had to grow six feet tall and work too hard to break the hold of that moniker, and there's only one person I allow that privilege."

His mother circled her arms around his neck, looking diminutive next to him. Her head was not far above his even though he was sitting and she was standing. She kissed the top of his head, mussed his already ruffled hair, and smiled. "You will always be my Markie – no matter how old and big you get. I earned the right to name you by carting you around inside me for nine months and for another twelve after that until you learned to walk."

She was grateful for Jack's little joke. It had pushed the building sob back down into her chest where she could control it. It had stemmed the flow of embarrassing tears finding paths down her cheeks. She couldn't do anything to help her son now the children had been taken, but she was determined not to make it worse. She would be strong for him as mothers should.

The senior Mark left the table and returned with a slim bundle of papers. "Here you are, Son . . . Markie," he said, eyes showing a small glint of their old sparkle.

"I said one person, Dad, and it wasn't you."

Mark rose to take the papers, and his father wrapped one arm around his son's shoulder, alternately squeezing and pounding his back. "Find your babies, son. I know you can do it."

Jack went to the door, shook hands with Mark's father and lifted his mother off the ground in a bear hug. "Thank you for the coffee and great pie, Mrs. Ramey."

"Mom," she said, then reached up and over to pat her son's face and left the room.

They were both silent in the buggy. Jack read the papers Mark had handed him, and then poked Mark in the arm. "Her address is here. We should start there first."

"Damn, yes. I should have thought to look."

They found Lorraine in a shabby room in an even shabbier neighborhood. After pounding on the door several times, a disheveled woman appeared. A satin robe hung open over a lace chemise which did little to cover her breasts. Her black hair hung loosely in ringlets brushing her shoulders. She tossed her head and stood in the open doorway, smiling.

"Well, look who is here," she cooed, her black eyes darting back and forth from Mark to Jack, then she held out her hand to Jack. "I don't believe I know you."

"I believe I know you, Ma'am, but you're right, we haven't met."

Lorraine was startled by his words, but quickly recovered and invited them in, waved the half empty glass she held in her hand, and asked if they would like a drink.

"So good to see you," she chirped to Mark. "It's been such a long time." Her words slurred slightly, but she kept on talking, filling the small space with babble. Jack saw the anger on Mark's face; his clenched hands, and quickly led Lorraine to a ragged, stuffed chair. She sat, flipped her curls back with a toss of her head, and posed for Jack, crossing her legs and running her free hand over a thigh, exposed when the robe fell away.

Mark was left standing immobile, unable to move without fear of throwing her against the wall or putting his hands around her neck and squeezing until she produced his children. Jack sat in the only other chair, opposite Lorraine. He silently surveyed the squalid room. A cluttered counter ran halfway down the wall next to the door and held a hot plate, several empty bottles, and a small sink filled with dirty dishes. At the end was a miniature icebox. The opposite wall was filled with an unmade bed. A third wall was covered with clothes hanging haphazardly on metal hooks. The only space left was where they sat in the two grubby chairs. Jack felt the broken springs reaching through the threadbare fabric when he sat.

He looked silently at Lorraine and calmly waited for her to finish fawning and babbling, then explained who he was, a lawyer, and he and Mark were there to take the children back to Hersey with them, to provide them with a good home.

Lorraine's response was a harsh, guttural laugh that chilled him. "You can't," she said, glaring at Mark who still stood just inside the door. "They are mine to do with as I choose. I have full custody – by court order. He . . ." she said thrusting her chin at Mark "has no say about them."

"Where are they, Lorraine?" Mark growled from the doorway. "They certainly aren't here in this one-room hovel!"

Lorraine leaned back in her chair, exposing more breast and leg, a wicked grin growing from her smeared, red lips. She tilted her head back, drained her glass, and then held it out to Jack.

"Fix me another drink, Mr. Lawyer. Then I might talk to you." She slowly turned her head toward Mark, her grin widening. "Mr. Ramey appears to be quite unreasonably surly."

Not knowing what else to do, Jack fixed the drink. "We need to see the children, Mrs. Ramey."

"Lorraine," she whispered coyly. "But, of course, they're not here."

"Then, we need to know where they are, and we need to see them. No court would make it impossible for a father to see his children. I will see to that," he said with deliberate, calm intensity.

The quiet battle continued for an hour, she as determined to punish Mark as Jack was to help him. But she became more intoxicated as the minutes passed and was alternately flirtatious and belligerent as Jack continued to refill her glass from the decanter he'd found on the cluttered shelf. He worked to control his disgust, contain his fury in order to get what Mark and his children needed, but it galled him to even pretend to listen to her. At times, he was aware an angry fire lit his dark eyes, and he was sure in those moments he would fail his friend, throw her booze in her face and walk out. But he didn't. He saw in her face she believed she had ensnared him by her female charms, and he let her think so.

In the end, they left after Jack had purchased her signature on a prepared divorce decree for a mere fifty dollars – a hell of a good deal for Mark's freedom from her – but no knowledge of where Jamie was living beyond some orphanage near Saginaw. She claimed not to know where Flossie was living – some fostor home, somewhere.

Mark never entered the room. He remained rooted to the floor at his spot just inside the door, too afraid of what he might do to her, and hating her with a force he would not have believed possible. It engulfed him. Red sparked in front of his eyes, nausea built in his throat until he thought he might lose his stomach. He watched her preen in front of Jack and knew only disgust – for her and for himself because he had once loved and lusted after the body she was deliberately exposing to Jack – as she would for any man who could give her what she wanted at the moment, or just for the fun of watching their reactions.

Somewhere deep within his embattled mind, he watched Jack who, from Mark's position at the door, appeared unaffected by Lorraine's flesh and behavior. He continued to maneuver her to give up what they needed. That he didn't entirely succeed was only due to her wickedness, her need to control men. Even through his anger, Mark could admire Jack's calm, his ability to maintain distance.

When they finally left, the silence was broken only by the sound of their boots on the broken sidewalk. Both men were deep in thought, reliving the nightmare of

Lorraine and all her kind. Grief, anger and shame mixed in their minds and formed a dark sludge from which they fought to surface, to be free of.

When they were back in the buggy, Mark picked up the reins and Jack finally spoke.

"Grand Rapids Court House, 24th street. We're going to file your divorce papers and for a retrial to overturn the custody decision."

"Do you think we can win – custody, I mean?"

Jack let out a tired sigh. "That will most likely take some time and a smart fight, but you will at least be free of that woman while we're in battle."

They found the courthouse, filed the papers, and tried everything they could to learn the whereabouts of Flossie. A stout man with double chins kept nodding his head in understanding of their plight, but determinedly claimed he was unable to help. Mark begged, showed old pictures of them he kept in his wallet, talked about Jamie's dark eyes and Flossie's blue fire-lit ones. He asked if the man had children of his own, tried to work on his paternal senses, but nothing would move him to reveal information the law said was private. The clerk's jowls wagged beneath his double chin as he shook his head again and again.

"No. I'm sorry," he whimpered, looking up at the two taller men. Then, feeling the sting and shame of his whimper, he tried to pull himself up, straighten his backbone, "You have no rights here. Your wife has sole custody, and, unfortunately, you have none."

Admitting their defeat at the courthouse, they headed toward Saginaw more determined than ever to find Jamie.

After days of searching the area surrounding Saginaw, and then the city proper, they finally tracked down Jamie. They only succeeded due to the kindness of a secretary at one of the orphanages near the outskirts of town. Apparently, the world of orphan care-givers was small, and she had heard of the Ramey children and their deposit at Smithton's. She knew Jamie was there, but not where Flossie had been sent.

Smithton's Orphanage was in the middle of downtown Saginaw. It was a large, three story, red brick building. The fence around it and the yard took up the entire city block. They saw young children in the yard, playing on the swings and slides near the side door of the building. Older ones stood in groups further off, at the end of the play area. Mark searched the faces of the older children, looking for Jamie's face in the groups. He tried to peer under the blonde curls to see if one might be Flossie even though they'd been told she was not there. Who knew what had been lied about?

They ran around to the other side of the fenced yard to get a better look at the boys and stood with their hands gripping the fence like war prisoners inside a compound instead of outsiders looking in. 'Same thing,' Mark thought. 'I'm a prisoner out here if they are on the other side of the fence and kept separated from me.'

Their faces pressed into the wires to get the best view as they searched, both silent, both intent with hope and need. Then Jack felt a hand claw at his arm.

"It's him. It's him, it's Jamie," Mark whispered hoarsely.

The yard butted up to a growth of trees and vines covered the fence at the end of the play area. Branches hung out over the yard and blended with small trees haphazardly scattered inside the barricade. They shaded those who loitered there and provided some privacy for boys who had no solitude in the orphanage building. Mark could understand why they would hang about at the woodsy end of the yard.

"There," he said, pointing to a slender, dark haired boy who was kicking at the base of a small oak and looking intently at a taller, bulky boy. "That's him; that's my son." Mark took off in a sprint, around the corner. He bent low to avoid the branches. Thorns tore at his pants, but he didn't feel them. Jack followed more slowly. If it really was Jamie, he wanted his friend to have a minute alone with his son.

"Jamie," he heard Mark call. "It's me. It's your dad."

For a few moments, it seemed Jamie was ignoring Mark. He turned his head, but no look of recognition was evident on his face, no welcoming smile.

"Son," Mark cried. "Please come nearer the fence."

Jamie suddenly smiled, and Mark's return beam lit his face. Tears made rivers of the dust on his cheeks, but his eyes leaped with joy. His fingers gripped the wires of the fence, and Jamie put his own over his father's. Jack stood back a few paces, watched and wondered how fatherhood could evoke such depths of feeling. He knew what brotherhood meant; he knew the love of a son for his parents, knew love for a woman, but he could not fathom the love of a father for his children. He could see it, though, and he knew it was uncharted territory for all who had not fathered or mothered.

"If hearts can really break," he murmured, "mine is now."

Jack vowed he would get Mark's children back – if it took forever.

"Dad, I knew you would come," Jamie said, a wide grin spreading across his face.

He was dancing up and down on his toes as he did when he was excited about something as a toddler. He gripped the wires of the fence and shook it back and forth, happiness flowing from his face. "I knew it! Go tell them you're here to get me and let's go."

Mark tried hard to hang onto his smile; not wanting to destroy his son's happiness, but Jamie could see anger and despair fill his father's eyes. "What's wrong?" he said standing back a bit.

Mark told his son what had been done with custody, how he no longer had any rights to his children, and begged him to understand and be strong until the mistake could be fixed.

"I will come get you, Jamie; you and Flossie, but it's going to take some time. It will have to go through the court system, and that might take awhile." He tried out the smile again, trying to show confidence, but the physical pain squeezing his heart made it hard to maintain. "I'll push them to hurry, Son. I'll push really hard."

"But you will do it, won't you? You'll come back?" Jamie asked, looking like he had as a very little boy when his hamster had died and he had gone to his father to fix it, make it live again. He had loved that little rodent. It rode around on his shoulder so much of the time, snuggled safely into the crook of his neck, Jamie would frequently forget it was there. It tended to startle some people who were afraid of anything even remotely rodent-like. But Jamie had loved him – hugged him, so much so his pet had died.

"Wake him up, Dad. You can do it," he'd begged. "I know you can do it!"

The confidence Jamie had had in him shamed Mark. 'I should have been able to at least keep my children safe,' he thought. 'I should have been able to do that.'

"We will be together again, Son; you, Flossie and me. I will never, ever give up. Will you remember that?"

Jamie, nodded. His chin tilted up, and he made a valid effort to straighten his shoulders as he had seen his dad do when times were troubled.

"I will remember," he said as bravely as his husky voice would allow. "I will think of us together every day. Maybe that will make it happen."

Mark nodded approval at his man-child. "I'm going in now to talk with the headmaster of the school. Perhaps he will listen to some sense, but I have to honest with you son, I don't believe he will. Jamie, if I can't get you out of here right away, I want you to know I will be back to see you as often as I can until the courts come to their senses. I have a lot to tell you, and I love you." Mark started to turn away, and then looked back at Jamie. "Do you know where your sister is?"

Distress crawled over his face, and he just shook his head then looked down at his feet. "I couldn't make them keep us together," he groaned quietly.

"It's going to be alright, Son. And you couldn't do anything about it. It's not your fault. I'll find her."

Jamie nodded, still holding back the tears threatening to demean his fragile manhood.

Mark waved an arm to Jack who had walked to the sidewalk and was waiting, giving them some privacy, and they headed into the building to face the headmaster.

"He's a good looking boy," Jack said quietly, not knowing how to ease his friend's obvious anguish.

Mark nodded and looked back toward the group of boys he had left at the fence.

"Damn her!" he exploded. "What the hell kind of woman would throw away her children?"

"The kind that sees them as personal, disposable property when they fail to suit her needs," Jack responded, as angry as Mark was about what he knew and had just witnessed. "Lorraine's a spoiled child, Mark, and sees people, no matter who they are, as a means to her own ends."

"And how can a judge just take away a man's children? Couldn't he see what kind of person she is? Have I no rights here?"

Jack put a hand on Mark's shoulder and turned him, stopping their progress toward the orphanage building.

"It's changing, Mark, but too slow. The courts still view mothers as the nurturers of their children. They birth them, nurse them, and supposedly teach them to be ethical, moral citizens. When confronted with a choice between mothers and fathers, judges still favor the maternal parent, not the father. It's a long standing tradition that is hard to break – even when the mother is a bad one."

Mark ran a shaking hand over his face, looked back at the boys again, and then turned to face Jack.

"Are you trying to tell me not to hope?" he asked. "Are you saying give up on my kids?"

"Nope, I'm just preparing you for a hard fight." Silence fell on them for long moments. It cocooned and separated them from the noisy chatter of the orphanage children. The two men stared at each other; years of battling hurt streaked their faces and streamed from their eyes. "I've seen enough to want to get into this battle myself," Jack said hoarsely, and turned toward the orphanage door.

The headmaster turned out to be a headmistress, a tall, slender woman with short, brown hair showing only a few threads of silver at the temples. She stood and walked quickly around her massive mahogany desk to greet them when the secretary led them in. Her handshake was as firm as a man's. Her back was ramrod straight – an 'I will tolerate no nonsense' kind of stance.

Mark began to explain the circumstances surrounding and leading up to why his son was in an orphanage and his daughter in some strange home for foster children until the headmistress, Miss Elder, held up her hand to silence his words as if he was a school boy who was inappropriately talking in class.

"Why this has occurred is not a concern of mine," she bluntly stated. "The custodial parent has seen fit to place Jamie here, and the courts have given her that right."

"But don't you see that this is not the place for him? That he should be with people who will love and care for him?"

"I understand your plight, Mr. Ramey, but that does not alter those facts. He is here because his mother could not properly care for him – perhaps due to the fact that she did not have the support of a proper husband," she said, looking down at Mark's frayed coat and the blackened creases in his hands where smith shop soot stubbornly remained no matter how much washing. "She assigned that care to us, and that is what we will do."

Mark's frustration grew; anger at his ineffective attempts flushed his neck and waves of heat crept down his spine. He wanted to pound his fist against the wall, at something, anything! Jack stepped forward, assumed his lawyer voice and asked to speak for Mr. Ramey.

Miss Elder nodded imperially, giving him permission to speak as if he was one of her orphans, and Jack laid out the plan to regain custody. He explained papers had already been filed, and said they were prepared to care for the children between now and the new trial. "Surely you can see that would be best for the children," he said confidently. "And isn't the whole business of family law about taking care of children?"

"What might be best is not in question here, Mr. Bay. The law is the obvious point. I have a signed document from Mrs. Ramey assigning responsibility for her children to Smithton's Orphanage. As a lawyer," she said stiffly, dismissing his request as ridiculous, "you must certainly appreciate the rules of law."

"Her children! Miss Elder," Mark shouted, "they are my children, more than they ever were, or will be, hers! She didn't want them; she gave them away! Can't you see beyond your pointed nose? Don't you care about the children at all? For God's sake, you are mistress of an orphanage. You're supposed to care about the welfare of your charges!" Mark had moved nearer to her until he was staring into her eyes, inches from her sharp nose.

"You are dismissed, Mr. Ramey, until you bring a court document that changes custody. Mr. Bay, control your client." She turned her back to them, emphasizing their dismissal, and returned to her seat behind the desk. She picked up a pen and began writing, ignoring Mark and Jack who were still in the room.

Jack took Mark's arm and turned him toward the door, but Mark pulled away and walked to her desk. Placing his hands on it, he leaned in to force her attention.

"Where is my daughter?" he said, each word a short, quiet burst of anger, a shot that pierced the room.

"I must at least have the right to know where she has been dumped."

The headmistress slowly looked up, a small satisfied look on her face. "No, Mr. Ramey, you do not."

The ride back to Hersey was long. A deep chill had claimed the growing dusk, and they sunk deeper into their jackets and personal thoughts. The rhythmic sound of hooves hitting packed dirt resounded in the surrounding quiet. Overhead, a flock of geese flew in perfect formation heading southward, the leader in control and the rest following contentedly. An occasional honk broke the silence.

They took a back way toward home, an eastward route, tree lined and with little traffic. The moon began to rise ahead of them even though there was still a pinch of daylight left. It loomed large at the end of the road and formed shadows in their path from the overhead branches. Intermittent noises in the brush whispered night critters were scurrying about, setting forth on their nightly quest for sustenance. All in nature was as it should be.

A bat darted across the road, its radar leading, guiding it where it needed to go. Mark looked up and tried to watch the bat as it flew erratically through the trees. It was so quick, so accurate in flight. Then it was gone, waiting in some tree for its special senses to indicate a new chase. He envied the bat its radar, the thing that told him where to go and when to go there. The bat would never be lost, without direction. The bat would know exactly what to do and how to do it. Mark had never felt so incompetent, so ineffectual, and so useless.

After watching Mark drag his hands over his face for about the sixth time, Jack reached back over the seat and fumbled around in his satchel. He grabbed the flask he always carried, and shoved it in Mark's face.

"I think it's time to get drunk," he said.

Mark looked up at his friend through fingers still covering his eyes, then sat up, grasped the flask and took a long swig. He returned the flask and sat up straighter, leaning against the cushioned leather seat.

"Here's to a good drunk," Jack said, and took a good swallow and sent it back.

"Here's to a good woman," Mark responded, and drank again.

"Here's to getting the best of a bad woman," Jack countered, and tilted the flask once more. "To hell with evil women!"

"Here's to a good whore, a thousand times better than a bad woman. I've known whores who are good women!" Mark's words slurred a bit, but his brain knew exactly what he was saying and what he meant. "I love a good whore," he continued. "She comforts a man and knows her business."

Back and forth the flask went, each drink needing a toast to precede it. When Mark tilted it back and the last of the whiskey drained into his mouth, he looked at the flask like it had betrayed him. He lifted it high into the air in front of Jack's face.

"I'm not drunk yet," he said matter-of-factly. "What now?"

"There's more where that came from," Jack said reaching behind the seat once more and producing another flask.

Mark almost giggled. "Good man," he shouted. "You're the best friend a man could have."

He unscrewed the top, lifted the flask to his lips, and then stopped. "I forgot, have to have a toast." He thought a minute, then seeing the horses in front of him, said "Here's to a good horse – and a big, mangy, faithful dog."

Jack laughed more than the toast should have called for and slapped Mark's back.

"You are drunk," he said, "if a horse and a dog are the best you can wish for. Give me that bottle. I'll tell you a good toast." He raised the flask again. The moon glittered off its silver metal. They both stared at the flask like it was a bottle of prophecy and had powers beyond mortal expectations.

"This is a good one. Here's to your Kate, a truly good woman. Oh, and I guess a good horse is not such a stupid wish because it's gonna take a good horse to get us home."

"I'm not drunk, yet," he said matter-of-factly, not offended Jack had said so. "But I intend to be." He looked slyly at Jack and raised the flask of prophecy toward the moon.

"Here's to Kate's sister, the other beautiful good Hughes woman. Besides Mrs. Hughes, I mean. She's good, too, but older, you know what I mean?" Mark stumbled around what he was trying to say, and Jack listened like his friend was actually making sense. He laughed, nodded, doubled over and snickered like a school boy.

Jack held out his hand, waiting for the flask to return. "I'm not drunk yet either. Not yet. Not yet, I'm not. Give me another swig. Here's to knowing what you want and knowing how to get it."

"Here, here," Mark responded. "I'm gonna be a bat."

Jack looked at Mark, leaning sideways to get a full view and almost tumbled out of the buggy. Mark grabbed Jack's coat and dragged him back in. The buggy swayed as weight shifted, and the horses automatically trotted to the middle of the road, innately knowing it was up to them to keep them all out of the deep ditch at the side.

"Almost lost you to the wolves, friend. Good horses, good girls," Mark cooed. "See? I made a first-rate toast. Now stay in the buggy."

"You're gonna be a bat?" Jack questioned, turning sideways in his seat to stare at Mark instead of leaning out.

"Yep, gonna be a bat, have radar that points the way, keeps me from bumping into things . . . like bad women."

"Oh, I see. Good idea. I could benefit from being a bat."

By the time the second flask was emptied, both men found the need to sleep. Jack, who had control of the reins by that time, pulled off the road and led the horses to the shelter of a small thicket, adequate providing a cold, autumn snow did not occur. They unhitched the horses, tied them to a branch and wiped them down, then collected dead scrub wood and brought it under a willow with branches that dipped to the ground and made a circle around them.

The small fire warmed them. Between the warmth and the whisky, the need for sleep was overpowering. Mark pulled some blankets out of the bucket behind the buggy seat and spread them on the ground under the willow with the fire between them. They lay with their heads on pillows made of their jackets and watched stars filtering through the willow leaves. The leaves would be falling soon, as the air was filled with assurance of Michigan winter about to come.

They drove the horses straight into the barn when they got to the Hughes' place. Night was just beginning to settle in for keeps, but the moon had either decided not to rise, or it was covered by clouds that threatened early snow. Mark was lighting the lantern, and Jack had just begun to unhitch the mares when Kate came flying into the room and leaped at Mark, almost tumbling him to the floor in a bear hug.

"You're back!" she cried. "I'm so glad! I'm so . . . so glad!"

"Somehow, I don't think you needed to say that," Jack said, leaning back against the buggy and grinning. "That, my dear, is pretty obvious."

Bug had followed and now stood with his paws on Kate's shoulders staring at Mark's face just inches from his wet nose. Kate ignored him; he was always so close to her she would only notice if he wasn't there, but Mark looked into Bug's eyes and knew his own presence was still only tolerated.

"Hi, teacher lady," he said, nuzzling Kate's cheek then added, "Hi, Bug, nice to see you, too."

Bug got down then, reassured his glare had done the job, and Mark was not a threat to his Kate. He strolled over to Jack, sat on his shoe and leaned against his leg. Jack absently stroked Bug's head and thought how good it was to be back. Much was right in this world of the Hughes family, right down to the huge, hairy dog now sitting on his right foot.

Will came in with a gust of cold wind and a big smile. Between solid embraces of homecoming and words of welcome for both men, sore hearts began the process of mending. Late autumn's chill had seeped into their bones during the ride home, but it was melting with back slaps and hugs, grins and care. Soon, Harley added his voice to the melee as he entered through the door that led to his small room off the stall area of the barn. Curls stuck out all over his head, and he rubbed his eyes trying to wipe away sleep. He had managed to pull a pair of trousers over his long johns, but no shirt.

"Sorry for the state of undress, Miss Kate," he said sleepily, "but I could not miss the merry homecoming. Welcome home my sons."

"Sons? We're your sons now?" Mark quizzed playfully. Jack just leaned back against the buggy wheel again and grinned.

"Of course," Harley said, trying to puff up his chest, but only succeeding in allowing his trousers to slide down because he had not stopped to button them or pull up the suspenders hanging down his legs - skinny legs, given the round, little belly that protruded over his trousers. He grabbed the belt loops and held them in place while he continued. "While you may not be of my seed, you are the sons of my soul because I see the child in you, the unfinished man in you; the promise of what you may become given the proper direction, the . . ."

Mark's groan interrupted the flow of Harley's words. He looked around the room, saw laughter bubbling in three other sets of eyes and grinned back.

"Okay, I'll save that bit of wisdom for later. Are we gonna put these poor horses up and celebrate with a nip of Will's famous nectar, or are you all just gonna laugh at poor, old Harley?"

"Who's laughing at you, Harley? I'll take 'em out for you!" Ruthie said from the door of the barn. Ruthie had obviously taken the time to brush out her long auburn curls and tie them back at the nape of her neck in a black velvet ribbon. She looked beautiful, radiant. Her cheeks glowed pink in the lantern light, and excitement poured from her eyes. She looked around the room, stopping briefly at each face; then lingering on Jack's.

"Welcome home," she said quietly.

"Thank you for the defense," Harley said, "as it appears, my dear woman-child, you are the only one to appreciate my presence, my wisdom – as odd as I find that to be. And you appear as a vision in the night wilderness. Doesn't she, Jack?"

"Yes, Harley," Jack answered, a bit uncomfortable Harley had focused on him and shifting his feet so Bug had to move from his seat on Jack's boot. "She is a vision."

Bug looked up at him as if to ask why he was forced to sit on the barn floor with the animals, but Jack didn't notice. Ruthie's cheeks flushed even more than when she pinched them just outside the door to give them color. She had heard pinching was what you did if you wanted to look beautiful. Now she regretted she had done so, as she was sure her face was the color of a vivid red sunset. Well, she thought, 'red sun at night is a sailor's delight,' and she wondered if Jack had ever been a sailor.

Will brought out his jug and passed it around. They toasted to good health, good friends, and family. Will deliberately passed the jug swiftly for a second toast.

"To the future and good things in it," he said quietly but firmly. A nod from both Mark and Jack said thank you for not asking questions.

"What about us?" Kate demanded, her hands planted firmly on her hips and glaring at the men in the group one by one. "Are the Hughes ladies not part of this celebration?"

"Aw, Kate," Mark said slowly, not wanting her left out but thinking the whiskey too raw for her taste. "The brew is good, but a bit on the harsh side."

"Kate's a big girl, Mark. If she wants a swig, pass her the jug," Will countered.

Kate took the jug from Mark, slanted it over the back of her hand and wrist like she had seen the men do, and tilted it up. It poured more quickly into her mouth than she expected and drizzled down her chin and onto her dress. She swallowed quickly, gulping rather than sipping as she had intended. It burned her tongue, then her throat and all the way down to her stomach. She coughed, sputtered and choked. Tears filled her eyes and streamed down her cheeks. She bent over at the waist trying to get her breath and succeeded in getting somewhat in control, so she just stayed there for a few moments. 'I've embarrassed myself again,' she thought. 'Damn!' Then, 'damn, did I do that out loud again?' It seemed to Kate she stayed bent over for several days until she could face them without tears, then she stood erect and proudly passed the jug to Ruthie.

"Thank you," she said firmly to her father. "That was tasty." She felt the warmth invade her body and tingled with the effect. Her brain was mellow and happy. "Good stuff," she said quietly.

Ruthie held the jug gingerly a foot away from her chest and stared at her sister. She wanted so much to be like Kate – not afraid of anything, but she was. This was whiskey, and she saw what it had done to Kate. Slowly she passed the jug over the back of her hand and tilted it. Head held high, she tipped it slowly to her lips. The whiskey trickled in, just a little bit, and Ruthie held it in her mouth before swallowing, getting used to the burn of the raw liquid. She swirled it around in her mouth, then slowly swallowed and handed the jug back to Jack. Looking him squarely in the eyes, she said, "Nice, thank you."

Her eyes were bright and her cheeks even more flushed, but that appeared to be the only effect. Her dignity remained intact, and the admiration in Jack's eyes was worth the struggle not to choke. Harley, of course, broke the silence.

"Ruthie, my girl, you are my whiskey queen. I've not seen a man do better, not even a giant, brute of a man. And you a mere slip of a dainty, little woman. I'd drink to that if Jack would pass the jug over."

Laughter once again filled the barn, and Jack raised the jug before passing it over to Harley, "To the whiskey queen and her strength."

They passed it again, and Kate and Ruthie merely put their lips to the rim of the jug mouth, tasting, but not really drinking. They were a part of the celebration, though, and both thought the whiskey drink had been worth it.

When celebration of their homecoming had died down, Mark told them about their trip, leaving out the details and giving them just the particulars of the situation. Jack filled in when it came to the future and what would need to be done to regain custody of Mark's children.

Ellen joined them and after hugging Jack, then Mark, she walked slowly by her daughters, sniffing the air. First Kate, then Ruthie and then back to Kate. She bent to her daughter's chest, sniffed again, and then looked her squarely in the face.

"I smell whiskey," she stated matter-of-factly.

"Yes, you do. Would you like some?"

"I certainly would not," Ellen bristled. "No God-fearing woman would."

After only a few moments of awkward silence, Harley came to the rescue.

"Miss Ellen, I regard you right up there with the saints and you know that, but I'm thinking if a woman feared God, she would need all the whiskey she could get her hands on. That's a powerful fear to deal with, but that's neither here nor there. This here passing of the jug is a kind of communion of friends and your wonderful daughters are part of this community of friends."

Harley heard Mark groan, knew it was because he thought Harley had begun another tirade, but he kept on. "I would take it as an honor if you would sip of the jug of friendship celebration with me Miss Ellen," and he handed her the jug.

Ellen didn't know what to do except take the jug. For some reason, she could not disappoint Harley. She held the jug like it was a poisonous snake, her arms outstretched, the jug dangling from her fingers as if it burned, but she couldn't drop it.

"To friends," Harley encouraged, "to friends, to the future, and to God-loving women."

Ellen grasped the jug with both hands, brought it closer, and looked into it as if fire would shoot from its open mouth. She sniffed, coughed just a little, and sniffed again. Deathly quiet filled the room. All eyes were on Ellen and every breath was held. If she had waited any longer, they would all have turned blue from lack of oxygen. She tilted the jug and sipped. Licked her lips, nodded, and sipped again, then handed the jug to her husband.

"So that's moonshine," she said. "It might be good with some wild raspberries in it, you know, left to soak for awhile with a little sugar added."

Will slapped his leg and roared with laughter. "You are the most impressive woman on earth, Ellen. No one can hold a candle to you, and here's to you," he said, then tipped the jug and promptly kissed her smack on the mouth, the whiskey taste still on both their lips.

All eyes were wide, shocked more than surprised and none more so than Kate and Ruthie. Never had they seen their mother take even the smallest sip of anything with alcohol in it. What was happening? What was changing her? They saw their father's joy, the public kiss, saw their mother bending to the winds of life, and recognized something was different. There was even a satisfied smirk on Ellen's face, and her eyes sparkled. That, along with the slight flush on her cheeks, made her look like a girl again.

Kate was the first to catch her breath and find her tongue. "Wow, Ma! I think you've been sneaking in here and sipping for years. That stuff just about killed me!"

"Why, I never . . . and I don't know what the big deal is. It doesn't go down very well, though," Ellen answered.

Mark and Jack were nodding with knowing looks teasing in their eyes.

"I always knew you were the tough one of this family. Here's proof," Mark said. "I toast to you, Mrs. Hughes."

"Maybe Kate and I can pick some raspberries next season, and you can make your own batch," Ruthie offered.

"Sure I'll help, and now the cat's out of the bag, mother, you won't have to sneak out to the barn for your nip," Kate added, laughter bubbling through the words.

Harley was unaccustomedly quiet, but a smile stretched across his face, until his eyes were almost closed. He just stood there holding onto his pants. He knew change was happening, and he also knew it was Old Harley who was doing at least some of the changing in this family. He wasn't egotistical, just assured. He saw people and understood them. He was a philosopher who didn't mind talking about what he knew, loved it in fact, and he wasn't afraid to speak the truth. That's what most people don't want to hear, he thought, just the simple truth and a new way of seeing things.

When the laughter and teasing died down, they noticed the doorway was filled with snow flurries, tempestuous evidence of Michigan's capricious nature. The moon was up now and almost full. It shined through the white shroud of flakes creating a magical place where the barn, with the Hughes family and friends plus two horses and Bug, was the only place in the world. Nothing else existed beyond the walls stacked with warm smelling hay, the floor scattered with musty straw, the stalls waiting for the horses still drying nearby, and the lantern which cast a small, warm light and drew them closer together.

Bug rose from his bed on a bale of hay and went to the door to stick his head out briefly and sniff the white air. He backed in, and then ventured out a bit further only to back in once more. His head was covered in snow, and only two huge, round eyes peeked through the white. He bowed down low, his rump sticking up into the air, and pounced at Kate, then whirled around to run out the door. He looked back at Kate, and then stumbled over his feet. He rolled, stopped and stood still, saw her watching and said, 'I meant to do that – Come on out. It's great. Let's play . . . let's catch this stuff.' Kate moved to the door and then they all joined her to watch Bug leap into the air, mouth open to catch snowflakes. Bug was pure maniacal joy out in the snow, a crazed, snowy fur ball, leaping and cart wheeling a foot from the ground, and then turning around to see if Kate was watching the fun.

Kate felt an arm at her waist and turned to see Mark's face just inches from hers. She reached around to put her hand over his, pulled him closer and snuggled in. 'It can't get any better than this,' she thought. 'I have almost everything.'

"I think so, too," Mark whispered into her hair.

"I didn't say anything," she whispered back.

"Not out loud," he said. "And I love you, too," he whispered, more softly than before, and squeezed her against him.

Will had moved behind Ellen and put both arms around her. He felt as he had when they first met, totally infatuated by this woman who never failed to surprise him. With each surprise, he became more in awe of her; her strength, her wisdom, her kindness, her capacity to love. But mostly, he gave thanks she had been tolerant of the whims of the man she had married, and she still loved him.

He didn't know Ellen gave thanks too, that her husband's fanciful nature had kept her from becoming what she thought of as a dried up old prune, a stiff, brittle old stick. Ellen giggled softly in the warm cocoon of his arms. The whiskey? The joy? Will tilted his head to look at her, and then nuzzled her cheek. Ruthie stood next to Jack, their arms just touching beneath their winter coats.

The scene around her wasn't lost on Ruthie, and she wanted badly to move in front of him, take his hands to wrap his arms around her, but she wasn't bold enough. So she stood as close as she could without being brazen and imagined herself enfolded.

Harley stood at the back of the group, his hands still occupied with holding up his pants and a self-satisfied smile on his face. 'My family,' he thought. 'My children – all of them.'

CHAPTER ELEVEN

I t was Christmas time. It was also one of the worst winters in history. Two feet of snow had already fallen, most of which stayed. November and December snows in Michigan typically melted in a few days while the weather was making up its mind to leave fall behind or to head firmly into winter. Some years, the weather teased and alternately sent heavy snow and then Indian summers with several hot days in between snow storms. It even threatened the possibility of having no white Christmas, making people plead for snow by the twenty-fifth.

This year, however, snow was showing its white furry face. The first real winter storm occurred while they were all gathered in the barn, continued for three days, piled in the fields, and stayed. By Christmas time, drifts had piled up to window sills and paths were shoveled to the barn doors like tunnels with four foot walls.

The stove at Nestor's was heavily used as men gathered to talk about the weather and make guesses when the next storm would hit or bets about when spring would come. It was a time for hibernation, whether in their kitchens around their own hearths, in the saloons, or in Nestor's store. Hersey folks still did their business, but they made short work of the treks to town and hunkered down to warm up when they got where they were going.

Mrs. Wellington still walked the few blocks from her home to the store every day, her layers of coats and hats making her look like a wooly mammoth – except for the tusks, of course, since she had no teeth. She still stopped at the door of each saloon to catch an unsuspecting man coming out so she could tell him a thing or two about his behavior – the behavior of all men. She caught Jack one day as he was leaving Sadie's.

"Wicked," she said, and then paused to chew. "Evil, wicked man. Screw, screw, screw, that's all you want to do."

Jack folded his arms across his chest, leaned back against the wall to listen and just nodded at her. He tried to appear interested in what she had to say and continued to nod and say "Hmmm," nod again, and then "hmmm."

Mrs. Wellington was confused by his attentiveness. Deep down she knew people didn't actually listen to her, but she continued her tirade until she wound down; then Jack patted her arm and smiled.

"You are an interesting woman, Mrs. Wellington. I hope you have a wonderful day."

Mrs. Wellington had been shocked by his words, and for a moment she had nothing to say. Her pinched little face peeking from under layers of hats jerked up to stare at Jack. Her mouth opened, but no words would come out. She began chewing faster and faster, then turned to scurry down the sidewalk, head shaking, shoulders hunched, her gate hurried. "Letch," she mumbled, "dirty letch, peeking under my coat and smiling. He just wanted to screw!"

Jack heard her words and laughed out loud. Aren't people wonderful? Well, most of them, he thought, then turned his face into the afternoon sunshine and snowflakes and headed for Mark's shop.

He heard the banging of hammer on anvil before he got to the door. Inside, the heat immediately melted the snow from his shoulders as he waited for Mark to turn away from the forge. Mark held up the tool he had been mending and then slowly dipped it into the barrel of water to cool.

"Well hello. What brings you here?" Mark asked, turning to pick up a scythe which had a badly gnarled blade. It looked like it had been twisted and then stomped on, and then twisted again. "Don't you wonder what happened to tools that come here so deformed?" he asked, not really expecting an answer.

"Well, no. Guess I never did," Jack answered. "I just thought I'd see if you were going to work all day and night or if you remembered you have a beautiful woman waiting to go to the tree lighting ceremony tonight."

Mark swung the scythe he'd been about to stick into the fire to soften for repair and then pointed it at the table that held the other tools awaiting the fire.

"I need to get these done first," he said. "Then I need to heat water for a bath, and then I need to spend about an hour trying to scrub the black off this body, and then . . . aw hell, I can't keep up."

"Where's Will?" Jack asked, looking around the cluttered room.

"Went home to clean up and sit a spell. He's doing his best, but he seems to wear out faster these days. He keeps trying though. Why aren't you back at the hotel getting spiffed up yourself?" Mark asked, and added, "as if you ever needed spiffing. You always look like you just got ready to go to church." He stuck the scythe into the fire and turned back to look at his friend. "You're going with us, right? I know another pretty girl who'd be darned disappointed if you didn't."

"Most likely not," he said, moving to the fire to watch the scythe grow red in the coals.

"Well why not? Even old Harley is going," Mark asked staring at his friend's back.

Jack kicked at the hearth like a schoolboy kicking at a rock in the road, but hearths stayed put, so he couldn't follow it down the road and kick it again, chase the rock wherever it landed and the toe of his boot pointed.

"Well, not that it's any of your business, my friend, but you just said it – a pretty girl. Since I assume you're talking about Ruthie, you must see she is just that – a young girl, and I, as you can plainly see, am not a young man."

Mark just stared at him, not sure how much he should say, how much interference Jack would tolerate. They had become good friends, but while Jack always seemed to be there when he was needed, sometimes appearing out of the blue to help like a fairy godfather when the times got tough, a part of him was closed off, private, and only the firm set of his shoulders indicated when you got too close. Mark looked for the signs and then decided to plow ahead.

He took the scythe out of the fire, picked up the heavy, blunt hammer used to bend steel, and began hammering the blade flat where it had been bent. He stuck it into the fire again when it began to cool, then placed it back on the anvil and began restructuring the original curve. It was a laborious process, swinging the heavy hammer and hitting the blade in just the right place, moving up the blade slowly, not going forward too quickly and creating a bend in the wrong place, perhaps doing more damage than it had come with, perhaps permanent damage. Mark thought as he worked, wondered how to explain his thoughts to Jack.

Finally, he began to speak in between hammer blows to the metal. "See this blade?" he asked. "It's a fine blade." Bang! Bang! Bang! "It requires careful handling." Bang!Bang! Bang! "If I hit too hard or go too fast, I ruin it." Bang! Bang! Bang! "But the metal lets me know just how hard to hit and how fast to move down the blade." He stopped swinging the hammer, stuck the blade back into the fire, and turned to Jack who stood patiently nearby. "It lets me know when it's too cool by its unwillingness to bend and too hot by its color."

"Yes, you have magic hands, Mark. You're a fine smithy," he said looking quizzically at his friend.

"No . . . I mean, yes I am," he grinned, "but this isn't about smithing."

"Has Harley gone to your brain, Mark? Why on earth are you going on about scythe metal like it actually thinks and speaks?"

"Because Ruthie is this blade. She is not a girl." Mark stopped and ran a blackened hand over his face at Jack's burst of laughter. He was confusing himself after thinking he had it all figured out. "Look, I made a mistake in saying she's a pretty girl. She is a young woman, and like this blade, she will let you know what to do, whether you move too fast and too hard, whether she needs warmth or cooling off. And if you listen, you will do no damage; you will only enhance her perfection." Mark stopped, picked up the scythe blade, made a few more corrections, and then slowly slid it into the water, careful not to change the temperature of the metal too quickly and make it brittle.

"Look, my friend," he continued. "I don't know if Ruthie is truly in love with you. What I do know is that she thinks she is, and so do you and that's why you're afraid – not because of her age at all."

Jack held up his hands in defeat. "All right, I'll go to the ceremony with all of you, emphasis on all, but I'm not buying any of what you're saying. You're crazy. Do you know that?"

Mark nodded; a satisfied smile lit his face. "Yes, I do. Oh, and by the way, if you hurt Ruthie, I'll have to kill you, bludgeon you with my trusty hammer."

Jack grinned back, tense shoulders now at ease. He playfully raised his hand like he was a witness in court swearing to tell the truth.

"I pledge to do no damage and will pay careful attention to what Ruthie's metal tells me. I will keep water nearby to toss her into when she says the time is right."

Mark slid the scythe out of the water barrel, carefully wiped it down, and held it up to the light. It shone brightly, and not an out of place bend could be seen.

"It's a thing of beauty," he said.

"Yes, it is. See what a bath can do? How about closing up here and heading for the hotel where bath water is heated for you?"

Mark punched him in the shoulder, gently, and attended to closing down the smith shop. "You can help, you know," he teased Jack, who responded by saying he didn't want to get dirty.

"You never get dirt on you. You are perpetually clean. You were born clean. I don't know how you do it."

On the walk to the hotel, Mark found the courage to ask if Jack had received a response from the court about their custody petition. He wasn't afraid to ask, but he was terrified of the answer. He closed his eyes waiting for Jack's words and almost stumbled on the rutted, snow covered ground.

"Nothing yet," Jack said, trying to put hope into his statement.

Mark nodded and opened his eyes. Silence lingered, and then Jack said, "These things take time, Mark. You know that."

Mark took a deep breath and nodded again because he couldn't speak.

The tree lighting ceremony was the best Kate could remember. In fact, all of the Hughes family and friends agreed it was the best. They gathered at the Hughes' house first; Willie was there with Mary and their little girl. He had come to know Harley well since the birth of the baby, and seemed to seek him out whenever he was at the Hughes' house. He never forgot the help Harley had given Mary. Jack had also become a permanent member of Willie's family after he and Harley had taken over the work of child delivery.

Mary hugged them both; good, strong hugs that hung on and told more than her words could say. She was still shy around anyone other than Willie and found it difficult to say what she was thinking and feeling. Instead of talking, she produced her daughter who was holding onto her dress behind her, having just learned to stand and take a step or two on wobbling, chubby little legs. She kicked when Mary picked her up, liking the independence of being on her own two feet, but quickly stopped when she saw Harley.

"Say hello, Ellie," Mary said, lifting the toddler who immediately smiled and reached for Harley. She grabbed his curls and hung on, then opened her mouth wide and placed it on his.

"Oh, I'm so sorry. That's her kiss," Mary said.

"And I couldn't be more grateful for anything in this mortal world," Harley answered when Ellie finally removed her mouth from over his lips. Then Ellie reached for Jack who snuggled her to his chest like she was a part of him. They sat around the Hughes' kitchen table waiting for dusk and the walk to the tree ceremony. Jack continued to hold Ellie who alternately closed her eyes in sleep and woke with a quiet smile on her face. Jack's face held the same contented smile. The rest saw and knew he pretended Ellie was his, if only for a little while.

Ellie made the rounds of arms on the walk to town, making a game of changing hands, but when they got to the center of town where the tree was, she perched on her father's shoulders and stabilized herself by holding onto Harley's curls beside her. They had picked up candles at the Congregational Church and quickly lit them when they got to the tree.

The Hughes group harmonized to all of the traditional Christmas carols with the others clustered around the tree, but when it came to *Oh Holy Night,* the town folks became silent, waiting for the Hughes family to sing. They looked forward to hearing them each year and waited quietly. When Willie sang 'Fall on your knees, oh hear the angel voices,' his mellow tenor rang out through the night, breaking hearts with its simple beauty. This year, Jack and Mark added their voices to the rest of the Hughes family, and strengthened the harmony. 'Oh night divine' was personally felt by each person listening. It was magical, and it truly was a divine night.

Then the candles on the tree were lit, each person finding one or more to touch with their own flame. Kate and Mark lit two candles by touching their own flames together to ignite the two on the tree. It was a symbolic thing for them, starting the flame of life together. When they were done, Mark kissed her – right there in front of the town where all could see. It wasn't a long kiss, but it was a kiss, and it showed the world he loved this woman, and she him.

He glanced toward Agatha Pennington, saw her flinch, and smiled to her, drawing Kate even closer to his side. As he looked around at the men, women and children gathered around the tree, he saw many people he had come to know, both before the jail sentence and after. Some still wore the same face of contempt they had during the trial, but many did not. People like Mr. Nestor and Jake the jailor had smiles for him and friendly handshakes. Those were the people Mark tried to remember when he received cold glares. He wouldn't care if it was not for Kate, but he still hurt for her.

Mel stood with his mother and two of his siblings nearly opposite the Hughes family, but visible to them. Mark saw him periodically look at them, his face wearing a detachment, pretended contentment. Mark's heart broke for him knowing Mel would take his place beside Kate given the slightest opportunity. He also believed Kate would be better off for it, but he could not release her. Mel nodded when he saw Mark's eyes upon him, and Mark nodded back, hoping his look conveyed warmth and Christmas cheer.

Ellen and Will lit several candles, one for each member of their family and three more for their adopted family members. Will squeezed his wife when they were done and beamed when she turned her face to his for a small kiss.

Harley took Ellie from her father so he and Mary could light their candles and held her high so she could see her parents. It was then he saw Mary would have a new one to hold before the next tree ceremony.

"Get ready," he told Ellie. "A new Hughes baby is coming to town, just like Santa Claus." She giggled, and Harley was sure he was speaking her language and she understood.

Jack and Ruthie went separately together, if that is possible, to light their candles, but Jack helped her by cupping his free hand around her flame when a light breeze threatened to blow it out. She almost lit the branch when he steadied her hand because she was nervous and looking at Jack who laughed and said, "The candle sweetie, not the tree."

Ellie's eyes widened at the sight of all the candle flames glancing off other bright decorations, and she almost lost her seat on her father's shoulders as she released Harley's curls to clap her hands in delight, but Harley was there to catch her as she tilted, and he kept his hand at her back from then on.

'That's my work,' he said to himself, 'to catch each one of these folks when they falter, before they fall. When they forget to hang on tight, I make a grab to steady them. Can't think of a better job,' he mused.

When they returned to the Hughes house, Will retrieved the 'good' jug from the pantry and out of deference to the celebration, poured the liquor into small glasses, even one for Ellen who staunchly smiled and took it. He knew better than to leave his wife and daughters out of the toast to Christ's birth. The hearth coals were rekindled, and warmth radiated throughout the room. Soon, they were warm inside and out, mellow from both the whiskey and friendly banter.

"Let's get a Christmas tree," Kate shouted excitedly. "Let's go chop one down now. It's a beautiful night. Let's do it."

"It's late, Kate," Ellen said, "and we have Ellie here to think of."

Mark smiled at Kate's exuberance, and Will's eyes danced at the thought of a night tromp through the snowy woods. Jack leaned back and watched all the faces. Ruthie nodded eagerly, hoping to walk beside Jack during the trek, and Willie looked at Mary who seemed a bit too tired for the journey, but wanting to go. Harley stood up, took Ellie from his mother and cuddled the sleepy child to his chest.

"If you promise to hold hands so no one gets lost in the snow, and if you promise to pick out the very best tree with which to grace this house, then you have old Harley's permission to undertake this journey. I will stay here with our child. We have not had the opportunity to have much conversation by ourselves, and we have been missing it. Haven't we Ellie?" Harley said, nuzzling the soft brown curls at the top of her head.

"I don't know, Harley," Ellen said, a small frown of concern on her brow. "Ellie might be upset being left alone."

"Alone?" he countered. "How can she be alone with me here? I am offended, Mrs. Hughes. I am deeply pained that you think I am not a proper caretaker for this beautiful child; I am . . ."

"No . . . no, I didn't mean . . ."

"Well, if you don't mean I can't care for our baby, then get your coat sweet lady. Go, now. Get your boots, too. It's snowy outside," Harley said gruffly, but turned on his sweet smile and looked around at the other grinning faces.

Ellen could do nothing else but take her coat from the hook, put on her boots, and wait at the door for the others to follow suit. When they were all dressed, with scarves around their necks, boots on their feet, and hats on their heads, Harley nodded his approval.

Will poured some whiskey into a tin flask and shoved it down into his pocket. "For medicinal purposes," he said, "in case of frostbite."

"Are you going to pour it on your fingers or toes, Mr. Hughes?" Ellen quipped, but she was grinning.

"Blasphemy, Mrs. Hughes, pure blasphemy."

When they were at the door and ready to leave, Harley lined them up for inspection, nodded satisfaction and told them they had his approval.

"Two by two, now," he said. "Each person must have a partner for safety's sake. Hold hands and don't let go."

"It's not a blizzard out there, Harley," Willie said. "We're not really going to lose each other in a storm."

"You never know what might happen, sir. You never know what a bright moon and a little snow could do. Why I've seen times when the strangest things have happened – almost magical things. One time . . ."

Mark's groan stopped him. "We'll hold hands, Harley. We'll hold hands. In fact, we'll like it." And he picked up Ellen's hand to put it in Will's, then Mary's in Willie's, and Ruthie's in Jack's. "There, are you happy now?"

"You're not done," Harley said, a fake scowl on his face, nodding at Mark's empty hand.

Mark laughed. "That goes without saying, you old coot."

Ellen was still concerned leaving Ellie with Harley and before she left asked him if he was sure about it, but Mary was content with her daughter's care and patted her mother-in-law's shoulder with her free hand.

"Ellie is in good care, Mother Hughes. She dotes on him, and he loves her. They'll be wonderful while we are gone."

So they walked into the moonlit, snow filled night, retrieved the saw from the barn and headed for the woods two by two. They spoke quietly, like the night demanded the respect of hushed words. Individual thoughts gathered in their heads, some contented musings, some nervous excitement. Some were peaceful, some unsure but happy with expectation.

"I'm not going to wander off in the snow, so you don't have to continue to hold my hand now that Harley is out of sight," Ruthie said, not wanting to force him into an embarrassing situation.

"No, I won't let you wander off, and yes, Ruthie, I do," he said grinning. "Harley said so, and I wouldn't want to go against what Harley says. You never know what that man can do, and I think he'd see us even if he's not here."

"Well, I just meant, you know, I wouldn't want . . ." Ruthie couldn't continue, didn't know what to say, and she felt foolish, like a silly girl. Since there wasn't a floor to fall through, she wished she could hide under a snow drift and not come out until spring.

Jack saw her discomfort and changed tactics. He was a bit uncomfortable himself and had hidden it under the paradox of Harley.

"Ruthie," he whispered, drawing her nearer. "I am thoroughly enjoying holding your hand. I want very much to."

Her sigh of relief was loud enough to be heard by the others, but they were wise enough to ignore it. She tingled all over with happiness, and after awhile grew warm enough and bold enough to remove her mitten and take Jack's bare hand in hers. He was startled by the move, but pleased and made sure she couldn't see his smile. She might misinterpret, and that thought unexpectedly pained him.

When they arrived at the place Jack said had the best choice of trees, they branched out, each couple searching competitively for the most perfect tree.

"This is it! This is perfect!" Will cried out.

"No, this one's better. Look, the shape is perfect, and it's the right height," Kate yelled back. "Come see it."

Back and forth the competition grew. "You don't know a Christmas tree when you see one, Kate," Willie countered. "You have to see the one Mary and I found."

Kate ran to where they were standing, leaped on her brother's back and tumbled him to the snow. Then she sat on his chest and piled as much snow as she could gather on top of him. His howls brought the others from their searches to find them rolling around on the ground, snow clinging to their clothes and turning them to abominable snowmen. Mark and Mary were standing back watching the fun. Then Ruthie leaped on the pile, and before long she was as snow covered as they were. Will joined the snowy heap. Then Mark and Jack, and only Ellen and Mary stood sentry and watched the fool-ishness. A snowball caught Mary in the shoulder. Then Ellen took one in the back. Soon they were pitching snowballs as fast as they could make them. If Harley truly could see them when he wasn't there, he was surely smiling now.

But at the moment, he was the most content man on earth and having a thoughtful conversation with his charge. His soothing voice went on and on, and Ellie never interrupted his flow of words. She never once looked at him like he was a crazy old fool. She looked into his bright eyes, heard his words, and seemed to ap-prove of his sage advice. At least, that's what he told himself. She understood the philosopher in him. "Wise little child," he said as her eyes closed in sleep.

Things were not quite as peaceful in the woods. Snowballs flew and found their marks until they were all exhausted. One by one they fell to the ground and sat defeated.

"I give, I can't stand for another minute," Will said, grabbing Ellen and lying flat on the snow. Jack was the last person standing and as the winner claimed the right to choose the tree.

"I hereby proclaim myself the victor," he said proudly. "Given that proclamation, I declare I have the right to sentence you to my choice of a Christmas tree, mine and my battle partner, that is," he said, taking Ruthie's hand and pulling her from the snow. Her mitten was still in her pocket, and her hand was wet and red. He pulled off the gloves he had put on for the fight and rubbed her cold hand between his until some warmth began to flow. Then he found the mitten still in her pocket. "You can take it off again later," he whispered as he slid it on her hand.

They found the tree he and Ruthie had chosen, and Will pulled the flask from his pocket to pass around the group.

"Your pick, you do the honors," Will said grinning and handing the saw to Jack.

"Not sure I remember that part in the verdict," he said. "Do you partner?" he said to Ruthie. But Jack sawed, and the others sat resting and sipping, the whiskey warming them from the inside out. When the tree toppled silently to the snow covered ground, Jack was given the last sip, and they started the long haul back to the Hughes house.

They stashed the tree in the barn so some of the snow could melt before putting it up, and headed for the house, tired, damp and happy. Harley lifted a finger to his mouth when they came in to silence them, nodding to Ellie who was deep in sleep on his chest.

"Was everything alright?" Ellen whispered.

"Of course," he whispered back, a satisfied smile on his cherubic face. "Ellie is a Christmas angel. We had a delightful time."

Christmas day brought more snow. It drifted slowly to the ground, huge flakes floating slower than usual. It was cold even though the sun shone brightly through the flakes, shining and glittering like it was decorating the world for Christmas. Smells of holiday dinner greeted them at the door when Mark and Jack arrived. Ellen was at the stove basting turkey and monitoring the pumpkin and current pies to be sure no sticky fingers snitched before dinner. Kate and Ruthie were setting the table, enlarged by the addition of two saw horses and an old door they'd found in the barn. A table cloth disguised it as a quite acceptable dining table, and was needed given the number coming for dinner.

The tree had been put up and decorated. It stood proudly in the corner wearing strings of popcorn and cranberries, as well as paper decorations made by the Hughes children years ago and saved by Ellen to be hung each year. Some were yellowed with age, but all were as precious as they were when they had been made by three and four and five year old hands years before. Willie, Mary, and Ellie sat on the floor by the tree, the parents trying to keep Ellie from grabbing the branches and toppling it.

Mark and Jack's hands were full of brightly wrapped presents which they placed beneath the tree and then turned to greet everyone with hugs or handshakes and ask their hostess what they could do to help. Bug stretched, walked over to Mark and stood to put his paws on Mark's shoulders. He stuck his nose in Mark's ear and stayed there for a minute. Mark just waited until he was done and was sure Bug was whispering warnings having something to do with Kate.

"I admit I saved the dried flower arrangement for you to do, Mark" Ellen said sheepishly. "I simply can't do it justice like you can. Other than that, dinner will be ready in about an hour."

"Where's Father Harley? I can't imagine him missing dinner." Mark asked, not seeing him – or more to his point, not hearing him.

"Blasphemy, Mr. Ramey," Ellen scolded, "on Christmas day of all days. Ruthie went out to fetch him, but he was busy finishing up some project he's been working on. He said he'd be in, in a few moments."

Harley kicked at the door when he arrived because his hands were full. He carried in an arm load of wooden objects, placed them in Mark's hands, and then went out for more. Bug bounded around the pile, nosed it, growled and then lay on it. Three times Harley went out and came back with large pieces of wood. The small area near the tree had grown even more crowded and cluttered, but he kept piling it up.

When he went out for the last time, Will shouted "there's no more room, Harley. What is all this?"

Harley just lifted a finger, nodded, and left again. When he came back, he didn't have an armful of wood, he was dragging a person with him by the hand, a short, stocky person of indiscriminate gender since a wool jacket went to the ankles, and a stocking cap and muffler covered the guest. A tiny red nose and bright, round blue eyes peeked from the cap. Every person in the room was silent, eyes wide and staring.

"What is all this?" Harley asked, repeating Will's question and pointing to the wood pile. "This, my friends, is a Christmas gift to the Hughes family and the Hughes family – the senior and the junior." He removed his coat, releasing the person he had dragged in, and moved to the pile.

All eyes turned to the pile, but went quickly back to the person still standing at the door. Harley ignored the stares and went on.

"I thought long and hard about what gift I could give to the people who have given so much to me, and came up with what I believe is the right gift for each. He began to sort the pieces, grown first foggy and then shiny after being wiped dry in the warm room. There were long, wide burnished pieces he set to one side, and several long, more slender pieces of different shapes he sorted, too, and placed together.

"They are, perhaps, not perfect, but they are made with great affection for the recipients, and isn't that what giving is all about?" he asked, not really expecting a response. He had their attention, now, and he was thoroughly enjoying it, drawing out his speech and taking advantage of their silence, but they were all staring at the person still standing at the door, covered in winter gear and as silent as they.

"Harley," Ellen finally said, "it is rude to leave a guest standing at the door."

"My mistake, I thought Will wanted to know about the gifts," he said, knowing full well their curiosity was for the guest. He was having fun watching their faces and loving the suspense. Harley was at his best when he was at the center of attention and was doing everything he could to stay there.

"I was rude, Mrs. Hughes," he said walking to the door. "This is Miss Verna, our Christmas guest. I knew you would not turn a person into the cold on Christmas day, so I took the liberty of inviting her to dine with us, since she has nowhere else to celebrate this glorious day." He helped her with her coat, hung it, her hat and muffler on a hook by the door and led her into the crowded room.

"I am not a hobo, Harley," she said, snarling at him. "I don't need charity, and I can go anywhere. . ."

"Of course not, Miss Verna," he interrupted quickly."I didn't mean to imply you are a vagabond."

"I was speaking, sir" Verna admonished. "When I am finished, then it is your turn."

"Of course. Of course. I didn't mean to interrupt," he said sheepishly.

The astonishment in the room was palpable. You could feel it, hear it, almost see it. This small woman had easily closed Harley's mouth. He was nearly groveling to please her!

Ellen took the lead by introducing herself, then the others, and invited her to share their Christmas meal. Verna greeted them all pleasantly and thanked Ellen for the invitation to dinner. Nothing was said about where she had come from or where she was going. Hearing her response to Harley, they were a little afraid to ask, not wanting to risk Verna's quick ire on themselves.

Mark's eyes nearly glowed; he was so tickled to see Harley in his current state. For once, Harley was feeling what all 'normal' people feel – a little unsure of himself, a little insecure. As much as he cared for Harley and actually liked him, it still felt good.

"Back to my original question," Will said pointing to the piles of wood, "what is all this?"

"Right," Harley said, regaining his composure and puffing out his chest, belly first as he tried to suck it in. "Clear the table and remove it, please."

"What?" the ladies shouted in unison. "It's all set for dinner."

"Please do as I ask," Harley said imperiously. "You will see."

Kate started stacking the dinner plates, and Ruthie gathered silverware. Mark moved his centerpiece, the table cloths, and then he and Will hauled the sawhorses and old door outside. Then they stood back, waiting further instructions.

"Would you take the kitchen table out to the barn so it won't get ruined in the snow?" he asked. Jack helped Mark move the table. When they got back from the barn, Harley was assembling a new table, the project he had been working on in his room at the back of the barn where no one could see.

Everyone stood to the side and watched it grow. When it was complete, it was beautiful; polished, golden pine with swirled knots periodically contrasting with deep brown. Four leaves stretched the table to hold at least twelve. It filled the room from end to end.

"The leaves are held in place by slides underneath the table," Harley said, "so when you don't have so many guests, you just pull on the table to separate the leaves, push the slides to the side, take them out, and magically you have a smaller table," he said, his eyes sparkling with the joy of his gift – and his own ingenuity.

Ellen's eyes matched his. She was in love with it. Her whole family, one that seemed to grow larger by the year, could sit at the table together.

"Harley, I don't know what to say. It is unbelievable. So much work," she said gently touching the table, caressing the gleaming top. "Thank you for the wonderful gift. I don't know what to say."

"Your beautiful face says it all, Mrs. Hughes. No words are necessary."

"Did you leave out some pieces, Harley?" Will asked, nodding at the pile still waiting by the tree.

"No, sir. That is for the other Hughes family. Let me show you." He began assembling the pieces. What appeared was a small bed with posts forming the frame for a canopy. The posts were polished, carved spirals, and on the head board the name 'Ellie' was entwined with flowers and leaves. "Sorry I don't have a mattress for it, but I don't know how to sew properly. I'm going to have to learn someday," he said.

Mary got up and ran her hands over the head board. "I can do that, Harley. I will love doing that, and Ellie will love her new bed. She's outgrowing her baby bed."

"I'm sure of that Miss Mary, but don't put that baby bed away. You never know when it will be needed again," he said, winking slyly at her.

Mary blushed and knew Harley was in on her secret. She didn't know how he knew, or why she hadn't said anything about her pregnancy. She had tried not to think of it. She was afraid of the darkness she had felt after Ellie had been born. She was terrified she couldn't take care of her babies if the darkness happened again, and she hated her weakness. The Hughes women were sturdy. They would never allow childbirth to defeat them the way it had her. She looked around the room, saw the faces staring at her, the love and strength in them, and clutched the bedpost tightly.

"Thank you, Harley," she said softly, then turned to Ellen. "We will have a new Hughes family member by June."

The room exploded. Back slaps, hugs, and kisses flew around the room, and everyone tried to find a chair for Mary all at once. The jug came out, and this time it was an ebony-colored cordial made from blackberries – a celebrating drink saved for special occasions and poured into small glasses.

Verna sat watching the activities. She tossed down her cordial when it was time for the toast and asked if there wasn't something a bit less sweet. Will was surprised by the blunt request, but complied by bringing out his moonshine jug.

"No offense, Mrs. Hughes," Verna said, "but a drink should be a drink. There's no need to disguise it as dessert." She refused the glass Will offered, tilted the jug over the back of her wrist in accomplished style and took a long drink. The silence was broken by a breathy sigh of pleasure when she was done. "Thank you, Mr. Hughes."

"Please call me Will, and it is my pleasure," he responded, grinning and bowing low in a grand gesture.

The table was reset in a flurry of activity, and Ellen announced dinner was more than ready. "Find a seat," she said, and then "grace please."

It was typical for the family to hold hands when grace was said. Willie squeezed Mary's hand willing strength to her in her fear. Mark held Kate's gently, one finger absently caressing her hand and feeling her returning caress. Jack held Ruthie's tentatively trying not to feel awkward doing so in front of the entire family. Kate stole a glance at her sister; saw a flush on her face and a small, almost contented, smile playing there too.

Kate nudged her under the table with her foot, and Ruthie peeked up to see her sister's eyes shining with merriment on her. When Harley's hand reached for Verna's, she slapped at it and scowled.

"When I want to hold hands with someone, I'll tell them," she said. "Don't touch me. I can pray without your hand."

"But it is usual when you are in someone's house to accede to their customs," Harley said quietly, unsure how to handle this strange woman. He wasn't used to such contrariness, or at the very least, he wasn't used to being unable to control or divert it, or to talk a person out of it. "I apologize, Miss Verna. Mrs. Hughes?" he said shrugging his shoulders.

When the dishes had been cleared and food was put away, they opened presents. All but Jack's presents to them had been handmade. Will had made a small box intended to hold cuff links and other trinkets for Jack, and Ruthie had sewn a deep purple lining for it and affixed it to the inside. The stitching was tiny and perfect, so intent was she that it would not have a single flaw.

Ellen, Ruthie and Kate had made a blue denim shirt for Harley so he could wear one while the other was being washed. He was overcome when he opened it; effusive with praise at its quality. He immediately stripped his old one off and donned the new one, pranced around the room and stopped before each person to show off the delicate stitching and how well it fit.

"I shall never remove this beautiful garment," he declared. "Never have I seen a better quality shirt. Never, I say, and I have seen many, many fine attire."

"Harley," Mark said quietly.

"Yes, quite right. Thank you so very much," he nodded to each Hughes family member in turn. "I will cherish my gift."

He sat down again, still wearing his new shirt.

Mark received a shirt, too; a white one with crisply starched collar and cuffs, one like he had worn with his suits when they had first met, before the edges of his shirts had frayed and grayed with age and wear. He no longer owned a shirt like the one he held in his hands, and his eyes misted in memory of the past and the wisdom of the Hughes women in their choice of a gift. He didn't care much for the person he had been in his youth, but he did miss looking clean, and he loved the look of crisp white shirts.

"Thank you," he said simply. "Thank you all so very much. Do you mind if I save wearing it for later?" he asked, grinning and looking at Harley puffed out in his new shirt.

Jack's presents for the Hughes family were yards of cloth for the ladies; blue print for Ellen, yellow for Ruthie, and bright red for Kate. The colors were thoughtful recognition of their personalities. Will received a shiny pocket watch which he promptly affixed to his vest, and the Hughes junior family received a wall clock with a kitten face intended to hang in their tiny kitchen. For Harley, Jack had purchased new suspenders that he indicated should be used to hold up his pants – "buttoned pants," he said in mock gravity.

"This is too much, Mr. Bay. You should not have spent so much money on gifts for us," Ellen reprimanded. "We cannot accept such lavishness, it's. . ."Jack interrupted her for the first and last time by kissing her squarely on the cheek. One just didn't interrupt Ellen Hughes, but she stopped trying to refuse her gift and held it close to her chest lovingly after the kiss.

Mark had forged his gifts at the shop; metal figurines of a variety of animals he hoped matched the personalities of the people he was giving them to. Kate's figurine looked somehow identical to Bug. The metal dog was standing; his paws perched precariously on the shoulders of a stick-man. The dog was a head higher than the man and looking down at him. Kate laughed and cried at the same time when she opened it.

"I have a second gift for you," he whispered when she hugged him. "But it's for later. Do you think we could make it through the snow to your cabin tomorrow?" he asked. Kate just nodded, excitement filling her eyes.

The next morning, it miraculously wasn't snowing when Mark knocked at the door. The sun was up and glistening on snow laden branches. It was a white world, a fairy land. He carried a sack tossed over his back which he left beside the door when he entered. Kate was busily packing food in a basket. She smiled when she saw him, her excitement too much for words to convey.

"Pa's out at the barn harnessing Penny. He thinks we should take the horse," she said.

"I don't know about doing that. It doesn't seem right to take a man's horse for a whim, even if it is a wonderful whim."

"It is right, Mark. Penny will get much more easily through the snow in the woods. It's not as deep there as in the fields, and the road to the woods has been hard packed."

"That's not what I mean. It's another man's horse," he said.

Kate gave him a quirky grin. "You sound like a cowboy, and in the words of philosopher Harley," she said, "know when to say thank you and take the gift someone wants to give."

"Okay, okay. I accept the use of Penny. Some day, I will have a horse of my own, and I will lend it to others."

They attached the bag and basket to the mare, climbed on with Kate behind Mark, her arms around his middle. This feels right, they both thought simultaneously. Right and magnificent!

Bug danced around the horse, alternately whining and growling. 'You're not leaving me behind,' he said. 'Whether you like it or not, I'm going with you. Hear my growl? Grrr...'

"Let's go, Bug. Of course you're going with us."

Kate snuggled close against him on the ride there, and periodically Mark put his hand over hers, pulling it against his chest. He was concerned about the deep snow, but not enough to put off their day at the cabin. It was what he wanted most for Christmas, and he knew it was what she wanted too.

The cabin was buried in snow, and branches of nearby trees were bent almost to the roof with heavy snow. They carried in what they had brought with them, lit the hearth fire, and stood chafing their hands and arms for warmth until the fire began to heat the small room.

The owner's clothes still hung on pegs near the door where Kate had left them, and everything was in its place. She lit a lantern, took a bright red table cloth from her basket and spread it over the scarred table. Bug found his place in front of the hearth and stared contentedly at her movements around the room.

When the room was warm, they removed their winter coats, pulled the two kitchen chairs in front of the fire and sat as contentedly as Bug who lay in front of them.

"I stole something," Kate whispered wickedly.

Mark jerked his head to look at her. "You stole?"

"Yup, I did. It's in my basket. Do you want to see it?"

"I'm not sure I want to be an accomplice to your thievery. What exactly did you steal?"

"A little bit of Ma's blackberry cordial. Just a little. I put it in a half-pint jar, thought we might need it – for medicinal purposes, you know. Frostbite and all that?"

Mark chuckled. How he loved this woman, he could never put it into words. She was a girl-woman; innocent and knowing, pure and mischievous, strong and soft, demanding and giving.

"A dichotomy, that's what you are," he said, "a dichotomous thief, but let me find your stash, and I will pour the demon drink for you."

He found a glass and the stolen cordial, poured a generous amount in since he intended to help her drink it and handed the glass to Kate.

"To us," she said, "and to the best Christmas I have ever had."

Mark repeated her words, but his mind went back to Christmas with his son and daughter, and a cloud darkened his enjoyment. He sipped from the glass after Kate and tried to dispel the cloud. "I have something for you," he said, and retrieved it from his sack. "It's not much, but I didn't want to give it to you with the rest of the family there."

Kate opened the small package. Inside she found a plain round silver band. She just stared at it, her usually mobile tongue stilled by the gift.

"Go ahead," Mark encouraged. "Try it on. You can't wear it on your finger yet, but I think it will fit. You'll have to put it on a ribbon and wear it around your neck for awhile – until later, that is."

Kate took it carefully out of the small box and held it up to the fire light. It had a deep, lustrous shine and glistened as she turned it around and around.

"Did you make this?" she asked, her voice husky with emotion.

"Yes, out of a silver dollar, at the shop. It's all I could afford to do right now," he said, hoping a hand-made ring wouldn't disappoint her. He had been so sure of her response when he was forging it, but now he was afraid – afraid what he could afford to do would not be enough. Kate deserved everything, more than he could give, more than him, an imperfect – sometimes fool.

"It's perfect," she said smiling and handing it to him. "Put it on my finger Mr. Ramey and ask me to marry you."

A sigh of relief escaped his chest and he began to form the words that would someday make her his wife. "Miss, Kate, you have made me so happy. Will you marry . . .?"

"No!" she interrupted. "Properly, Mr. Ramey, on your knees please," a Cheshire cat smile lighting her face.

Mark went to his knees in front of her, took her hand, slowly slid the silver ring on her finger and repeated his words.

"Yes! Yes, I will marry you," was Kate's response even before he had finished his speech. Her words were accompanied by a hug that tumbled them both to the floor beside Bug.

Mark's kiss was long and slow, his hands gentle on her back. Kate responded with longing built massive over time. She pushed him down and rolled next to him, displacing Bug and not caring. Her arms circled Mark's neck and tried to pull him closer when there was no space between. Her body moved against his and she felt his growing desire. She wanted nothing more than to melt into him, deep into his body and him into hers. His tongue licked at her lips and neck, his hands were fire sliding over her hips. The heat of their embrace consumed them, and both were frantically lost in burning need for each other. Then Kate jerked up, her face inches from his, her rasping breath stopped instantly.

"What?" Mark asked fearfully. "I'm sorry. I shouldn't have. . ."

"Does this mean . . .?" she blurted incoherently.

In the moment it took for his brain to clear, he knew exactly what she was asking.

"Yes, it does. "We can marry as I am a single man."

Kate slugged him. "When? When did that happen?"

"Ouch! A few days ago. I was saving it for now."

"You rotten person," she shouted. "You louse. Damn it, you could have told me! Sorry. For the damn it, not the other!"

"Yes, I could have, but with everyone around I wouldn't have been able to do this," he said, pulling her down against him and kissing her again. When they momentarily separated, he said "I wouldn't have missed holding you like this for anything."

They lay for a long time in front of the fire, both wishing clothes did not separate them, wanting to taste more of the deep pleasure they found in each other. Kate ran a hand over his face and under the collar of his shirt. Mark's skin tingled, and he tensed with need, but he grasped her hand and kissed each finger. "Soon," he whispered.

Bug reclaimed his place nearest the hearth and stretched the full length of Kate, snuggling as close to her as Mark was to her other side. They talked of the future and the past, their wants and their dreams. Lots of children were what they both wished for, but money was an issue for Mark. Kate didn't care. Money didn't care for children, love did, and they had plenty of that.

They ate Kate's food by candlelight, sipped more of Will's cordial, and were content. "We could live here," Kate said. "It's a long way to school and the smith shop, but we could buy a horse and get there faster."

"In good time, Kate. We'll find a way in good time."

"I don't want to wait. I want to be Mrs. Ramey now – this minute. You don't know how long I have loved you, Mark. Since I was sixteen, that's how long, and that was a long time ago."

Kate pleaded her case, told him she didn't care about money, about a big house, about anything other than being his wife, and Mark couldn't refuse her even though he felt wrong in doing it.

"I should be able to offer you more," he said. "I want desperately to offer you the world, and right now everything I have goes to getting my children back. You know that, don't you? I need them. They need me."

She nodded, not dissuaded by his words. "You are everything," she said. "You and Jamie and Flossie are everything I want and need, and we will get them home – to us."

Kate looked contentedly around the room. The soft light from the fire hid its shabbiness and gave the room a warm glow. She glanced up at the man's clothes, and a twinge of sadness crept into her eyes, for she hoped the man would never return to his tiny cabin, and the thought made her feel selfish and wicked. In the same breath, she pictured him wandering the land and then returning, happy to be home and safe. She wanted to feel good about that – for him. The candle on the table flickered, and Kate watched it dance, letting her mind create pictures of his return. The mixture of emotions flickered through her like the candle flame. She shook her head to erase the thoughts and spotted the bag Mark had brought with him.

"What's in the bag?" she asked quietly, still coming out of her reverie.

"Just some stuff."

"What stuff?"

Mark was uneasy and shifted in his chair, then went to the bag and carried it to the table. He didn't open it right away. Instead, he looked at Kate, a question in his eyes.

She sat waiting, thoroughly confused and curious.

He took a deep breath and plunged in. "Mel brought in some tools for mending awhile back. Some he couldn't fix himself without a forge." He paused and Kate waited. "Did you know he gave Bug to you because he knew you came here by yourself and was concerned about your safety?"

"That's what I've always thought, but he never said why. Bug was just waiting for me at home one day."

"Well, he did. He's a good man."

"What does all this have to do with your bag?" she asked, confused by the direction of the conversation.

"We got to talking at the shop, and eventually he asked about the cabin. I told him I had seen it and described it to him – and how you loved it. When he came back to pick up the tools a few days later, he brought this bag with him. Told me his mother had cleaned out the cupboards and was tossing out old stuff. He thought you might want to use it here. I didn't believe him – about the old stuff," Mark said thoughtfully, running his hand through his hair and over his face.

Mel disturbed him and he pretended to himself he didn't know why. It wasn't that he obviously cared so deeply for Kate. He knew Mel would never act on his feelings inappropriately. He was too honorable a man. He loved from a distance in apparent contentment, but the wounds were deeply etched in Mel's eyes. The man had loved only once, Mark thought, and it had been for his Kate. But something else ate at Mark from deep inside where he had hidden it, and he wasn't about to unearth it right now.

"Do you want to see?" he asked.

"Yes, I'm really curious. What was Mel thinking?"

"Who knows, Kate? Whoever knows what Mel Bronson is thinking – unless he tells you, and he doesn't often enlighten."

The bag held two sets of curtains, a long hearth rug, a mat for in front of the door, a bright red table cloth, and four blue kitchen towels. Kate was childlike in her exclamations of joy as she held each item up to the fire light, tossed it on the table and dug into the bag for the next one.

"Look at this, Mark! It's perfect for Bug to lie on, and it looks so new. So do the curtains and they'll fit perfectly. I won't even have to refit them." Mark nodded, enjoying her enthusiasm, but not responding.

"Damn! It almost looks like he knew what colors to pick out of Mrs. Bronson's cast offs, and everything looks so new."

"Yes, they look good, don't they," he said, smiling with a tinge of sadness he didn't want to think about, and he didn't know whether to tell her what he was thinking or not. Then he thought of Harley and what he said about gifts and the givers and receivers. "Honey, I think they are new. I think this is Mel's Christmas present to you, given the only way he knew how – through a small white lie."

"You mean these aren't his mother's cast offs? He bought this stuff?"

"That's what I believe, yes."

"Well, then I'm not sure I should keep it. Why would he do that?"

"Because he wants you to be happy, and he wants to be a part of your happiness. He knows you can't afford these things."

"Well, why not just bring them to me? Why give it to you at the shop?"

Mark ran his fingers through his hair again, paused, and tried to sort out what he thought. "I'm not sure, Kate, but I think Mel sees us together, and he doesn't want to interfere, wants to respect boundaries. But he had to find a way to give you a Christmas present – through me and a bit of subterfuge. Harley would say do not disrespect the giver of gifts by questioning. Merely accept and say thank you. Remember? You once told me to follow that advice – today, in fact," he said grinning at turning the tables on her.

Kate grinned back and punched him lightly on the arm. "You're not supposed to use my own advice against me!" Her face lit up in anticipation of seeing her treasures in their proper places.

"Go ahead," he said. "Try them out."

Kate bounded around the room, dislodging Bug and replacing the old rug he had been laying on with the new one. Bug sniffed at it, stood in the middle, turned three circles, and lay down. 'Nice,' he said with sleepy eyes, 'and soft.'

She placed the mat in front of the door, cleared the table quickly and spread the new red cloth on it before placing the candle in the center. It cheered the room with its brightness. She hung one of the new towels on a peg by the sink, and took the old curtains down. When the new ones were up, she stood back and swung her head from side to side taking in the changes.

"I love it. I love this place, and I love you," she said, putting her arms around his head and pulling him against her breast. Mark snuggled against her and tried hard to silently thank Mel for the joy he saw in Kate. 'One day,' he vowed, 'one day I will give her everything.'

CHAPTER TWELVE

The century turned. By the end of the 1800's, Michigan had become the richest lumber state in the country, thanks in part to the expansion of railroads. Michigan's hard, straight maples and oaks were in demand for use as the ribbons that formed tracks. A hundred and fifty miles or so southeast of Hersey, Ransom Olds had founded the state's first auto company, and industrialization began to take hold. Iron and copper mining was still available for the more northern Michigan workers, but the Hersey area still depended on its trees, which were vanishing from the forests, and its small farms.

The latter half of the century had seen market crashes and panics, almost decade-long depressions, laborers' pay move up and down the scale several times in a decade, to as low as a dollar a day, when a barrel of flour sold for thirteen and a bushel of potatoes for one and a half. Lumberjacks didn't earn a lot, but those without families got room and board at the camps, so they had ready cash when times were hard. The married ones sent their wives and children to work wherever they could find it. Male children went to the camps as soon as they could handle the heavy tools or found seasonal work on farms large enough to require hands. Even small farms needed periodic help when crops were ready. You couldn't take your time getting them in by yourself. Heavy rains could ruin an entire year's harvest. The females cooked and cleaned for others, took in washing, or went to the saloons to wait on men with money.

Hersey felt the impact of the flighty nineteenth century, not as much as some areas of Michigan, but felt it nevertheless. However, Hersey continued to grow and eventually became the county seat, a prideful thing for many Hersey residents. They were a real city; had a white painted courthouse, a bigger jail, a firehouse, a post office, all the trappings of prosperity, and they didn't want the kind of industry Mr. Olds had built. They wanted things just as they were.

It sounded strange on the tongue, and Kate kept trying it out to see if it would ever sound normal.

"Nineteen hundred," she said to Bug who lay on her bed watching. "I will become Mrs. Ramey on May 1, 1900. Only two months, Bug!" He perked his ears, rolled his eyes and seemed to say 'It still sounds strange, Kate.' She knew what he was telling her, but wasn't sure whether he was referring to the date or the marriage. Bug really didn't like sharing her with anyone.

The 1800's had slid quietly away. Winter continued to cover the earth with new snow every few days, and its great mounds muffled sound in the valley of Hersey. The crack of an axe could be heard from the camp if you stood still and listened carefully, but you never heard the tree fall as it ploughed into the deep snow. Even in town sound seemed muted. The mill saws still ran. The high pitched whirring was softened by two feet of snow that covered the mill roof and was stacked high up the walls. It was hard, slow work sledding logs to the mill instead of floating them down the river, but it meant the camps and the mill still ran, although slowly, throughout the long winter. They stacked much of what they felled, waiting for a thaw and high water in the river, but what they sledded down kept the mill open.

Since daylight work hours were short, Sadie's business was strong and the hours long. Patrons started early and stayed late, growing more boisterous as the hours passed. Saloons were the only businesses prospering in a hard winter and perhaps even increased in their patronage. Everything else seemed to slow down as if the town was in partial hibernation.

Mark made trips to Smithton's Orphanage as often as he could. Sometimes he was able to see and talk with Jamie, and sometimes he waited for hours for the children to come outside, but it grew harder and harder to leave him there. At times he felt like cutting the fence, grabbing him and running away. But he knew the authorities would find him. Running wouldn't work. The miles were long and cold during the wintertime, and he was grateful when spring grew near and made traveling to Saginaw more tolerable.

"I'll be back in a couple of weeks, Son," Mark said, holding Jamie's hand through the fence.

"I know that, Dad," Jamie responded, his clear, dark eyes trusting his father's words. He ran off when the mistress rang a bell for the children to go in, and Mark watched him turn back to wave to his father with a brave smile. Mark stood for a long while, his hands gripping the fence, his forehead pressed into the slats.

Farmers came to town more frequently as winter began to hint spring could be just a month or so away. They had mended what they could mend, tended to their livestock, listened to their wives and children in the close confines of their kitchens, and sought the company of others. "Cabin fever," they said. "I just had to get out of there for a bit." They gathered at Nestor's and purchased a single item – the excuse for heading to town, and sat by the stove.

Some of the small farms had run out of feed for their livestock due to the early, harsh winter. They hadn't planned on the snow coming and staying in November. They had parceled it out carefully and their cattle were thin, but doing alright. Now, though, some had stopped giving up their needed milk, and the feed was gone.

"Hell," Jackson said to no one in particular. "I can't even let 'em out to forage on their own. Snow's too damn deep in the pasture."

"Don't I know," Thompson added. "I got enough left for about a week and that's it. Don't know what I'll do then."

"Tried the feed store?" Nestor asked. "It's not hay, and they'll surly think they've gone to heaven if they get good feed all day, but it'll get you through another month of this."

"Can't," Jackson grunted. "Been there."

Mr. Nestor didn't push it. He knew feed was available, but knew, too, credit was not. Small farms were having a hard time everywhere, and Hersey was no exception. Times were changing, and a man couldn't raise a family easily on forty acres like he used to, especially when the family had ten mouths to feed as Jackson did, twenty feet to put shoes on. Even when you passed them down like Jackson and almost everyone else, shoes eventually gave way to the toes pushing through the leather. Material only stood up to so many patches, and then what's left is just one big patch.

Nestor pondered silently for a few moments, wondering if he should tell what he knew, if it was the right thing to do. He looked at the group gathered near his stove, the ragged coats, the coarse gnarled hands, the pride in their faces and the fear in some eyes. He took a solid breath, cursed softly, and left his counter to walk closer to the men.

"This isn't for public knowledge," he said to the small group, "and you didn't get it from me, but I heard Mel Bronson gave some hay and feed to a man who needed it just last week."

"What, he just gave it away, to who?" George Simms asked, a look between awe and disbelief distorting his face.

"This is not for discussion at Sadie's, George, and I really shouldn't have said anything at all. But no, he lent it sort of, and I'm not saying to who. None of your business. He told the man he could pay for it with chicks in the spring, or with a pig or calf, or whatever they had to pay it with. Mel's a good man. Big heart."

Jackson pondered the idea, his elbow on his knee and his fist holding up his chin. It's a thought, he mused. He sure as hell hated going begging, but he might have to. He didn't know what else to do. He knew Mel, and knew also he wouldn't try to make him feel like a beggar, but he sure as hell hated asking for help.

"I'll mull over it," he said to Nestor. "I'll think on it."

"Hell, man," George blurted, "if Bronson's giving stuff away, get in line. He appears to be good at it. He gave his girl to that man Ramey without even putting up a fuss. Did you all know that? Kate's a stupid girl. She could be living in Mel's big house by now if she had half a brain, but she got goggle-eyed over a fancy man – a jailbird no less."

Ed Miller, George's drinking buddy, was as much of a tongue wagger as George, but a bit kinder. "I heard they're getting married come May," he offered to no one in particular.

"I thought he was already?" George questioned. "Wasn't it his wife who ran off with Landmark's money, or so he says?"

Nestor didn't like the turn of conversation. He put up with the group who always gathered by his stove, even enjoyed them when business was slow, but George was a perpetual gossip who sometimes showed a nasty streak. Nestor liked Mark, and he had a special place in his heart for Kate. He didn't know why. Maybe it was because he had watched her grow up in his store, always lurking near where things were happening, and hiding behind the pickle barrel so she could eavesdrop on conversations, quick to respond with a retort and a toss of her head when she was caught. She was spunky, not to mention beautiful. That didn't hurt.

"Ramey paid his debt, George. He's working hard, so give the man a break. And leave Kate out of your gossiping or do it somewhere else."

All heads looked up at Nestor, and most nodded agreement. They'd been forced to listen to George many times in the past and hadn't cared for his snide comments.

"Gossiping old woman," Ed said playfully. "Old biddy."

Later, Mel had gone into Nestor's with a grocery list his mother had written out for him. She found it difficult to move about in the deep snow and left it for Mel to do. She also played up her age a bit, wanting her son to leave the chores for awhile and see people in town, do something other than work.

When Nestor had gathered everything on the list, he asked if Jackson had been out to see him. He felt guilty for suggesting Mel might be able to help and confessed his guilt.

"I shouldn't have said anything," he said, "but Jackson looked so damned beaten, I couldn't help it."

"It's alright," Mel said. "I probably need to clear out some of the old hay in my barn. Make some room in there. I've got plenty. Last year was pretty good."

On his way home, he stopped at Jackson's place and found him in the barn. He looked around at the space where straw and hay should be and found it empty. Five cows stood with their heads low, their noses snuffling around the ground for stray pieces of hay. Jackson threw a handful toward them, stuff he had raked from the floor of the space where it had been stacked.

Jackson greeted him distantly, wondering why Mel would show up this day of all days. He'd been arguing with himself for hours about going to Mel for help. Now here he was. Mel shifted his weight around, unsure how to go about helping a proud man.

"Sorry for breaking into your work," he said.

"Not much to do right now anyway. Haven't seen you around lately; what can I do for you?"

"I was wondering if I could unload some hay on you, since you're close to my farm. I'm trying to clear out some space, and wondered if you had any."

Jackson, not much for a lot of speech, looked around his barn. "You see anything taking up space?" he said. "That's just about all that's here. Space and some skinny cows."

Mel didn't know how to respond to his words, couldn't think where to go with the conversation, how to proceed.

"Well, if you could get a wagon over to my place, we could load up about twenty bales or more and move them here. I'd appreciate it." Mel stammered, kicked at the hard packed dirt, and looked anywhere but at Jackson. "Of course, I wouldn't expect you to just store it. You could use whatever you want."

Jackson stared past Mel through the open door, saw the deep snow, and then looked at his scrawny herd. He was tired and discouraged. He kicked at the small pile of hay he had raked up and closed his eyes for a moment. Then he took a deep breath and swallowed his pride.

"Yeah, I can store it. I guess old Nestor got to you," he said gruffly. "You're a hell of a bad liar"

"I'm sorry, Mr. Jackson. I should have just said so, but I have plenty, more than enough for my herd, and you need some."

"I'll pay. I don't take charity."

"I know that," Mel said, relieved the truth was out. "You'll pay when you can. I know that." He turned to leave then, saying he'd see Jackson with his wagon later on.

Two more desperate farmers showed up at Mel's later that week. He gave them what he could spare and hoped spring would come soon. He couldn't let their cattle starve, and hated the mere thought they would even be hungry. He looked at his own fat herd and was pleased by the sight of their shiny coats, their contented lowing. When he squatted on his milk stool and braced his forehead against their warm sides, their content soothed him.

He thought of Kate then, of the time he had found her on his milk stool, her head braced in the same way as she milked one of his cows. That had been a long time ago, just after the camp fight, but he still thought of it every time he sat to milk. He no longer tried to dispel the picture. He found some comfort there and knew he would continue to allow the scene to come to him. It would not go away, and he had given up fighting it.

Mel had talked to Kate shortly after Christmas. She had stopped him on the sidewalk and thanked him for the things he had given to her for the cabin.

"It was just some stuff Mother was going to get rid of, Kate. I thought you might be able to use it."

Kate's eyes softened at his lie, but she let him have it. "Well, please tell your mother I am grateful and that the cabin looks beautiful wearing her things."

"I'll do that," he said, hoping Kate didn't run into his mother and find out the truth.

"Mel," Kate said, reaching out to put a hand on his arm. "I was going to walk out to see you. I need to talk with you about something. Tell you something, I mean."

Alarm leaped into Mel's eyes. "What's wrong?" he asked, quick fear for her evident in his voice.

"Nothing's wrong, Mel. It's just . . . I felt I needed to tell you . . . Mel, Mark and I have set a date to be married. May first." Kate rushed the words, wanting to get it over with as quickly as possible, not wanting to say them to him at all, but knowing the news had to come from her. He deserved that.

Mel looked like he'd been struck with a two-by-four. He knew they were together, that Kate loved the man, had loved him from the first moment she'd seen him. He knew Mark had been the silent intruder between them even when he'd been absent, knew he'd been the barrier Mel had never been able to cross over with Kate. But the news still struck him a heavy blow. He was silent, letting her words fall over and around him, but not letting them in. That would come later, when he was alone and she could not see his eyes.

"Congratulations," he managed to say. "I hope you will be very happy."

"Will you come to the wedding . . . please?"

"Kate, don't ask that . . . please."

Mel remembered those moments on the sidewalk all too clearly, but he chose to think of other, more pleasant pictures of Kate while he milked his cows. He saw her by the river dripping wet after falling off a tree branch, in his buggy with her head on his shoulder, or lying exhausted in the straw pile after running to him for help. Mostly, though, he liked to picture her squatted on his milk stool, her forehead pressed against one of his cows, her face smudged with their dust, the things he loved so close together.

The wedding was small, just family and a few close friends. They held the ceremony at the Congregational Church, and Reverend Havens performed the service after all. He tried his best to put roadblocks in the way, and Kate almost sought out the Presbyterian minister, but he eventually gave in when he saw she was determined to marry a married man.

"Mark is not married, Reverend. He has a divorce decree signed by a Grand Rapids court. You've seen it."

"That means nothing in the eyes of our Lord. Why on earth do people believe they can part what God has put together – as man and woman are in marriage – until death, Kate. Don't you hear that? Until death parts you, not man and a court hacking away at matrimony! In the eyes of God, he is still married."

"Well not in my eyes and not in the courts eyes, Reverend," she said icily, standing to leave his office, "and if you cannot perform the service, then at least provide my baptism certificate so I can ask the Presbyterian minister to marry us. I will be singing in his choir from now on."

Her words made him step back as if he had been struck. "I – it will take some time to find it, Kate, and you don't want to be hasty."

"Hasty?" she asked. "Yes, I do want to. I've waited too long already. By May first, I will be married to Mark, and if you choose not to marry us, that is just fine."

Kate's words spit fire. There was much she didn't like about Reverend Havens. First and foremost was he had singled out her father one Easter Sunday, at least that was how she had interpreted his words, when during the sermon he castigated the people who only went to church periodically. Will was not much for attending church every Sunday, but he went on special days when he knew it meant a lot to Ellen, and when his daughters would be singing duets for the congregation. He had gone that Easter when the reverend saw fit to demean people like Will. Since then, Kate had difficulty seeing him as a very Christian man. She would have changed churches, but Ellen dissuaded her.

"Reverend Havens is just afraid of losing his flock, Kate," she had said. "And he needs us in the choir and you at the piano. So many young people have left his church."

"That's because he's an old curmudgeon!" Kate said. "And he's so boring."

"Kate! Your tongue!" her mother said, shocked by her daughter's words.

"Sorry."

Reverend Havens finally agreed to marry Kate and Mark, most likely because what Ellen had said was true; he was afraid to lose the few in his choir who could actually carry a tune. And he was certainly not going to lose them to that upstart, modern preacher at the other end of town.

Ruthie was her maid of honor and looked beautiful in a yellow dress she and Ellen had made from the material Jack had given her for Christmas. Her hair was drawn back with a matching yellow ribbon and flowed down her back in lustrous, deep brown curls. She walked down the aisle with Jack, Mark's best man, and pretended to herself it was her wedding – to the man at her side.

Willie ushered the few guests to their seats at the front of the church where Mary sat with Ellie. He walked Ellen to the front pew, and then Harley who held Verna's arm carefully tucked under his.

They'd been together frequently since Christmas. Verna had been taken under Sadie's wing and was now a server at the saloon and a favorite among the customers. Her cantankerous humor and biting manner seemed to suit them. When Sadie smothered them with cushioned hugs, Verna cuffed them and told them to drink or get out.

"Your glass is empty," she'd say. "Order up or leave this table to a paying customer."

"Verna," Ed Simms had said to her one day, "why are you so ornery?"

"Because I'm old and because I want to be," was her response. "Why are you so mouthy?"

Harley puffed his chest and tried unsuccessfully to suck in his belly as he walked Verna down the aisle. His new red suspenders managed to hold up his pants as he did so. Verna's look seemed to say 'I own this place. It's nice isn't it? Thanks for coming.'

Mark entered and stood nervously opposite Jack who twinkled at him and smiled.

"You sure you have the ring?" he whispered to his best man.

"Quit stewing. You're going to give yourself a heart attack old man," Jack whispered back.

Willie had already taken his seat next to Mary when Mrs. Wellington walked in, the door slamming behind her. All heads turned to see who was there, surprised because no one else except Mel had been invited.

"Go get her, Willie. Sit her down somewhere," Ellen whispered.

Willie almost ran back down the aisle, then took Mrs. Wellington's arm elegantly and led her to the pew behind the family and next to Harley and Verna. She talked all the way.

"Bet you all thought I forgot, didn't you?" Chew, chew, chew. "Knew you wouldn't start without me; ain't a marriage til I say it is; doesn't matter anyway; this one's a man, no different than the rest, and that other one looks down my coat."

Willie's eyes rolled, and he hurriedly handed her off to Harley's care. If anyone can handle Mrs. Wellington, it's him, he thought.

Harley nodded in greeting and put his finger to his lips to quiet her. When she opened her mouth to speak again, he just patted her arm and raised his eyebrows, and she stopped.

Then the music started and Kate floated down the aisle on her father's arm. Mark stared, in awe of her beauty. The veil over her face was thin enough he could see through it to her shining eyes. Ellen had made it from her own veil which had been packed away for many years. The dress, too, was made of fabric from the dress she had worn.

When they stopped in front of Mark, Will lifted the veil, carefully folded it back and kissed his daughter. He started to place her hand in Mark's, but stopped and held it for a moment.

Then he held her close and whispered into her hair, "You will always be my Kate, my beautiful, wonderful daughter. I couldn't love you more, or be more proud of you."

Tears welled in her eyes as she looked at her father, and she heard Reverend Havens clear his throat, trying to move things forward.

Will looked up at him, "This is my moment, Reverend. You'll have yours in a minute."

The preacher looked shocked, but simply nodded. The few guests laughed uneasily, and Ellen just smiled. That was Will. She knew it would be hard for him to turn his daughter over to someone else. There was a special relationship between them, one that couldn't be defined simply as father and daughter. They thought alike, loved alike, and were similarly untamable. Will had encouraged her willfulness and spirit, loved to see it springing from her.

When he finally released Kate's hand to Mark, he quietly said "I am not giving you my daughter. I am sharing her with you. Take care of her." His eyes were pools of water he willed himself not to shed. Ellen saw, and her own eyes filled.

"I will, sir," Mark said gravely, and hoped with all his heart he could.

As Reverend Havens began to speak, Mel quietly slid into the last pew. He hadn't meant to be so late, but had made the decision to attend just minutes before. He had dressed carefully in his black suit and ridden to town, but just wandered around, still undecided. He was still wondering about whether or not he should be there when he found himself at the steps of the church and heard the music begin. He'd heard Will's words to Kate, and it could have been himself talking. No, he thought, I am not giving Kate to you either. I can't, and you damned well better take care or her.

The ceremony was brief. They were married. Kate laughed out loud in joy when the preacher pronounced them man and wife and even louder when he emphasized the part about letting no man put asunder the union of man and woman. He just can't help himself, she thought, but she was too happy to care.

When they walked back down the aisle as man and wife, Kate saw Mel and her face split into a huge grin.

"You came! I'm so glad," she said when they were across from him.

Mel merely nodded and waited for the rest of the party to follow Kate and Mark into the entry.

He shook hands with everyone, was introduced to Verna, hugged Ruthie and Mary, even held Ellie for a moment. Ellen invited him to the house for a small reception, but he said he had chores to attend to and then turned to Mark and Kate.

He slapped Mark's back and shook his hand firmly.

"I'm happy you're here, Mel," Mark said. "It means a lot to Kate."

"I couldn't help it. She said please," he said trying to joke, but the reality was he meant it and his lips could not force a grin.

Kate stood on tiptoes to kiss him on the cheek. "Thank you, Mel. It really does mean a lot."

"Do I get to kiss the bride?" he asked Mark, then took his kiss before Mark could respond and hurried down the steps.

Mark was left wondering how he had been blessed with Kate's love. Why had she chosen him over this strong, good man who obviously loved her completely? He hoped he would prove worthy of it to Kate and vowed to shower her with love until the end of his days.

The reception was larger than they expected. People kept stopping by and staying. They didn't intended to stay, but once inside, they were greeted warmly and encouraged to sip from Will's home brew. John Nestor was the first at the door and went back to his buggy a second time to bring in gifts he had brought.

Kate was embarrassed he had not been invited and confused he had brought gifts, but she ripped open the packages, obvious joy written on her face. Inside were two red wool blankets with beige and blue stripes across the ends and a set of blue print plates with matching cups and saucers.

"I love presents!" she said laughing. "Thank you!"

"I couldn't help it," he responded, the second person in a short while to say those words. "I kept seeing you behind the pickle barrel. You're the pickle princess, and here you are getting married."

She wrapped her arms around him, flinging the veil aside to kiss his cheek. "Can I take this off now?" she asked her mother.

Bessie Dunn arrived next and shyly put her present in Kate's hands. "It's not much," she said, "but I thought you should have pillows with your monograms on the cases."

Kate tore into the brown paper they were wrapped in, and then paused to look at Mark. "You want to help?" she asked.

He shook his head, happy to just watch her having fun.

Jake the jailor came. Ed Miller, Gordon Tilmann and several of Kate's students showed up at their door. Each one of them brought gifts, from a simple basket of eggs to beautifully stitched linens. Sadie even showed up and stayed for a few minutes. She sipped at Will's jug, nodded approval at his moonshine prowess and gave Mark a huge, buxom hug.

"You've caught yourself a good woman," she said. "I like that girl."

Mark knew that was high praise. Sadie didn't like just anyone, and he agreed with her.

"Yes, I have and believe me, I know it Sadie."

"Don't forget it," she said firmly and hugged him again.

When people stopped coming to the door, when the uninvited but welcomed guests had gone and the excitement died down a little, Will produced his special brew, a cordial made from raspberries like Ellen had described. He poured the deep red liquid and passed glasses around, then asked his daughter and her husband to join him in the center of the room. He lifted his glass high and looked at Kate. Then he looked at his wife, his eyes soft with remembrance of their own wedding day.

"I make this toast to love. You for your husband, and he you," he said, formally.

"Many years from now, love as completely as I do my beautiful wife today." He raised his glass to Kate and then to Ellen. "Now get out of here."

Kate changed into suitable traveling clothes, and they packed Will's buggy with gifts, clothes and things they would need for a short honeymoon at the cabin. Mark had already stocked the shelves with enough food for a few days. Will would follow them to the edge of the woods, help transfer their things from the buggy to the horses' backs; leave one horse with them, and then take the buggy home.

Ellen joined her while she changed, helped her gather up a few last minute things and tried to talk with her about marriage, but couldn't say the words. Ellen stammered around the subject until Kate hugged her mother and told her not to worry.

"I know you're a mature woman, Kate, but I've never talked with you about things between a man and a woman. I know I should have, but somehow I just put it off."

"It's alright, Ma. I'll be fine."

Ellen nodded, still not sure, but leaving it to her capable daughter, trusting she would deal with whatever came her way. She always had. Why should it change now?

It was dark when they began their journey to the cabin. The three of them were silent, enjoying the quiet and the crisp, cool night. They hauled their gifts and luggage to the cabin, said goodnight to Will, and then they were alone.

Mark asked Kate to wait outside for a few moments, and went in to light the fire in the hearth. Then he went outside to his wife. He placed both hands on the side of her face and drew her to him. His lips were gentle on hers, caressing and soft. He scooped her up with one arm, lifted her to his chest and carried her across the threshold.

"I love you Mrs. Ramey," he murmured. "Let's go home."

"I love you, too, Mr. Ramey. I always have."

He held her close, soaking up the warmth of the fire in the hearth and their bodies. Kate felt no need to stand on her own. She melted into him, knowing she no longer had to separate from him. She kissed his neck, felt him tremble, and knew only a small fear about what was to come.

When he put her down and removed their coats, Kate looked around the cabin and shivered.

"Are you cold?" he asked.

Kate shook her head, no, and looked around again. Their gifts lay piled on the table. Luggage was by the door. She would normally have scurried around to take care of the clutter. It usually disturbed her not to have everything in its place, but she didn't want to. It didn't matter. It will be there in the morning, she thought and, looking shyly at her husband, took his hand to lead him over to their bed.

He kissed her gently, felt her response, and caressed her. His tongue flickered at her lips, and Kate sought it, let her own tongue taste Mark's lips. She boldly rolled onto him and buried her face in his neck. Her hands slid down the length of his body as far as she could reach, to his hips, felt hard muscles flexing under her hands. When Mark's breath grew ragged, he paused, lifted Kate from him and rolled her to his side so he could look at her, kiss her eyes, her ears, her neck. She watched his face, entranced by the passion she saw there, and knew it was reflected in her own.

Kate was unsure of what was to come, but her anticipation mounted. She knew what she felt, but didn't know what to do with it; feared her lack of knowledge and yet knew what she felt was what Mark wanted. She trembled with desire and reached for him.

Mark pushed her gently back on the pillow and began to slowly remove her clothing and then his. His mouth followed each button and Kate felt a slow burn course through her body. She could not get close enough to him. Their bodies were woven tightly together, but what she wanted was to slide into him, enter into him through his skin. Numbness took over her brain and nothing except sensation, the tingling of her nerve endings, had meaning.

Later, they sat in front of the fire, Kate's flush still lighting her face, her smile of contentment glowing. Mark held her hand. Every few moments, he kissed it, still awed by the fact that Kate was his wife.

"I miss Bug," she said. "Why didn't we bring him with us? I love you, but I still miss him," she giggled.

"Want to go get him?" Mark asked.

"In the middle of the night?"

"Why not? Are you ready to sleep or do you want to take a ride?"

"Let's ride!"

Bug woke up the Hughes house with his barking, but Will and Ellen just rolled over and went back to sleep. He bounded out the door as soon as it was opened and ran to stand by Penny the horse, not willing to be left behind again. He scowled at Mark and then looked at Kate with reproach. 'You should never have gone off without me,' he said rolling his eyes with disdain. 'You should know better.'

Ruthie came to the door in her nightgown, said she knew they would be back for Bug, quickly said goodnight and shut the door.

They rode back in the moonlight, Kate in front with Mark's arms around her. She was content with his caresses, melted back into him and thought of nights to come. A sparkle lit her eyes. Bug barked at shadows and valiantly led the way, scaring off robbers and freeing the world of errant raccoons and other noxious creatures.

They spent three idyllic days and nights at the cabin, roaming the woods to pick early wild flowers and mushrooms, watching the squirrels chase each other or hide acorns, sitting outside at midday when the sun found its way through the thick canopy of leaves or sitting by the hearth fire mesmerized by its red and orange flames. In the early morning, three deer came into the small clearing between the cabin and creek, grazed happily and drank at the stream. Their heads tilted curiously at the strange sounds coming from the cabin, but once accustomed to the clink of a coffee cup or clatter of silverware, they resumed their forage for food. Kate watched them quietly from the window over the sink, careful not to make a sound that would scare them away.

"Look, Mark," she whispered softly with her finger to her lips the first time she saw them. "You have to see this."

Mark moved lazily from his chair by the fire and stood with his arm around her to watch the deer. Their fur was still thick from the winter cold, but patchy in places where nature was shedding the heavy coat in preparation for warm weather, and they were skeletally thin.

"They're hungry. Their backbones are sticking out."

"Well, the snow is finally melting in the woods, so they should be getting some good food now," he said, trying to help Kate feel better.

"But two of them are going to be mamas soon. They're too skinny to be mamas."

Mark felt her sadness and knew nothing he could say would take away the look in her eyes – unless he could find a way to fatten them up. She'd been outside feeding the birds, squirrels and a variety of woodland rodents everyday with scraps of bread and dinner leftovers. He'd swear the number of birds and small animals around the cabin had multiplied by at least four in the three days they'd been there.

She even trained Bug to sit quietly when she fed them even though Mark was sure it practically killed him to do it. His eyes darted back and forth following the chipmunks as they ran across the opening to grab scraps and scamper back with it tucked in fat cheeks. He whimpered when they got too close and trembled with the desire to give them a chase, but he just looked at Kate, questioning her command for him to sit.

When she finished feeding and the critters had scampered back to safety, Kate patted Bug's head, told him what a great dog he was, and he was off, his long red hair flung out in a wild circle surrounding him. He flew around the clearing several times, ran full tilt, barked and growled, reestablished control of his domain. Mark laughed out loud the first time he saw it, especially when Bug came back to sit by Kate, in the same place she had commanded him to sit before, but this time he wore a satisfied look on his face that said he was the master here. He was in control.

Mark was thinking about Kate's love for all nature's creatures as they stood at the window watching the deer. That was just one of the special qualities he loved in Kate.

"Maybe I could buy some hay or beets to haul out here," he said. "Maybe that would help fatten up these mamas. I'm pretty sure they've got beets at the feed store."

"Let's do it," she said happily. "Let's get some today." As quickly as she had been saddened, her spirits lifted and she flew around the room getting breakfast, cleaning up, and was ready to go before Mark could eat and get the mare saddled.

On the way to town, they talked quietly, warm in the growing sunshine and each other.

"I don't want to leave the cabin," she said.

"We don't have to leave today. We have one more day before we need to get back to work."

"No, I mean I want to stay there, live there."

"Kate, it's a long way to work – for both of us. And in the winter, it will be worse. We might even be snowed in and not be able to get to town."

Kate was silent, knowing he was right, but not yet ready to give it up.

"It's not really ours. Do you remember that?" he asked.

Her back stiffened at the thought. "It is too," she blurted. "It's ours . . . until the man comes back anyway."

"And if he comes tomorrow, what then?"

"Then . . . I don't know, but that's tomorrow, and he'll like what we've done to it."

"We'd need a horse, and we'd have to go into work and come home at the same time. I need to put in some long hours at the shop, Kate"

"I won't mind, and if I want to go home earlier, I can walk. I like walking to the cabin. I've done it a lot. That's how I found it." Kate's voice rose with excitement; she was already visualizing their life in the woods, with her critters, the creek, the sounds of wildlife coming in through the open windows.

Mark sighed, knew it was not the most sensible thing to do, but felt himself giving in to Kate's growing excitement. He did love being there, loved the solitude and quiet of the forest. But they were really only squatters. What had begun as a bit of naughty trespassing on a dilapidated shack had turned into something else entirely. Mark silently vowed to find out who owned the place and try to make some arrangements if Kate really wanted the cabin to be their home. But he'd need to buy a horse, too, and money was short. As hard as he worked at the smith shop, he never seemed to be able to get much ahead.

He paid Jack every week, a small amount, but he was determined to pay what he owed him as soon as he could. Jack hadn't charged much for his legal work, had tried not to charge anything at all, but Mark wouldn't allow it. He still owed for the futile search Jack had undertaken years before when he was looking for Lorraine, and Jack was still working to gain custody of Flossie and Jamie. He would continue, must continue, until he had them safely in his home. God, how he wanted his children with him! The ache was always there, nagging at the back of his mind, a seed sprouting thorns and barbs at any given moment.

Once or twice a month, he made the long trek to the orphanage to see his son. Sometimes Jamie was there, and then the many night miles meant nothing. At other times he was gone – fostered out to only God knew where — and the trip was futile. It was those times Mark's anger boiled making the drive back to Hersey long and empty. But he had no way to know in advance, and the disappointment in not seeing his son haunted him all the way home.

Still, periodically he was able to meet with Jamie through the fence at the orphanage yard. The meetings were brief, but he carried Jamie's face home with him, refreshed by the light in his son's eyes, and it was all worthwhile. Those times, he left with hope and Jamie's smile in his heart.

Kate was silent and watched Mark's face as his thoughts covered all the possibilities and pitfalls. She wanted life to be good to Mark, to see only joy in his eyes, not worry and sadness.

Gently, carefully she said, "I have a small income to add to yours, Mark, and a little saved. It's not much, but I think it could buy a horse – maybe a small horse," she added playfully.

Mark couldn't help but laugh with her. "I can just see us sitting on a Shetland pony, our feet dragging the ground. Besides, that money is yours, Kate."

"Hold on there, Mr. Ramey. I think we're about to have our first quarrel," Kate said, her head tilting back to stare at him. "You are not the only one who can earn a living. I can too, and have been for some time. Why should your money be the only funds we use?"

"Because it is my job to take care of you, not the other way around."

"Excuse me. We work together, Mark. We build our family together, take care of our home together, and do what needs to be done together. If that's not the way you see things, then I think you should just stop this horse and let me walk – alone, because we're not together."

Mark held tightly to Kate, feeling her try to slide off the mare. She'd do it too, just hop down and walk off.

"Let me go," she commanded.

"No, Kate. Never, and I'm sorry. I didn't mean we aren't together in this. We are, it's just that . . . sometimes I feel like such a failure that . . . my pride jumps up and gets in the way, makes me stupid."

"Well, damn! Oops, sorry, don't let it."

Mark smiled. She was forever swearing and apologizing for it. The word sounded strange coming from her lips, incongruous with her style and grace, and it always made him laugh.

"You never have to apologize to me Kate," he whispered softly.

"Well you do," she whispered back.

"Is this a double standard?"

"Yes. I like my double standards, thank you very much," she answered briskly, her shoulders thrown back in mock severity.

"I'll make a deal with you, Kate. We'll stay at the cabin, providing the owner doesn't return, until the snow flies. Then we move to the rooms behind the shop like we had planned. Does that suit you, my dear?"

"Yes!" she squealed happily, turning on the saddle to throw her arms around him. "Yes, it does!" After a few moments she continued, "We've gotten our first quarrel out of the way. Aren't you glad?"

"Yes, I am, but what about the kissing and making up?" he said, raising his eyebrows and leering at her. "I can stop this horse anytime."

He slid off the saddle and pulled Kate after him, wrapped his arms around her and nuzzled her neck. After he had thoroughly kissed her and felt her body slacken to melt against his, he drew back to look at her. Her lips were swollen and wet, her face rosy with passion, and her blond curls wild in the breeze. Her shirt had come open at the top, and his finger traced the swell of her white breasts. He wanted to nibble there where her skin was so creamy and soft, but couldn't take his eyes from her. She looked like a wood nymph and belonged to the forest.

"I think we'd better go, Mrs. Ramey."

"Are you quite sure, Mr. Ramey?" she said, a teasing glint in her eyes.

"Very sure."

They stopped at the Hughes house, surprising Ellen and Ruthie who wanted to know all about their days since the wedding. Kate talked with them while Mark went to find Harley. Will was at the shop, taking over in Mark's absence.

When Mark told Harley their plans to stay at the cabin, Harley thought it perfect.

"Why not," he asked. "No one else is using it, and Kate has been taking care of it for a long time."

"Well, there are little things like getting supplies out there with just a narrow path through the woods, buying a horse, winter, the fact we don't own it . . ."

"Mere opportunities," he said, his eyes squinting in a grin, "merely a wonderful chance for you to show your beautiful wife how clever you are. If you continue to look at the down side of everything, my boy, you will only see the ground. Look up. See the sky and look around you; see what is there waiting for you to touch."

"Harley," Mark said trying to stop the flow before he was too entrenched in his sermon. "Harley, wait, please. I just came out to say hello while the ladies caught up with each other."

"I know where you can buy a good horse for not a lot of money. Do you still want me to be quiet?"

Mark sighed, fearful of letting Harley get hold of the conversation again, but wanting to know.

"Yes, I do. I mean, no, I don't, please tell me. You confuse me, Harley."

"I heard one of the camps was clearing out their corral, culling out all the old horses. They've been worked hard and should be put to pasture, but they've still got a lot of use left in them if they're cared for properly. Check them out. I think they'll go cheap."

"Thanks, Harley. I don't know how you happen to know things like you do, but I'm glad you do."

"I keep my pretty eyes open, son, and my ears, too."

"How's Verna?" Mark asked, grinning at Harley, but soon wished he hadn't.

"She's a mighty little firecracker, that one. She can topple a man twice her size with just her tongue and a glare from her baby blues. Let me tell you what she did the other day . . ."

He was still talking as Mark shook his hand, said he had to be off, and left the barn. He knew Harley would not be hurt. That wasn't his way. Thank goodness.

Mark and Kate went together to look at the horses. Kate picked out a grey mare, not the sturdiest looking one of the bunch, but one that caught her eye, and then haggled with the foreman of the camp to get the horse for pennies on the dollar. She told him the horse was hers all along, had always been.

"Can't you see it?" she asked. "Look at the way her big, brown eyes stare at me. She knows me and wants to come home." The foreman just grinned at the crazy lady.

"Sure, lady. She's your long, lost sister. She knows you," he said, grinning and eyeing Kate appreciatively.

Mark watched Kate work her charms on the poor foreman, wondering if he should step in to help and wisely deciding to leave it alone. Kate needed no help; it was the poor man who was beaten before he even began. Perhaps he should have warned him in advance. Mark almost felt sorry for him.

She tossed her curls and laughed. "Of course she does. You just don't speak horse like I do. What do you think, Bug?"

"You speak dog too?" he asked.

Kate lifted her eyebrows at him and watched as Bug went into the corral, looked around and then went over to the grey. He sniffed at her chest and she let him, then she pushed her muzzle into Bug's face and snuffled around leaving wet marks on his fur at the top and sides of his head. When they were done, Bug walked back to Kate with a satisfied look on his somewhat horse-slimed face and sat at her feet.

"Well, what do you think?" Kate asked, looking down at Bug and then back to the man.

"I think you got yourself a horse, crazy lady."

Kate walked the horse back to town, stroking her flanks and talking to her all the way while Mark led the other mare. We have a horse, Mark thought. An old one, but it's a horse, and he had to admit the old girl did look happy to be with Kate.

"God, Mark," he said to himself, "you're losing it if you really think a horse can have a happy look."

"I believe you said that out loud, Mark, and yes a horse can. She has to have a name. Who does she look like?"

"I think you will find the perfect name for her and that you are reading my mind."

"Then be careful what you think when you see other women on the street," she said laughing into the sun.

They stopped at the shop to show their mare to Will. He was just closing up for lunch so they walked to the house together, leading their charges. Will showed appropriate approval of the new horse – and of the flush on his daughter's cheeks. It was obvious to him that

Kate was deliriously happy, and joy was all he had ever wanted for her.

When Mark told him what they had paid for the mare, Will said, "Let me guess – Kate did the haggling, right?"

"How'd you know?"

"Never mind," he said, a prideful grin spreading across his face. "You'll learn soon enough,"

They told him of their plans to stay at the cabin, and together with Harley, they devised a way to haul supplies. In fact, Harley had already begun to fashion a sled that could be pulled down the narrow trails leading through the woods. It sat on two metal runners that made pulling it over the ground easier than hauling a flat piece of wood or one with wheels, and attached it to an old harness he had found in the barn. Will gave them a saddle bag that hung over the horse's back, with two compartments to hold small items needing to be transported when the sled wasn't used.

"Sorry I don't have an extra saddle," he said to Mark.

"No, don't be. You've done too much already and we'll be just fine riding bareback."

Ellen had lunch ready and plates set for all of them. She was not entirely happy about their decision to live at the cabin, though, and vowed to see it for herself as soon as she could. Kate saw it in her mother's face, and invited them all out for dinner the next day.

"I can't wait for you to see it," she said, her face bright with anticipation. "You are going to love it, Ma. It's quiet, except for the birds, and there are chipmunks and squirrels and deer that come right up to the house, and a family of raccoons live in the biggest tree near the clearing, and . . ."

"A family of raccoons?" Mark asked.

"Yes, I saw them there last night when I went outside to watch the moon."

"You went out to watch the moon?"

"Yes. You were sleeping, and I couldn't because the moon was full, so I just wandered around the clearing a bit and saw them. They're so cute, little balls of fur with bandit eyes."

"You couldn't sleep because of the moon?" he pressed.

"Do you know you are repeating my words back to me?" Kate asked, smiling because he looked so confused.

"She's a were-woman, Mark," Harley volunteered. "It's a phenomenon sometimes suffered by women who are closely connected to the natural world. It's rare." He went on to describe the symptoms in detail with a great deal of scientific evidence backing his theory. Mark for once didn't try to quiet him. He just stared from Harley to Kate and back again, trying to understand Kate's affliction.

Harley continued until he could not stop the roar of laughter growing in his belly. Kate, too, was doing her best to stifle her mirth. When Harley couldn't contain it any longer, Kate let loose and the rest followed suit with Mark looking even more confused. Then it occurred to him he'd been had and graciously allowed himself to be the butt of their joke.

"I'm a fool," he said, laughing with them, "but I believed you, you old goat."

"Well, some of it is true," Kate said through giggles spilling out of her. "I do have difficulty sleeping during a full moon, so maybe some of Harley's tale is true."

"Right, Kate. I'm onto you now. Just don't go wandering alone in the woods at night, okay?"

"I didn't. Bug went with me."

"Good luck getting Kate to behave herself, Mark," Ellen said, a little pride sneaking into her voice. "I tried for years and never succeeded; you can't tell Kate what to do. Well, you think you can, and she'll listen and nod like she understands and agrees. Then she'll ask, 'why is the moon yellow?'" They laughed again, and each had a response to Ellen's question.

"She just wanted an answer, Ellen," Will said. "Did you give her one?"

Mark smiled, picturing Kate as a little girl with golden curls. He wished he had known her then. He'd heard tales of Kate's youthful escapades from Mr. Nestor and others who loved Kate's unquenchable spirit, even from Kate herself. She would do what she thought was appropriate for her, and that was the determining factor – what she believed was appropriate, no matter what he or anyone else said. That was Kate, and he thanked God or he wouldn't be her husband now. She was fearless, much more so than he, he thought. The forest creatures were her companions, and perhaps she knew them well, felt connected to them. Perhaps her lack of fear meant they wouldn't hurt her because they didn't fear her either.

They left with their new horse pulling Harley's sled laden with a bale of hay and sack of beets they'd bought at the feed store. They rode until they got to the path through the woods, then walked beside the horse. She didn't seem to notice she was pulling a load. Most likely it was nothing compared to the heavy work she'd been doing at the camp. He tied her to a large willow that would provide some shelter if it rained and then put out some of the food for the deer.

The next day the Hughes family – minus Willie, Mary and Ellie, but with Harley, Verna and Jack bringing up the rear, arrived early, surprising both Mark and Kate. They all had their hands full of apple pies, freshly baked bread, and a large crock of butter Ruthie had churned that morning. The men carried tools and lumber, dropped their loads, and went back to the wagon left at the edge of the woods for more supplies.

"What is all this?" Kate asked, clearly not understanding what was going on.

"It's a shed for your horse. You can't leave her out in the rain," her father said, his face lit with pleasure in the surprise.

"Will, I can't let you do all this," Mark said, running his hand over his face as he did when he was disturbed.

"It's just scrap from the mill, son. If it doesn't get used, it will get burned in somebody's hearth."

Harley pulled on Mark's shirt sleeve and mouthed an almost silent 'say thank you' to him. Mark obeyed and they built a shed.

Inside, the women inspected the cabin, approved its charm and asked about the man's clothing hanging near the door. Ellen sighed, remembering her daughter had only informally adopted the abandoned cabin for her own. They didn't own it. But she refrained from saying anything to put a damper on Kate's obvious delight in the place she felt was home.

They went out to help in the building of the shed, Verna strapping on a tool belt, sawing and hammering with the best. She was strong for a small woman and kept up with the men when it came to throwing around the heavy lumber. Before long, the frame had been made, the trusses up, and they were nailing the wall and roof boards on. Jack laid tar paper down over the roof boards and promised to return with shingles the next day. It was finished, and in plenty of time for a drink before dinner to celebrate, by Verna's command. First things came first, according to her, and next things next.

Mark pulled the two kitchen chairs outside for Ellen and Verna, and the rest sat on the ground, but Verna soon joined the group on the grass because that was where the jug seemed to hang around the most. Her pixy-like gray hair was cropped short. She wore pants, like a man, and sat cross legged like one, too. You didn't see women wearing pants around Hersey, but it seemed to suit Verna. She noticed them looking at her as she sat, and grabbed the jug as it went by.

"Yup," she said. "I wear pants. I like pants. Is that a problem? I don't get stick-tights stuck to my bloomers either. "

Everyone said no, no problem, at the same time, rushing to put her at ease, and agreed it was certainly not a problem for them, embarrassed Verna had seen them looking and read their minds. Harley patted her arm.

"You are a vision in your trousers," he said, "a fetching vision, I must say, and if you had stick tights attached to your bloomers, I would gladly pick them off for you."

"Harley!" Ellen said, gasping, shocked that undergarments would be discussed in mixed company.

"My apologies, Mrs. Hughes. You are a fetching vision, too," he said, teasing and pretending to misunderstand her shock just to watch her blush grow.

Kate considered Verna's pants thoughtfully. They were just the thing for working in the woods.

"I think they're great," she said. "I don't know why I didn't think of it. Why should women have to wear skirts that get in the way, snag everything and fly about when you run or climb trees? Or ride a horse?"

Ellen wanted to respond to her daughter, but closed her mouth quickly as words of reprimand were ready to fall from her lips. She would not make Verna uncomfortable by directing Kate to remember she was a lady, but could see the idea of wearing pants was blossoming in Kate's mind.

"Let's put dinner on the table," she said, diverting attention to food.

A huge pot of stew simmered at the hearth. They brought out the kitchen table and loaded it with the fresh bread, pies, pickles and chowchow they'd made from whatever was left in the garden late last fall. Plates were filled and refilled until the stew pot was empty and bellies full.

When they left, the sun was just high enough to give them light until they reached the edge of the woods. Kate and Mark stayed outside, sitting in the small clearing, holding hands and talking quietly in the growing dusk. Their first guests had left happy and full. Their dinner party had been a success, and they both felt a glow of pride – and a little relief it had gone well.

"You were wonderful, Kate, and your stew was delicious."

"Thank you, kind sir. I think I will make a pair of trousers."

"You didn't need to tell me that, Kate. I could see it in your eyes. But I really like you in bloomers," he said, running his hand over the back of her neck and through her hair, loosened from its ribbon and flowing free.

"You like me out of them," she teased. "Now wouldn't Ma be shocked at those brazen words? Poor Ma. I know she really wanted to lecture me, but didn't because of Verna."

"Your mother is a kind, patient woman. My guess is she had to practice a lot of patience with you for a daughter, my sweet."

"Would you care?" she asked. "About the pants, I mean."

"Would you care if I cared?"

"Don't answer a question with a question."

"Kate, I would love you if you dressed like Mrs. Wellington, and chewed and cussed."

Kate smiled sweetly and drew her lips in to cover her teeth. "Screw, screw, screw," she teased, mimicking the old woman. Mark covered her tight lips with his own drawn in as if he was toothless, tipped her back into the grass and then kissed her properly.

Much later, they checked out their new shed, put some of the hay and a couple of small beets in a corner, and then led the mare to its new home. She balked at the door, stopped to peer inside and, as horses will do, seemed to consider the structure a possible danger, a strange, predatory beast. 'This wasn't here when I first came. Where did it come from? Is it dangerous?' the mare asked.

Kate patted her flank and moved inside ahead of her. "It's okay, fraidy cat. It won't hurt you, come into your new house."

The mare nickered at Kate, flared her nostrils and pounded one foot on the ground in indecision.

"Come on," Kate repeated, "or your new name will be Kitty Cat, fraidy cat."

At that, the horse followed Kate into the shed and nonchalantly nibbled at the food in the corner, then looked up at Kate. 'I wasn't afraid, just careful.'

When Kate told Mark what the horse was saying, he just laughed. "So you really do speak horse," he said, "and dog."

"Of course. What did you think?"

CHAPTER THIRTEEN

I t was January 5, 1907, and her cries were as fiery as her hair. She flailed her tiny fists and kicked her legs. When they laid her on her mother's breast, Kate uncovered her, looked at the small body, counted toes and fingers, and marveled at her bright auburn haired daughter, laughing at the large sound coming from such a tiny girl, their fourth.

She was still yelling when Mark went in to see his newest daughter. He kissed Kate gently, looked at her tired eyes, and squeezed her hand.

"You've done it again, Mrs. Ramey; you've produced the most beautiful girl in the world."

"You've said the same about each one," Kate said, a tired smile playing at the corners of her mouth.

"And it's been true every time. Our babies are all the most exceptional, most beautiful in the world."

He took the infant from her mother and walked to the window, cradling her in his arms. Jeannie stopped crying and stared at her father, trying to focus her dark brown eyes on his face.

"What do you see there, little copper top?" he crooned. "My sweet copper penny, I'm your scruffy, old father, and you are another miracle."

Ellen bustled around the room, cleaning up. She paused, looking around at the soot covered walls and window panes, the tousled bed where Kate lay, the shabby furniture filling the small space. It was impossible to keep their winter home clean with the smith shop just outside the door. She knew Kate tried, but the forge fire spit smoke constantly, and no matter how many times you washed the walls, the gray was too deeply ingrained in the wood from soot that seeped under the door closing off the shop from the house and stealing in through the smallest cracks.

It bothered her to see her daughter living this way. Mark and Will, with Jack's help, had added a room at the rear of the building when the second baby came, so there were three now; one living space, a tiny bedroom for Kate and Mark – where Jeannie had been born – and another bedroom for the other three girls; Rachel, Katherine, and Rebecca.

Mark brought Jeannie back to Kate who opened her gown to suckle her new daughter. Each time she had given birth, she was newly surprised by the overpowering love she felt for the little stranger at her breast.

"I couldn't love you more," she whispered. "Whatever life brings to you, remember. I couldn't love you more."

"And I you," Mark said, hearing her whispers. "You are so beautiful and so brave."

"Let the hounds in, Mark," she said.

He looked at her like she had temporarily lost her senses. "The hounds?" he asked.

"Pa, Jack, Ruthie, Willie, all the people waiting in the shop for this baby to be born."

Harley was already in the birthing room. He had helped by Ellen's request. While she didn't quite approve of his methods, they had worked with Mary's two deliveries, and with each one of Kate's. She didn't know how he knew what to do, but he did, and knowing was all that mattered to her – propriety be damned when it came to her children and their babies. Ellen didn't even apologize for thinking the cuss word. She meant it.

"Mark," Kate said, reaching for his hand. "Before you let them in . . . I'm sorry."

"For what?" he asked, thoroughly confused. "What have you done to be sorry for, run around the woods in your pantaloons again?" he teased.

"I have not given you a son."

Mark would have passed off her words with a wave of his hand because he was so totally in love with his girls it didn't occur to him Kate wouldn't know, but he saw tears well at the corner of her eyes and roll down her cheeks. Kate didn't cry, not when anyone could see her. He couldn't dismiss her concern with a wave of his hand. He also couldn't say at this moment that he had a son – Jamie, and he cherished him from a distance even though all his efforts to be a father to him had only brought frustration and agony. He didn't want to take anything away from Kate and kept his thoughts to himself.

"Kate, do you have any idea how much joy our daughters give me, how much I would not trade them for sons? I was meant to have girls. I was meant to wallow in their adulation. In fact," he said with a grin of satisfaction. "I was feeling a little sad for you because I am the only male in the house and get all of the attention from all of my girls. I mean that, Kate. I have never hoped for sons and not daughters. Look at our Jeannie," he said. "Could anyone be more perfect, more outstanding?"

"She is, isn't she?" Kate said, beginning to feel Mark was telling the truth, not just trying to make her feel better.

"Girls are the best, Miss Kate," Harley said, sliding into place beside Mark. "And you surely are the best at producing the best of the best."

Mark went to let the hounds in then, assured that Kate felt better.

Will's shout of glee shook the room when he saw Jeannie's bright auburn hair and brown eyes. "Look at her! She a beauty!" and led in the three sisters.

Rachel, the oldest, asked if she needed to be diapered, asserting her right as the eldest, even though she was only six, to mother the youngest child. Rebecca, who was two and used to be the youngest, looked grimly at her new sister and mumbled something Kate interpreted as wanting to play with her new baby. Kat, their four year old second daughter, looked disinterested and probably was. She only cared about what happened outdoors with her critter friends, not babies.

"I'm not sure where this came from," Kate said, nodding to Jeannie's thick thatch of deep red curls.

"I'm thinking the neighbor," Will teased.

"Will!" Ellen said, "Shame on you."

"You just had to show me up with four to my two," Willie said, but the truth was he had tried hard to make sure Mary did not get pregnant again. She found it difficult after the birth to regain her strength and get over the strange depression that engulfed her. He never wanted to put her through it again. Two children were enough – one girl and one boy. Life was perfect.

Ruthie picked up Jeannie without asking permission, held her close and kissed her soft cheeks. She had been an aunt many times over and cherished her responsibility, but a deep yearning gnawed at her. She wanted her own babies.

Much had happened over the past seven years, yet a great many things had not changed. Lives were lived, sorrows dealt with and joys rejoiced in. They worked, they loved and they laughed.

Jack had finally proposed to Ruthie three years before, and they'd been married the following year. They lived in town in a small white house near the smith shop, just where the Hersey River began to curve away from town. It was so close to the river you could hear water rippling over the riverbed rocks just across the narrow street from their house. It had needed a lot of work, but there was a large unfinished upstairs they planned to turn into bedrooms for the flock of children they wanted to have. Jack had fixed up the downstairs rooms and put in running water and a new wood stove, but left the upstairs until later. It was still unfinished, waiting for the first signs of pregnancy.

Harley still lived in the back of the Hughes' barn, but he'd done some renovating there, too. He'd divided the space into two rooms, one for living and one for sleeping. He saw no reason to leave, and Will and Ellen had given no indication they wanted him to. Periodically, he picked up an odd job in town, like sweeping up at Nestor's or Sadie's, which everyone suspected was because Verna worked there, but mostly he worked around the Hughes' place doing things Will never got around to. It worked for Will. Ellen was happy to have repairs done, and he didn't have to do them. He was busy at the mill and sometimes at the smith shop. Harley had become a deeply ingrained part of the family, and it never occurred to them he could leave or would want to move on.

Frequently when Will came home, he found Harley and Ellen at the kitchen table talking and drinking coffee, sometimes even at midday when Ellen would normally have been hard at work around the house or in the garden. He knew they talked about things Ellen found difficult to accept or understand given her belief in the Bible as the ultimate word. Harley's philosophical bent sometimes grated against her teachings, but he was gentle with her and patiently let her talk for long periods of time about her beliefs before battling her ideas with his philosophy about the ways of the world and the Lord.

"Did it ever work for you to tell our Kate she was not allowed to do something?"

Ellen shook her head no, but wasn't really convinced it was the same thing.

"Well, we are his children, most imperfect ones at that, and he wants us to experience life; to love, to learn, to grow, to respect each other, and most especially, he wants us to be happy children. He wants us to laugh. He

certainly does not want to tell us what to do every moment of the day, as you found impossible with your own
children. We are to learn what is right to do, to feel what
is right. Let me ask you, Ellen, did you want your children to be copies of you?" When she shook her head no,
he said "Of course not. You wanted them to be better,
wiser, richer, and so does He – richer in the best kind of
way," he added.

Ellen would go for days thinking about a tiny question she pondered before finally finding a way to bring it
up to him, and Harley would watch her gnaw at an idea,
knowing eventually she would casually toss it out for
his conjecture. And she eventually, always did.

They had formed a special relationship, and Ellen
cherished talks with him, especially now her children
were grown, and her house was empty of their laughter. He confused her, unsettled the firm foundation of
her beliefs, but when she felt herself bending to his
words, she'd get up to pour more coffee and call him
an old fool.

"And I'm an old fool, too, for listening to you," she
said. But she laughed when she said it.

Will watched his wife grow mellow and appreciated
the smile that came more easily to her eyes and lips. She
even teased Harley and was slowly learning to tease her
husband about his small faults instead of gritting her
teeth and bearing with them. He knew part of her growing tolerance and ease was due to the security she felt.

The mill was still running – with the typical ups and
downs of businesses depending on weather, supply and
demand. It didn't make a lot of money once the profits
were split between Tom Reeves and Will, the men were
paid and overhead taken care of, but it continued to put
food on their tables and, most importantly, it had not
failed. They'd not had to move again. Her children were
settled; they had homes of their own, even if she was not
comfortable with Kate's situation, and her own home
was well taken care of.

But Will knew Harley was responsible for much of his wife's growing contentment. For that he owed Harley more than he could ever pay. He had been blessed by an angel the day Mark dragged the wanderer to the Hughes house like a stray dog who had followed him home, and Will thought of the words he had been taught as a small boy. He couldn't remember exactly, but it had something to do with 'entertaining angels, unaware.' It suited the situation perfectly. Harley certainly did not look or act like an angel, more like a chubby, curly haired rag doll with button eyes, but the results were the same. He touched their lives and healed their inner wounds. If that wasn't angel-like, then Will didn't know what was.

He snickered to himself thinking of Harley as the Hughes family midwife. A more bizarre appearing one would never be found, but he had been for all six of Will's grandbabies. Mark and Kate had been staying at the cabin when the first three had been born, and when her time was close, Kate asked her mother to move in until the birth.

Ellen arrived with Harley in tow. The first time, Kate and Mark had been surprised, wondering what to do with him in their small cabin. Where would he sleep? But Harley produced a canvas tarp, draped it over a branch and staked down the corners.

"Right here in God's great outdoors," he said smiling broadly and crinkling his eyes. "I've slept under the stars, under trees, on benches, just about anywhere you could think. This is more than adequate and, actually, quite lovely. I will be very happy here."

Mark brought a small table out to his makeshift tent and a kitchen chair. It felt good to know he and Ellen would be with Kate when he went to work each day. He was nervous leaving her alone, but she refused to move into town until the first snows came, just like they had planned, and it was only September.

"We can't let a little thing like a baby change our plans," Kate said, grinning. "Women give birth every-day, some even out in the fields. This is where I want to be, Mark. This is where I am happiest, and our baby will know."

He couldn't refuse her.

Neither could the school board, although some had tried. Directly after their marriage, on the day they had both returned to work following their brief honeymoon, Agatha Pennington arrived at the school house just as the children were leaving. She led the rest of the board, who looked embarrassed to be there, but Agatha's firm frown brooked no argument. Ed Miller, Bessie Dunn, George Simms and John Nestor stood a few feet behind her, waiting.

"Since you are now a married woman," she said, "we assume you are prepared to vacate your teaching post. We've considered a replacement, and you'll be happy to know it is your sister, Ruth, although we have not yet broached the subject with her. She," Agatha said imperiously, "is unmarried."

Agatha crossed her skinny arms over her flat chest and paused, waiting for Kate's response and assuming quick capitulation.

Anger lit Kate's eyes with fire. She crossed her own arms and looked at each face in front of her. Bessie's eyes had filled with tears that threatened to spill. George Simms alternately smirked and snickered and kicked at the dirt. Ed Miller poked George in the ribs and told him to shut up. John didn't say a word, but glared at Agatha. She didn't need to be so bitchy about it, he thought.

'I need this job,' Kate thought. 'We need it.' But she would never admit it to the group in front of her. She took a deep breath, looked out over the top of their heads and took another breath.

"Can you show me a board policy saying a married woman suddenly loses the ability to teach children when she gains the license to marry?" she asked.

Agatha, the obvious leader of the group, responded. "That has always been the policy, Mrs. Ramey. Women are meant to be in their homes, raising their own children, not out working. The Lord made women to bear and nurture; the man to provide for his family. If yours cannot provide properly, it is not the board's problem. It does not alter the board's position – or the Lord's," she added.

Kate was furious when she mentioned Mark. "This has nothing to do with my husband or his ability to provide!" she growled in anger. "And the Lord, also, has nothing to do with my teaching!" She looked again at the other faces.

"I believe the Lord has something to do with everything, young woman," Agatha replied, her pointed chin raised, her small, black eyes glaring.

"Your beliefs be damned, Miss Pennington! And I do not apologize for swearing. You have tried to interfere with my post for years, and I will not stand for it." She put her hands on her hips, glared back at Agatha, and said, "Do your best. I will fight you." To the others, she softened her tone. "I don't think this was your idea, but I will fight you, too, and I feel sorry for you if you let this bitter, old woman lead you around by the nose. I feel sorry for her too, because she lives a lonely, miserable life and the only happiness she finds is by controlling other people or making them as wretched as she is."

Agatha was gasping, had been since Kate swore, and was almost choking by the time she'd been called a bitter, old woman. She tried to speak, but couldn't.

"Kate," John Nestor said, "I don't like this at all, but it has been past policy. I don't know what to do."

"I do know, Mr. Nestor. Show me a written policy. If it's not there, then we don't have a problem, do we? If it's there, then change it. It's a stupid policy."

Bessie's tears were streaming down her cheeks. Conflict of any kind was more than she could bear.

George had stepped back and looked like he'd been slapped.

"She needs a man who can control her," he whispered to Ed Miller. "Feisty," he continued, eyeing Kate's chest as it heaved in anger.

"Shut up, George," Ed said again, then seeing the leer on George's face continued, "or I'm going to have a little visit with Mrs. Simms."

George had the decency to blush slightly, and stepped back a little further behind Ed so he could continue to eye the beautiful woman at the door. She stood defiantly, fists firmly planted on her hips, her feet spread in a combat stance, and silently waited for them to leave. She refused to turn around, refused to let them see her fear over the possibility of losing her small income – what it would mean to her and Mark.

When they left, Kate flew around the school room, swept the floor, cleaned desks, washed the chalk board, and vented her anger in a furious bout of cleaning.

"Damn! Damn! Damn!" she cried, tears streaming from her eyes. She swiped angrily at them, hating that they came so easily, but not able to stop, and as long as no one was there to see them, she let them flow – and didn't apologize for swearing.

She waited until all trace of tears had gone before walking to the smith shop like she did every day after school. Outside, she put on a false smile before going in to see her husband. There was no need to worry him until she'd done battle. She would see this through to its end by herself.

Mark sensed something was wrong in her smile, but let it go after asking if she wanted to talk about it.

"No," was all she said. "Later."

She left the shop, saying she had a little shopping to do at Nestor's and would be back before he was ready to leave for the day. Once there, she paused, her determination faltering, but she looked in the dusty window as she had done as a young girl, and saw the pickle barrel she used to hide behind, saw the men sitting around the stove, and then her face staring back at her.

"What's the matter with you, Kate, you cry baby?" she said out loud. "You're not afraid of Mr. Nestor. What is there to fear? And you know you are right about this, damn it! Sorry," she said to no one, then grinned at herself. "Alright, the old Kate's back!"

She felt a hand at her back and saw John Nestor's face in the window beside hers, not looking at her, just staring into the window as she was doing.

"That's what I did when I got back today," he said.

"What? Swear at yourself?" she asked, sure he had heard her.

"No. I looked in this dirty window and saw you hiding behind the pickle barrel." He paused, looked down at his feet and then back at Kate's face.

Kate giggled, and her face looked like the child she had been then. "I did that, didn't I?" she asked.

"Almost every time I turned my back. I never really knew when you would show up or what you were doing there," he said.

"Learning. I discovered a lot of things just hiding there and listening."

John's face was a mixture of sadness and memory. His hair had grown white since Kate had been his pickle princess. The lines on his face told a story of good times and bad; of hard work and conflict; his desire to help those in need and the need to care for his own family. Kate remembered years ago when he'd turned Mr. Jackson away as he begged for spring seed. She thought – no, she knew –he would not do the same today.

Kate impulsively hugged him. "I came to see you for a reason."

"I know, and there is no written policy, Kate. The board has no policy book, I looked, and I think it's time for some young blood on the school board," he said with a small sigh.

"Thank you," she said, and went back to the smith shop with a lighter heart. Kate knew she would win this time.

Kate taught school right up to the birth of her third girl. Until Ruthie got married, they dropped the girls off at the Hughes house, and Ellen and Ruthie cared for them while Kate was at school. Mornings were hectic when they were living at the cabin. They rose before dawn, fixed a quick breakfast, packed up the girls and loaded them on Kitty Cat. The girls went instantly back to sleep as Kitty Cat's rolling gate lulled them. The mare seemed to sense she had babies strapped into the saddle bags hanging down her sides, and her walk was more gentle, her step more sure.

Harley had fashioned carriers for the girls that sat securely inside the bags. They became accustomed to their early morning beds, even eager to nestle inside, their little faces peering out at the stars still twinkling between the branches. Eventually, Rachel thought she was too old to sit in a baby carrier and insisted on riding on Kitty Cat's back. Most frequently, though, she soon fell asleep and Mark slid her off the mare's back before she could topple and held her in his arms the rest of the way.

Bug danced along beside them, guarding them from night animals on the prowl. He'd run ahead, make sure the path was safe, and then run back. During the day, he stayed at the Hughes house and guarded the girls. Periodically, he made a trip to the school house to check on Kate, and then went back to guarding his charges.

When Rebecca, the third girl, came along, Kate admitted it was time to leave her teaching post. She handed her resignation to Mr. Nestor though, not Agatha Pennington.

"The children are losing a wonderful teacher," he said, "and an even more wonderful role model, but I understand. You have two beautiful girls. Is this another?" he asked, nodding at her swollen belly.

"We'll see," she answered, hoping for a son – for Mark.

Jamie, Mark's son, was a guest at the cabin shortly after copper penny Jeannie was born. Mark brought him home with him after he showed up unexpectedly at the smith shop. He was seventeen and he'd had enough of foster care. Jamie had been in one foster home after another over the years, and the story of his life brought physical pain to his father. He had run away from some of them; had been returned to the orphanage by others.

Jack's work to gain Mark's children had been in vain. Jamie knew they had tried. Mark had visited the orphanage as frequently as possible, and talked with Jamie through the fence when he was there. But many times his trips were useless. Jamie had been 'fostered out,' they said, but would not say where, and he never found out where Flossie was staying.

Jamie was a handsome young man; tall, with penetrating hazel eyes and a quick, clipped humor. His eyes were wide-set, his shoulders broad. Intelligence was an aura around him. Wide cheek bones and high brow gave him a bit of an exotic look, like you might expect if he was from a foreign country, or from this one when Native Americans freely roamed the land, and, like them, he treated the earth like it was alive and all its creatures were special.

He made over all of his half sisters, told them how beautiful and smart they were, and then picked up Jeannie, held her in his arms, and only reluctantly let her go when it was time for bed. Jeannie was in love. She patted his face, snuggled against his chest, and watched him. When he laughed, she giggled. When he scowled, she frowned. When he talked, Jeannie babbled, her words unintelligible, but obviously making sense to her.

Kate watched her husband's face as he and his son talked together. His pride was obvious, and the sorrow he felt in his failure to be the parent he'd wanted to be was even more so. But Jamie didn't show any resentment. In fact, it was he who comforted his father.

"You did your best," he said. "You tried, and that's all you could do." He looked around at Mark's family. "I like these people," he said, grinning. "I'd like to come back to visit when I'm out of the Navy."

During the time Jamie was with them, he spent much of it outside drawing. His tablet was always within easy reach. He drew the forest, the cabin with branches touching its roof, the squirrels and the deer, and many, many sketches of his sisters – most especially Jeannie with her curls glowing in the sunlight, which made her hair look more red than auburn, and dirt on her face as she crawled through the grass in the clearing.

The only time Jamie showed despair was when Mark asked if he knew where Flossie was. Jamie's hands clenched into fists and the look on his face hardened.

"They would never say. They wouldn't tell me even when I begged," he said. "But I will find her . . . that I will do." He paused, saw the grief lining his father's face and added, "She has been in one home, Pa, just one, and I have been told it is a good one."

The story of Jamie's foster home life was too horrible to be described. He'd been used as slave labor, been strapped to his bed to lie in his own excrement, forced to live like he was a sinner in the home of a Lutheran preacher who saw his duty was beating the sin out of Jamie. He tried to describe it gently, but there was nothing gentle about how he had lived. He had run away when he was thirteen, but was caught and returned by authorities bent on doing 'the best for the child'. He had run away again and again, and at fifteen he joined the Navy, lying about his age until they discovered the truth. He was returned again and given back to the Lutheran preacher.

Kate sat silently, listening to Jamie's story and wondered how Mark could live through it. His anger showed in his hands as they tugged at his hair and ran roughly over his face. She wondered how she would deal with this story if it was one of her girls telling it.

She knew the pain of it would kill her, just as the grief she saw in Mark's eyes was killing him. He had tried so hard, and like him, she knew without a doubt she would do anything if her children were in jeopardy, or her husband.

Jamie spent close to a week with them and then left. But he had made his imprint on them, especially on Jeannie who would find him later in life and be as in love with him then as she was now.

It was strangely lonely when he left, but Kate loved her life, loved being in the forest, tending her garden and children, feeding her creatures. She found ways to make their lives glorious and their dollars stretch. Monday was washing day, which she did in a metal tub by the creek. Tuesdays, she baked, filling all of her baking trays with bread, buns, and sweet tarts from the leftover dough. She sewed continuously, remaking clothes to fit the next youngest child and patching Mark's. His were always filled with burn holes from the forge fire and in constant need of patching. Wednesday was garden day, and Thursday was town day when she shopped for supplies and visited her family.

Much of her time, though, was spent outside with her girls. They picked berries and wildflowers, talked with the animals, and played in the grass. She made trousers for them all, and in them they freely climbed trees, hid from each other, and rolled in wildflowers.

Harley and Verna visited often and joined in the fun. At night, Kate would cajole them to stay. When they did, they built a small fire in the clearing, and Harley entertained them with stories. Rebecca always claimed his lap and lay back against his arm, staring up at him, intent on his story and his face.

Kat sat by Verna, quietly and unobtrusively holding her hand. Kat had adopted Verna, kindred spirits in their innate blunt natures. Jeannie tottered around, poked at the fire with a stick, making everyone lean forward at once to prevent a disastrous fall into the flames if she got too close. She investigated the ground for strange creatures and brought them back for approval. Rachel sat by her father, not touching, but watching his face, and was properly sophisticated and silent.

Kate thought of herself when she watched her oldest daughter, and wondered if she was feeling the same kind of insecurity she had felt when Mark had first come to dinner. Wasn't Rachel too young to feel like that? Kate didn't know if a boy was involved in what her daughter was feeling, but what could be going on in her beautiful head that made her insecure in this safe environment? Kate smiled at her daughter and wondered if Rachel was growing up, was trying to figure out how to cross that bridge between childhood and young womanhood. Give it time, sweetheart, Kate thought. You are so young yet, and there are too many trees to climb before you cross over, and I hope you'll climb them forever.

"Kate, you're getting maudlin. The smoke has gone to your brain," she said out loud.

"No," Mark whispered, "your brain isn't smoked. Your daughter is growing up. I see it too."

"You're reading my mind again. Stop that."

"Never. It's a fascinating place," he said, smiling at her a bit sadly. Mark didn't want to see his girls grow up either, possibly even more than Kate. He had missed the childhood of his first two, and perhaps that was why he cherished every first step, every first word, every discovery each of his girls made.

He was as excited as they were when they discovered dandelions made your chin yellow. He ran out to the yard to pick as many as he could find, brought them back and covered all their faces with yellow. The pieces stuck to the stubble of his beard, and he just rubbed it again, covering his face with the small yellow petals. When the dandelions changed to white fluff, he dragged the girls all over the clearing to search for them, make wishes, then blow the fluff into the breeze and watch as it floated away.

When a storm thundered, he gathered the girls in the middle of the clearing, away from the trees, to watch the lightening as it streaked across the sky. He pointed at the gold streak and counted the seconds before the thunder arrived.

"That one is just over town," he said, "probably right over the smith shop." Each time lightening lit the sky, Mark pointed, counted, and told the girls where it was and where it was heading next.

"I'm not sure I like it," Rachel said. "It makes me nervous, like it's going to strike us right here."

"Well, it wouldn't do that," he said, patting her back and snuggling her closer.

"Why?" she questioned, not accepting his words as truth.

"Because, I know the people who make the lightening," he joked, "and I've told them where to put it. I also told them to give us a good show tonight."

When the lightening receded and the storm seemed to blow away, Rebecca picked up her father's hand and pointed it at the sky. "Do it again, Daddy. Make it lightening again."

Mark laughed and realized his daughter thought when he pointed at the streak of light, he was causing it to happen. It was a sobering thought, their belief in his power, and he was unsure how to respond. It also filled him totally. He could not find it in his heart to dispel Rebecca's belief, to tell her he was just a mortal man. For his girls, he would sell his soul to the devil to become a power strong enough to keep them safe and happy.

But Mark didn't know the devil, except as the pain growing in his stomach. He felt it now as he sat holding his girls and watching the storm blow across the night sky. He rubbed his hand where the dull ache gnawed, and prayed it was ulcers. He had been worried a lot lately, and he knew worry was sometimes the cause of ulcers. Who wouldn't worry? He had four children to feed and clothe, plus Kate. He had no real home for them except filthy rooms at the back of the shop and someone else's cabin, and work at the shop was dwindling as folks traded in their horses for automobiles. He couldn't seem to get ahead and it ate at him. He should be able to do more. He hadn't gone to see Dr. Cheston, wouldn't until he had to; and hadn't told Kate. He wouldn't until he had to, and maybe it would go away. He prayed it would go away. It had to.

CHAPTER FOURTEEN

O range light filled the eastern corner of the sky this time. Fires had begun to slowly eat away at the town of Hersey. Homes far from town were piles of ash before the fire truck could get there. Those in town were damaged close to collapse. The last few winters brought too little snow. While hard winters took its toll on the animals and forced people into hibernation, heavy snowfalls were needed to moisten the earth, to hold the ground firmly in place as summer took hold and the sun dried everything in its heat. But snow hadn't fallen heavily in the last few years, and the earth was dry. Crops were sparse in the drought, tempers flared, and money was once again in short supply.

Mark worried about the fires, worried about everything, as he rode Kitty to Mel's farm, still unsure what he was doing was right. He continued to ponder it as he rode. The sun was high in the sky, and dust swirled on the road with each of Kitty's steps. He rode slowly, not in a hurry to get there and not wanting the heat to get too much for his mare. She treated them well, had been a good, sturdy horse and hadn't been young when they bought her ten years before.

When he saw Mel in a field near the road, Mark almost turned the horse around, changing his mind once more about talking with him. But what he wanted from Mel wasn't for himself; it was for his girls, for Kate.

Mel looked up, nodded when he saw Mark, and it was too late for him to turn and leave unnoticed. Mel was surprised to see Mark. While he ran into the Ramey family in town once in a while, Mel had never been to their home and had made a point of not being where they were. It wasn't difficult to do; he didn't leave the farm much unless it was for a purpose. He wasn't angry or resentful; he was merely saving himself some heartache. He didn't feel good about it; it just was. His philosophy was simple; if you don't like what you're doing, change it. Same with what you see. If what you see bothers you, make sure you see something else. So he did, and he loved his farm, was content there. He waited for Mark to speak.

"I wonder if I could talk with you a minute," Mark said, getting down from his horse and trying to quickly get to the point of his visit.

"Sure. I've got a few."

"Can we sit?"

Mel led them over to a maple at the corner of the field, and they sat in the shade of its branches.

"I'm not quite sure how to go about this," Mark began.

"Then why not just say what it is you're thinking. What brought you here?"

Mark took a deep breath. "I'd like you to come out to the house. Visit us, see Kate and the girls."

"Why?"

His bluntness gave Mark no room to wiggle around the reason. He shouldn't have been surprised; it was Mel's way to get straight to the point, but he hadn't thought it out, didn't really want to give his reason and had hoped he could find another way.

"Well, you and Kate were good friends, the best, and she's missed your company. You haven't gotten to know our daughters, and you would love them. Kate would like to show them off to you, and . . ." Mark ran out of silly reasons, but he couldn't say the real one. It was too stupid, too presumptuous. He ran his hand through his hair and over his face and felt drawn with the effort, exhausted by the energy his emotions expended.

Mel watched Mark blunder around and began to see he was deeply troubled. He looked tired, and the etching around his eyes grew deeper as he squinted in the sunlight. He was thin; more so than he had been the last time Mel had seen him. Even though Mark had always been slender, it had been an elegant slenderness. Next to Mel's brawn and size, Mark now seemed diminutive, and suddenly Mel understood. The gray pallor, the body bordering on gaunt.

He didn't say anything, and for long moments Mark was silent too. They looked out over Mel's hay field. It was golden, the shafts heavily tasseled and ready for the first cutting.

Finally, Mel spoke. "I'm not sure what you want from me."

"Just to be the friend you were. That's all." He looked Mel straight in the eyes. "Am I asking too much of you?" he asked sincerely. He truly did not want to cause Mel pain, but concern for his family came far above his concern for Mel's feelings, and that is what had led him to Mel's farm.

"I'll think it over," he said simply. No questions, no caveats. He got up from the grass and held his hand out to Mark.

"Thank you, appreciate your listening," Mark said.

It was a while before Mel made it out to the cabin, not because he hadn't made up his mind if he was going to, but because he hadn't figured out how to do it. How could he make it seem normal to visit a family he hadn't called on since it had become one? He stewed about it, knowing instinctively Mark's visit to him had been covert; he had not told Kate about it, and it was intended to stay between him and Mark.

He also guessed Kate didn't know Mark was ill, and he was trying to set up a way for his family to be taken care of – at least that was what Mel suspected – and he wanted Mel to know and love his daughters. It seemed strange Kate couldn't see he was sick, but she saw him every day, so the change in him most likely had come gradually, and love was blind. She wouldn't want to see it. The pain he felt for her was a physical one, deep in his gut, and he wished he could change places, take Mark's illness for Kate. "I don't have a wife and little ones who would grieve if it was me who was ill," he said looking up at the sky. "Lord, I don't understand you."

He didn't like subterfuge, but this one protected Kate, and that he did appreciate. He knew he would eventually run into Ellen Hughes in town if he hung around long enough, and she was going to be his reason for going to the Ramey house. She was going to 'drag' him there.

He didn't run into her quickly enough, though, and Mel finally had to ask Mr. Nestor when Ellen did her shopping. Nestor looked at him a bit strangely when he asked, but didn't say anything about his question nor ask questions Mel couldn't answer.

The next time Ellen shopped, Mel was at the door of Nestor's. "Mrs. Hughes," he said happily, "how are you?"

Ellen was always glad to see Mel and it showed in her face. "I am just fine, Mel, and it's good to see you."

"And your family?" he asked, easing into questions about the Ramey family.

"They are well, too, Mel. Thank you for asking."

Ellen didn't expand on the family, thinking Mel usually wanted to skip that part. Eventually, Mel had to just come out and ask.

"Doesn't Kate have four daughters now?"

"Yes, four beautiful girls."

"I'll bet they are," he said, still wondering how he was going to get her to ask him to accompany her to the Ramey home. He wasn't used to playing around the outer edges of the truth. His way was straight forward, not hedging and conning people into doing what he wanted. He shuffled his feet and looked everywhere but at Ellen's face as he tried to figure it out.

"Are you alright, Mel?" Ellen asked, confused by his behavior.

"Yes, sure, I'm fine."

Ellen nodded slowly, peered into Mel's eyes trying to read what was there, and waited for him to tell her. Mel decided to tell half the truth, keeping Mark's secret, and take the blame for the deception on himself.

"I've not seen the babies," he said. "I guess I'd like to, but it feels strange to go barging into their home after so many years. I'm chicken," he said grinning.

Ellen nodded again. "Chicken you've never been, Mel, and they're not babies anymore. The youngest is three now, and the oldest is nine. But I understand, and it's long past time. Perhaps I can help. Why don't you come for dinner tonight?" she asked.

"I'd like that," he said, relieved Ellen had quickly seen his dilemma – or part of it, anyway.

"Come a little before six."

Will and Harley were not there when Mel arrived, and Ellen quickly described the plan she had come up with.

"I will go see Mark at the smith shop and tell him I am longing to spend a little time with my grandchildren and would like to go out on Sunday. He never denies me my visits, so it will not be an issue. You will stop by this house on Sunday to say hello on your way home from church, and I will insist that you go with us. I can be very pushy when I want, and I believe on that day, I will be a bit forceful and unwilling to take no for an answer."

"Mrs. Hughes," he said smiling, "I think you have become tricky and just a little bit deceitful – in a good way," he added quickly. "Thank you."

Harley came in then, saw their conspiratorial faces, and he raised his eyebrows in question.

"Mrs. Hughes, if I didn't know better, I would say you were having a clandestine meeting with young Mr. Bronson."

"Well, Harley," she quickly responded, "did you really think you were my only admirer?"

Mel was startled. He had never known Ellen to tease, had not watched her grow playful throughout the past several years as the others had, but he admitted it looked good on her.

Ellen put her finger to her lips for silence. "Shhh, I think my husband's coming."

They were laughing when Will came in, but Ellen and Mel didn't let them in on their plan. Harley and Will would be witnesses to Ellen's dragging of Mel to the Ramey cabin next Sunday, and they would be honest when they told how she forced the poor man to go along.

Mark stewed over what he had done, still not sure if he had done the right thing, and he was truthfully surprised when they showed up on Sunday with Mel in tow. He knew how much he had been asking of Mel, and didn't really think it would happen. Will teased his wife when he told them how she had brow beaten poor Mel into coming with them. He never suspected it had been planned – who would suspect Ellen of duplicity? And Mel's entrance into their lives appeared to have just happened. Kate was stunned, but happy to see him.

She introduced their daughters, delighted to show them off to her old friend. Mel politely shook their hands and asked each one a question or two about what they liked, what they wanted to be in a few years – when they were grown up. He asked Kat if she had a boyfriend. She told him boys were yucky, but bugs and worms weren't. She liked them best. Rebecca asked if he had a girlfriend. When he said he didn't, she suggested he could marry her.

"I would like that," he said, solemnly, "but I will have to ask your father for your hand, and I'm afraid he might say no."

"Not my hand, me," she said confused and pointing to chest. "Would you say no, Daddy?"

"Absolutely. You belong to me my sweet Rebecca. Only me."

Rebecca was satisfied by his answer and went to sit on Harley's lap.

They sat outside for a long time after supper. The sun was beginning to drop behind the treetops, and the air lost some of its heat. It was comfortable. The unease Mel expected to feel, and had worried about, had fled after the first shock of being there. He was glad Mark had asked. It didn't hurt like he expected. In fact, as he watched Kate in her home with her family around her, he felt peace. She was happy. Perhaps he had finally come to terms with it.

Conversation drifted easily from place to place, from weather and heat to crops and lumber camps, from the disappearing forests to the noisy automobiles beginning to chug and fume down the roads, and finally to the fires that were close to becoming a frightening probability instead of just a possibility.

Mel turned to Kate, "If you even smell smoke in a breeze that is going your way, or even if it's not blowing toward you, load up your daughters and get to town," he said grimly. "Don't pack anything, just go. The forest is a tinderbox, and wind can change direction in an instant."

"We'll be fine," she said. "I know it's a long way out to the road, but we truly will be fine."

"Mel's right, Kate. You must be vigilant in your watchfulness when I'm at work. Maybe we should move into town for awhile, at least until we get a good rain."

Mel was sorry he had spoken. He hadn't wanted to start anything. Kate looked distraught at the thought of leaving the cabin and determined not to go.

"Houses burn in town too," she said. "In fact, they're so close together that one catches fire from the other."

"That's true, but they are not surrounded by a forest as dry as tinder. You've no place to go to get away from it."

"What if we had a place?" she said.

"Like what?" Mark asked. He wasn't being stubborn; he was afraid for them, and as the pain in his stomach worsened, the more fearful he became. He knew part of it was his fear about what would happen to them if he should become too ill to care for them any more, but he couldn't make his fear stop, and the threat of fire was a reality he couldn't deal with.

"I don't know," she said, "a place we could hide in until any fire went past us. Maybe a hole in the ground or something like that."

"You know, that's not a bad idea," Harley said. "I've seen undergrounds; so have you. Your root cellars. We could dig one here and cover it with a thick wood roof. We'd make it deep enough to hold lots of air, and if a fire really threatened, you'd douse the roof with lots of water kept nearby in rain barrels. It would work," he said eagerly.

"It might," Mel said thoughtfully, "if you had a lot of barrels and if you drenched the area around the hole too. I have a bunch at the farm you can use if you want."

"You can have scrap from the mill to make the roof and line the walls. I wouldn't want it to crumble in on my grandchildren."

Kate looked brighter thinking she might not be forced to leave her home for the rooms behind the shop. She knew she was being stubborn, even selfish, but she could not bear taking her girls to those hot, dingy rooms during the summer. This was their summer world, where they could see nature at their fingertips, where crickets put them to sleep each night and they woke each morning to see deer at the creek.

This was their school room, too. They spread a blanket on the grass, and learned to read and do math in the sunshine. Kate knew her daughters were far ahead of the other children their age. Even Jeannie was learning to read and was already doing simple addition. They didn't even take summer vacations from school because out in the fresh air, school was fun and nature was their teacher. She told Mel about their school in the clearing and bragged about how smart her girls were. Mel assured her he could tell just by looking at them, and Kate lightly punched him in the arm.

Mark grinned, agreed their daughters were exceptional and ran a hand through his hair. He dragged it over his face, and for what seemed a long while to Kate, he let it cover his eyes.

"Okay," he said. "Let's see what we can build." He smiled at her, but it was a thin smile and didn't erase the worry lines on his brow.

For the first time in a long while, she really looked at him. She didn't see the handsome strong man she had met so long ago, or even the man she had married, and was shocked at what she did see. He was pale, and his broad shoulders drooped. He was so thin. When did that happen? How had she not seen? What was wrong? Fear crept into her heart, and she wanted to run to him, cradle the face she so loved, and kiss the lines etched around his beautiful eyes.

Mel and Harley began making plans, and Will joined them. Mark listened, adding a thought or two when he could. They would begin tomorrow.

"I have work that needs to get done," Mark said. "I can't tomorrow."

"Well, we all can. Who needs you," Harley teased. "We have enough brawn here to dig circles around you anyway." He turned to Kate. "Will you feed us if we dig?" he asked.

"Of course, as much as you can eat," she said grinning at him, but looking quickly back at her husband, trying to understand what she saw.

Mel knew the moment it hit Kate, and knew, too, it had hit her hard. She was distracted and quiet, and her blue eyes were filled with liquid she would not shed. It was time to leave.

"I have to get back," Mel said. "Sorry to break up the party, but I'm late for milking."

Mark stood quickly and shook Mel's hand. "Thank you for coming," he said simply, "please come often," and when he looked into Mel's eyes, he saw Mel knew what he meant.

"Is tomorrow soon enough?" he joked quietly. "I'll be here digging with Harley and Will."

Mark grinned and nodded. They took the girls inside, carrying Jeannie who had fallen asleep on Will's lap and Rebecca who slept soundly on Harley's. Kat, who had listened intently to their plans for a shelter and was wide awake, told Harley Verna should come with them tomorrow.

"She's the best digger," Kat said confidently. "You should have brought her today. Where is she?"

"She had to work today," Harley told her, "and how do you know Verna's the best digger? Even better than me?"

Kat nodded, assured in her knowledge. "She can do anything. She's as strong as a man, and she wears pants."

"Yes, sweet girl, I think you are right. She can do just about anything she puts her mind to. I'll see if Verna can come out and dig tomorrow. Will that suit you?"

Kat nodded solemnly, and then tugged on his arm. When he bent down to her, she whispered in his ear. "I wear pants too."

Harley pretended to be shocked and widened his eyes. Kat put her finger to her lips to silence him, and he nodded conspiratorially.

When the girls were tucked into their beds, Kate and Mark went back outside into the silent night. They sat on a swing Mark had built and rocked gently back and forth. Mark's hand rested across her shoulder and his fingers played with the tendrils of hair at the nape of her neck. It sent shivers down her back and made goose bumps on her skin. Kate grew warm with yearning that began deep inside and spread throughout, all the way to her fingers. It amazed her Mark's touch never, ever failed to arouse her. He was the same, she thought. He hadn't changed. She had imagined things earlier, and the dusk had played tricks on her eyes.

She kissed him and then drew back to look into his eyes. "You're not ill are you, Mark?" she asked. "Tell me you are not."

Mark was silent for a few moments. They had never lied to each other, couldn't because too often they read each other's minds, and they didn't want to lie, had never felt the need to.

His stillness began to scare her, and she grabbed his hand. Maybe the dusk had not played tricks. "Tell me," she said bluntly. "I can take the truth, but I can't take your silence."

"I am sure it is nothing," he said, seeing fear creep over her face.

"What is nothing? What do you mean – it?"

"Probably just an ulcer. I have some discomfort in my stomach, and that's usually all it is, an ulcer. I drink some milk, and it feels better."

"How long have you had this ulcer?"

"Awhile."

"Have you seen the doctor about it?" she asked.

Mark shook his head and looked off into the distance. He would give anything not to have this conversation, to assure Kate everything was fine. How could he tell her what he really thought?

"Well, you will. You will make an appointment with him tomorrow."

Mark didn't respond. He looked up at the stars twinkling between the leaves and then around the clearing. He spotted one of the raccoons living in the hollowed trunk of a huge maple at the edge of the clearing. They were so quiet for their size, and almost ghost-like in their ability to appear next to you in an instant when they had not been there the moment before. The coon stood on its hind legs holding an acorn, rolling it in his agile hands.

"Look, Kate," he said quietly, "there's one of your babies. Not so little anymore, are they? I believe he's looking at you."

"And I am looking at you, Mark. You've lost weight. You look tired. Why haven't you told me?"

"Because I love you too much."

"Please see Dr. Cheston tomorrow. Please?"

Mark nodded and kissed her. "For you," he said.

He started for the smith shop while darkness still shrouded the forest. He left Kitty in her shed as he had been doing so Kate would have her to use if she needed. The walk was long, but he didn't mind. It gave him time to think, and the quiet was soothing. This morning, he pondered his life, remembered a time when no hill was too high to climb, no obstacle too great for him to overcome. Obstacles were merely challenges, and he loved a challenge. When did I grow old?

"Kate didn't earn this, Lord," he whispered out loud. "All she's done is to love me."

He was at the outskirts of town, and the sun was skimming the edge of the horizon when he heard them. The wagon squeaked as it rolled over hard packed dirt and was the sound he heard first. Then he heard their laughter. Will and Mel sat on the seat, and Verna and Harley rode on top of the lumber stacked on one side of the wagon bed. Several shovels were wedged in between four large wooden barrels that stood on the other side. They sloshed water as they bumped down the road and were part of the reason for the laughter as Verna and Harley tried to dodge the spray.

"I took my bath," Harley yelled.

"Obviously Will didn't know that, or you smell!" Verna yelled back, and hid behind him to avoid a bath of her own.

Mark stopped to watch as they rolled toward him, wishing he didn't have to go to the shop. They were all having fun at Harley's expense, and he wouldn't mind being part of it.

When they were abreast of him, Mark said, "I'd like to go play with you all, but some of us have to work. Looks like you rose before the roosters this morning, Mel."

"I have to admit my herd seemed confused when I milked early this morning, especially since I was a bit late milking last night. One even objected, rolled her big, brown eyes and said 'I just gave. Leave me alone.'"

"Sounds like a wife," Will said, not really meaning it, but it had sounded funny in his head.

"So you talk cow?" Mark asked. "Hmmm. . . Kate talks horse and dog. Interesting languages."

"I must admit that few people have the ability to converse in the language of nature," Harley said, wiping the drops from his face. "And," he continued, "not everyone believes a language exists, but it does. However, one has to be open to subtle nuances in order to understand natural languages like cow and horse and dog."

Verna slugged him then. "Be quiet, you old coot. Don't you understand a joke?"

"Of course I do. I just thought they might want to benefit from my knowledge of languages," he said, and then sat quietly for a moment, trying to look hurt. But it was hard for that face to appear wounded. The light in his eyes betrayed him.

Mark had laughed loudly when he saw Verna slug him, and even louder when he saw Harley close his mouth.

"I never thought to see the day," he said.

"What day?" Will asked.

"The day anyone could still Harley's tongue. Let me know how long it lasts."

"We'll keep track," Will offered, "and we won't keep you from your work. We'll probably see you at the cabin when you're done."

When they had rolled down the road toward the cabin, Mark went off to work feeling comforted they had such good friends – friends and family who were helping take care of his family. He smiled and his step was lighter.

He hurried through his work, and was finished mid-afternoon. Even though he could not have put off the work he had to do that day, the load was light and had been growing lighter each year. Mark didn't know how long he could continue to make even the small living he did at the smith shop. Demand was no longer there, and he couldn't create it when it didn't exist. He had to think about what to do when there was no need for a smith shop at all. Could he swing an axe? Would any of the lumber camps even hire him after the mess he'd been involved in? He knew they wouldn't, but he didn't know what to do either. He hated the idea of moving his family, but the thought kept nagging at him that he might be forced to.

Mark had not made an appointment to see Dr. Cheston, but he did walk over to his office after he left the shop, hoping he would not be there and he could honestly tell Kate he had tried. The door was open, so he went in. The old man was sitting at his desk and looked up when Mark entered, smiled somewhat grimly at him, asked about his girls and then about why he was there. He had never quite forgiven them for not letting him take charge of their deliveries, especially when he heard Harley had been the midwife.

"I told Kate I would see you," Mark said. "She thinks I should ask you about this little pain I have in my stomach."

"But you don't think so?" he asked.

"Well, maybe, but it's probably just an ulcer."

"So, you're a doctor now? Why don't you tell me about it?"

Mark did, and Dr. Cheston checked him out, had him lay on the table and poked and prodded at his stomach. Mark winced when he pushed two fingers deep into his belly just above his hip bones, and the old doctor nodded and pushed again.

"Well?" Mark asked when he was done poking.

"You seem to have something going on in your stomach," he said, "but I can't feel any growth in there, anything like a tumor."

"Could it be just an ulcer?"

"Could be that, I just can't tell."

He gave Mark some medicine to drink when he felt pain, and told him to come back if it got worse. Mark left feeling a little better –it could really be an ulcer - and he could tell Kate what it was.

He was smiling when he got to the cabin and saw the group still digging in the hard-packed earth, and covered in dirt - all except Jack, of course, who was still spotless in his white shirt. Mark hadn't even known he was there because he had not been part of the group early that morning. He'd shown up later having been told by Ellen what they were planning.

Mark shook his friend's hand, glad to see him, and asked how he did it.

"What?" Jack asked, knowing full well what Mark meant.

"Remain the only clean person in a group of groundhogs."

"I'm sure it's because he leaves the real work to the rest of us," Harley said.

"He's afraid to get his hands dirty," Verna volunteered. "What kind of man doesn't get dirty?"

"I think we're about done with the digging, thanks to Miss Verna. She's a power with a shovel," Will said. "We can probably build the frame right inside the hole, get it done tonight and finish the rest of it tomorrow."

"Good," Verna said, leaning on the handle of her shovel. "I'm ready for a drink," she added, "and the rest of you can build. You've all been slacking, and now I'm gonna supervise and drink." She smiled broadly, her teeth looking white against the skin of a face darkened by black dirt.

"Sounds like a plan, Verna. I'll just get the jug and then take over your shovel, if that meets with your approval. These lugs need a good supervisor; I know that for a fact."

Inside, he kissed Kate who was busily making food for the workers. She lifted her eyebrows at him, waiting anxiously to hear if he'd gone to the doctor.

"I went," he said, not making her have to ask. "It's most likely just an ulcer like I figured."

"Oh, thank God," she sighed and went limp against him. The fear she had felt melted away and made tears well up in her eyes and slide down her face. "Thank God," she said again. "I couldn't lose you, Mark. I would die."

He tilted her chin up with one finger and kissed the dampness from her face.

"Smile, sweetheart. You are stuck with me for as long as you'll have me." He patted her bottom and turned to leave. Kate smacked his bottom with the spoon she'd been holding.

They finished the hole, shored it up with a two-by-four frame, and fell to the ground by Harley and Verna. Kate came out to see if they were ready for food and saw them sprawled on the ground, bantering about who had done the most work.

"You look like a bunch of hobos," she said, "well, except for Jack."

"Hey there, Miss Kate, there's nothing wrong with a hobo. We're a good lot; kind, wise in ways others cannot fathom, able to live where life lands us and bless strangers with our presence, our wisdom . . ."

"Sorry, Harley. I didn't mean to insult you. You truly are a wise one."

"Don't you mean wise ass?" Mark said.

Kate cuffed him and said, "No, I did not. I don't cuss."

"Yes you do," they all said at once.

"Damn," Verna said, an impish grin on her dirty face. "Just because you say 'sorry' afterwards doesn't mean you didn't say it."

"Sometimes I don't even say I'm sorry," Kate said, lifting her chin proudly and tossing her curls.

They sat in the grass and sipped at the jug. Kat was close by Verna's side, and Rebecca perched on Harley's knee. Jeannie skipped around them all, peered over the edge of the giant hole, wanting to slide in to see what was at the bottom. Rachel sat next to her father, her skirt spread neatly around her, her back erect, her eyes watchful. He patted Rachel's hand, looked up at her from his half-prone position, and quietly told her how beautiful she was.

"Thank you, Daddy," she whispered back.

When they went in for supper, Harley declared they needed a bigger table.

"Where would we put it?" Kate asked.

"Well, maybe it would come with a room around it."

"And would the room come with a couple of bedrooms attached?" Jack asked, playing into Harley's thought process.

"I've been told sometimes you can't get a table without all of the rooms and stuff that comes with it," Harley added.

Mel sat back, listened to the banter of words, watched eyes sparkle in the lantern light, and felt the warmth in the room. These people love each other . . . all of them. It warmed him, too, and he knew he could have been a part of it years ago. 'Well, I am now,' he thought, 'and I'm thankful that I am. Maybe Harley has a good idea. Maybe they could use more space. No, they definitely could use more space.'

They finished the cellar the next day. It had two thick wooden doors across the opening and met in the middle. They were almost level with the earth, but slanted upward slightly following a gentle rise in the ground. Two ropes were attached to the handles, which made it easy to open the doors. The rain barrels stood like soldiers lined on the ground along the top edge of the doors. Grass had been cleared around it so if a fire did come close, it had nothing to burn and would be forced to move around their underground space or die out. They stood back and admired their work.

"It's a thing of beauty," Harley said.

"Yes, it is, and I pray my family never uses it for anything more than storing garden vegetables," Mark said soberly. "Bless you all for what you have done."

When they were leaving, Mel asked if he could visit Mark at his shop. He'd been thinking about Harley's table suggestion and wanted to feel him out about some help in expanding the cabin. He couldn't believe they had been living for so long in such a small space. It was basically one room with a patched on space at the back where the girls slept. It was tricky trying to help people out, but, "Hell," he said to himself. "Mark came to me, so now I'm sticking my nose in." It took a couple of months for Mel to actually say what he'd been thinking, periodic days of casual conversation, of learning to know Mark and his family, of watching Mark's slow deterioration, but eventually he brought up the idea.

"What do you think," he asked after tentatively describing the plan to expand the cabin.

"Hell, Mel. We don't even own that cabin. Did you know that? We're basically squatters there. I just couldn't take Kate away from it. She loves it."

"I know, but would it hurt to make it bigger? How could the owner care about that? And if he hasn't shown up in all these years, he's probably not going to. He's probably dead."

"I don't know, Mel. I appreciate your concern, but I can't afford it, and . . . and I just don't know," he said tiredly.

"You could get lumber from the mill, you know that, and Harley and I can do the work – with your help, of course, and approval. I'm not talking about a mansion, just a little more space. We could also make a real road through the woods so you wouldn't have to move into town during the winter. I could bring my field team out and drag a road. Your family wouldn't have to leave the place they love just because of a little snow."

It was a long speech for Mel, but he wanted it badly – for Kate, and now for Mark and the girls. He had grown to care about them all, even Mark, and as time passed, he watched Mark grow thinner and more tired. He was afraid for him.

Like Mel had said to Mark months before, Mark now said, "I'll think about it."

He knew his hesitation was based largely on pride, but it was hard to face his own deficiencies and accept help because of them. When he went home, Jeannie ran up his legs and planted herself firmly in his arms. He grinned at her and rubbed the stubble of his beard into her neck. She squirmed in delight and giggled.

"I love you, Daddy," she said breathless with her giggles.

He lifted her high into the air and twirled around with her, watching her face light up and grow rosy.

"Who do you love best?" he whispered in her ear.

"You, Daddy, but don't tell Mama."

"Never!" he said seriously. "It is our secret."

Jeannie always jumped right down and ran to her mother who scooped her up in her arms and asked the same question. It was a game they had played with all the girls, and they had all loved it as much as Jeannie.

"Who do you love the best, my sweet Jeannie?" Kate would ask.

"You, Mama, but don't tell Daddy."

"I won't. It's our little secret," Kate would say, her eyes glinting with delight in their game.

Mark made his decision. It wasn't fair to his girls to let his own foolish pride interfere in their comfort. They deserved more. He rode out to Mel's farm the next day and told him he would like his help in adding some rooms to the cabin.

CHAPTER FIFTEEN

T hey made plans for the cabin addition, talked with Will about lumber and Harley about drawing up the design. He claimed architecture was his specialty, and to tell the truth, his drawings were intricate and detailed, so maybe he was right.

"We need the road first," Mel said to the group gathered around Kate's small kitchen table. "Unless you want to haul everything into the woods on your back."

"That makes sense," Will said. "Are you sure your team can handle it?"

"We'll have to cut some trees, but the ground in the woods is softer than anywhere else. It hasn't been baked by the sun, so I'm pretty sure they'll do fine."

"And your drag. Is it up to the task?" Mark asked, thinking of the huge drags they used at the lumber camps to make roads for hauling logs to the river. And those were pulled by teams of four huge horses used to heavy pulling.

"Well," he said, hesitating for a moment. "I borrowed a drag. It's already loaded on my biggest wagon back at the farm."

"From who?" Will asked.

Mel hesitated, and then said slyly, "I know a man who works at Landmark. I'm storing it for him for awhile."

Mark nodded, understanding. "And the foreman has agreed to this 'storing' of the drag?" he teased.

"Yes. The man I know assured me they needed a place to store it, and I believe for at least a little awhile it will be stored in the woods near your cabin," he added with a grin.

Mel, Harley and Verna cut trees from the path in a wide enough swath to accommodate the borrowed drag, and Mel's four work horses pulled it easily. It took almost a full day of traveling up and down what was once the path in order to turn it into anything resembling a dirt road, but eventually Mel stopped at the clearing, unhitched the team and went inside to get Kate to come look at the new road.

She clapped her hands like a girl and giggled, calling for her daughters to come see what the road looked like. Jeannie and Rebecca jumped around, delighted in the change. Kat was more entranced by Mel's four large horses grazing quietly at the edge of the clearing. They stood taller than any horse she had ever been close to, and their feet were monstrous and hairy. She and Verna edged close enough to touch the muzzle of one and ignored the noises the rest were making over the road.

Rachel nodded her approval of the new road, but her eyes were bright as she thought ahead to a time when she might have some place of her own in the cabin when they added on the rooms they talked about. She prayed for it, for just a corner big enough so she could curtain it off from her sisters and she could be alone. That was what the road meant to Rachel, and for that she loved it.

"Can we walk down it?" she asked quietly.

"We can run down it if we want," Mel said, looking at the quiet girl next to him. She's on the verge, he thought, of wanting to grow up, and it is such a difficult a thing to do.

"Let's do it," Kate said, and tried to call Kat from the horses. "We're going to walk the new path, Kat. Let's go."

Mel pretended to be offended. "It's now a road, Mrs. Ramey – a real road."

Harley, with Rebecca's hand in his, and Verna, who had to drag Kat away from the horses, led the way. Mel and Kate followed, with Jeannie at one moment in Mel's arms or riding his shoulders and in the next prancing ahead with Bug racing beside and in circles around her. Rachel walked next to Kate.

"It's wonderful, isn't it?" Rachel said.

"The road? I'm a bit surprised the road excites you, sweetie."

"No, it's just a road, but now we can have a bigger house." She looked up at her mother, a question in her eyes.

"What is it Rachel?" Kate asked.

"Do you think there will be enough space in the new room for me to have my own?"

Kate's happiness momentarily fled. She suddenly thought of how crammed in her girls were. She hadn't given it much thought before, had continued to think of her daughters as babies or at the very least little girls. Why hadn't she seen it before? She looked with new eyes at Rachel and knew she needed what Kate had as a young girl in the loft – a place to call her own, a place for her to dream and grow.

"I am sure there will be, Rachel. You will have a corner that will be just yours."

Rachel took her mother's hand then, and they were quiet as they walked behind the rest. When they reached the end of the road, where the new one met the old, a surprise waited for them. Mark was waiting there, quietly sitting in a buggy attached to a large, light brown horse. He looked up sheepishly when they drew near and pretended surprise.

"Well, hello. Fancy meeting you here," he said.

"What are you doing here?" Kate asked. "And what are you sitting in?"

"It's a buggy, Kate," he teased. "This is called a buggy. One sits in it, and it is pulled by a horse."

"Brat," she said. "I can see that. Where did it come from and whose is it?"

"It is yours, my sweet. It is all yours." He puffed out his chest and lifted his chin proudly. "I made it."

"You made it?"

"Yes, that is what I said, from old buggy parts."

"Old parts?"

"I believe you are repeating my words as questions, Mrs. Ramey," he teased. "Want a ride? I expanded the rumble seat to hold four, so climb in girls." He got down, lifted Kate up on the seat, and put the reins in her hands. "Please do the honors, Kate."

She did, and the smile on her face filled him completely. When they got to the clearing, she jumped down before Mark could get to her, and then ran around the buggy inspecting it.

"It's beautiful. You did a wonderful job, Mark. I love it," she said throwing her arms around his neck. "I didn't know you could do anything like this."

"You'd be amazed at what I can do," he said, kissing her ear and nibbling just a little.

She stepped back from him, blushed, and looked again at the buggy.

"Whose horse is that?"

"It's yours and Mark's," Mel said coming up behind them.

The look on her face was confusion, then wondering, and then chagrin. Mel knew immediately she was having a problem with it. She'd accept work from others and cast offs, but not charity, and the gift of a horse felt like charity. Mark had responded the same way when he had first mentioned it, but eventually, Mel had convinced him he needed to accept the horse, that it meant a lot to Mel to give it.

"Did you buy this horse for us, Mel?" she asked, her brow lined in a frown.

"Yes, I did."

"Girls, please leave us for a moment." She turned to Mel, "Why?"

"Because I wanted to," he said simply.

"We cannot accept," she said as tersely.

"Why?"

"It is too much, too expensive, and we . . . I . . . just can't."

"Again, Why?"

"I don't know," she said, whipping around to walk a few feet away.

Mark stood still, his hand on the wheel of the new buggy. Harley and Verna had walked away with the girls. He looked at Kate's face and was torn by what he saw. She wanted the horse, badly, but did not want something they could not pay for, not from Mel. Will's lumber was one thing. Will was her father. Mel was a friend, and perhaps she felt she owed him, not the other way around. Perhaps, too, she felt she was presuming on his past love for her. It would be an uncomfortable place to be, and he understood.

"If you don't want to take the horse, Kate, then we won't. I am sorry Mel, please understand."

"Well, I don't. No, I do – but I don't want to," Mel said sadly. "And I don't think you understand, Kate. I missed out on almost ten years of giving gifts to your girls, for their birthdays, for Christmas, and hell, just because I wanted to, because I'm Uncle Mel. I want to give them this." He paused. "Should we ask them?" he said pushing a little.

"No," Kate said, deflated by his reasoning, and Kate thought of Harley's words. 'Don't disrespect the giver of gifts by refusing. Just say thank you.'

"Damn Harley!" she spouted. Then after a moment, she smiled a little and added "Thank you, Mel, for the wonderful gift. She is beautiful."

"Did I hear you call my name sweet Kate?" Harley called from across the clearing.

"Yes, Harley, I was merely cussing at you."

"Told you, you swore," Verna said, satisfaction suffusing her face.

They introduced the new horse to Kitty who immediately raised her head, walked around it, and then placed her head over the other's shoulders, just inches from it, and stood there. The new horse backed away, lowered her head and stood quietly. Kitty pawed at the dirt with one hoof, snickered, and walked into her shed. The other one stood at the door, peering in until Kitty whinnied loudly. 'Back off,' Kitty was saying, 'until I say you can come in – if I decide that you can.'

Mark laughed. "She's tough isn't she?"

"She sure is," Mel agreed.

"We are talking about the horse, right?" Mark asked.

Mel gave a little grin that said 'maybe.'

"I am not!" Kate growled, giving her husband a little punch and then asked what the horse's name was.

"They called her Dusty because of her muddy brown color, but you can rename her," he said.

"I think Dusty is a fine name," Kate said. "Let's find something to tie Dusty with and give them a chance to get to know each other. We can leave the door open; Kitty isn't going anywhere. We let her just wander around as she pleases. Is there really room in the shed for two of them?"

"Sure," Mark said. "They'll cuddle up soon."

Just days later, an orange glow lit up the eastern corner of the sky about the time Kate was setting the table for supper. She walked outside, stared at the glow, and called Mark.

"It's near Mel's farm," she said, and then turned into the cabin. "I'm going."

"Kate, you can't. What about the girls?" he said. "I'll be going, and that's the best we can do to help."

"I'm going," she said, and began packing the supper food into baskets. "Please harness Kitty and Dusty. I'll be ready when you're done." She called to the girls, "You're going to stay with Grandma for a few hours."

Mark knew better than to argue with her when she had made up her mind, so he did what she asked. He loaded the back with rakes and shovels, threw in some old blankets, and filled the rest of the space with Kate's food and a couple of buckets.

"Kat," he said when they came out ready to go, "you ride on Kitty. Rachel, please take Dusty. Your spots in the buggy are full. Jeannie and Rebecca, come up with us. You can sit on our laps."

They were quiet in the growing darkness and watched the orange glow grow. Mark slapped the horses gently with reins to hurry them along. They seemed to sense the urgency and kept up a steady trot. Kat and Rachel hung on, leaning forward on their horses and grasping their manes. They would never fall. They were used to riding bareback, and the horses were sure footed.

They pulled up to the Hughes house hoping Ellen was there. If not, Kate didn't know where to leave the girls. Ellen was packing supplies when they went in, her face grim and her eyes full of unshed tears.

"Will you stay with the girls, Ma?" Kate asked.

"I'm needed out there, Kate."

"I need you here," she pleaded. "Please?"

Ellen looked at her daughter's distraught face and nodded.

"Bring the girls in and take this stuff then. Will has already gone, but he left the wagon and horse for me to bring supplies in. Use that if you need it."

Mark ran to the barn, hitched the mare to the wagon and brought it around. They quickly loaded it and were ready to go.

"You take the buggy, Kate. You're familiar with our mares. I'll take Will's rig."

Kate's fear grew as she watched the sky on the way there. The closer they got, the more she could see flames dart into the darkness, and sparks, like fireflies, flared bright and then went out, only to be followed by bigger clusters of sparks blowing in the wind. She followed closely behind Mark's wagon and wished she was beside him instead of driving alone. It wouldn't do any good; it didn't really matter, but it would have made her feel better.

Her heart sunk when it became clear the fire truly was at Mel's farm. They turned up his drive, and saw one of his barns was totally engulfed in flames, and men were trying desperately to save the house and a second barn and still control the blaze at the first one, all at the same time. The fire truck was there, its spray not quite reaching the roof of the house. There was so much fire and too few people for the work even though it seemed all of Hersey was there.

"Pump harder! Harder!" she heard them shouting, trying to make the water reach the roof. They worked frantically, running with buckets to the creek, filling them and running back. A line had formed, and as it filled in, they passed the buckets from man to man, the rhythm uninterrupted as bucket after bucket sent water over the sides of the barn that had not yet become tinder for flames from the other barn. A full bucket in one hand swung forward and was grabbed by a waiting hand, while an empty one was passed toward the creek to the hand waiting for it. Kate grabbed the buckets from the buggy and ran to give them to hands only momentarily empty. Their rhythm was still uninterrupted by the addition of more buckets.

She got the blankets, doused them with water in the creek and ran back with the heavy load and passed them around. Mark had given the shovels and rakes to anyone who looked in need of a fighting tool and was in line already passing buckets. When a man had to stop, breathe air that wasn't fouled by smoke, Kate took his blanket, rewet it and began slapping it against the ground around the burning barn. She coughed, choked, and pounded the fiery ground, ran to rewet the blanket and slapped some more.

"Damn you! You will not win! Damn you!" she growled. It had become a chant; "Damn!" Slap. "Damn!" Slap. "Damn!" Slap. It seemed she beat the ground and sides of the barn for hours, swearing and choking, eyes blinded by smoke momentarily washed away by tears. "I will not cry, damn it!" Slap! "Damn it!" Slap! She felt a hand at her shoulder, dragging her back.

"The men need water to drink and coffee, Kate. Give me your blanket and go back to the wagon. Set up a place for the men to take a brief break whenever they can."

Her arms and back burned from swinging the heavy, soaked blanket, but she couldn't stop. She flung it back and slapped again. Will grabbed her arms as they flung the blanket back over her shoulder again, ready to beat the burning ground.

"Stop, Kate," he said. "Do as I say." He hugged her to him, his arms firmly around hers, to stop her from continuing to beat the blanket on the ground. He held her tight and then looked at her filthy face, at the places where her hair had been singed by sparks, at the streaks her tears had made through the soot and grime on her cheeks.

"We need you to set up the wagon, Kate. Please give me your blanket."

Kate threw her arms around him, and sobs broke from her chest. She cried hard, hugged her father harder, and then gave him the soggy blanket.

"I love you, Daddy," she said, and turned to do what he had asked. She put out the food, the container of coffee, the water bucket and some cups in a daze, moving to do what had to be done, but watching the flames and the men and the desperate effort to fight something so much bigger than they were. Her legs were leaden and her arms, too heavy to lift, hung woodenly. When she was done, she leaned against the wagon wheel and watched. She wanted to be back there fighting the nightmare, but knew her father had sent her away – to safety, not because they needed the refreshments right then, but because he loved her. For the moment she would do as he asked.

The men did come for a fast glass of water, and then they rushed back to the inferno they fought. Verna came by. Kate might have expected she would be fighting alongside the others. She saw Willie, his face black and grim. The hair on his arms was singed and he limped when he hurried back to his post.

"Be careful," Kate shouted after him when he ran back to the bucket line.

Jack appeared next to her, gulped a drink, squeezed her, and ran back. Kate saw just about everyone she knew. She thought about them each briefly, loved them all, and then threw the ladle into the bucket and went back to the burning barn to find a blanket or a rake or something she could use to fight with.

She found a blanket on the ground, grabbed it, and hurried as fast as she could to throw it into the creek and drag it back to the fire. He arms screamed as she raised them to heave the blanket against the sides of the barn. Her back cramped instantly, but as she lifted and slapped it against the barn, she didn't feel it anymore. Numbness crept in and the rhythm of her work kept her from seeing and thinking. She lost track of time until once more, a hand grasped her shoulder, turned her around, and forcefully took away the blanket she was mindlessly hurling. She jerked her head around to see who had interrupted her and saw Mel. She started to jerk the blanket away, and then saw his face.

"What?" she asked, fear already freezing her.

"You need to come with me, Kate." He grasped her hand and pulled her away from the fire and over toward a grassy place at the edge of the lawn. She saw a man lying on the ground. Someone was kneeling by him. She looked up at Mel and then ran.

Will lay still, his eyes closed. He coughed, and then tried to sit. Kate knelt next to him and cradled his head in her lap.

"Pa?" she whispered. "Pa? Are you hurt? Don't move. Get him some water!" she shouted at Mel.

"Do you want some water, Pa?"

Mel came back with a cup of water and a damp cloth and handed it to her. She held the cup to her father's lips and then looked at Mel. "What happened?"

Mel couldn't look at her. Her face tore at his insides, a scythe slashing at his guts.

"Mel," she demanded, "what happened? He's alright, isn't he?" She begged for assurance, smoothed Will's hair back from his forehead, caressed his cheek and wiped his face with the damp rag.

"One of the horses tried to run back into the barn. They're so damned stupid," he growled angrily, punching the tree next to him. "I got the horses out of the barn as fast as I could when I saw the smoke." He paused, not wanting to say the words. "I didn't get a blinder on that one, she was going so crazy. I just got her out of there as quick as I could pull her. She jumped the fence. Will saw her run back to the barn, tried to stop her from going in and got dragged into the barn with her. I saw it happen, screamed at him to let go, to stop, but he didn't. When I got inside, one of the stall rafters had pinned Will to the floor."

He knelt beside them, looked at his friend's face, his stillness and was afraid. "I'm so sorry, Kate. It's my fault. It's all my fault." Tears ran down Mel's face. He felt the weight of responsibility as heavy iron shackles pulling him under water, drowning him.

Will opened his eyes briefly and looked at his daughter. His lips formed a little smile and he tried to reach for her hand. She took his hand and lifted it her lips. "I love you, Pa. I love you so much. Please just lie still."

Mel left to find Willie and Mark. He pulled them from the bucket line and walked back to Kate and her father, telling them on the way Will had been hurt and Kate needed them.

When they drew near, Mel knew Will had died. Kate's stillness told them. She held her father in her arms, cradled him as if he was her child and stared into the still burning flames of the fire.

Mark didn't speak. He just sat next to her and put his arm around her. Her back stiffened at his touch. She squared her shoulders and looked toward the darkness. He heard a sharp intake of breath and then a small choking noise in her throat. He removed his arm and sat silently near. He knew Kate. She was trying to find the strength to deal with her loss. She was digging deep within. She needed to stiffen her back, to fight against the screams threatening to erupt from her chest, and any touch meant to share her sorrow threatened the control that kept the screams inside, shallowly buried.

Mark waited. It was difficult to sit silently by when she was in such pain, difficult not to hold her, to let her wail against him. But he knew she would deal with this pain in her own way.

Willie sat at Will's other side, softly touching his father's hand. Tears streamed down his face, and an occasional sob forced its way into his breath. They were silent in their grief.

When the flames finally subsided and danger to the other buildings seemed under control, the men began to pack up. One by one, they walked to where they sat with Will. Despair gripped their faces, sorrow and despair made tears in many eyes. They were tired – from fighting fire, some from fighting to feed their families, and some tired from losing people they cared about. Exhaustion made tears flow freely when normally men would have died before letting them fall in front of people. They swiped at them with angry hands and walked away.

Mel had ridden to the Hughes house and took Verna along to stay with the girls. He knew Ellen would insist on coming back with him. When she walked over to her husband, her back was straight, her head high. She would not cry now. That was for later.

Ellen directed them in transporting Will home. She rode in the back with him, making sure his ride was comfortable. She had told Verna to prepare a place for him at the far side of the kitchen and it was ready, but that was for later. too. Now she needed to wash him, dress him in his suit, and make him presentable.

"Please put him on the table, Mark." Jack, Mark and Willie moved him from the wagon, Ellen asked them to leave.

"Mrs. Hughes," Mark said respectfully, "There are others who will do this for you."

"I know that, Mark. I will do it myself. Will is my husband."

"I will help, Ma," Kate said from the doorway.

"Kate," Mark said, "Please don't . . ."

"Go get Ruthie, and then take the girls home, please" she said quietly.

He didn't have to go get her. Jack and Ruthie walked in just then and stood at the door still and silent, then walked to where Will lay on the table. Ruthie lay her head on her father's chest, her eyes closed, but tears still crept out from the corners no matter how tightly she clenched them shut.

"I'm so sorry," Jack whispered to him. Mark could do nothing else but what Kate asked. He touched Kate's hand gently for a moment.

"Sleep well, my good friend," he said to Will, his own tears threatening to spill. "I will miss you." Then he went to gather his daughters.

They were quiet and subdued on the way home. Jeannie kept asking why Mama wasn't with them, but Mark wasn't prepared to respond. Then she asked why Grandpa was on the table, and knew he had to. He told them the truth. He had died helping a friend. He tried to quiet their tears with assurances that Grandpa was surely on his way to heaven, and their mother would be home tomorrow. He wasn't sure about that, but he hoped.

Kate stayed with her father for the three days before the funeral. She refused to leave his side and slept in the rocking chair by the hearth. Ruthie and Willie stayed with them. It was like they had been when they were children – just the five of them alone together, except the light that had been their father had gone out, and each in their own way felt diminished by its extinction.

After the funeral, she went home directly from the graveside, bypassing the gathering at the house. She felt badly leaving her mother alone with all the folks who would come to the house to pay respects, but she just couldn't be there, couldn't listen to all of the well intended condolences. She would break, and it would kill her. She needed the woods and her cabin, her girls and Mark. It was time to grieve, and she would do it in the forest, alone.

She walked home, having sent Mark and the girls ahead in the buggy, and she thought about her father, what he had given her, what he had made her. She thanked him fervently and said, "But I'm not done, yet, Pa. I still need you," and her tears began to flow.

When she arrived at the clearing, Mark met her outside.

"Where are the girls?" she asked.

"Inside. Rachel's reading to them. They don't quite understand it all, except Rachel."

Kate just nodded, too tired, too drained to speak. Mark held her gently while quiet tears ran down her face and dampened his shirt.

"It shouldn't have happened," she finally said, her voice still husky with the build up of tears that were still unshed.

"No, sweetheart, it shouldn't have." He held her for awhile longer and then pulled back a little. "Mel's mother told me to give you something. May I?" he asked. "I think she might be right."

Kate nodded, not wanting anything at the moment except her father. Mark walked to the woods at the edge of the clearing, searched for a moment, and then came back with a long, stout branch and handed it to her. She looked at him, confused, but took the branch and just stood with it dangling from her hand.

"What am I supposed to do with this?" she asked.

"Take it into the woods, start beating it against a big tree, and don't come back until it's just a short stick. Scream, swear at anything and everybody you can think of. And cry, Kate, get angry and cry hard."

"This is what Mel's mother wanted me to have?"

"That's what she said."

Kate turned to go, dragging the branch behind her, and she didn't stop until she was far enough into the woods that her screams would not be heard. She smacked the branch against a tree trunk. The tip of it broke off, and she smacked it again; then again and again and again, faster and harder, beating the tree, shouting at God, damning the drought and the fires, damning the world that had taken her father. Damning everyone and everything. She lost track of time, wasn't even aware that her branch had been beaten to a short stubble, until she no longer had anything left to beat the tree with.

She sat down then, looked at the stick in her hand, and a sad laugh gurgled from her throat. And she cried, talked with her father about beating a tree, and she was sure he laughed too, with her. Then she went home. She would have to remember to thank Mrs. Bronson.

Mark had begun to worry, Kate was gone so long, but when he saw her coming out of the woods, he knew that she had begun the healing process. It wouldn't be over quickly, but it had begun. She hugged him when he met her at the edge of the woods, and her hug was real. Her spine didn't feel like it would break if he hugged too hard. He smiled when Kate showed him the stubble that was once the branch he had given her.

"That's what's left?" he asked.

"That's all," she said, and smiled back. "I'd like to keep it."

"We will. It will remind me how tough you are."

"I am not," she said, then added "I need to see Mrs. Bronson – and Mel."

"Today?"

"No, but soon. I know Mel, and he is feeling responsible. I need to tell him he isn't."

"He must know that he isn't, Kate," he said, not wanting her put through any more grief.

"His logic says that, but his feelings don't agree. He needs to hear it from me."

"I understand. You just say when."

Mark held her again, her head against his shoulder. "It will take a lifetime to get over, Kate. But it won't always hurt so bad," he whispered.

"I couldn't hurt like this for a lifetime, Mark. It would kill me."

"Your pain will last for awhile, sweetheart, but it will abate. I promise. You'll just keep him in your heart and most likely miss him for a lifetime."

The fires continued, erupting in town, at farms, in the fields, and anywhere there was something to burn. A periodic rain would create hope, but the little dampness it engendered was soon dried up by summer heat. The courthouse burned, and the post office next to it. They built a temporary place in Nestor's store to hold mail. The feed store disintegrated when flames caught the dry feed that was stored in the tall silos, and the feed store was gone almost before the fire hose could be unwound. Three homes on Main Street burned together. Only the concrete steps remained, sticking up in front of the narrow lots as reminders that houses had once been there.

Mel had not rebuilt the barn that burned. He made do with the one that was still standing, saying that the time was not right, and he would wait for better times, wetter times. Perhaps he didn't want to rebuild just to lose it again in another fire.

Kate and Mark had driven out to see him a week or so following Will's funeral after dropping the girls off to visit with their Grandmother. He had not been to their cabin since Will's death, and Kate needed to see him, needed to convince him that he was not responsible. When they drove up, Mel was poking around in the rubble of his burned barn. He threw a black piece of metal onto a pile of similar looking pieces and smiled a bit grimly when they grew near.

"How are you?" he asked Kate who nodded that she was doing well, and then asked about him.

He agreed that he was well, too, but the slope of his shoulders denied it.

They went to the house for a cool drink. As soon as they sat, Kate said what she had come to say.

"Mel, I know you, and I know that you have taken on the responsibility for my father's death."

When he started to deny it, she stopped him with her hand in the air and a look that said, 'let me finish.'

"My father died helping his friend. That is what he did, and that is what all of us do when friends and neighbors are in need. If the fire hadn't been here at your farm, it would have been somewhere else. He was doing what needed to be done – what he wanted to do."

"He didn't need to get that horse," he said huskily.

"Yes, he did, Mel. He wouldn't have willingly let any animal die like that. He couldn't."

Mel just shook his head sadly, not ready to let go of his responsibility.

"You know, some things you just can't control, Mel. I know that you think if you work hard enough, do all the right things, you can take care of everyone and everything. You can't. You're not God."

JuliAnne Sisung

Mel looked as if she had slapped him. His back stiffened. His eyes grew dark.

"I never thought I was God," he said.

"Well then, don't act like it."

Mark put his hand on Kate's, trying to tell her she was being too hard on Mel. She shook it off and leaned across the table closer to Mel's face.

"Harley would tell you to bend before you break, Mel. He would say if you try too hard to control things, they and your efforts will begin to control you." Then she was silent for a few moments. "And," she continued, "when you try to control people – to make up their minds for them, you take away their dignity, their right to their own minds. You could not control what Pa needed to do. It wasn't your right or responsibility."

"Is that what you think, Kate? That I try to control things? People?" he asked quietly. He waited, a long sigh escaped his lungs and he slumped a little in his chair.

"Well, damn it, yes! Isn't that what I just said?"

He smiled then, and said, "Aren't you sorry for swearing – and yelling at me?"

"No, not this time."

"I'll think about it," he said quietly, but he smiled again, and Kate knew that he would. Mel always did what he said he would do, and if he couldn't shake off feeling responsible, maybe he would begin to forgive himself if he knew that Kate did not hold him responsible.

They tried to get Ellen to move into Ruthie and Jack's little house in town, told her they would finally finish the upstairs and she could have it all to herself, but Ellen refused. She would not leave the home she and Will had shared. It was home.

Willie took over his father's place at the mill as partner with Tom Reeves and shared the income with his mother. Money was tight, though, and trying to maintain both his house and his mother's was a strain. Harley picked up more odd jobs around town and always gave

410

the money to Ellen for his board. She tried to refuse at first, but knew how hard it was for Willie to support both his family and her, so she unhappily took it.

"Just say thank you," he said grinning at her. "How many times do I have to say that? Besides, you've been feeding this big belly for years. Now it's my turn."

Nothing changed at the smith shop; it had been in both Will and Mark's name, so Mark merely continued as the owner. But work just got slower as more and more automobiles came to town and horses were put out to pasture. Mark didn't know what he would do even if there had been more work. He seemed to tire out so quickly that each job took longer to finish. He tried to pace himself, told himself he was just getting old, and kept going back to Doc for more of the pain medicine.

He loved the automobiles, though, even if they were the reason his shop was dying. He loved the sound of them as they chugged down the roads, the smell of the fumes they left behind, loved the ornery engines that started grumpily when you cranked them over. When he heard them nearing the shop, he'd walk to the door to watch them bump down the road toward him. Then he'd watch until they were out of sight and were nothing but dust in the distance. Kate was at the shop with him one day when he heard the sound and ran to the door.

"Aren't they something?" he asked.

Kate watched the machine, then watched his face light up in anticipation of its approach.

"I guess they are," she said, smiling at the little boy in his face. "Why don't you ask Mr. Nestor if you could drive his?"

"I couldn't do that," he responded.

"Well, why not? I'll bet he'd love to show it off."

"I don't know. It's kind of like begging to play with another kid's toy. And it's an expensive one, too."

Kate smiled and vowed that Mark would ride in one of them – sometime, maybe even own one.

CHAPTER SIXTEEN

It finally rained, a good, long rain, one that sent mud sliding down into the valley from hills that had been cleared of the huge trees that once held the soil in place. But folks in Hersey lifted their faces to the sky and let the rain wash over them, smiling and breathing sighs of relief. They didn't run for cover into Nestor's or Sadie's; they stood on the sidewalks getting drenched and talking with others who wanted to savor the rain, their clothing sopped and clinging to their bodies. They pointed to the black clouds in the western sky and made guesses about how long the rain would last and how much would come down. When they finally entered the store, their hair hung in dripping strands and their clothes smelled like freshly turned fields of beautiful damp loam. But the grim faces of yesterday were gone. Instead, there were tentative smiles and jokes. Their fears were at least momentarily quelled, and inside each raindrop grew hope.

Jeannie toddled beside Kate. At not quite four she thought she was too old to be carried and wanted to do everything by herself. She, too, looked up at the sky with joy written on her face and opened her mouth to catch the drops. Her auburn curls stuck to her cheeks and darkened as they grew wet. Bug danced around them, his shaggy coat spraying water as he leaped and pranced. Even Bug was ecstatic over the rain. Rachel had raced into the store when the first drops fell, and Rebecca waited by her mother, looking at the clouds for signs of lightening so she could count the moments until thunder bellowed and she could tell exactly where the storm was. Kat looked for worms that she knew would come out of the ground if enough rain fell. She'd sneak them into her pocket to take home with her to fish in the creek by the cabin.

John Nestor came out of the store to watch with them. "This is good," he said quietly, looking around at others gathered on the sidewalks watching the sky and hoping.

"Is this the end?" Kate asked.

"The almanac says so. This should be a better year. I pray it is right."

"I'm praying with you," Kate said, laughing. "But right now, I'd better get the things I need and take my soggy daughters home. And dog."

Kate searched the meat counter for the cheap pork steak she would split between her husband and daughters and carefully counted out the pennies in her change purse.

"Three today, Mr. Nestor, to celebrate the rain." It took all the coins she had. A small frown creased her brow, but it was fleeting. This is not the day to worry, she thought. Things would change, and the rain was just the beginning.

Kat and Jeannie stood at the glass counter that held penny candy. They didn't ask for any. They just wanted to see it all and savor the imagined sweetness. Mr. Nestor saw them look from one piece to the next, pointing and whispering to each other.

"That one," Jeannie said to her sister. "That's the best one. I'll bet it's chewy."

"Maybe it tastes better," Kat said, and since she was older and wiser, told her she should always get one that lasts longer. "A hard one, so you just suck on it for a long time, because you can't chew it up," she explained.

"That's very wise of you," Mr. Nestor said to Kat who nodded at him with a look that said 'of course, what did you expect?'

"I'm almost eight, you know," she said, staring into his eyes earnestly.

He reached into the case and brought out eight pieces of candy; four of the ones that Jeannie thought would taste better, and four of the ones Kat believed would last longer – peppermint sticks with red barber pole stripes that curled around the long stick. He put them into a small sack and reminded them to share with their sisters. Jeannie reached eagerly for the bag, but Kat looked at her mother for permission.

Kate's face was a mixture of longing for her girls to have the sweets and wounded pride that she couldn't pay for them. Nestor forestalled her objection.

"It is my little celebration," he said. "You wouldn't deny me that pleasure, would you? It's a small thing." Kate looked at the joy in Jeannie's eyes and shook her head. "No, I guess not." She stood silently for a moment, thoughtful, and John watched knowing Kate was deliberating something that she couldn't come right out with. Something was on her mind.

"Do you want to tell me?" he asked.

Kate shook herself lightly, took a deep breath, and said, "Well, damn, I guess I'll just say it. Sorry."

John smiled. He'd been hearing her say damn since she was a little girl, and it still made him smile. Long ago she'd stomp her foot along with it, but she always apologized and then went on to do it again and again.

"Well?" he said.

"Yes, well," she stammered. "As long as you are in a celebrating mood, I have a favor to ask. It's a really big one."

"You can ask anything, Kate, and I'll more than likely do it. You know that."

"I want Mark to drive an automobile." Once started, Kate babbled on. "I mean, he wants to. He loves them so much. They drive by the shop, and he quits whatever he is doing and runs out to watch them. He is in awe of them."

She would have gone on, but John held up his hand for her to stop.

"Why didn't he just ask? That's an easy favor."

"He wouldn't ask. I told him to do that a long time ago."

Kate danced around him like Bug had done out in the rain. She wrapped her arms around his neck and hugged him.

"Oh, thank you. Thank you so much. When can we do it?"

"As soon as the rain quits and the roads are dry enough," he said, grinning at Kate and loving the gleam in her eyes. Kate had been special to him from the time she was a little girl lurking in his store, and he still saw that girl in the woman in front of him.

"Is Mark feeling any better?" he asked, and then wished he hadn't because Kate's eyes clouded and the joy he had seen there moments ago fled.

"He says he is," she answered quietly. "But I don't think it's true."

"I'm sorry, Kate. Maybe this rain will help. Everyone has suffered in the heat," he said, trying to make her feel better.

"It will be alright," she said, stiffening her spine in Kate fashion and smiling at him. "Mark will be fine. About that drive . . ."

"It's done. I'll take it over to the shop as soon as the weather allows and tie him in the driver's seat."

Kate giggled, clapped her hands and gathered her daughters. They ran out into the rain laughing and stomping in the puddles. They were soggy, muddy messes when they stopped at the shop to see Mark. Jeannie ran into her father's arms. Her wet dress soaked him, and his black soot streaked her wet face. He nuzzled each of his daughters, smearing his forge dust equally among them. He had to chase Rachel around the room until he caught her, but he did, and she finally let him. He couldn't lift her in his arms as he did the others, but he snuggled and rubbed his face against hers until she was at least a little smeared.

"There," he said when he was done. "Now you look like proper smithy children!" he said laughing at their still damp faces. "But you, my dear," he said turning to Kate, "are entirely too clean." He lunged for Kate, and when she saw his intent, she tried to scamper away.

"You beast!" she yelled.

"I am the beast you married!" he cried back. "And you will do as I command!"

"Never!"

Kate put the table between them and danced back and forth to stay away from him. The girls giggled as they watched their parents play like children.

"Get Momma, Daddy. She's too clean," Jeannie screeched.

"Well, help me, ladies. Barricade her. Don't let her escape!"

They did as he said and before long Kate was the grimiest of them all. He nuzzled Kate's wet face with his own, ran his blackened hands over her cheeks, got more dust from the edge of the hearth and smeared it where he saw pink skin peeking through.

"There. Now we are a complete smithy family," he said.

"Thank you, Mark. I was feeling left out," Kate said with a grim smile, "and I appreciate your efforts to make us whole."

"You forgot Bug, Daddy," Kat said.

Mark grabbed Bug, ran his hands over him until his red coat was darkened by the soot, and asked if Bug was now a proper smithy dog. They laughed and nodded, and Bug stood on his hind legs to stare into Mark's face, saying it's a good thing Kat reminded you that I am part of this family or I'd have to do something, and you wouldn't like it if that happened. He drooled on Mark's face, and his look said 'There, now you're a proper dog owner.'

"Are you about finished here?" Kate asked.

"I will see to it that I am finished if I can drive home with you lovely, scurvy looking ladies."

"Then the scurvy ladies will wait for you."

He tied Kitty to the back of the buggy, and they piled in. Rain was still pouring down, slanting sideways in the winds. It washed away some of the soot and drenched them even more than they had been, but they laughed for the joy of it. They sang songs, told Mark about the candy Mr. Nestor had given them, and loved the wonderful day.

On Saturday, John drove his auto to the shop. Mark had heard the engine and was standing in the doorway when he drove up, surprised to see it stop at the shop instead of continuing on down the road. The sun was shining, and the land looked green and lush from the rain. It was a gorgeous day.

"What can I do for you, John?" Mark asked, believing that he needed some small work done in the shop.

"Well," he drawled, "It's a great day for a ride, and I like a little company sometimes. Wondered if you had time to take a spin with me."

Mark just stared at him, the words not really sinking in.

"If you're too busy," John said, filling in the pause, "I can come another day."

"No – no, I'm not busy at all. I'd love to go," Mark said quickly. "I'd really like to."

"Well, then, close up shop and hop in."

Mark did. He sat gingerly in the passenger seat and ran his hand lovingly over the dash in front of him. He looked around the inside of the auto, taking in everything. He peered over at the pedals in front of John, unsure what exactly they were for, tested the door handles and carefully touched the knobs on the dashboard. The grin on his face spoke loudly.

"My God," Mark said in awe. "Isn't this something!"

"It is. It surely is a thing of wonder," he said, smiling and proud of his auto.

"Let's go." He got out, went to the front to crank the engine, and explained how it worked as he fiddled with the awkwardly bent bar. When the engine sparked and roared to life, he ran back to his seat and jumped in.

Mark's hair blew back in the breeze, and he felt unbelievable joy as they rumbled down the road. He felt the vibration of the engine through his seat, the bumps in the road as the wheels ran across them, and his excitement mounted. They didn't speak for a long while. Mark was savoring the joy, and John was alternately watching the road and Mark's face.

They finally stopped at a crossroad. John turned the car around, and then got out.

"Okay," he said. "This is how you do it. The crank goes out there in front and is what turns over the engine. You have to be careful not to break your arm when you spin it around because when it catches, it tends to bounce back. Listen for it to catch and hold tight. When you hear the engine rumble, get in the driver's seat fast and push the throttle forward just a little. Push in on the clutch so it doesn't stall when you put it in gear, and then let it out slowly so the car doesn't leap forward. Got it?"

Mark just stared, not believing he was about to drive. "Are you crazy? I don't know how to drive one of these things."

"Nope. Not at all. It's easy." He explained again about the choke and the pedals, the brake and the gas. "Now, just do what I said, and it will all be good."

Mark got out, went to the front and put the crank in its slot. He tested it by pushing it until he felt some resistance. Then he looked at John again. "Are you sure?" he asked.

John nodded and Mark turned the crank, felt it engage the engine, pulled the crank lever out and threw it in the rumble seat, then leaped into the driver's seat. He shoved in the clutch, put it in gear. He let the clutch out slowly and pushed on the throttle just a little. The rumble increased, and he released the throttle a bit, fear squeezing his heart – fear that he would do something to harm this wonderful machine.

"You're doing just fine," John said. "Relax with it, cause you're not going to do anything to it that I haven't already done."

Mark tried to relax, and his joy made him feel like his heart was about to burst. He released the clutch slowly, inch by tiny inch, and felt the car move slightly forward. Then it was moving down the road. His hands were tight fists on the steering wheel, and his body was forward in the seat, intent on keeping them firmly on the road. Then he began to really relax and felt the breeze again, the freedom and the power. He drove all the way back and through town, nodding at the people on the street and even waving when he thought he could take one hand from the steering wheel. He turned it around at the other end of town and drove back through to the shop. When he stopped, he turned to his friend.

"I can't thank you enough," he said, and his hand unconsciously went to his stomach. "This has been a dream of mine for a long, long time. I love your automobile. Not as much as my family, but really close," he said, laughing.

"I'm glad," John said, then asked "are you alright?"

"Sure. I'm fine."

There was silence for awhile, and then John felt he had to speak. "You are losing weight, Mark, and you are clutching your stomach. Are you sure Doc is treating you properly?"

"It's just this damn ulcer," Mark said. "It gets worse when I get excited or upset. That's all."

John heard the words, but, like Kate, he didn't believe what they said. Yet, he couldn't pry, even if he didn't believe.

"We'll do this again soon," he said.

Mark got out, ran his hand lovingly over the fender and said thank you again. He managed to stand erect while he walked into the shop and then sank into the nearest chair, the pain in his belly doubling him over. He sat there for several minutes, sweat beading his face, bile rising in his throat. Fear racking his brain.

When he had recovered, he saddled Kitty and rode home. Kate knew when he came through the door that something wonderful had happened. His face was aglow. He wrapped his arms around her, whispered thank you in her ear, and hugged her.

"For what are you thanking me?" she asked in her most imperious school teacher voice.

"For the most wonderful drive," he answered, grinning into her face and kissing it at the same time. "I don't believe for a second that John just happened to come by needing someone to ride with him."

"Well, he could have," she said.

"Well, he didn't. You," he said, holding her close and whispering in her ear, "convinced him that he needed a friend in the passenger seat. I love you, Kate. Thank you."

"Did you enjoy it?"

"I can't even begin to tell you how it felt. It was unbelievable. A carriage moving down the road with the rumble of an engine, not a horse. I . . . I can't explain."

Kate hugged his head against her breast as he sat at the table. She smiled, one smile for John Nestor and one for her husband. Then she saw Mark move his hand to his stomach, and fear gripped her.

"Are you alright?" she asked.

"It's just excitement. Ulcers do that," he said.

They went to bed that night with many thoughts passing through their minds. Mark's was the thrill of the automobile – and the increasing pain in his stomach – his fear for his family – and his determination to provide for them.

Kate's were happiness for Mark – that he got to drive the amazing machine, but also fear for him, and determination to see that he got treatment for whatever it was that hurt him.

But when they fell into bed together, their thoughts centered on their love and desire for each other. Kate nestled into the crook of his arm, her body closing the gap between them. She felt lust for him, and he knew it by the tingling of his nerve endings. Kate caressed his face, let her hands roam his slender body and they loved each other. Mark's hands slid over her hips and pulled her to him.

"I love you more than life," he whispered in her hair.

"You are my life," she whispered back.

Before breakfast the next morning, Mark told her. The girls were still asleep in their tiny space at the back of the cabin, and other than the occasional honk of geese beginning their flight southward, it was quiet.

"I'm going to close the smithy and look for work in Reed City," he said softly. "I've made inquiries already, and I think there is a possibility at a print shop."

Kate stood stunned, holding a spatula in the air that she'd been using to stir pancake batter, her mouth open, but she couldn't respond.

Mark sat with his hands wrapped around a coffee cup and stared into the liquid as if it held answers in the grounds, like tea leaves did for the gypsies. When the moments stretched in silence, he tried again.

"I just can't make enough anymore, Kate, and it just keeps getting worse."

"But it will pick up now. We had a good rain, and if next year's crops are good, people will come back to the smithy," she said hopefully.

"Look around Hersey, Kate. The people are gone. They gave up and left. Have you seen anyone rebuilding? And even if they did, and if they had the money to spend, it's not going to be on horses and the old kinds of machines that horses pull. It's on automobiles and engines."

"Reed City is so far away, Mark. Maybe I can get some work in town to add to what you make."

"You have a job, Kate. Our family."

"I can do more than that. The girls are older now, and Rachel can help with the younger ones. She's ten years old now."

"No," Mark said emphatically. "Your work is here."

Kate's back stiffened and her chin lifted. "Since when do you command me, Mark?"

"Be reasonable. You can't do everything, and it's my job to take care of this family," he said softly, trying to make her understand. His hand ran through his hair and over his face.

Kate stomped her foot. Anger infused her face. She turned back to the bowl she'd been mixing pancake batter in and began to beat at the mixture. She knew they were in trouble at the shop, but she just kept hoping things would turn around, and she definitely didn't want Mark so far away every day. He was not well no matter how many times he claimed that he was fine, and it horrified her that he wouldn't be near.

"What if I found work that I could do at home – something like laundry? I could do other people's washing and ironing. I could go out to the camps, pick up their things and take them back to them all freshly done."

Mark groaned at the thought of his wife doing others' wash, and of her at the camps with all the lumberjacks. There weren't as many now as when the lumber boom first hit Hersey, but the ones that remained were the same rowdy bunch.

"God, Kate, do you know what you're saying?"

"Yes, damn it, I do. I am saying that if this family needs help, and if I can give it, why shouldn't I? You're treating me like a child, and as you can plainly see by this face, I am not. And," she continued, her anger growing as she spoke, "you will not tell me what I can or cannot do!"

Mark ran his hand over his face again and knew it would do no good to talk sense to her. He knew, too, that what she said was right. He couldn't tell Kate what to do. She would do whatever she thought was necessary and appropriate in her mind. That was one of the things he loved about her.

He paused, thinking desperately about what could be done, what he could do, and came up empty. It seemed hopeless, and he was so tired and angry at himself.

"Let's wait, Kate. Let's just wait it out a little longer – through the winter. Can we make it through the winter? It will be really tight. If things are the same come spring, we'll talk about it again. Is that all right with you?"

"Yes," she said grudgingly, still irked with him, "just don't tell me what to do."

"Never again," he said, smiling a little. "Except this one last time. Come here," he commanded.

Kate's head whipped around, the spatula raised, then she saw his grin and went to him. He wrapped his arms around her waist and nestled his face against her bosom.

"Aren't you going to apologize?" he asked.

"Me? What for?"

"The cuss word."

"Sorry," she said, giggling, and then added while he nuzzled, "I've got bushels of potatoes and beets and carrots put away in the underground cellar. I canned tons of tomatoes and beans and jams and – we can make it," she said, hope rising with her words. "And you might have to take one of the deer that come to the clearing. I'd hate it, but the meat would certainly help. I can put that up in jars, too."

"You are a miracle," he said.

"Yes, I am, and don't you forget it."

"I love you. Can I have some pancakes now?"

For the first time in the last few years, winter brought heavy snows. It came early, mid-November, and stayed. Mounds piled up to the windows, and deep trenches had to be dug to make paths to the cabin and shed doors. They shoveled lanes wide enough for the buggy to make it out of the clearing and out to the narrow road Mel's horses had dragged. Fortunately, branches canopied the road and prevented snow from piling up, and the woods kept it from drifting too deep. The horses could manage to pull the buggy down it easily, so Kate and the girls could get into town. They made a day of it when they did, bundling up in heavy blankets and singing all the way. Kate had taught them how to sing harmony parts to many of the hymns she knew. Even little Jeannie, who wouldn't be left out of anything, could sing a part if she plugged her ears with her fingers so she wouldn't hear the others and be thrown off. Mark loved to hear them sing *In the Garden*. It reminded him of the night he had met Kate when she was just sixteen, and he thought he could conquer the world.

In town, talk was always of the weather; some grumbled about the massive amounts of snow, and some had gleams in their eyes because it meant a moist earth for planting come spring. Even more, it meant that the forests and buildings were too snow covered for fires, and that filled many hearts with peace they had not known for years.

Harley rode out frequently and sometimes brought Verna or Ellen with him, snuggled up behind him on Will's old horse. Kate loved the winter solitude in the woods, but was happy when company came out. Harley always said he needed some frosty air, but Kate knew he was checking on them, making sure they were snug and safe. Ellen usually brought the soft, sweet cinnamon rolls she was famous for and that the girls loved, or mittens and scarves for them all.

"You don't need to bring anything when you come out, Ma," Kate said. "You don't need to do that every time you come."

"I know that, but I need to keep busy, and crocheting helps pass the time." But she was making sure her grandchildren stayed warm and knew that Kate could not afford the luxury of sweet rolls.

Jeannie climbed on Harley's lap and held his face between her two newly red-mittened hands.

"I miss you, sweet girl," he whispered in her ear. "And you are growing so big you almost don't fit on my lap anymore."

"It's not me; it's your belly," Jeannie said honestly. "It takes up so much room."

"Jeannie," Kate admonished. "That's not a nice thing to say."

"She is merely telling the truth," Harley said. "And the truth is always best. I have worked on this belly for many years, and it's enormous," he said proudly, sticking it out even further and almost pushing Jeannie to the floor. She grabbed his suspenders to keep from falling and giggled.

"Where's Verna?" Kat asked. "Why didn't you bring her with you?"

"Well, old Bessie would have a hard time carrying three of us, but now that I see the new road is still pretty clear, maybe we'll hitch up the buggy and bring out a whole slew of people next time. How would that be?"

"Good," Kat said matter-of-factly.

Kate agreed and then got excited with the idea. "Why don't we do that? Let's plan a winter party out here! We could go sledding on the big hill or ice skating on the creek. We could make a bonfire and have a real party! What do you think?" she asked growing more thrilled with the idea.

By the time Mark arrived home from work, the party was already well planned. Harley would spread the news to Willie and Mary, Jack and Ruthie, Mel and Verna. Next Saturday they would have an old fashioned winter party.

Mark fell tiredly into a chair after chafing the chins of his daughters with a day's growth of beard stubble and listened alternately to Kat telling him he felt like a porcupine, Jeannie waving her new mittens in his face, and everyone telling him the plans for the party.

"It sounds like just the thing," he said, grinning broadly at his family. "I haven't been sledding or skating for at least a hundred years."

"Are you a hundred, Daddy?" Jeannie asked.

"Sometimes more, sweetie. It depends on the day," Mark kidded. "I think this special day calls for a sip of my special home brew. How about it, Harley?" They raised the jug to winter and good times.

"It's not as good as Will's brew," Harley said grinning at Mark, "but it's not bad, and you'll probably learn in time."

A shadow clouded the room at the mention of Will's name, and Mark looked around at the somber faces.

"That probably wasn't the best thing to say, Harley," Mark said.

"Well, are we never to speak his name again? Are you all trying to wipe away his memory? Cause if that's so, you do him a disservice. Speak his name with joy," Harley went on. "That's what he gave us, not sadness. Wallow in the joy."

"Harley," Mark said, trying to stem the flow of words, but Kate intervened.

"He's right, you know." She got up, poured a small amount of the home brew into a glass and lifted it, waiting for the others to join her. When Ellen poured one for herself, Kate touched hers to it and continued. "Here's to my Pa. I miss him terribly, but I want to say his name gladly. I want him to be with us at our party, and he can't be there if we're afraid to say his name."

Harley smiled and nodded at Kate. "Here's to Will, to a good friend, a wonderful husband and father; simply an excellent man and worthy of the adoration of this family!" He tipped the jug and drank. His eyes watered as he swallowed, but he stifled the cough that threatened to choke him. "Good," he said, clearing his throat.

"He would have liked that very much," Ellen said, a small smile creasing her cheeks. "Thank you, Harley."

"Will helped me more than any man has ever done," Mark shared when the jug was passed to him. "I will be beholden to him always."

"And now, my friends, since Will is happily with us again," Harley said, his eyes squinting in a deep grin, "let's plan a party!"

Jeannie and Rebecca jumped around, energized by the excitement in the room, and Bug rolled his eyes from one person to the next still sprawled on his rug in front of the hearth. Kat sat next to him just watching, and Rachel hovered nearby.

On Saturday, four buggies rolled down the road to the clearing. Mel led the way, his buggy full of food from the farm. He brought a huge smoked ham, jars of pickles and sauerkraut his mother had canned, and a huge bag of penny candy, four of every variety from Nestor's candy case. He carried it in and deposited it on the table then looked around for the girls.

"Where are they?" he asked.

"Out gathering wood for the bonfire. What is all this?" Kate asked.

"Just some stuff I had."

"You just happened to have a bag of candy? Do you have a sweet tooth that I never knew about?"

"Well, no. John Nestor just happened to have it, and then I did, and now your daughters do."

Kate cuffed him. "You spoil the girls."

"That's what uncles do. And even a mother can't take away that right. It's a law."

Harley, Verna and Ellen followed with a buggy just as full as Mel's. Jack and Ruthie arrived with more food and Willie brought up the rear with Mary and their two children.

Kate put away all the food, trying to find space for everything and alternately salivating at the thought of smoked ham and feeling a little bit sad about wanting it so much. 'For the girls and Mark,' she thought to herself, and then grinned. 'Okay and me. This is the way life should be.'

"Get out of here," she said, "while I finish up. Go help gather wood. Get the sleds and skates out and I'll meet you by the creek."

Mel lingered as the others left. "Are you alright?" he asked.

"Yes," she said simply. "Yes, I am. Are you?"

"Yes, I am too."

When she got to the creek, they were trying to decide which to do first – skate or go sledding. Harley opted for sledding since he wasn't sure he could stay up on a pair of skate runners. Jack thought skating might be more fun since he'd like to see Harley navigate the ice. Mel had brought several pairs of skates that had belonged to his brothers and sisters. They were the kind that strapped on to your boots and could be adjusted for size. Jack brought his and Ruthie's. Between them all, there were enough skates for everyone.

Jack put his on and was first on the ice. He twirled in circles and raced down the creek bed and was back before anyone else was on the ice.

"Smarty," Harley said. "Show off. There's usually one in every group," he said confidentially to Rebecca who was sitting next to him.

Mark joined Jack, and they spun off to race down the ice again.

"I didn't know if I could still do it," Mark said. But he was graceful on the ice, and skidded his skates sideways to stop in front of Harley with a spray of ice that had been shaved by the runners and now covered him.

"Make that two in every group," Harley growled. "Two smarty pants, show offs. Well, I'll just have to show you how it's done." He got up from his seat on the snow and inched over to the creek. Tentatively, he placed one foot on the ice, and then the other. He stood still, unable to move, afraid to upset his precarious balance.

Mark and Jack stood together, arms crossed, huge, satisfied grins on their faces.

"Well come on, show us how it's done," Mark said.

Harley inched one foot slowly forward, his arms held out for balance, tottered, then fell with a resounding thud to the ice. He landed on his rump and bounced, then sat still. He carefully brought his feet in and tried to scoot them under him. They slid out again, but since his bottom was still at ground level, his fall was short.

"You didn't bounce that time," Jeannie said. "That was fun! Do it again!"

Kat skated over to him and held out her hand. Harley took it, trying not to pull too hard as he rose again, and they slowly made it over to Jack and Mark.

"See?" he said when he got to them. "Told you I'd show you how it's done."

"And that snail's crawl is how it's done?" Jack questioned.

Harley grinned broadly, "I don't see you holding a pretty girl's hand. This, my sons, is how it is done."

When they had all skated their fill, they removed them and grabbed sleds and the toboggan that Mel had brought. At the top of the hill, Mel said he would sit in the front of the toboggan to take the brunt of the snow. Verna took the last seat, with Kate and several of the children in the middle. Verna flew off the back end about half way down the hill and rolled the rest of the way, laughing and swearing that Mel had deliberately unseated her. She seemed to gather snow as she rolled and looked like a snow ball when she got to the bottom. All you could see were two sparkling blue eyes, a rosy little nose, and two red cheeks peeking out from under her knit cap.

"He did that on purpose. I know it," she said and tackled his legs low, tumbling Mel to the ground. "Don't mess with Verna," she said, sitting on his chest. "Say 'uncle' and I'll let you up." Kat helped her by piling snow on top of him until he complied and yelled "Uncle! I give up."

They had races, lying on their bellies and flying down the hill as fast as they could go. Mel and Harley won those and were chided that their size meant they didn't really win.

"It's your weight, Harley. That's the only reason you're faster," Mark teased.

"It's a skill; one I have never spoken of."

"Do you mean to say that there is one thing you haven't talked about? I don't believe that for a moment!"

Kate intervened, "Don't pick on Harley, Mark. He beat you fair and square."

"Old coot," Mark whispered, poking him in the belly playfully.

"Silly, callow youth," Harley said back.

They hauled the sleds up and down the hill until they were covered with snow and exhausted. Then they hauled them back to the creek bed where they had piled the wood for the fire. When it was roaring and providing heat, they gathered around holding their hands close to the fire for warmth. Mark brought out the jug of home brew and passed it to Harley.

"First sip to the winner," he said grudgingly, but inwardly pleased that Harley had won. "I'm calling you runner-up, Mel. I make the tie-breaking decision, since I made the whiskey."

"It's not as good as Will's," he said teasing, "but it will warm you from the inside out."

Kate made hot chocolate for the kids and brought it to them in tin cups, then sipped from the jug, too. They passed it back and forth, thawing out with the heat from the fire and the warmth of friendship and family.

Kate was about to go into the cabin to prepare food, when Mark abruptly sat down and bent over, clutching his stomach. Every head turned toward him. Conversation suddenly stopped, and they stared, each person with a different kind of fear growing in their eyes. Rachel backed up a few steps not wanting to see her father hurting, and knowing that he did. Kat reached for Verna's hand and held on tight. Rebecca inched closer to Harley until she could feel him next to her. He stroked her head and pulled it close to his side. Willie reached for Mary and wrapped his arm around her back, snuggling into her.

After a brief moment of silent shock, Kate raced over to him, and Mel was by Mark's side even before Kate could get there.

"What's wrong? Are you alright?"

"Just a little stomach ache," he said, gripping it with both hands.

"Don't lie, Mark. It's more than a little ache," she said. "We need to get you to the doctor."

"I'll be fine. Just let me sit here a bit."

"Damn it, Mark! You're in pain. Something is wrong, and it's not just an ulcer."

Mel touched Kate's shoulder. When she turned to him, he saw the raw agony on her face, anguish mixed with fear.

"Make him go to the doctor," she begged to Mel.

"Why don't you go into the house and get some dinner started, Kate. Let me talk with him a bit."

Kate stared at him, looked at her husband and then back to Mel.

"I'll be fine in a minute or two, Kate. Do what Mel said – please?"

Kate went, and soon after, the other women followed, dragging the girls with them. Mel squatted by Mark and was silent for a few moments. Then Jack wandered over with Harley and Willie along side.

"So, how long are you going to play with Doc Cheston?" Mel asked.

"I don't know what you mean."

"Yes, you do. You need to see a specialist, someone from Blodgett Hospital. You know damn well this isn't an ulcer."

Mark ran his hand over his face and grimaced, but he didn't respond. He couldn't. He didn't know what to say and didn't want to spoil the fun by being sick.

"I can't imagine that you would willingly die and leave this family, but if you don't take care of yourself that is exactly what you might do. You're sick. And you're stupid if you don't take steps to get better. I don't think you're that stupid, and I'm telling you, man; it makes me mad."

"It's none of your business, Mel. Back off! I appreciate your concern, but I can handle it."

"You are my friend. I love this family. That makes it my business," Mel said quietly, but anger bubbled through the words.

Harley, who was unaccustomedly silent, tapped Mel on the shoulder and tilted his head for him to walk away with him. He did the same with Willie, leaving Jack with Mark.

"I figure he might listen to Jack, take some advice from him," Harley said when they were at the other side of the fire. "They've been in tough spots together before, and neither man feels beholden to the other. Let Jack take over from here."

Mel saw the wisdom in Harley's words and just nodded, but his irritation with Mark lingered.

"Why the hell hasn't he gotten some real help?" he asked quietly.

"Probably a variety of reasons," Harley said. "Money, pride, foolish hope, fear that he really is too sick for help. Name any reason you can think of, and it's probably a part of it."

Mel nodded, knowing what Harley said was likely, but still not really understanding.

"The man has pride," Harley added quietly, "and he took a fall when he went to prison for that woman's crime. Think about it. Here's a man who could manage to do just about anything he set his mind to, and one day that's gone, but he keeps on trying. He keeps thinking if he tries hard enough, wants it badly enough, he can make it happen."

"Well, I understand that thinking," Mel said, "but it doesn't work."

"No, it doesn't, but if you quit hoping and trying, what have you got left?"

Mel nodded. He was uncomfortable talking about another man like they were and somewhat unsettled by Harley's words. But he understood what it felt like to be unable to make things happen, to be forced to sit with your hands tied. Hadn't Kate accused him of thinking he was God just a short while ago? It was hard, though, to sit back and just accept the way things were without trying to make them better, to do something.

When Jack stood up, Mark stood with him, the pain having receded to a dull ache. They walked over to the other men who were still standing at the other side of the fire.

"I'll be going to Blodgett with Jack in the morning," he said. Then he turned to Mel. "I'm sorry, friend. Didn't mean to bark at you."

Mel stood quietly for a moment. "Well, I did – mean to bark, that is – but I guess I'm sorry I had to," he said smiling at Mark. "Are you feeling any better?"

"I'm okay, and you're right, I don't ever want to leave my girls."

"And Kate," Mel added.

"She is one of my girls, always will be." He leaned closer to Mel, and with a tired grin, he poked him lightly in the chest. "Don't ever forget it."

"Go show Kate you're feeling better," Harley said, "and then let's have some fun." He leaned toward Mark and looked him in the eyes. "Are you up for that?"

Mark nodded yes and walked slowly to the cabin. Kate's sigh of relief stabbed him. "I'll go to Blodgett, but can we talk about this later?" he asked. "Can we just enjoy the party right now?"

She nodded yes, but asked "Do you feel up to it?"

"You're at least the millionth person who has asked me that, and yes, I do."

He put his arms around her and squeezed, then picked up Jeannie and Rebecca, winked at Rachel, grabbed Kat's hand and headed out the door.

"I am strong like ox!" he bellowed to the giggles of his girls.

CHAPTER SEVENTEEN

B lodgett Hospital was imposing, a huge concrete block building that terrified Mark. They sat outside just looking at it for a long while. He didn't want to go in, was for some reason afraid he would never come out once he stepped foot in those doors.

"Come on, old friend. Let's get this over with," Jack said, throwing off the blankets they had been covered with during the long ride. It had taken a full day to get there, and they had stayed the night at a hotel near the hospital so they could be there first thing in the morning.

The place smelled antiseptic and sterile. White painted walls, people in white clothes, everything glared at him, but it was a world without a speck of color. They checked in at the desk and sat down to wait. Eventually, they called his name, and he tensed when he heard it, then got up, shook Jack's hand and went into the small examining room.

"I can't be sure," the doctor finally said after much poking and prodding, "but this could be very serious. It's definitely not just an ulcer like you think."

"Well, how can you figure it out for sure?" Mark asked, not really wanting to know.

"Surgery," the doctor answered simply. "There's a mass in your abdomen, and that mass needs to be removed at the very least. Then we'll biopsy it to see what it is. If it looks like cancer to me when we're in there, we'll try to get it all during the surgery, but we'll know more with the biopsy."

Mark ran his hand over his hair and face, looked out the small window at the bare, dark branches that were silhouetted against a grey sky. He couldn't think, couldn't respond. The doctor waited. It was never easy telling someone they had a tumor; never easy to say what it could be. He had found that the best way was to simply wait silently until what he had told them finally sunk in, until the horror of his words could begin to register in the brain and not just the heart.

"When?" Mark finally asked.

"In the morning. We'll get you checked in today, run some tests, and be ready to go in the morning."

"Do it today."

The doctor was quiet, then nodded. "I'll see if I can get you in. I'll order the tests as soon as I leave you and send in a nurse to help you get settled."

"I need to see my friend first, and then I'll be ready."

When Jack went into the small room, he knew immediately that the news was not good. Mark told him about the surgery scheduled, hopefully, for later that day and what the prognosis might be. Jack couldn't speak. He looked at Mark and knew he was holding it together with thin, ragged twine.

"Schedule the surgery for day after tomorrow and I'll go get Kate," he said finally.

Mark shook his head firmly, tears finally welling up in the corners of his eyes. Jack looked away, unable to witness his friend in such torment.

"She'll want to be here," he said.

Mark shook his head again. "No. I want this done today. It's too far, and she has the girls to think of."

"Don't do this without Kate," Jack begged. "I know she'll want to be with you."

"No. Let's get this over with."

Jack waited while Mark was in surgery, alternately pacing the room and staring out the windows. Periodically he pounded his fist against his leg and swore quietly. He thought about Kate and the girls and swore again. He wanted to wire Kate, let her know what was happening, but then thought he should wait until they had some more definitive information.

He started when the doctor came out of the swinging doors leading to the waiting room, then leaped up to speak with him. "Well?" he asked.

"Mr. Ramey is in recovery right now, and he is stable."

"Well, is it cancer?" Jack asked.

"It is," the doctor said abruptly. "I'm sorry."

"Were you able to remove all of it?"

"We won't know right away. For now, he needs rest."

"That's it? He just needs rest?" Jack said, frustrated and angry, wanting to blame someone and taking it out on the man who was only the bearer of bad news.

The doctor motioned Jack to sit and then tried to explain.

"We don't know a lot about this type of illness," he said. "We're learning, but it's very difficult to predict different kinds of cancers. We don't know how much it has spread or where it began."

"What else can be done?" Jack asked.

"Well, obviously good nutrition, peaceful rest, and the medicine I'll send with you." He paused for a moment. "Some illnesses also respond well to warm climates. Perhaps Mr. Ramey could move south for a period, see how his recovery goes there."

"How long before he can go home?"

"About a week," the doctor said, and then stood to leave. "I wish I had more definitive answers," he said grimly, "but we know so little. I'm sorry," he repeated.

Jack sat in the chair by Mark's bed, waiting for him to wake up. Periodically, he touched his friend's hand and talked to him. He hated what was happening, was angry that it was happening to Mark, and it boiled in-

side of him. Hadn't he gone through enough? He had a
family, little girls who needed him, who loved him. He
tried not to think of Kate – of having to tell her. Maybe
the doctor was right, though, he thought hopefully.
Maybe they took all the cancer out. Maybe rest and
warm air would fix him up.

When Mark began to stir, Jack rushed to him from
the window he had been staring out of. "Hey, old man,"
he said, "glad to see you're awake,"

Mark tried to smile, but his mouth was dry and his
eyes had difficulty focusing.

"You don't need to talk," Jack said. "I'll just sit here
for a bit, and then I'm going to go get Kate. She'll want
to be with you while you're recovering from that old
sawbones' work."

"How long will I be here?" he croaked through the
dryness.

"About a week, the doctor said."

Mark shook his head. "Leave Kate there with the
girls. She doesn't need this," he said, and then drifted
back to sleep.

When he woke again, he was more alert and able to
talk. He convinced Jack that Kate was where she needed
to be, and they decided to wire Harley with the news of
the surgery and when Mark would be released. Harley
could ride out to tell Kate and be with her.

"You go on home, Jack. I'll be fine here until I can
get out." He paused. "You will come back to get me
won't you?" he teased, a weak smile on his lips.

"Naw, with you out of the way, I can have both
Hughes sisters all to myself."

Jack wired Harley, but he didn't go back to Hersey.
He got a room near the hospital and waited, visiting
every day and watching Mark gain back some strength.
By the second day, he was sitting up, and on the third he
was actually walking – slowly, but he was on his feet
and moving around the room. Then he began walking

the length of the hallway, back and forth, determined to build up his strength.

"You're pushing it, Mark," Jack admonished.

"No, I'm doing fine. I feel alright."

And he did look like it. Jack began to be hopeful that Mark really would recover completely. Each day he wired Harley with updates. When Mark could move about comfortably and the doctor said he was healing well from the surgery, they prepared for the long drive home.

Outside, Jack led him to a shiny, black automobile instead of the buggy they'd come in. Mark stopped, looked at his friend. "Where on earth did this come from?"

"I just borrowed it for awhile. Did you really think I'd haul your sorry ass home in a buggy?"

Mark ran his hand over the fender lovingly, a warm smile lighting his face. "It might have been worth it all just to spend awhile in this," he said.

Jack tucked him into the car on top of a pile of blankets he'd put there to cushion the seat. He was like a mother hen caring for her chicks as he made sure Mark was completely covered by more blankets and would stay warm. He drove slowly so he didn't hit the bumps too hard, grimaced and swore when the wheels hit one and surprised him.

Mark laughed. "At this rate, we'll get there in about a month," he said. "Can you speed it up a bit? Can I drive?"

"Not right now. Let's see how you fare just sitting there, okay?"

Mark was content to do that. He watched the trees go by and was comforted by the rumble of the engine. He slept sometimes because he was still on medication that made him drowsy, but mostly he just lay back against the door and rested.

When Harley rode out to the cabin two days after their sledding party he had Jack's first wire in his pocket and a heavy stone in his heart. He would gladly have changed places with Mark, would have died on the spot if it meant Mark could come home to his family healthy. For the first time in his life, Harley could not think of the right words, didn't want to talk at all.

Kate was fixing dinner, heard the horse coming up the road and ran out to meet him. He tied the horse to a nearby tree and asked where the girls were.

"They're studying in their room," Kate said, nervously plucking at the wrap she had thrown around her shoulders on the way out. "You've heard something, haven't you?"

"I did, Kate. Jack sent a wire and asked me to come see you. There's no other way than to just say it, Kate. Mark has had surgery – for stomach cancer."

Kate blanched like she'd been shot. Harley reached out to grab her arm to keep her from falling backwards and held it.

"He is recovering well and should be home in about a week."

Kate couldn't speak. Her tongue was thick in her mouth, choking her, and her throat felt tight and swollen. Harley let his words sink in for a few moments, then he turned her around and led her to the cabin. He sat her down in a chair and then went to the cupboard to find Mark's moonshine. He poured a generous amount into a glass and put it in front of her, then took a swig from the jug.

"Drink it," he said. He stood watching her and his eyes watered. He widened them trying to stem the flow, trying to give the water some space so it wouldn't fill up his eyes and spill out. When Kate just sat there, he picked up the glass and held it to her lips. She sipped from it, like a little girl, doing as she was told. The burn of the whiskey didn't even faze her. She merely swallowed as Harley had asked and stared.

"What else do you know?" she finally asked. "Tell me."

"Only that Mark has cancer, but they have done the surgery to remove it."

"Is it gone, then?"

"That will only be known with time."

Kate looked up at Harley, saw him struggle to maintain his own composure, and she stiffened her back. Her lips quivered and she blinked her eyes, and her heart pounded in her chest with the effort to gain control over the raging storm that was in her.

Then Harley put his arm around her. She buried her face in his stomach, and her chest heaved with quiet sobs. Harley's tears could no longer be held in check. They washed over his face and fell on Kate's hair. He tried to wipe them away, but they fell harder the more he tried.

"I'm so sorry sweet Kate."

When Kate could, she pulled away from the shelter of his stomach and shoved the chair next to her out for him to sit.

"Tell me everything," she said. And he did.

"I need to go to him. How can I get there?" she asked.

"Mark prefers that you stay here. The wire made that clear."

"That's not fair."

"Life isn't sometimes, Kate. Think about the girls."

She just nodded, too torn to argue with him, too exhausted to think. They talked about what they would do when Mark came home, about how to tell the girls, about the possibility of moving where the climate was warm. Kate drank the whiskey in her glass, and then drank more when Harley poured it, but she didn't feel it at all. She was numb. Her back was stiff from trying to keep her body together, to keep it from flying apart, and her mind was in turmoil.

Harley slept by Bug that night so he would not leave Kate alone. She slept in the rocking chair beside him. She could not make herself to go to bed, not where she and Mark slept. She would do that when he came home. Harley didn't argue with her. He knew better. He didn't even talk much. He let her talk as she rocked, and he just listened.

The next morning, Harley told her he would ride into town and wait for the next wire. Jack had said he would give them news every day, and he would be back at the cabin as soon as it came in.

"Will you wait until the girls get up?" she asked, "until I tell them?"

"Of course. May I make some coffee?"

"I'll get it, Harley."

"You sit. I know my way around a coffee pot."

When they told the girls that Mark was in the hospital, they sat as stiffly as Kate had, holding in their question and fears. They did not say the word cancer. That would come later, if it had to come at all. Jeannie, sitting on Kate's lap, looked up at her and asked if Daddy's belly would feel better when he came home, and Kate honestly said "we hope so, sweetie."

Kat stood next to Harley, her arm around his shoulder, her hand gripping his shirt. Rebecca was on his lap. Rachel sat erect at the table near her mother, her eyes wide with fear and tears she would not shed.

"Are you telling us everything, Ma?" Rachel finally asked.

"That's pretty much all we know, honey. Jack said he'd wire every day to let us know how Daddy is doing."

After Harley left, the house was silent. Kate moved around the room doing things she needed to do, making the motions of living, but her heart was a boulder that weighted her down, and it was an effort to pick up one foot and place it in front of the other. She was just marking time until Harley came back with more news. She got books out for the girls, and they quietly read – or pretended to. She fixed breakfast, and then lunch. She swept and scrubbed the floors, polished the table and chairs. She washed clothes and took them out into the frigid air to hang, relishing the painful bite of winter on her face. She put a pot of soup in the kettle and hung it at the hearth.

The smell of ham and peas released a false scent of security and well-being into the room, and Kate remembered how excited she had been thinking about all she could do with the ham when Mel had brought it to them just three days before. 'Was it only three days ago?' she asked herself. How could that be? How could anything like food ever be important? She never wanted to eat again.

Toward evening she heard Harley ride into the clearing and ran again to meet him.

"What have you heard?" she asked breathlessly.

"Mark is recovering well. He is sitting up in bed and eating. Says he'll be walking around by tomorrow. What's for dinner? I smell ham!"

"Yes, you do, some of Mel's. It's split pea soup with lots of leftover ham."

"How are the girls?" Harley asked.

"Quiet. I wish they would fight or something."

"Maybe we can play a game after dinner. Checkers. I'm good at that. I'll whip their little butts and make them mad."

Kate laughed, surprised that she could, and said that was a good idea.

"I went to see Willie and Mel," Harley said, "and told Ellen what was happening. I thought you'd want me to do that."

"Damn, Harley. I didn't even think, about letting them know, I mean. I feel badly about that."

"Ellen wanted to come out, but I didn't know where she would sleep," he said. "Do you want me to bring her out tomorrow?"

Kate thought for awhile, and then shook her head. "I hope Ma understands, but I really want to be alone – except for you, that is. Do you think that's okay?"

"Right now, for the time being, anyway, whatever you want is okay," he said smiling at her.

Harley came every evening and spent every night sleeping by Bug. He couldn't convince Kate to go to her bed, and finally gave up. She slept in the rocking chair and watched the flames in the hearth. She tried to see Mark getting well in the flames, thinking if she visualized him healthy and strong, it could help it happen. She talked to her father as she stared at the flames, and wished so badly that he was here to hold her. It was a throbbing ache deep in her chest.

Willie drove out for a visit and brought Ellen along. They didn't stay long, and Ellen seemed to understand Kate's desire to be alone. Mel came, too, and didn't know quite what to say. He stammered around some words and fidgeted with his hat.

"It's alright, Mel. I know what you want to say, so there's no need to say it. Want a cup of coffee?"

"That would be nice."

"I brought the girls some candy," he said as she went to the stove.

"They still have candy left from that huge bag you brought to the party!"

"I didn't know what else I could do," he said with a groan. "What can I do?"

"Pray, Mel," she whispered, fighting tears that always seemed there waiting to spring to her eyes. "Damn eyes. God, I hate that!"

"You always did," Mel said with a sad, tender smile, "and I do pray for him, Kate."

It helped the girls to have people in the house, people they loved. As usual, Rachel stayed her distance and watched, but the other three either climbed on their laps or stood snuggled close, holding a hand, touch bringing a sense of safety and security, a sense of normalcy that had gone with their father in the buggy that carried him away. They all seemed to be in limbo, waiting, and the girls watched their mother for clues. Kate pretended confidence she didn't feel, but they knew better, and they tried to cheer her up. She tried to smile for them, but her laughs were hollow, and they knew that, too.

Days went by, and they all seemed to blend into one another. They lived for Harley to come with the wire, for news of Mark.

Then, late one evening, she heard the chugging of an automobile in the distance, a faint sound that only registered as another sound. It stopped, and soon after she heard the crunch of wheels coming up the road. She ran outside, wondering why Harley had brought the buggy instead of riding Bessie. And then she knew.

She flung herself at him, touched his face, felt his arms and legs like she was checking to make sure all of him was there. When she was sure, she backed away, tears rolling down her face.

"Damn," she said, swiping at the tears. "It's about time you came home!"

Harley grinned from the driver's side of the buggy, and Jack chuckled from the rumble seat. He was scrunched in, but he looked happy.

"Sorry," she said. "Are you feeling okay? What can I do? Do you need help getting out? Are you in pain? Oh, God, it's so good to see you!"

"You're babbling, my sweet. And no, I will be fine if you just help me get out from under the ton of blankets Jack has me swaddled in. You'd think I was his little baby."

"You are, Mark. A baby, that is, but not mine," Jack said. "I don't claim you. Maybe you could help me, Kate. If you just grab my hand and pull to help unplug me from this hole I seem to be stuck in."

She grasped his hand, pulled, and Jack extricated himself from the small space. Then he went around to lift the pile of blankets from on top of Mark. Harley jumped down, stuck his belly out and beamed. Then they noticed the four girls at the door, just standing there, watching, waiting.

"Hey," Mark yelled. "Have you forgotten your Pa in this short time? Get over here and give me some hugs."

They raced to him, scrambled on his lap, and smothered him with hugs and kisses. Even Rachel shoved her way in to claim a place by her father, but she wrapped her arm around his shoulder and squeezed, letting the others climb all over him.

"Careful, girls. Please don't push at your daddy's tummy. Don't hurt his tummy."

But they didn't hear her, and Mark just ignored it. "This is the best medicine ever," he said grinning hugely. "My girls could never hurt me."

When Mark got out, he tried to straighten without looking like it was an effort, show how strong he was, until Bug sniffed at him, stood to plant his paws on Mark's shoulders, and lapped at his face. Mark stumbled a bit, but then spread his feet wide and held on, letting Bug lick him.

"Well, I'll be damned. Now you like me?" Mark said in amazement, "and I get a kiss?"

"Get down, Bug. Down!"

"It's okay, Kate. He didn't hurt me. I am pretty much healed. And," he said smugly, "I got a kiss from the dog who never liked me much. He must be feeling a bit bad about the way he's treated me all these years – or he's going senile and forgot who I am."

"He loves you," Kate said. "He always has."

"Yeah, he just doesn't like me because you love me," he said, a huge grin spreading across his face.

"I surely do love you, Mark."

Harley and Jack stayed a short time while Kate scurried around trying to make Mark comfortable in the rocking chair, getting slippers for his feet and putting them on the footstool. She brought a pillow from their bed, and covered him with an afghan, then stepped back to see what else she could do.

Jack and Harley sat at the table just smiling at her. It filled their hearts to see her so happy. Finally, Harley tapped on the table.

"Hey, you have guests over here. Remember us?" he asked.

"Get it yourself, Harley," she said, laughing. And he did.

Jack poured a small amount of the moonshine in a glass, and Harley tipped the jug. When Kate was finally content that Mark was comfortable, she joined them at the table, but she sat where she could look at Mark, make sure he was still there with her and that he was not in pain. Jack watched her as she talked with them, one eye constantly on her husband, her face lit with happiness, and he knew that no matter what their future held, they had this, and nothing else could compare. The girls surrounded Mark, sitting on the floor at his side, holding his hands, touching his legs, and Rachel stood behind him – his guardian. Her hands rested lightly on Mark's shoulders, not moving, just lying still; touching him was enough.

Before they left, Kate reached over to Harley and covered his hand with hers. "Thank you," she said. Then with her other hand, she covered Jack's. "And you, Jack. I don't know how . . ." She couldn't finish. Jack scooted back his chair and stood.

"It's time to go, Harley. The horseless carriage still sits at the end of the road."

The cabin was quiet. Mark fell asleep in the rocking chair. She put the girls to bed and went to sit by him. She went outside to get wood, stoked the fire, and sat beside him again, quietly staring into the flames. She awoke in the middle of the night with her head on his lap and clutching his legs. He was awake and just sitting there watching his wife sleep. He stroked her hair and whispered "Come to bed, sweetheart."

They did, and their love making was passionate and gentle, sweet and slow. She was afraid to hurt him, and he just wanted to prolong the moments. She tried to say no, it's too soon, but his determination won out. She was so afraid of losing him, and he was so determined not to go. Her fears intensified her need of him, and he released himself to her desires.

When they awoke, the sun was already up. She heard the girls in the kitchen, but snuggled back under the covers to snuggle up against Mark.

"Rachel can handle it," she whispered, afraid they would hear her and come running. Mark just chuckled.

"I am sure she can. She's her mother in a lot of ways. They all are."

They stayed at the cabin until March, living quietly, each of them healing from their own wounds. They read and watched the birds feeding on scraps that Kate threw on the snow for them. The snow was so deep that the deer couldn't dig deep enough with their hooves to get at the grass. They stood tall on their hind legs to nibble at the lowest branches of the evergreen trees. Kate remembered their first year at the cabin when they had brought out hay and bags of beets for the deer and wished they could do that now. She worried about the raccoons and opossums, all of the forest creatures that were struggling to find food, but there was little left over to give to them.

Mark recovered from the surgery, had healed well, but it was difficult for him to eat, and Kate was concerned. There had been a brief respite, during which he had seemed to get stronger, but it was brief, and then he began growing even thinner than before the surgery.

Kate made soothing soups and then just thin broths from chickens that Mel brought out, and beef stock when she could get it, but that was about all he could keep in his stomach. Doc Cheston came out to see him, had even been in contact with the doctor at Blodgett. He gave Mark the medicine that was recommended to him, but all that seemed to do was ease the discomfort that gnawed at his stomach when he ate.

Mark read to the girls, helped them with their studies, and played quiet games with them. There were times when everything seemed good, times when Mark's face looked serene and happy, even healthy, and Kate held on to those moments, telling herself that he was improving, he was getting better. But those were fleeting, and deep down she knew that he was not.

She sat at the table mending and watching the snow melt from the trees. The sun was shining, and spring seemed about to make its appearance in the clearing even though it was only March. Normally, she loved spring. It exhilarated her. But this year, it did not. She knew they would have to leave their cabin in the woods, travel south looking for warmer climates and that they couldn't wait for summer to bring warmth.

Mark's son, Jamie, was in South Carolina. They would go there, live for a time with him. She would find some work, and Mark would get well. He must, she thought; he has to because I can't bear anything else. 'I waited a lifetime to be with him,' she thought, 'and he cannot leave me.'

When she told Mark her plan, he refused at first. It killed him to think of Kate and his daughters leaving the cabin, the home they loved. But as he grew weaker, he agreed that it seemed to be the only hope.

Kate borrowed some of the ticket money from Mel and the rest from Jack for the train that would take them there. It was painful asking, but both Mel and Jack had the money in their hands and were handing it to her before she could even get the words out. There were tears in her eyes as she hugged them, and sobs choked her words of thanks.

"Just get him into the sunshine, Kate. When Mark gets well, that will be thanks enough," Mel said in a voice husky with feeling. Kate left before she came apart and made a fool of herself.

Jack merely turned and left, not trusting himself to a hug or word of thanks.

They wrote to Jamie, hoped he got their letter, and then packed to leave. Harley came out with Will's buggy, and between that and their own buggy, they loaded everything they could find room for and drove into town. Ellen and Ruthie had said goodbye the day before when they drove out to help Kate pack and spend some time with her.

Willie, Jack and Mel met them at the train station. They carried the luggage up the steps of the train and stowed it in the compartment. They had one with a bed on one side where Mark could rest and a bench on the other. It was crowded, but at least it was private. They helped Mark in, and he fell onto the bed, exhausted with the effort of walking. Mel shook his hand, squeezed Kate's arm, and quickly left. Kate saw him walk across the station platform through the small, dusty window of the compartment. His head was bowed, and he was swiping angrily at his face. Kate knew what he was feeling, and fought the tears that choked her.

Jack sat on the narrow bed by Mark and talked softly, teased him about finding a sneaky way to get a vacation in the sunny south. Harley interrupted now and then, helping to find an easy way to say goodbye. But there wasn't one, and they were all glad when the whistle blew and they had to leave.

Willie hugged them all and lightly punched Mark's arm. He didn't know what to say, and Mark told him he didn't have to say anything. So he didn't. He just left.

Harley turned back at the door of the compartment. "I never thanked you for finding my family," he said.

"What are you talking about, old coot?" Mark whispered weakly.

Harley came near again, "For bringing me home with you from the train that day. I never thanked you." He clasped Mark's hand in both of his.

Mark waved his hand and tried to smile. "You wouldn't stop following me. What else could I do?"

"God bless you for not kicking away a stray dog." Then he left, and Harley's tears flowed freely. He didn't even bother to wipe them away when he hugged Kate and the girls whose tears matched his. Verna waited for him on the platform. Kate smiled sadly when she saw her take his hand and kiss his cheek.

The train chugged, the whistle blew, and they pulled out of Hersey. Kate watched the landscape roll by, and watched Mark as he lay on the bed. By the second day, his breathing was labored, and his hands clutched his stomach almost constantly. His face contorted in pain with each bump, and each time the train slowed to a stop, he opened his eyes to ask if they were there, tried to smile, and closed them again. The girls tried to sleep or read, but mostly they watched their father and mother, looking for signs in their faces, anything that would make them feel better about where they were and would explain what was happening.

The clanging of the train wheels on iron tracks went on interminably, mile after mile. It seemed they would never make it over the hills in southern Ohio as they slowed to a crawl going up and then raced down. Kate pointed out the walls of slate and red clay on either side of them, like tunnels that had been left when they burrowed through the hills to lay the tracks – trying to divert their interest outside of the small, dingy compartment.

"Look, girls, the snow is going away. It's green here. I'll bet it's warm."

They looked and nodded, but only briefly, their gaze falling back to Mark.

"Do you want to get off at the next station to stretch your legs and see how warm it is?" she asked. They agreed that would be good, but Rachel said she would stay with her pa, and Kate couldn't say no. She didn't want to leave him alone, either, and didn't want the girls to go off by themselves among strangers. Just over the border into Kentucky, they left the train. The air was warm, and the sunshine felt good after so long on the train. They used the restroom which was much easier than trying to manage the one on a moving train, walked around the platform, and got a drink of water that Jeannie said tasted like medicine.

"I think it's from all the minerals in the mountains," Kate said, glad to be thinking of something other than Mark, even for a moment, glad that Jeannie could, too.

"It's icky anyway."

"But it's cold and good for you," Kate said, "so drink it while you can."

"See, it is medicine if it's good for you. It is medicine in a fountain," she declared with a small grin.

Kate smiled at her youngest daughter whose hair glowed in the sunshine and framed her chubby face.

"Don't be dumb," Kat said. "They don't put medicine in fountains, even here, and if you think it is, maybe you should take some to Daddy."

The brief moment of freedom from Mark's illness vanished, and Kate blanched.

"Don't talk to your sister that way, Kat. She's not dumb. No one in this family is dumb. Let's go back now."

They filled two small paper cups with water for Mark and Rachel and wearily trudged back up the steps of the train. She lifted him gently and held the cup to Mark's mouth. Most of it dribbled down his chest, but he licked the damp from his lips and whispered thank you.

They never made it to South Carolina. By Nashville, Tennessee, Mark was too ill to go on, and they both knew it. At Nashville, they got off the train and took him to the hospital.

After Mark was settled in a hospital bed and being cared for, Kate started looking for some place she and the girls could stay. She hated leaving him, but they couldn't stay in his room all night, and they were all exhausted.

They found a place in the basement of a building with a sign that said 'rooms for rent.' It was tiny and dingy; the concrete walls damp, but it was near the hospital. She counted out the money carefully, knowing if they didn't get to South Carolina soon and find Jamie, it would be gone.

She and the girls had carried their luggage up and down the streets and could hardly move another step by the time they found the place where they could afford to stay. They flopped on the two small beds and looked around. The blankets were grey with grime and dust, and cobwebs hung from the walls. It smelled like mildew. There was a wash bowl on a rickety stand, a hot plate, and that was it, their home until Mark improved enough to go on to South Carolina and Jamie.

"Where do we go to the bathroom, Mama?" Kat asked.

"I think it's out back, honey. We'll all go together, okay?"

"I don't like it here," Jeannie volunteered. "It's scary." They listened as a rodent scampered across the room, and they all lifted their feet to get away from it.

Kate slumped, and tears filled her eyes. She couldn't keep them from falling, and soon all of them sat together, holding each other with tears running down their faces. Kate tried to gather all of her daughters in her arms and hold them, cried with them and for them, and for herself.

"Damn it," she said.

"Mama, you cussed," Rebecca said through her sobs, her six-year-old voice too wise for her age, and way too sorrowful.

"Sorry," Kate whispered. Then she straightened her back, sucked in her stomach and sniffed back the tears.

"Let's get out of here and go see Daddy," she said. "I know this place is awful, but we'll be at the hospital all day and only have to sleep here at night."

They were there for two weeks, listening to the mice and rats crawl around in the dark and watching roaches scamper into the walls when they came in and turned on the light. Kate shuddered every time she opened the door and was afraid to turn out the lights knowing they would come back out of the walls when she did. And she thought of her own sparkling clean home, the woods instead of concrete, the creatures she loved instead of

455

those that bit and carried diseases, and crawled over their blankets at night.

They lived on little, bread and oatmeal with some milk for the girls. Kate's money was running out. She looked for work that she could do for a few days, anything that would tide them over while they were there, but no one would hire her with four daughters and a husband in the hospital. She thought about lying. She was coming to the end of her strength. A conversation with the doctor made the decision for her.

"Your husband is not going to get well, Mrs. Ramey. He is dying. You know that, don't you?" he said softly but firmly.

"No." Kate answered. "He just needs to be warm and in the sunshine."

"Mrs. Ramey, take your husband home. There is nothing we can do for him, nothing sunshine can do. Take him to his home where he belongs, where he can die with people who love him."

Kate put her face in her hands. She bent forward like she'd been kicked in the stomach, and it felt like it. "Nooo!" she wailed. She stayed that way for long moments, and then braced herself and sat up rigidly, her back so stiff it might break with the slightest movement.

"I can't. I have no money for tickets, no money for food, no money for anything. I looked for work. No one will hire me." She sat still, the horror of her situation too much to think about. "I went to the courthouse for help, to the police station, and this hospital. I've begged, but they can't or won't help us," she said angrily.

"Try Red Cross," he said, gently. "They are there to help people in dire circumstances." He told Kate where to find Red Cross, and she and the girls walked there.

The lady was kind, her face motherly and surrounded by blue-gray curls that bobbed when she nodded her head. She had the large, soft bosom that made children want to snuggle on her lap and rest their heads against her breasts. She listened quietly while Kate explained what had happened, how they had planned to go to warm weather so her husband could get well, how they had ended up in Nashville without food or money. It was humiliating and painful, but she patted Kate's hand and said they could help. She gave her enough money for a compartment on the train back to Hersey and for some food for the trip. Kate was too emotionally drained to feel ashamed.

"Bless you, thank you so much. I really didn't know what we were going to do, and . . . I, we . . ." she couldn't finish. She was too tired, too wretched. The woman just patted her hand again and gave her a sad smile.

"Go to your husband," she said. "Take your beautiful daughters home."

Before they left, she hugged Jeannie, Rebecca and Kat, then shook Rachel's hand sensing the girl would not like being hugged. Rachel held out her hand and took the woman's firmly in her own, her back as stiff as her mother's, and Kate was saddened at the sight. She was only ten, and she was trying so hard to be an adult, to be strong. What was happening to her babies? Kate wondered. She resolved to take good care of them, give them the childhood they deserved. She didn't know how, but she would do it, damn it!

Mark died on the train somewhere in Ohio. Kate didn't know exactly where they were, but knew when he was leaving her. Rebecca was curled up at one end of the bench, asleep. Rachel sat at the other end holding Jeannie while she slept. Kat was cross-legged on a suitcase on the floor and leaning her back against the wall. Kate sat on the narrow bed next to Mark and watched him. They'd been like that for a long time.

He slept fitfully, alternately trying to sit up and falling back into a troubled sleep. His breathing was ragged, and he tossed his head and mumbled. Kate tried to give him a little of the morphine the doctor had given her to ease his pain, but he kept pushing it away. He tried to speak, and Kate leaned forward to listen.

Then she lay down next to him and curled around him, trying to keep him still and comforted. She wrapped her arms around him and held his head on her breast.

"Don't talk, Mark," she whispered. "Save your strength."

He tilted his head back and smiled at her, his eyes opened and were soft and loving.

"You are so beautiful, Kate. I'm so sorry."

"Damn. You said sorry, did you cuss?" she sobbed, smiling through her choked words.

He shook his head no and closed his eyes. His face was peaceful.

She laid her head on Mark's silent chest and held his hand. "Sorry," she whispered. "I love you, Mark."

Rachel watched and knew. Tears fell from her eyes and streamed down her cheeks, but she sat silently holding her sister. She didn't know what to do, and she didn't know how to help her mother. Kat waited, perched on the suitcase. She wanted to hold her father's hand, but so much more desperately she wanted him to lift her in the air and ask her if she loved him best.

After a long while, Kate sat up and looked at her daughters. "Daddy feels better now. His pain is gone, and he is with your grandpa, my Daddy."

Kat and Rachel nodded, understanding.

The conductor sent a wire for her; and Harley, Jack and Willie met them at the station. The girls went back with Jack to stay with him and Ruthie. They took Mark to the Hughes house and laid him on the same table that had held Will such a short time ago, or so it felt. No one argued that neighbors could take care of Mark; they knew better and quietly left them alone.

Ellen and Kate, talking in monosyllables only when necessary, washed him and dressed him in his white shirt and suit. He looked much like he had when they first met, so elegant with his starched cuffs and collar framing his hands and handsome face. He looked almost youthful and without pain or sorrow. When they were done, they waited for Harley and Willie to return and help move him to the place Ellen had provided at the back of the room – again the same place her own husband had lain in rest before his funeral.

Kate sat with him, could not leave him alone once the others had gone. Ellen moved about the room quietly, not interfering in Kate's last hours with her husband. Every once in a while Kate slept, her head resting against the back of the rocking chair so that when she woke, she could see him. She talked to him and imagined he answered her.

She told him that she had been so instantly in love with him the first time he came to the house that she had wanted to slide under the floor boards and live with the raccoons that stayed there. She reminded him how he had so stunned her when he showed up after his years in prison that she tripped, fell down the last step and tumbled him to the floor with her. "And you deliberately tipped the chair at the smith shop when I was hanging the curtain," she accused, "so I would fall and you could save me – or get back at me for the other one. But I dragged you down with me, didn't I? Somehow, we always seemed to end up in a heap on the floor, you and me."

Kate smiled, talked and sat silently. She held his hand and stroked his hair. It curled around his ears and over his collar, and she messed it up a bit so it looked like he had just run his hands through it. She liked being with him at night when other people weren't coming by and Ellen was in her room sleeping. When the day came, she was ready.

They laid Mark to rest near Will in the cemetery outside of town. After the funeral, Kate walked home as she had done after her father's funeral. Harley drove the girls in the buggy and was there long before she walked into the clearing. She spent the rest of the afternoon reading with her daughters and talking quietly about what had happened. She tried to find some way to ease their pain, but she didn't know how. She couldn't even begin to look into her own heart. It was too shattered, too broken.

Harley stayed, but much of the time sat outside in the sunshine. The snow was melting. It was going to be an early spring, but Kate couldn't see it, and couldn't care. Before dusk, she heard someone coming into the clearing and looked out. Mel got off his horse and strode to the edge of the woods. He came back dragging a long, stout branch. He knocked on the door and said, "Get your coat. I'll stay with Harley to watch the girls."

Kate remembered the other branch, and did as he said. She walked a long, long way into the woods, heard the robins and woodpeckers announcing spring. Saw squirrels scamper down tree trunks, dig in the ground to retrieve buried acorns and scamper back up. They didn't run away when she passed by them, just watched warily, mouths holding their treasures.

After she began, the only sound in the forest was Kate's wail and the crashing of the heavy branch against a tree trunk, again and again and again, and then she collapsed on the forest floor, spent.

She came back quietly, held up the stubble of a branch and said, "Thank you. I'll put this with my other one," and she smiled. It was a weak smile, but her back was no longer bent and brittle.

"It will take a long time, Kate."

"Yes. A lifetime," she said.

CHAPTER EIGHTEEN

K ate washed the clothes and linens in tubs outside by the creek, then strung it on long lines to dry. She ironed outside, too, because it was cooler than in the kitchen. It meant that she had to run back and forth to the stove hundreds of times to keep the iron hot, but it was better than being in the stifling cabin. She folded the shirts carefully, stacked them on top of the pants, wrapped them in brown paper, and tied the package with twine.

She alternately looked at the shirt on her ironing board and at her daughters as they did their school work in the shade of a tall willow. Rachel was helping Jeannie with her spelling. Kat and Rebecca worked alone on their slates. Kate smiled and wished she didn't have to leave them while she went to the camp, but Rachel watched her younger sisters carefully. She mothered them as if she had given them birth since her father had died. Kate tried to tell Rachel she didn't need to, that she was still a girl herself, but Rachel only nodded and continued to hover over them. And truthfully, Kate didn't know how she could do what was necessary if it wasn't for Rachel. She had to leave them for brief times when she picked up and returned laundry, and she had to trust that her oldest could take care of the younger ones.

When all the laundry was done, she loaded the packages in the buggy to take them back to the lumberjacks at the camp to collect her money. Her hands were red and chapped from the lye soap and hot water. Her back ached as she hitched Dusty and then climbed in.

Bug rode in the seat beside her, his nose high and sniffing the air, his long, red fringe waving in the breeze. Bug was torn by a need to stay and guard the girls or go with Kate and guard her. The first time, he had walked back and forth, from the blanket to the buggy, until Kate laughed and lifted him to the seat. He rolled his brown eyes at her, asking 'are you sure?' She patted his head and told him the girls would be fine.

"I need you with me," she said. "Maybe we need two dogs; one to stay and one to go with me." He rolled his eyes again, not believing Kate would ever bring another dog into the family.

"I'll be back as soon as I can," she called to her daughters who looked up briefly, and then went back to their studies. They were used to the routine by now and had grown comfortable with Kate's brief absences.

It felt good to sit and rest against the seat back. The sun was shining and just beginning to dip in the western sky. Periodically it was blocked by the trees that lined the road, and the shadows cooled her skin. Even though she didn't like leaving the girls, it was a time of peace and rest that she relished. She had no choice but to do what she must to make a living for her family. She would not move them to town, would not take them away from the comfort of a home they loved, so Kate took these moments as small gifts, refused to worry about something she could do nothing about, and cherished the brief respite.

She pulled into the camp and began unloading the packages, each marked with the name of the owner and the amount they owed her. They were finishing their work for the day, and Kate saw them heading toward her and the cook tent where she had stacked their things. Jack led the group. He'd been watching for her and always made sure he got there before the rest of the men.

"Kate," he said. "It's good to see you. How are my beautiful nieces?"

She gave him a tired smile. "They're well, Jack, sitting under the willow studying – I hope, but you never really know what happens when you're away from them, do you?"

"How about their beautiful Mama," Tommy Thompson asked, eyeing Kate appreciatively.

"Shut up, Tom," Jack said. "Just get your money out, boys, and pay the lady. Don't be stingy, either."

Jack stood sentry when Kate was in camp. He didn't trust any of them where Kate was concerned, and hovered nearby as she collected her money and more dirty laundry. He hated that she had to wash their filthy clothes, hated that she had to work so hard, but didn't know how to help. He had tried, but Kate was stubborn and said she could take care of her family, thank you very much.

"I was just being friendly," Tom whined.

"Do you remember the hickory switch by my desk, Tommy?" Kate asked, grinning at him. "I recall from my school teaching days that threatening you with a switch works wonders. Do you want me to find one?"

Tommy had the good sense to blush and back off, not that he feared Kate would actually do what she threatened, although she might, but because he knew Jack was not a man for idle words. He knew also that Kate was under the protection of others, like her brother, Willie, and Mel Bronson. But she did look good, even with her long hair messed and coming loose from its tie and her face reddened from long hours outside.

"I didn't mean nothing," he said to Kate. "You know that."

Jack helped her load up the dirty clothes, separated the piles with brown paper and labeled them.

"Come out to visit," she said. "The girls would love to see you and Ruthie."

He said they would and watched as she drove out of the camp.

When she got home, the girls were already in the garden weeding. Kate unloaded the buggy, unhitched Dusty, and went to join them. They still had some time before total darkness fell to get some work done in the garden.

They pulled weeds around the plants until they could no longer see, talking quietly at times, and sometimes singing softly. They needed what the garden would produce and took good care of it, watered it with buckets filled at the creek and made sure no bugs ate the plants before they had a chance to produce. Kate didn't know how she would find the time to do all the canning, but it would have to be done. 'Probably the middle of the night,' she thought. 'It will be cooler then anyway.'

Mel was visiting one day after the garden began to really flourish when Kate flew out of her chair and ran yelling across the clearing, waving her arms. She came back panting and angry.

"Damn deer! Damn rabbits!" she said.

"I can't believe what I'm hearing!" Mel said. "You? The woodland fairy scaring off her creatures?"

"They're eating my garden! I can't guard it all the time just to run them off."

The next day, Mel came out with posts and chicken wire. He spent the day critter-proofing the garden. He had been afraid the first time he visited following Mark's death. He didn't want to see Kate's devastation, didn't know if he could handle seeing the deep sorrow in the eyes of the girls. He waited a long time after he had given Kate the tree branch to beat out her anger and loss, and only went the next time because Harley demanded that he ride along with him one day. It wasn't that he didn't want to go, but he was afraid.

Harley made it easier. Even though Harley was a frequent visitor, Rebecca and Jeannie climbed all over him, they were so happy he was there, and Kat held his hand, not wanting to let it go. Even Rachel hugged him and then hugged Mel. Soon Jeannie was on his own lap, having given Harley's over to Rebecca, and they sat comfortably at the kitchen table and talked.

That was when Kate had first told them her plans to earn money by taking in laundry, by gardening and selling what they didn't need in town. Mel had tried to discourage her, told her she could consider moving into Ellen's house. His advice was met with a stony look that clearly said, 'keep your advice to yourself. I know what's best for my family, and we're not leaving here unless the man who owns this cabin actually comes back. Maybe not even then.'

"I'm sorry, Kate. I didn't mean to . . ."

"I can do this, Mel. I don't need help."

They talked long into the evening after the girls had gone to bed, and Kate convinced them that she would survive, that she could do nothing except stay where they were and try to rebuild their lives. The stiffness of her spine said it, and the grim determination on her face repeated it.

Willie and Mary, with their children, visited as often as they could, but their lives were busy, too. And Ellen and Verna came out with Harley. They spent time with the girls and talked with Kate while she continued to work. Ellen tried to help her, but Kate said "Go spend some time with the girls, Ma. They need their Grandma."

Jack stopped sometimes on his way from the camp into town, but Kate had so much to do that she kept turning the clothes in the tub, wringing them and tossing them into the rinse water. After the first time, it became his habit to roll up his sleeves and wring the clothes for her. Then they both strung them on the lines. He was good at it, and pinned the shirts from the

bottom edge at the seams, just as it should be done. He
didn't ask. He just did it. For some reason, she didn't
mind accepting his help. Maybe it was because Mark
had trusted Jack enough to accept help from him. Jack
had been there from the beginning; they had helped
each other, and he was a connection to Mark that was
almost palpable.

Once, when they were done washing and the
clothes were all on the line, he went into the cabin and
brought out two small glasses of Mark's moonshine and
handed one to her. The sun was drifting into the trees at
the west side of the clearing. They sat outside, not talking, just enjoying the night air. Kate sipped at the home
brew and tasted Mark. Her throat contracted, and she
swallowed the tears that threatened.

"I know. I miss him, too," he said.

Kate just nodded, unable to talk.

After a few times, it became their ritual. At least
once a week, Jack would show up, help her finish up the
laundry, and they would relax with a small glass of
whiskey while the girls played nearby.

"I'm just tired," Kate had said when she could
speak.

"I know," he said. "You work too hard, Kate, but
you know that, and I can't tell you how not to."

Ruthie came out by herself after that, at least once a
week, and helped her do the washing and ironing. It
was good spending time with her sister, and they began
to know each other better than they ever had.

Kate listened to Ruthie as she talked about the pain
of not having babies of her own. They talked about their
father. And Kate finally began to speak of losing Mark,
loving Mark. Their conversation flowed easily back and
forth, and silences were comfortable. The sisters com-
municated as no others could; they filled in words that
weren't said, needed no touch to feel the empathy of the
other, and when Ruthie left for the day, they both felt
more whole than when she had come. They had helped

in each other's healing. Their bond had strengthened them both.

"I love you, Ruthie," Kate said as Ruthie climbed into her buggy. "Thank you for coming."

"I know. I should have done this a long time ago."

And that is the way the next years passed. Friends and family visited and tried to help as best they could, as much as Kate would accept. She mourned Mark, and the pain of losing him never left. She just learned to live with it, the dull ache that was so much a part of her. She learned to laugh again, and she learned to remember their love with a smile. Eventually she could even talk about him without sobs catching her throat. During the day, she could.

At night she lay in darkness on the bed they had shared. She lay motionless, quieting her breath in order to still the sobs chocking her throat, to be silent, waiting. Hot tears flowed down her cheeks in salty rivers. She didn't wipe them away and felt liquid pool at her temples. She didn't try to stem the flow, and in the morning there would be streaks of white crusted salt in paths from her eyes. She felt his lips in the dampness on her cheek, his mouth seeking her lips. She felt the fever of his touch as his fingers gently caressed her face and brushed hair from her eyes. She inhaled deeply, held it there to cling to him in the whisper of her breath. Morning always came too soon.

The man had not returned to claim his cabin, yet, but twice each year Kate washed his clothes and hung them back on the hooks by the door, just in case.

A second dog came to live with them, and Bug, who was growing old, merely tolerated the puppy Mel brought out. He rolled his eyes at him and gave a small growl that said 'get away from my rug. I get the hearth. You find some other place to lie.' But he let the new dog chew on his ears and romp on top of him. Kate thought he was tolerant of the pup because it was young, or maybe he knew the girls needed a guard dog to stay with them while he guarded Kate.

The first time Jeannie saw the puppy, she ran to it and scooped it in her arms. "It's a poochie," she squealed. "Mel, you brought a poochie!" and that became his name. Poochie started out small and grew into a huge, hairy Saint Bernard who followed Jeannie where ever she went. It had been love at first sight that continued for years.

Mel continued to visit and grew comfortable being there several times a week. He even started doing some work around the cabin, like fixing the roof that had sprung leaks and building a small corral for the horses. He worked with the girls on their homework and sat with Kate after her long hours of work were over.

Once, when they were sitting in front of the fireplace after the girls had gone to bed, he gently tucked her loose hair back behind one ear, a loving, tender touch that said more than words could do. Kate looked at him, and he stopped, squeezed her shoulder and smiled.

"Maybe another time," he said softly, and then he leaned back in his chair, content to be right where he was, comfortable waiting for her to be at peace with the past. 'I'll be here when there's no elephant in the room, Kate. Right here.'

CPSIA information can be obtained at www.ICGtesting.com
Printed in the USA
BVOW04s0021160914

366910BV00007B/9/P